Mistletoe Magic in the Highlands

Mistletoe Magic in the Highlands

BELLA OSBORNE

HEAD
of ZEUS

An Aria Book

A catalogue record for this book is available from the British Library.

ISBN (PB): 9781837930043
ISBN (E): 9781837930029

Cover design: Gemma Gorton

Typeset by Siliconchips Services Ltd UK

Printed and bound in Great Britain by
CPI Group (UK) Ltd, Croydon CR0 4YY

Head of Zeus Ltd
First Floor East
5–8 Hardwick Street
London EC1R 4RG

WWW.HEADOFZEUS.COM

For my nieces Emma Taylor-Smith and Mollie Smith.
Luv ya x

Liv looked at her newly inflated boyfriend and his perpetually surprised expression.

'Thank you,' she said to her sister, Charlotte, and her best friend, Abigail, who were struggling to control their laughter after a tad too much Prosecco.

'We thought we'd get you the perfect boyfriend. He's silent, low maintenance and wipe clean. We've called him Plastic Stan,' said Charlotte coyly. Liv did have a disastrous track record when it came to men, so the birthday gift wasn't completely unjustified – although still quite embarrassing. Even still, she was glad to be at home. With only a week until Christmas, Liv had decided a takeaway was considerably better than sharing her evening with umpteen office parties and a multitude of Christmas decorations – which was often the downside of a December birthday. In Liv's mind, Christmas celebrations could properly start *after* her birthday.

'If you do *this*…' said Abigail, fiddling around the back of Stan. 'There's an extra surprise.' With the flick of a not-so-discreetly hidden switch, Stan's nether regions began to vibrate. The girls returned to hysterics as Liv frantically tried to turn him off – which was surprisingly harder than with real men. When it came to the human variety, Liv seemed to have a knack for instantly turning them off. At last she found the switch and the inflated doll stilled.

'It had very good reviews on the internet,' said Abigail, who was in full make-up and dressed for a night out.

'I don't think I'll be using that feature, Abi, but thanks anyway,' said Liv.

'That cost extra, you know,' said Abigail, looking a little hurt and quite flushed from the alcohol.

'It was um… very thoughtful,' Liv said, choosing her words carefully.

'We also got you this,' Abigail said, producing a large box.

'If this is a lifetime's supply of batteries…' began Liv, which was met by two shaking heads. 'Shame,' said Liv, opening the box. Inside were several presents all individually wrapped in birthday paper. It was a small gesture, but it meant a lot to Liv that they used birthday paper and not Christmas wrapping – as so many did and which drove her slightly potty. Her argument was that you'd never wrap a present for a June birthday in Christmas paper so why do it with hers?

Twenty-five felt like a bit of a milestone. It was making her reflect on her life and compare it to others – something she knew wasn't the most healthy thing to do. Abigail was already happily married to a lovely man who doted on her. They were both dentists and had just bought a large four-bedroomed house on the fancy side of Blackburn.

Her sister was only a couple of years older, but by twenty-five already Charlotte had her own place and an amazing job that allowed her to work with the world's biggest musical artists and travel all over the world. Liv once overheard a friend describing her as a lot like Charlotte, only shorter and not as pretty. Unhelpfully, that was also how Liv thought of herself. Liv was living in Charlotte's spare room in Brownhill, just on the outskirts of Blackburn. Or as Charlotte liked to say, bordering the Ribble Valley, as that sounded posher.

Liv felt she was a bit of an 'also-ran' compared to her sister, and always had. On the plus side, she did have her own company. Although that sounded more glamorous than the reality, which was that it was just her and her laptop trying to improve the visibility of small businesses online. But at least she was her own boss and could go to work in her pyjamas; not many people of twenty-five could say that.

After a few minutes of unwrapping, Liv had a pile of all her favourite things: chocolate, bath bombs and books.

'Thanks, you guys are the best.'

After a gushy group hug, the girls nestled on the sofas with topped-up glasses of Prosecco, with Stan taking pride of place next to Liv.

'Aww look at you two,' Charlotte said. 'The perfect couple.' She winked.

'Actually,' Liv said, concentrating on the bubbles in her glass, 'I am dating someone.' She'd planned to stay quiet for a bit longer but she couldn't resist an opportunity to shut Charlotte up.

'What?! When? *Who?*' Charlotte cried, putting her glass down and leaning forward. Abigail joined in an almost synchronised motion.

'A few weeks now,' Liv said with a wince. She braced herself for their reaction.

'*Weeks?*' was the chorus of disbelief.

'Why didn't you tell me?' Charlotte asked, looking more than a little put out.

Liv reached for her hand. 'Because after last time I didn't want to call it too soon.'

'I understand,' said Charlotte.

Abigail made exaggerated puffing sounds. 'After the last arsehole I don't blame you! To have told you how much he loved you only to ghost you – boy was that harsh. He deserves to have his balls roasted on a barbecue. Oh, how about we order a barbecue chicken pizza?' Abigail looked around but nobody seemed keen.

Liv didn't need the recap. She had taken quite a few months to get over how awfully Pierre had treated her and what a blow it had been to be ghosted. The initial shock of Pierre not replying to texts or calls and then blocking her from his socials had been quickly overtaken by a feeling of worthlessness. How boring and insignificant must she be that he could so easily cut her from his life? If she was being honest, it was still playing on her mind. But she had put herself out there again and was trying hard to move on.

'It's early days but it's good so far,' Liv said.

'Tell us more about him,' said Charlotte. 'Where've you been hiding him for a start?'

'Well, we met online.'

'What's his name?' asked Abigail.

'Fraser,' said Liv, feeling a squirm of something in her gut at the sound of his name. They were still getting to know each other but there was something about his messages and their connection that made her feel this could be the start of something special. After her last dating disaster she was trying to be cautious, which was difficult given Fraser ticked all her boxes.

'Tell us more,' urged Charlotte.

'He's from Scotland. He's a chef with his own restaurant. We both like reading, Mariah Carey and holidaying in Spain. He had a bad break-up so he wants to take things slowly, but he's kind and caring and he sends me the cutest messages.' Just talking about him was giving her all the feels.

'Photos! We need photos,' demanded Charlotte.

'Not dick pics though,' added Abigail quickly.

'He's not like that,' Liv said. In between Pierre and Fraser there had been two men who had quickly introduced themselves and sent her a close-up of their favourite body part. Why men thought that was attractive was beyond her.

Liv got her phone out and opened up the dating app they'd been using to chat. He'd had an issue with his phone so they'd not exchanged numbers yet. But the app was fine and at the start it had actually been reassuring that she'd not had to give out any personal details other than her full name – Olivia Bingham. Only people she was close to got to call her Liv, although Fraser was fast approaching that status.

They messaged every night and whilst she'd been keen to talk on the phone, he'd admitted that he wasn't much of a talker – so the messaging worked just fine. That little bit of anticipation as she waited for a response was oddly exciting. She was chatty, some might say gobby, so it was probably best that they didn't talk directly. The messaging meant it was a more balanced exchange. There were also frequent exchanges during the day. Some encouraging her if she was feeling a bit down, some flirty, and others were quite funny. It wasn't a conventional relationship but after what she'd been through this felt like a safer way to get to know someone. And while she didn't like to think of herself as superficial, he *did* look hot in his profile picture. She'd initially been attracted by his auburn hair – a very similar shade to her own. He had the most stunning blue eyes she'd ever seen and a well-groomed beard.

Fraser had a sort of ruggedness about his features, not that she'd studied his tiny picture for hours on end. Okay maybe a couple more hours than was healthy, one of the many dangers of working from home. She was keen to show him off to her friends and was speedily navigating the app. For some reason Liv couldn't get his details to come up. She also couldn't seem to find their lengthy message thread. The app was likely playing up so she refreshed it and waited impatiently for it to reload. Still nothing. His profile, along with their messages, was gone.

An icy sensation crept over her and settled in her gut. 'What's wrong?' asked Charlotte, quickly sensing all was not well.

'It's gone. His picture has been deleted and all of our messages,' Liv said in a small, defeated voice.

'Ghosted again?!' said Abigail with a hiccup.

The phrase shot alarm through her. This couldn't be right. It couldn't have happened *again*. Could it?

2

After a fitful night's sleep, Liv woke with a dull pain in her head, thanks to the Prosecco, and an acute ache in her heart, thanks to Fraser.

She also had a whopping great dent in her already battered ego. She huffed and flopped back on her pillows. Reality was not being particularly kind: she was living in her sister's spare room, driving a clapped-out Fiesta, working her backside off at a job that never quite took off, and to make matters *even* worse, she had a love life worthy of any agony aunt column. She felt like a complete and utter loser. She really wanted to believe everything Charlotte and Abigail had said last night; it wasn't her fault, it was men being horrible, and she wasn't a shit magnet. Being ghosted once was clearly bad luck. But to have it happen twice – it was hard not to conclude that she was the common denominator.

She wasn't the prettiest but she also didn't look like a cow's backside. She frequently received lovely comments about her long, auburn hair. The remarks were somewhat in contrast to the teasing she'd endured at school – where she had been called everything from 'ginger nut' to 'Ron Weasley', none of them very original. She was a bit of a talker, perhaps that was what put them off. She wished she knew because all she could see stretching ahead of her was an endless cycle of her being dumped and having no idea why. Actually, being dumped would have been a whole lot better than being ghosted. When they just disappeared she didn't even get the chance to ask why, or to vent her anger and hurt.

There was a tap on the bedroom door and Charlotte's face appeared.

'Hey, you. I made you some toast and a large cuppa.' She put the offerings on the nightstand and sat down. 'How are you feeling?'

'Like I've won the grand prize for biggest loser in the world – ever.'

'Seriously? It's not that bad. It's just some random bloke. What does he know?'

'Apparently the same as Pierre.'

'He was another idiot. Liv, you are better than them. You need to pick yourself up, dust yourself down and get on with your life.'

Liv harrumphed from her pillow. 'I think I'll be doing some wallowing first. A day in bed is probably what I need. I'm owed some wallowing time surely?'

'That won't make you feel any better,' Charlotte said, sounding all school-teachery.

'I sure as hell can't feel any worse.'

'I've just been to the gym so I'm going to have a shower,

then I've got a work call for an hour or so. After that I'm expecting to see you up and dressed.'

'Why?' asked Liv.

'Because life goes on, little sister,' said Charlotte, and she almost skipped from the room.

Liv grabbed a slice of toast and munched on it in her horizontal position. Then she started to choke and had to sit up. It would be just her luck to die from choking on toast. It wasn't exactly a life-flashing-before-her moment but if she were to die, what had she achieved in her twenty-five years? *Bugger all*. She finished her toast, had a swig of tea, lay back down again and snuggled under the covers. She was feeling sorry for herself and bed was the best place to do that. Even losers deserved a day off.

A couple of hours later she was scrolling through her phone having rebooted the app and searched the database for Fraser. Still no sign of him. It turned out her low point had a few more levels down than she'd realised.

'Are you not up yet?' Charlotte's less understanding face poked around the door.

'I said I'm not getting up today. I'm busy wallowing.'

Charlotte came in and put her hands on her hips – never a good thing. 'Now listen to me. This man is not worth it. Dwelling on what's happened will only make you feel worse. You need to seize the day.'

Liv would have quite liked to have seized Charlotte by the ponytail and slung her into next week. 'I appreciate the pep talk. I do. But I'm going to get over Fraser *my* way.'

Charlotte pulled a number of different facial expressions.

None of them boded well. 'Get over him? You've not even met him. What is there to get over?'

'We *met* online,' said Liv trying not to sound niggled. 'I thought we had potential. We were a good match because we liked the same things. He was always there with a text when I needed him. And I liked him.'

'But you know nothing about him, apart from the fact that he *allegedly* likes Mariah Carey.' Charlotte rolled her eyes – she wasn't a fan. 'And he says he's a chef in Scotland. It's probably all lies. Did he even say where in Scotland he lived? It's a whole other country.'

'Yes,' said Liv. 'He lives on the banks of Loch Lochy.'

Charlotte belly laughed. 'Loch Lochy? And you didn't think that was a made-up place?'

'Not until now.' Liv was feeling like a proper fool.

'Chalk it up to experience and move on. Hey?' Charlotte had that 'I'm so clever' big sister look about her – it was very annoying.

'You can't just delete someone from your mind like an unwanted computer file. Relationships don't work like that.'

'Apparently you can because that's exactly what he's done to you,' said Charlotte. 'And it was hardly a relationship. You probably couldn't pick him out of a line-up. And if you'd been in touch with him anymore that may have been the next place you'd have seen him. He's most likely a con man.'

Liv could feel that familiar sense of going into battle that she only ever felt with Charlotte. Was it a stubborn sibling thing? She wasn't sure but it was a definite sensation reserved only for her sister.

'Online relationships are still relationships you know. We had feelings for each other. I know it was early days but there was definitely something. We had a connection.' Charlotte gave a derisory snort and Liv was further riled. 'He was kind and thoughtful and I'm going to miss him.'

'Sure. It was definitely kind and thoughtful of him to ghost you like that.'

'Before that part he was really nice to me. Not that you would understand because you're too busy for a boyfriend. You barely noticed when Ricky buggered off to Ibiza.'

Charlotte gasped. 'That's unfair, Liv. I love my job. And I couldn't give a shit about Ricky.'

'He owns a bar in Cyprus now,' shot in Liv.

Charlotte's expression changed to interested.

'Does he? When did…' She shook her head. 'I don't care about Ricky. But I *do* care about you. We don't need men in our lives. Look at Mum. She's happier now than she's ever been.'

It was true their mother did seem to be happy being single but it had taken countless tears and a lot of useless men for her to finally embrace it. 'But Mum's in her fifties. I don't think I'm ready to be permanently single.'

'Take my advice. Forget about Fraser and focus your energy on something else.'

Liv puffed out a breath as she lay in her bed. 'What energy? I don't have any.'

'That's a hangover. Get some juice and a vitamin C tablet down you and you'll be right as rain.'

'Why are there so many men with arsehole tendencies in this world? Why can't someone gather them all up and send them off somewhere like an island?' said Liv.

'Maybe they did. We are on an island after all. Perhaps someone needs to invent a dating version of TripAdvisor so you can leave one-star reviews to warn the next woman. Anyway, worse things happen in Wetherspoons.'

'Why are you always so bloody jolly?' asked Liv. 'It's zapping the last of the energy I actually had. Look I'm going back to sleep. That's your fault.'

'Liv, don't be ridiculous. Liv!'

'Zzzzzzzz.'

'You are such a child sometimes,' said Charlotte and she stomped out of the room.

Liv barely left her room for the next few hours, only to forage for a pot noodle and scoot back to the safety of her pit. She must have nodded off because she was woken by the sound of high-speed chatter, and that could mean only one thing. She sat up in bed just as Charlotte let herself in. She was not alone. Liv pointed at her accusatorially. 'You called Mum!'

Her mother came bustling into the room and immediately began straightening the bedcovers with Liv still under them. 'Of course she did, Olivia. What else was she to do? Hmm? You're refusing to get out of bed. Mithering about some lad who probably doesn't even exist. They set up fake accounts on the internet just to get your money. Marjorie at number seventeen was scammed by an Elbonian prince. Awful business. You've had a lucky escape. Now you hop in the shower and I'll get you out something nice to wear. Okay?'

It was very much not okay but when faced with her

mother's wall of words it triggered a deep desire to flee, so a shower was a safe alternative. Liv slunk out of bed and glared at a smug-looking Charlotte as she left the room.

When she came back her mother had put out the only dress she owned. She would not be wearing that. She brushed her hair and gave it a quick blast with a hairdryer, threw on a long-sleeved top and her favourite jumpsuit. Feeling marginally better, she went to face the verbal equivalent of a firing squad.

'Ah, here she is,' said her mum, getting up to wrap her in a hug. She squeezed far too tight, as if she hadn't seen her for ten years rather than the ten minutes she'd been in the shower. 'I've made you a nice brew. Now come and tell me all about it and we'll work out what to do.' Her mum tilted her head as she ran an eye over what she was wearing. 'That's not what I put out. Maybe you wearing boiler suits all the time gives people the wrong impression.'

Charlotte tried to hide a laugh with a cough. She was sitting at the dining table pretending to work on her laptop. Liv scowled at her.

'It's a jumpsuit, Mum. And it's fine. People wear them all the time.'

'Do they? I know *you* do, but other than workmen, I can't say I know anyone else. Anyway, let's not dwell on the overalls. Tell me about this chap and what's happened.'

Liv went over the whole sorry situation again whilst sipping her tea in between rants. Her mum did make the best cuppa going, and she listened attentively and didn't butt in. Liv concluded with: 'I know it's not the end of the world and I'll be fine and all that. It was just a bit of a blow it happening again. I was taking the day to recalibrate.'

'Uh, men are the worst,' said her mum. 'Look at your father. He was gone before I'd even brought you home from hospital. The placenta stuck around longer than he did.'

'Eww, Mum!'

'My point is, you need to know this really isn't about you. You are a beautiful girl and whoever he is, or was, he doesn't deserve you.'

'Thanks. I'd not go that far but I know I'm not Quasimodo.'

'You can't say that love, it's racist,' said her mum.

'It's not racist, Mum.'

'I think you'll find it is. He was French and you know first-hand what they can be like. Odd race. But never mind. What we need to work out now is what you do next.' Her mum looked at her hopefully.

'There's nothing I can do, Mum. He's ghosted me. It's like it sounds. He's now a ghost. Gone, no trace of him anywhere.'

'I don't believe that.' She got out her ancient mobile phone. 'What was the restaurant called?'

'Um something Scottish, I think. It's in a hotel.' Liv couldn't remember any details. She wasn't even certain that he'd shared that much.

'Where was it again?'

'Loch Lochy,' said Liv in a small voice; she glared over at Charlotte, willing her to snigger. 'But that's obviously a made-up—'

'Here it is,' said her mum turning her phone screen around to show her. 'Bonnie Scott's Restaurant, Lochy House Hotel, Great Glen Way, Glendormie, Inverness-Shire.'

'Bloody hell,' said Charlotte coming from behind her laptop. 'He *does* exist.'

'Of course he exists!' Liv threw up her hands. Charlotte was infuriating. Although a little part of her was hugely relieved as she had been starting to think Charlotte was right.

'Well, the place where he *works* is real. *Him* we don't know about. Why don't you call and ask to speak to him. Tell him what you think of him and put the phone down,' suggested her mum.

'Tempting but it's likely as soon as I start ranting he'd hang up.'

'Definitely,' said Charlotte. 'Forget about it, Liv.' She shrugged. 'Do what you usually do – dodge the difficult situation and carry on with your life.'

'What does that mean?' Liv glared at her sister.

'It wasn't a dig. I simply meant that you are more carefree than me, and while I couldn't stand by and be treated badly you are able to pretend it's not happening. It's a good thing.' Whilst it was hard to hear, Liv did know this about herself. She loathed conflict. Whether it came from the many shouting matches she'd witnessed as a child between her mum and countless useless boyfriends, she wasn't sure. But she did know that the very thought of challenging someone brought her out in a sweat.

'Oh well,' said her mum, intervening before things turned into an argument. 'Now did you want to come to mine for tea? I could do your favourite: tinned beans and sausages. You can help me wrap your nanna's presents if you like. Now your birthday is over we can start getting full-on Christmassy. You should immerse yourself in all things festive and forget about that nasty boy.'

But it wasn't that easy. Besides, an idea was forming in Liv's mind, charged by a bubble of anger that had taken hold in her gut. She wasn't going to wallow in tinsel and eat beans and processed sausages, no. She was going to do something about it.

'No thanks, Mum. I'm going to Scotland.'

★

Effie was sitting on the window seat and scrolling through messages on her phone. This was her favourite place. It was peaceful but it was also warm and had a smidgeon of a phone signal, unlike the rest of Lochy House Hotel, apart from the middle of the kitchen, which was the most inconvenient place to use your phone. The view out of the window was stunning at any time of day but she liked it the most at midday, when the sun was high in the sky, assuming it was making an appearance at all. The lawns and the run of stone steps drew her eye down to the water's edge and the hills beyond. The light was just perfect, the way it created a halo around the clouds that scattered a glow on Loch Lochy.

Her cousin walked in and she hastily put her phone away. 'What are you up to?' he asked.

'Nothing.' Effie plumped up the cushion next to her, somewhat alarmed by the puff of dust it released. 'Up to implies I'm doing something that I shouldn't be doing, which I'm definitely not because I'm allowed to sit here and look at the view and check my messages. And you can't stop me.' She glared at him. She didn't have any siblings, so he was the closest thing she had to a big brother.

'Euphemia Douglas, I've known you your whole life and you are the world's worst liar.'

'That's not a skill I'd want to be good at anyway. And who says I'm lying? People can have secrets, can't they?' She knew as soon as she'd said it that it was the wrong thing to say.

His eyebrows arched. 'Oh now I'm interested. What's the secret?' He sidled over and tried to get a look at her phone screen.

'You need to get a life of your own. I thought you said you were crazy busy. You can't be if you're wandering around bothering folk. Anyway, some of us have important things to be getting on with.' And with that Effie left the room. She'd walk around for a bit and then sneak back to the window seat and see if any new messages popped up. It wasn't like she had anything better to do.

3

Liv threw some clobber and her wash kit into an overnight bag whilst her mum and Charlotte hovered, sharing the many reasons why her hotfooting it to Scotland was a bad idea.

'Liv, listen to sense,' said Charlotte. 'I've googled the journey. It's three hundred and forty miles and it's going to take you at least six and a half hours. Probably nearer six days in your old car. I'm not sure you've thought this through.'

This fact did at least make Liv pause with a pair of pants in her hand. 'Blimey that is a long way. Still. I need to do this face to face so it's worth it.'

'Liv, it's okay to change your mind,' said Charlotte.

'Don't try and talk me out of going. This is the only way I will get proper closure. I *have* to go.'

'Olivia, sweetheart,' began her mum. 'I know this was my idea but—'

'Was it?' questioned Liv. 'I think this was *my* idea.

It was me who said I need to have it out with him face to face. Prove to myself that it's not me who has a problem. It's him.' She needed to do this for her own peace of mind and then she could move on. Plus after what Charlotte said about her dodging difficult situations she felt it was about time she faced this one, however uncomfortable it might be.

Her mum wobbled her head. 'It was me who found the restaurant and suggested that you speak to him so...'

'On the *phone*. This is different.' She waved her pants at her before adding them and a spare pair to the bag.

'I don't think you should go alone,' said her mum, biting her lip and looking at Charlotte.

'I would go with her but I've got this big thing in London tomorrow. I could cancel?'

'I don't need babysitting, thank you very much.' Liv was indignant. She'd made her mind up and wouldn't be swayed.

'Then *I'll* come with you,' said her mum. 'We'll need to stop at mine so I can pack a case and—'

'Definitely not,' said Liv, feeling a nerve twitching in her neck. Even Charlotte was shaking her head. 'Thank you but I really have to do this on my own.' Her mother opened her mouth but Liv continued. '*Completely* on my own. I'm a grown woman and you brought me up to look after myself. I'll be back before you know it.'

'Liv, you'll have to stay overnight somewhere,' said Charlotte. 'If you leave now you'll have to stop a couple of times so you'll likely not get there until about eight or nine o'clock tonight. You can't turn around and drive all the way back again – that's madness.'

Annoyingly her sister did have a point.

'Fine. I'll find a bed and breakfast somewhere.'

'Be careful,' said her mum. 'You read about people being murdered and chopped up in places like that.'

'No you don't, Mum. That's only in novels and they're usually set in remote parts of America.'

'That's true it is usually in America. Maybe go for a Travelodge in a town somewhere to be on the safe side,' said her mum.

Charlotte and Liv exchanged knowing looks. They loved their mum. As a single mother she'd been amazing at bringing them up on her own but sometimes it was a wonder how she'd managed it with her blurred view of real life and fiction.

'Okay, Mum. I'll make sure I stay somewhere legit. Okay?'

'Thank you.' Her mum gave her a hug. 'And if you hear a strange noise. Don't go to investigate.'

'Mum!' Liv's patience was being tested.

'Charlotte, have you still got that large torch?' asked her mum. Charlotte nodded. 'Please give it to your sister; she can use it to defend herself.'

Liv needed to finish packing and escape this madness. She grabbed cola and crisps from the cupboard. That would tide her over and she could always stop at a Greggs on the way. She'd be fine. She headed to the front door with her bag and snacks.

'It's seriously cold up there right now. They're expecting minus eight tonight,' said Charlotte. 'Take my torch, and my car.' Charlotte handed her the keys.

'Really? Are you sure?' Charlotte loved her BMW. It was her pride and joy.

'Yours will never make it and I need my little sis safe.

I'm getting the train to London so I don't need it. Plus, it has something yours doesn't have – acceleration, so you can escape the bad guys. I don't want you getting carjacked by some mad axe murderer.'

'Oh my word, Charlotte!' said their mum looking horrified.

'Mum, I'm joking. She'll be all right. It's full of petrol so it should get you there but keep an eye on it.'

'I'm not a complete moron,' said Liv, taking the keys and getting pulled into a tight hug.

'Remember he doesn't know you and you'll never see him again. So you can be the person you want to be and say all the things you want to say,' whispered Charlotte.

'Blimey, Yoda, that's a bit deep,' said Liv.

'Fine. Give him hell and then come home safe.' Charlotte gave her a final hug.

'I'll be fine,' said Liv, feeling buoyed by the anticipation of her adventure. Especially now she was going in Charlotte's BMW as opposed to her vintage Fiesta.

'Take care,' said her mum, getting teary as she gave Liv a hug. 'I love you.'

'Love you too, Mum. Don't worry about me.' She waved them off, put her bag in the boot and went to get in.

'Argh!' she yelped, spotting someone inside the car.

Charlotte and her mother appeared at her side. 'I thought you'd like some company for the drive,' said Charlotte with a grin.

Liv pointed at Plastic Stan, propped up comfortably in the passenger seat. 'Stan? And what is he wearing?' asked Liv.

'I couldn't leave him naked. I put him in my old gym kit

so at a quick glance it looks like you're not alone,' explained Charlotte.

'Oh that's a really good idea,' said their mum, nodding furiously.

'I'm not taking Stan with me,' said Liv leaning in to undo his seatbelt.

'Think about it,' said Charlotte. 'You've no idea if this place is a nice area or well dodgy. This way thieves might think twice about nicking my car. Think of Stan as a theft-prevention device.'

Liv studied her sister. There was little point in arguing. 'Fine, I'll take Stan. Now clear off because I need to get going.' She could always put him in the boot at the first services.

'Call when you get there,' said her mum.

'No, because if I forget you'll have air-sea rescue out after me. If you don't hear anything then I'm fine. I'll see you tomorrow.' With that she got in the car and set off for Scotland.

The first couple of hours went well. The satnav was helpful, Stan was quiet and there were no traffic jams. She'd eaten three packets of crisps, sung her heart out to Taylor Swift, Mariah Carey and McFly, drunk two of the cans and now she was more than a bit bored. She'd been driving for two hours. It was dark and she was still on the M6 and quite fed up with the monotony of it now. Seeing the *Welcome To Scotland* sign was exciting but when she saw how far she still had to go, that excitement soon evaporated. She tried a game of I-Spy with Stan, but sadly he proved quite useless.

A few more miles and the effect of the cola was starting to make her need a wee. She could see the petrol gauge steadily declining so started to plan her pit stop like a formula one driver. She wanted to get to Loch Lochy as quickly as possible. Liv decided that a one-stop strategy at roughly the halfway, or three-hour point, would be her best option.

Whilst her strategy might have been sound, she hadn't considered the possibility that her bladder would feel like an overfilled water balloon. But she was determined to hold out and now saw it as a challenge. She pressed buttons on the satnav in the hope of finding a nearby services. The next one on the route was near Glasgow and another twenty-four minutes away – there was no way she was going to make that. But there was a garage two miles from the next exit, which would have to do.

She swung onto the garage forecourt like a getaway driver. Then had the dilemma of whether she should use the loo first and then fill up with petrol. Many loos were designated for customers only, and a discussion would only delay her getting to the toilet. She decided she would bung some fuel in and then make a dash for the loo.

Cross-legged, she stuck the nozzle in the car and squeezed the handle at the same time she squeezed her pelvic floor muscles, hoping that they'd hold. The slosh of liquid exiting the nozzle did not help. She watched the numbers on the pump whizz up. How much petrol did this car take? She couldn't wait any longer, that would have to do. She returned the nozzle and as quickly as her full bladder would allow she made it into the garage shop.

There were a couple of people in the queue – she couldn't

wait. She'd got some petrol even if she hadn't paid yet so she weaved her way through the aisles as 'Christmas Wrapping' by The Waitresses blared out. She followed the maze of shelves until she came to a printed sign and an arrow that said 'Toilet'. She felt like an explorer on the cusp of her quest. A few more steps and she could see the loo but she could also see a sign on the door that said, 'Out of Order'. Nooooooo!

Liv looked in all directions for inspiration. She had no more contingency plans left and definitely did not have time to go back to the car and find the next services. She had to go here. Liv tried the loo door and it opened. She dashed inside and locked it. There was a toilet and a sink. What was the worst that could happen? She lifted the lid, sat down and had the biggest wee of her life. The relief was immense. She also felt like a bit of a hero for completing her mission of a single pit stop without wetting herself in the process. She was winning at life today.

Liv was surprised and grateful that the flush worked – clearly not out of order at all. They probably just didn't want people using it. She washed her hands, unlocked the door and went to leave the cubicle. That was when she discovered why the toilet was out of order. The handle on the inside of the door was all floppy and had no impact at all. She tried it a few times but the door remained firmly closed. She locked and then unlocked the door. Liv tried the handle again – nothing. She put all her strength on the door handle and it came away in her hand. She was trapped.

4

Liv couldn't believe her master plan had been derailed by a toilet. Was she ever going to make it to Loch Lochy? She'd been calling for help for ages, and had now reached shouting stage, but nobody had come to rescue her. The music was still blaring out so it was likely they couldn't hear her shouts. At least she had her phone so decided to see if she could work out where she was exactly and call the garage. She put the toilet lid down. If she was going to be a while she might as well sit down.

It wasn't the nicest place to be trapped. It was a bit smelly and small with dark grey walls scrawled with graffiti such as 'One star – wouldn't pee here again' and 'Banksy woz ere'. The latter she very much doubted. But at least she had a loo and a sink so she figured she could survive quite a while if she had to. She was scrolling through garages near Glasgow when the door suddenly opened and she jumped to her feet. She was saved by a rotund man in an egg-stained T-shirt – not exactly a knight in shining armour, but he'd do.

'Pump four?' asked the man in a thick Scottish accent.

'Sorry?'

'Are you pump four?' He pointed over his shoulder. Liv had almost forgotten that she'd filled up with petrol.

'Yes.'

'You've not paid.' He scowled at her.

'Because I was locked in your toilet.' She didn't like being unjustly accused of something.

'Can ya not read?' He rapped a knuckle on the sign.

'I thought it meant the toilet, not the door. And it was somewhat of an emergency. Anyway, this has delayed me for a very important meeting.' She strode past him with as much dignity as she could muster.

'You've not paid,' he yelled after her.

'I'm going to pay now!' she yelled back as she rummaged in her bag for her debit card.

She went to stand by the till point and waited for the large man to squeeze himself behind the counter. He came to stand the other side of the counter but said nothing. There was an odd moment where they looked at each other, expecting the other person to do something. At last he spoke. 'What pump?'

Liv put her hands in the air.

'Number four, *obviously*.'

He grumbled something inaudible. She paid with a wave of her card.

'Thank you so much. It's been lovely to meet you,' she said. 'And this is yours,' she added placing the toilet door handle on the counter.

'For crying oot loud!' he grumbled. 'I should charge you for vandalising my loo!'

'Sorry,' she said, and she walked out wishing now that she had left something floating in his toilet.

The next leg of the journey was thankfully less eventful. Glasgow was busy, there were queues at each motorway junction where people were hopping on and off. For a while she sat stationary, but Liv decided to keep the last can of Coke as an emergency.

The satnav display taunted her with the anticipated arrival time. She'd been elated when she'd crossed the border but that had been ages ago. How long did restaurants stay open? If she got all the way there and it was closed, she'd have to wait until the next day to confront Fraser. Although she had no idea what time it would open again, maybe only for dinner the next evening. She needed to face him tonight because the adrenaline that had fuelled her slightly rash decision to travel all this way had suddenly dissipated. Now she was having a few second thoughts.

It had seemed like a good idea when she'd been charged up by her mum and sister, hell-bent on righting the wrong. But now she was in the car with only Plastic Stan as backup she was starting to question her choices. What if Fraser was aggressive? Having a go at him could be very unwise. Although from what she knew about him and their interactions he'd not seemed like that at all. He'd come across as a mild and gentle soul. She reminded herself that this was the same person who had cruelly ghosted her – maybe she didn't know him at all. But then there would be other people about as it was a public place. She should be fine. Worst-case scenario there would at least be a few witnesses. She had a fleeting thought that if she somehow went missing, her last known whereabouts could very well be a grainy picture from the garage of her handing over a door handle.

Charlotte's words came back to her. She liked the idea of being the person she wanted to be. Charlotte was right, nobody knew her in Scotland and how well did Fraser really know her? Question was: who did she want to be? She didn't want to be the person who dodged difficult situations. She wanted to be the sort of person who spoke their mind and said out loud all those things that went through her head. But that would land her in uncomfortable situations and was precisely why she avoided them. She tried to push the actual encounter to the back of her mind and focus on getting there.

The last part of the journey seemed to go on and on. It started to rain. Not a light drizzle, it was like someone had a hose on the windscreen. The wipers had to really fight to clear it. She was also getting tired. She gripped the steering wheel and focused on the road ahead; she just needed to get there and verbally shred Fraser so she could move on with her life. The satnav told her she needed to take a half right turn.

'What's half right? What does that mean?' she shouted at the satnav. A quick glance at the display told her she was almost on it. Then she saw a sign half covered by vigorously waving trees, which said Lochy House Hotel with a large arrow to the right where there appeared to be a narrow gravel track.

Liv braked and pulled hard on the steering wheel in the hope of making the turn. The car was going a bit too fast and skidded as it hit the gravel.

'Shiiiiiiit!' She righted the car, thankful there was no one else on the road, but there was a large pothole filled with water that she didn't notice until she was driving over it. The hole wrenched at the tyre, causing her to fight the steering wheel. A few feet further on, with the car tugging to one side, she knew she had a problem. Liv pulled over where there was a passing point on the narrow track. The rain continued in sheets but she had to see what the damage was. She jumped out of the car and went around to the passenger side. She could see it even before she knelt down that the tyre had a whopping great hole in it.

'Bugger it!' she said and she dashed back around to the other side, dodging puddles as she went.

Liv sat in the car for a bit, rain dripping off her hair and thundering onto the windscreen. What should she do now? She turned to her passenger.

'Stan, any ideas?' He didn't reply, which was probably a good thing – that was a whole level of horror film she wasn't ready for. 'Nope, I thought not,' she said. She'd have to figure this out on her own.

The rain wasn't going to ease. It was almost ten o'clock now, and according to the satnav the hotel and restaurant were just a few more yards up the road. Liv decided she hadn't come all this way to get derailed by a flat tyre. She pulled up her hoodie, grabbed her phone and got out of the car. She was going to tell Fraser Douglas what she thought of him! On second thought, perhaps she'd ask if he knew anyone with a tow truck first.

Liv set off with the driving rain soon soaking through her clothes. Helpfully there was another sign further up for Bonnie Scott's, which she followed down a long, winding driveway. The walk gave her a chance to go over her rant in her head, which fired her up a little more. There were lots of trees but as she made it around the last bend the hotel came into view. It was a large grey stone building with gables and a turret. It looked more like a fairy-tale castle than a hotel. There were no lights on anywhere, which did not give Liv hope, but having come this far she wasn't giving up yet. She was thankful there was a small portico where she could shelter from the rain. She knocked on the door and waited. Her knuckles on the solid door didn't make a lot of noise but she waited and knocked again but harder – still nothing.

Frustration drove her back out into the rain, and she trudged around the outside of the hotel in the hope of finding some signs of life. Had this all been a waste of time? She was about to give up when she saw a dim light further around the back. She followed it, tripping over undulations in the lawn as she went. There were a couple of lights on up ahead and the signs of life buoyed her a little. As she neared the lit window she took in her surroundings: outside it was pitch-black, freezing cold, and there wasn't another soul about. Suddenly she wasn't quite so bold. What if Fraser was a madman? She could almost read the newspaper article – *Lone woman, who vandalised toilet, disappears from remote Scottish location.*

She was feeling vulnerable so decided to see if she could get a look through the window first. If she could ascertain if there was anyone else inside, and ideally if Fraser didn't look like a serial killer, that would help inform her next decision.

The nearest window was thin and horizontal, higher up the side of the building. Higher than she could see even on tiptoes. Thankfully there were a number of crates that looked to be steady enough for her to climb up on. She got on the first one, which felt robust, so she stepped up onto the next one. A little more precarious but at least now she could grip the stone window ledge and peer inside the window.

She found herself looking into a small room that was either a kitchen or utility – it was hard to tell. There was a run of worktop, a rack of coats and some long cupboard-style doors. A door was open at the end of the room but that was at the furthest limits of her vision. She inched along the crate and felt the structure wobble. She froze and again leaned in against the window. Briefly she saw someone beyond the small room but it was so fleeting she wasn't even sure if they were male or female. She was intrigued and keen to see who was there. She was watching intently, waiting for somebody, ideally Fraser, to appear when something thumped her on the backside.

'What the actual—' Fury shot through her as she twisted around to confront whoever had inappropriately clouted her. But as she turned the sight that met her was unexpected. A bull with horns like a curtain rail was preparing to give her another shove.

'Argh!' she yelled, which startled the bull and caused it to turn around and swipe her a second time. She tried to hang on to the windowsill but it was no use. The force of the animal's rump sent her flying off the crates. Her head bashed into the window ledge as she fell. Unable to stop herself, Liv landed awkwardly on the concrete below with an unpleasant thud. Everything around her turned to black.

5

Effie was on her way to answer the front door when she heard a distant cry followed by a clatter. She whipped open the front door to find her friend Robbie.

'Hello,' he said awkwardly. 'I was just passing.' He pointed up the very long private driveway. 'And—'

'Quick, I heard someone scream and then a loud bang,' said Effie almost dragging him inside and through the hotel. 'I think something awful has happened. Perhaps a plane crash, some sort of natural disaster, or it could be the ghost soldiers from the Battle of Lochy risen up. Or maybe—'

She was interrupted by the hum of a mobility scooter. They heard the sound long before it appeared and blocked their way. Effie's grandmother, Dolly, rode the scooter into the hallway like she was leading a charge of the clan. The elderly lady sat on the vehicle with her back ramrod straight, her white hair in a neat bun and a shawl draped nonchalantly over her shoulders. It looked like it should be flying behind her; that is, if she was to travel any faster than three miles an hour.

'What are you two standing there for?' asked Dolly in her thick local drawl.

'You heard something too then?' asked Robbie.

'See! I didn't imagine it. And before you say anything about last time, I'm still sure that was a bear.' Effie stared him down.

'Aye, I heard something all right and it wasny any animal I've ever heard of,' said Dolly.

'Could have been Janet,' said Effie. An icy sensation trickled through her system at the name. She savoured it for a moment.

'Hmm.' Dolly seemed to ponder this. 'I believe Janet is more of a wailer than a screamer. I'd wager that cry was the sound of the living.'

'Maybe we should check they're okay then,' suggested Robbie pointing to the back of the hotel.

'Aye, hop to it,' said Dolly, but as Effie and Robbie went to walk through the doorway Dolly set off on the scooter, promptly blocking the way. They slow-walked behind Dolly as she trundled through to the back door. 'Well, one of you will need to open it,' said Dolly with a tut.

'Sorry,' said Effie trying to squeeze past the scooter and get to the door.

The weather was keen to join them inside as soon as the door was opened – although still mild for the time of year, the rain was unrelenting. The back portico provided a useful shelter for them to survey the backyard. At first the three of them saw nothing as they squinted into the darkness but as

Effie turned her head to the right, she spotted something – or rather *someone* sitting on the ground.

'There they are!' she shouted, running towards them. This was the most excited she'd been since Dolly had upgraded her wheelchair. Not a lot happened in Glendormie.

When she reached them, she could see it was a young woman in her twenties who was absolutely soaked through. Effie crouched down and touched her arm.

'You're real. Not a ghost. I just needed to check.' She looked her over and quickly noticed a mix of blood and rain trickling down her cheek. 'My gosh, you're injured. Robbie, it's a girl and she's hurt! Call the air ambulance.'

'Oh no, no. I don't need to go to hospital,' said the woman blinking slowly as if trying to focus.

'What hurts?' asked Effie.

'Everything,' she said. 'My head and ankle are doing the most throbbing. But I don't think anything's broken.'

'Hold the air ambulance,' called Effie feeling quite disappointed.

Robbie gave her a thumbs up.

'I'll get the first-aid kit,' he shouted.

'Bring her into the warm!' called Dolly. 'I can see from here she's drookit.'

'Come on, let's get you inside,' said Effie, trying to help the stranger to their feet. Whilst she didn't like to see anyone hurt, she was beyond delighted to have a visitor.

*

Liv had heard the phrase 'dazed and confused' but never before had she fully understood what that felt like. She reached for her phone but it was no longer in her pocket.

She glanced around but it was so dark she had no hope of finding it, and she was feeling a bit sick as her head was thumping so hard. The kind young woman helped her to her feet, and she instantly noticed one of her ankles was tender to stand on.

They made their way inside once an old lady on a scooter had very slowly reversed out of the way. Liv now found herself sitting on a chair in a wide hallway clad in dark wood panels, dotted with what she could only describe as odd items. Next to her, leaning against the wall, was a giant spear type thing and on her other side there was what looked like a stuffed giant turkey. High on the walls sat a variety of mounted deer heads, punctuated by an elaborate chandelier that appeared to be made from the antlers of another bunch of unfortunate wildlife. This wasn't like any hotel she'd ever been in and definitely wasn't the Travelodge.

'Jings, did you hear the crash as she went down? She's cracked her skull open!' said the young woman. 'What should we do, what should we do?'

'Now what *you* need to do is calm down, Effie,' said the older woman, inching her scooter closer and closer to Liv. 'You've been watching too much *Casualty*. There's some ice on the way for her bumps. She'll soon be right,' she added before turning to face Liv. 'I'm Dolly. Can you hear me?' she asked.

Liv nodded.

The young man who had gone to get the first-aid kit stepped forward. Liv looked him up and down. He was thin with a shock of dark hair and suspicious eyes. He wasn't Fraser.

'I want to know what she was doing around the back of

the property. Very suspect behaviour. Do you think she's a criminal or possibly a spy?'

Dolly backed the scooter up and she and the man had a not-so-hushed conversation. 'Goodness, Robbie. She'll not be a spy. Probably just a lost tourist.'

'She's wearing a boiler suit. Some sort of tradesperson perhaps?'

It's a bloody jumpsuit, thought Liv defensively, but she wasn't brave enough to voice it. Charlotte's words floating into her mind – nobody knew her in Scotland; she could be whoever she wanted to be. She opened her mouth but thought better of it, and then the moment passed. Maybe she needed to build up to being brave and speaking her mind.

'I'm Effie. What's your name?' The young woman loomed in front of Liv, making her pull her chin back and wince. The pain in her head was making it hard to function. Plus, she was so tired, and she knew she couldn't give her real name. What if they knew Fraser? How could she explain what she was doing? Oh, I'm just snooping around so I can shout at a man who ghosted me – nope she couldn't say that. Her addled brain had no answers.

'Umm... err... Sorry, I can't think straight,' said Liv.

'She's taken an awful blow to the head. She's probably concussed. She must have amnesia,' said Effie, seeming quite excited at the prospect.

'Do you know your name?' asked Robbie, looking a little more concerned.

Liv shook her head. It wasn't that she didn't know it, obviously, but she really didn't want to tell them.

'See!' said Effie. 'That's amnesia. I told you. Didn't I?'

'How about you track down Doc McLeod,' said Dolly, wheeling over and narrowly missing the large spear thing. All Liv needed was for that to land on her head and she would be off to hospital – or possibly a shallow grave in the woods.

'Okay.' Effie dashed off.

'Where's the ice!' shouted Dolly making Liv recoil.

'Coming!' called back a deep voice.

Dolly was quite close again. Her voice a gentle burble of accent.

'Now, can you remember anything? Who you are? Why you're here? How you got here?'

This was beyond awkward. Liv bit her lip and slowly shook her head. Once she felt okay to drive, she'd have to get the tyre sorted and just leave. Then she had a flash of something she did remember, and that she should definitely share.

'Oh I remember what happened outside. I was attacked by this huge bull.' She gestured with her hands so they could get an idea of the size of it. She didn't want it attacking anyone else. 'He had these massive horns. I thought it was going to gore me with them. It was the bull that knocked me off... um... over. He knocked me over and I must have banged my head.' She looked to Dolly and Robbie for a response. What she wasn't expecting was for them both to start laughing. A laughter that built up into belly laughs. Liv sat there soaking wet, with her head throbbing and her mind whirring. Were these people insane?

Effie returned and while she seemed to have an air of the dramatic, she did seem fairly normal.

'What's going on?' asked Effie as Robbie was now

holding on to Dolly's scooter for support while clutching his side with the other hand.

He finally got his laughter under control.

'She said she got attacked by a giant bull with big horns.' That was all he could manage before he and Dolly cracked up again. This was weird.

'Were both horns pointed in the same direction?' asked Effie turning to Liv.

Probably the oddest question she'd ever been asked apart from someone who stopped her in town to ask if she'd seen any recent signs of alien life. Liv had to think back to the bull. She'd only caught a glimpse of her attacker and that had been enough to scare the life out of her. But now she thought about it the horn nearest her was slightly pointing up but the other not so much.

'I don't think so. Sort of one up and one down. What does that mean?'

Effie started to giggle. This was an epidemic. Liv shot her a look and Effie put her hand over her mouth.

'Sorry. We're not being mean. It's just that it wasn't a giant bull.'

'It flaming well was,' said Liv, feeling indignant. She might have banged her head but she knew what she saw. 'It was right in front of me. I thought I was going to be a human kebab.' This triggered another burst of laughter from Robbie and Dolly.

'Actually I think you just met Ginger,' said Effie.

'What now?' asked Liv starting to wonder if she'd taken a harder bang to the head than she thought and she was imagining all this madness.

Dolly cleared her throat and gave herself a shake to quell the laughter.

'I'm sorry,' she said gripping her shawl. 'Ginger is a wee Highland cow, not much more than a calf, and she's the gentlest soul you could ever hope to meet. Although she has no idea about how big she is, so sometimes she's a bit...'

'In ya face,' added Effie. 'It's possible that she thinks she's a dog. She loves to steal a bucket and kick it around the yard.'

Robbie nodded. 'Like she's playing centre forward for Rangers.'

Liv wasn't sure what to make of all of this. A football-playing Highland cow – that was beyond weird.

'Right,' was all she could manage. When she thought her head couldn't take any more, a door at the end of the hallway opened and out strode Fraser Douglas.

6

For a moment Liv wasn't sure if it was her head playing tricks but as Fraser strode towards her, she knew it was him. Although he was even hotter in real life. He was certainly beefier than she'd imagined. He had the faintest smile on his lips, but he was coming straight at her with an outstretched fist and she panicked. She felt vulnerable sitting on a chair, so she jumped to her feet once he was within arm's reach. Pain shot through her ankle and she immediately hopped onto the good leg, accidentally kicking the long spear-like object. She watched it, in what seemed like slow motion, as it fell, striking Fraser on the head.

'Pissing hell!' he said grabbing the pole before it hit anything else.

'Careful,' yelled Dolly somewhat belatedly. 'That's a genuine Scots pike from the Battle of Pinkie Cleugh.'

Liv was none the wiser about what the thing was other than bloody lethal and she was now face to face with a cross-looking Fraser. What was going to happen? Her heart thumped almost as hard as her head and ankle. But in that moment it felt like it was exactly the right time to start being the person she wanted to be.

'What the hell did you do that for?' he said touching his head and checking his hand for blood – thankfully there wasn't any.

'I didn't do it on purpose.' Liv tried to take the weapon from him to put it back against the wall but he wasn't letting go.

'English?' said Fraser, taking a step back as if she'd announced she had leprosy mixed with a raging dose of bubonic plague.

'She can't help that,' said Effie. 'Can I have the ice?' she asked.

Fraser returned the pike to where it had been, all the while keeping a watch on Liv.

'You can have half the ice,' said Fraser to Effie, unwrapping what he was carrying in his hand and reluctantly handing half of the contents to her along with a cloth he pulled from his pocket. 'I need the rest now she's tried to brain me.' He glared at Liv. Instead of being intimidated she was surprised. How did he not recognise her? He was looking right at her. The profile picture she'd used was from last summer when her hair had been highlighted and she'd made an effort with some make-up. Maybe it was a best version of herself, unlike the wet and bedraggled version in front of him now, but the photograph did look vaguely like her, unlike so many of the men she'd encountered on dating apps. Why wasn't he frantically pointing at her saying: *You're Olivia Bingham!* Or was this his poker face? She was so confused. What was going on?

'Shouldn't something like this be on a wall where it can't hurt anyone?' asked Liv, checking the pole couldn't fall over again.

'It may have escaped your notice but this place is in need of repair.' He looked at her like she wasn't the sharpest crayon in the box.

Liv glanced around at her surroundings: damp patch on the ceiling, peeling wallpaper, and a threadbare tartan carpet. On the wall above them was a single bracket and a mark on the wallpaper in the shape of a long pointy pole.

'I'm guessing it fell off the wall and nobody's put it back.'

'Got it in one. You're smarter than the average Sassenach.'

'What did you call me?' She'd not stand there and be called names. Especially now she was being the new improved Liv. That Liv wouldn't dodge being insulted.

'It just means an English person,' said Effie, stepping between the two of them. 'We should get this ice on your head.'

Liv and Fraser went to sit on the same chair. Liv got there first, but as she sat down hard her wet clothes emitted a strange wet fart-like sound. Fraser huffed and sat on a chair to the side and fixed his glare on her. Still not even a flicker of recognition. Had he taken a much harder thump to the head than it seemed or was she that easily forgotten?

Effie wrapped the ice in the cloth and placed it gently on Liv's head.

'Thanks,' said Liv.

'You're welcome.'

Everyone was silent but Liv felt like all eyes were on her.

'Who is she exactly?' Fraser looked at Dolly for an answer.

'Lass has bumped her head and does nay know who she is,' replied Dolly.

'It's amnesia,' said Effie. 'She had a run-in with Ginger in the yard and she banged her head really badly. Did you not hear her scream?'

'I heard something. I thought it might be an owl.'

'I think I've done all I can,' said Robbie. 'I'll leave you good people. If there are any issues.' He indiscreetly pointed a finger in Liv's direction. 'Then just give me a call. Goodnight, everyone.' He strode off creating a bit of a draught as he passed, and Liv shivered.

'She was sitting in a puddle when I rescued her. She can't remember who she is. I've left a message for the Doc,' said Effie.

'Amnesia?' Fraser snorted a laugh. 'Really?'

'Well if I don't know who I am, maybe you do,' said Liv jutting out her jaw in challenge. She was fast warming to the new ballsy Liv.

'Not a clue,' said Fraser.

Effie gasped. 'Maybe you've got amnesia too.'

'No, I'm fine,' said Fraser kindly. 'What was she doing in the yard?'

Dolly wheeled herself forward. 'We think she's a lost tourist. Probably a wee dram and a good night's sleep will bring more answers in the morning.' She turned her scooter towards Effie. 'It's late. You'd best get me home,' she said as she disappeared up the hallway.

'Here you go,' said Effie, passing Liv the ice bundle.

'Hang on!' Fraser got to his feet. 'What's happening with her?' He pointed towards Liv like she were an item of lost property.

This was the point where she should say she could sleep in her car or she'd get a hotel room but seeing as she wasn't meant to know who she was, she was limping and she'd lost her phone when she fell – she was a bit stuck.

'You live in a hotel, Fraser,' said Dolly. 'You work it out.'

'But she can't stay here,' he said.

'I can't stay here,' repeated Liv standing up and wobbling slightly. She stopped herself from reaching for the pike as support.

'Why not?' asked Effie. Fraser also turned to give Liv a questioning look despite what he'd just said.

'Because… he's a stranger.' Liv pointed at Fraser.

'No, he's not,' said Effie with a laugh. 'He's my cousin Fraser.'

Liv leaned forward to whisper. 'But I don't know him.' She hoped her expression underlined her point.

'But I do,' said Effie, with an earnest nod. 'He's sound, is Fraser. You'll be grand. But watch out for Janet.'

'Who's Janet?' asked Liv.

Effie's eyes widened and her expression took on a theatrical quality.

'Janet was a local woman who made herbal potions for the sick. But after a few people died she was tried as a witch and strangled on the shores of the loch. At night you can hear her ghost wailing,' she said. 'Legend has it that she is looking for another poor soul to replace her so that she can return to the living.'

'Okay, wasn't expecting that,' said Liv. She didn't scare easily but that was one creepy tale.

'I have to go.' Effie pointed up the hall after Dolly. 'Bye,' she added cheerily.

'Thanks a bunch!' called Fraser as Effie strode after the scooter.

They returned to their respective seats; Liv lowered herself down more carefully this time to avoid any embarrassing noises. They sat in silence. This was awkward.

'They say that an Englishman's home is his castle and you actually live in one,' she said.

'I'm not an Englishman. I'm a Scot.'

'Whoops, sorry. No offence.' But she had a nasty feeling he was very much offended. They sat in silence for a moment. Liv decided that perhaps she should swap her ice to her ankle as that was still throbbing too. She rolled up the leg of her soggy jumpsuit, and undid her boots, revealing a very puffy ankle. She reached down and held the ice in place. She heard Fraser huff. She looked up and he was watching her.

'Look,' she said, 'I don't like being in this situation any more than you do.'

'Here,' he said getting up and handing her his ice. 'If you're stopping…' He paused, probably in the hope that she would contradict him but she didn't so he continued. 'Then I've things I need to sort out. I'll lock up, so we don't get any *more* intruders.' She tried not to react to his pointed comment. 'And then we'll go to bed.'

Bloody hell, he doesn't waste any time, thought Liv, more than outraged.

'Not so fast!' Liv was on red alert. If she hollered would the other women still hear her? 'I don't need a place to stay that badly. I'll sleep in the rain with the bull or cow or whatever it is, if I have to. But I am not sleeping with you!' She wondered for a moment if this had been his plan all along. Ghost her and get her to track him down then she was at his mercy. Or was that just her tired brain overreacting?

'Stop!' Fraser held up his palm. 'Not go to bed *with me*. I meant I'll fix you somewhere to sleep. Trust me, it will be nowhere near me. All right?'

Liv felt a bit foolish. 'Oh I see. I thought… you know… I'm all a bit woozy and extra wary. Sorry.'

'Forget it. If you want a dram, there's whisky in the cabinet in the library. It's good for shock.' He pointed down the corridor to the left before heading in the opposite direction and leaving her alone.

'Thanks,' she said but he'd already gone. She waited a couple of minutes as the ice was easing her ankle, but her curiosity got the better of her and she decided to go and investigate the library. It sounded very grand. She got to her feet easily enough but her ankle was unhappy and she didn't want to aggravate it more, so she virtually hopped up the hallway, moving from one piece of ancient furniture to the next for support.

She pushed open the door. The room was dark. She felt for a switch and found an old-fashioned metal one. Above her a chandelier sparkled into life. She blinked at the brightness. The initial dazzle soon faded as she noticed the many missing crystals and damaged state the light fitting was in. Looking around the room, she saw that the chandelier wasn't the only thing with bits missing. Some faded but fancy-looking chairs huddled around a redundant fireplace. The room was lined with dark wood bookcases; there were a few rows of dusty encyclopaedias and a row of cloth books that she'd never heard of but there wasn't a single normal book in sight. At one end of the room was a large built-in cabinet in the same dark wood; so dark it was almost black. She made her way towards it and was grateful to grip its ornate beaded edge for support. That was until with a small creaking sound the beading came away in her hand.

'Shit,' she muttered as she held on tight with her other hand. This place was a death trap. She tugged open a drawer, which was full of papers that were keen to escape their confines and seemed to burst free. 'Bloody hell!' She rammed them back, popped in the piece of beading and shut the drawer quickly. Bottles weren't going to be in there anyway. Her mind was a mush. She opened the cabinet-style door below and was met by the smell of old alcohol; like it had seeped into the very structure of the cabinet. She crouched down as best she could and peered inside. There was something that looked like a shiny silver fire extinguisher, a glass in the shape of a skull and a bottle of whisky. She pulled out the bottle. A bit of rummaging in the other side of the cabinet uncovered a tumbler. Usually Liv wasn't a spirits drinker but Fraser had said it was good for shock and she'd definitely had one of those. She poured herself a small measure of the honey-coloured liquid. She gave it a sniff. It smelled a bit like TCP.

Leaning against the end of the cabinet she looked around. It was a big room and quite chilly but that was likely because her wet clothes were sticking to her. There were high ceilings and ornate cornicing, which was still pretty, even if some bits were missing. She would have loved to have seen it when the shelves were full of books and could imagine this was quite a grand room in its day. Straight ahead was a large window and a padded window seat with cushions.

She wondered what the view was like. All she could see out of the wet window now was darkness. She left the safety of the cabinet and hobbled over to the window and sat down. There were large white-painted wooden panels on either side of the window that she supposed were shutters.

Liv swirled the liquid in the glass and watched it adhere to the side. She peered through the window and knocked back the whisky. The harsh liquid hit the back of her throat, making her gasp. With that a hairy ginger face loomed out of the darkness.

'Argh!' she yelled as best she could as the whisky seemed to have stolen her voice.

She heard the thud of Fraser's feet before he came flying into the library. 'What did you do now?' he asked, scanning her and the room.

She pointed at the window, which was being licked clean by a very large pink tongue.

7

Liv was laughing now she could see the hairy face was the young cow they'd told her about. It looked soaked as it methodically cleared the rain off the window. She looked at Fraser. He didn't seem amused.

'It's just Ginger,' he said.

'I know that now,' she said, her voice sounding all hoarse thanks to the whisky.

'How much have you had to drink?' He glared at her accusatorially.

'One tiny measure,' she croaked. 'And it wasn't very nice anyway.'

'That is a Highland Malt. It's one of the best whiskies made. It's fifteen years old.'

Liv screwed up her nose. 'Then it's probably gone off.' That would explain the taste. She stuck her tongue out in a futile attempt to get rid of the aftertaste.

'And they call us heathens,' he muttered as he shook his head.

She didn't like his attitude. 'What have I done now?'

'Never mind. Let's get you to bed. To your own bed,' he said carefully. 'Then I'll round up Ginger and tuck her in for the night.'

He walked out leaving Liv to push herself up onto one leg and hobble from the room. 'Are you coming?' he called.

'Bloody hell. Have some patience, would you? I've knackered my ankle.'

His head appeared around the door. 'Did you want a hand?'

'No thank you,' she said as she clung to the cabinet and hopped her way to join him at the door. She didn't want anything from Fraser Douglas. 'I can manage just fine,' she added.

'So I see,' he said and he left her.

Liv followed him out of the room and turned left, past a reception desk to where Fraser was waiting at the bottom of a sweeping staircase. Despite the worn patches on its carpet, it was seriously impressive.

'This way,' he said, taking the small steps two at a time until he was soon at the top.

Liv watched with her mouth open. 'Do you not have a lift?'

'No. The main building is seventeenth century with Victorian additions. They weren't so big on lifts back then.'

'Thanks for the history lesson. I'll just crash on the sofa.'

'What sofa?' he asked.

Liv sighed heavily. 'No sofa?' He shook his head. 'Anywhere downstairs I can sleep?'

'Ten bedrooms…' he began and hope bloomed inside her.

'Are all on the first floor. Downstairs, there's the library, dining room, kitchens, drawing room, toilets and snug.'

'Maybe I'll curl up on the window seat.'

'Up to you but you'll not be that comfortable and likely to fall off in the night if you roll over.'

He had a point. 'Right.' She set about taking the stairs slowly and one at a time. She felt ancient. Even her great-granny moved a lot quicker than this and she had an arthritic knee.

'You may as well stay down there. At that rate you'll not make it up here before midnight,' he said, leaning his forearms on the banister at the top and watching her slow progress.

'Have you thought about stand-up comedy?'

'It's been suggested before,' he said, 'but I quite like being a—'

'Smartarse?' she offered.

He did at least chuckle at her retort. 'Are you sure you wouldn't like me to help you?'

She was tired, grumpy and she ached all over. 'Assuming you can't perform levitation then yes, please.' The last word she had to force out. It was hard to be polite to someone who had ghosted her. The whole situation was odd but she was a big believer in listening to her gut and whilst Fraser had done the dirty to her online she wasn't getting any mad axe murderer vibes from him.

Fraser swept back down the staircase and without warning lifted Liv into his arms and set off back up to the first floor. 'What the actual—'

'You were taking far too long, this is the quickest option.' He held her securely in his arms. Her wet-jumpsuit-clad body instantly heated up at the contact with him. 'This way we can both get to bed. Separately,' he added with emphasis as he put her down carefully at the top and she clutched the rail. The unexpected contact had winded her. Her senses were awash with the scent of him, which was a confusing mix of bergamot and garlic. 'This way.'

He led her along a corridor with a deep red carpet and dim lighting. He opened a door and stepped inside. 'Actually I'd forgotten there was a leak in here.' Liv popped her head around the door to see water sploshing into a bucket from the ceiling. 'I'll empty that later,' he said, more to himself than Liv. 'It's fine – there's lots more to choose from.'

'Ooh do I get to choose?' This was starting to feel almost fun. The choice of bedrooms in a hotel wasn't something you got offered every day.

'I guess,' he said opening another door and walking in. 'This is smaller but the view is great because…' Liv pointed at a picture on the wall. 'What?' he asked.

The dark painting was of a hunched woman all in black. The hooded eyes seemed to lock onto Liv and she felt a sensation like cold fingers creep up her spine. 'Is that Janet the witch by any chance?'

'It is,' said Fraser sounding pleased. 'It's a copy of a famous painting. Well, famous in these parts.'

'Can you move it please? Because I don't think I can sleep here with Janet staring at me.' Liv tried stepping a few feet to the left but the eyes were definitely following her.

'Err, no I don't think so. For health and safety reasons the pictures are screwed to the walls. Let's look at the next room. Perhaps that will be to madam's taste.'

'Sorry,' said Liv getting out of the way as Fraser turned

off the light and came out. The next two rooms had either boxes of stuff on the floor or things piled on the bed, so Fraser quickly moved on to the fourth room where the bed had no mattress, making him huff a bit more.

He took her off down another corridor and opened the door to the next bedroom, switched on the light and stepped back so that she could look inside. The first thing she saw was a line of mounted stags' heads above the bed.

'I know you're not going to like this and I'm really sorry to be a pain. But no way,' she said shaking her head and turning around.

'What do you mean, *no way*?' When he repeated it in his accent it almost sounded comical.

'I mean I can't sleep in here with them. I'd be awake all night worrying about one falling off. And if one of those did fall on me I'd be skewered by its horns. That's not how I want to die. No ta.'

'Oh deer,' said Fraser. She gave him her best withering look and he stopped grinning. 'They're not horns,' he explained. 'They're antlers and, like Janet, they are firmly secured to the wall.'

'Like the pointy stick thing once was? Still I won't be able to sleep with butchered Bambi staring down at me all night.'

Fraser snorted a laugh. 'Do I need to *buck* my ideas up?'

Despite all her aches she was quite liking the battle of the puns with Fraser. 'I don't expect you to be *fawn*ing over me, but if there's somewhere else I could sleep that would be great.'

'Fine,' he said with a shrug. 'That rules out a couple more rooms. But I think there's some bats taken up residence in one of those so that probably wasn't your first choice anyway.' He wandered off and she limped after him. He opened another door. 'Here you go. This is the last option. The lock doesn't work but otherwise I think it's fine.'

She had a tentative look inside. 'No murdered animals, that's a good start. But blimey it's cold.'

Fraser marched over to where the window was wide open and there was a small puddle of rainwater on the floor. He pulled the window shut. 'Dodgy catch, that's all. I'll get some bedding,' he said. As he went off, Liv hopped into the room. There was a four-poster bed, which she couldn't help but be a bit wowed by. Dust sheets covered all the furniture so she scooted over to the bed and began pulling sheets off the things nearby. First to be uncovered was a bedside table, then a plump-looking chair, followed by a large camera on a tripod.

Fraser stepped back into the room with an armful of white bedding. 'What the hell is that?' she asked.

'It's a camera.'

'You don't even deny it.' She scratched her head. What sort of pervert was he? 'Do you film people while they're sleeping? Having sex? What?'

Fraser closed his eyes slowly and opened them again. 'If that was what it was for, do you not think guests might notice? If I wanted to film people, which I definitely don't, I'd go for one of those tiny spy cameras you can hide inside anything.'

She studied him. 'I guess but why's it pointed at the bed like that?'

'It's an antique from the golden age of cinema, and it doesn't even work. But I'll move it.' He plonked his armfuls of bedding down, snatched up the camera and stomped out of the room. 'Worse than the princess and the bloody pea.'

'Thank you. I appreciate it,' she called after him and she received a grunt as a reply.

He returned with some extra blankets and Liv tried her best to help him make the bed but he tutted at her as she was too slow moving around the bed. Eventually it was ready. She looked about her. 'En suite?' she asked.

'You have one of those at home do you?' he asked with a tilt of his head.

'No, but this is a hotel so I assumed—'

'It's not a hotel if it's not open and if guests aren't paying. And you assumed wrong. Again the Victorians weren't big on their plumbing but there is an alternative under the bed.'

Liv crouched down to see a large china pot. 'Eww, gross.'

'It's for comedy value. Toilet is next door...' He paused and seemed to be considering something. 'I'm in the next room along after the bathroom. If there are any more cow, Janet or camera emergencies please do let me know.' He tugged at his auburn fringe and made for the door.

'I'll be sure to do that. You're on your way to a great star rating on TripAdvisor. Goodnight,' she said and she shut the door behind him. Liv breathed a sigh of relief, then she had another thought. She opened the door again, and this time her tone was a bit more contrite. 'I don't suppose you've got a towel?'

'I'll bring you one in a minute.'

She stuck her head out of the door to see he was further along, standing with his back to her. 'Thanks, and something to sleep in?' She noticed his shoulders tense up.

He turned around. He didn't look happy. 'Would you like a nightdress or pyjamas?'

'Ooh pyjamas would be great, thanks.'

He stared at her and shook his head. 'Unbelievable. Completely unbelievable.' He was still grumbling to himself as he walked away.

A few minutes later there was a tap on the door and Fraser handed her a large white towel, a pair of men's underpants and a Meatloaf T-shirt. She took them.

'Didn't have you down as a Meatloaf fan,' she said, thinking about how much Fraser's profile had said he liked Mariah Carey.

'Funnily enough we don't carry nightwear for random passers-by but I'll put it in the suggestions box. You can keep the trunks but I want that T-shirt back. Intact.'

'I'll try not to put bumps in it,' she said with an overly enthusiastic smile. 'Thanks. Goodnight.' And she closed the door. Now she just had to find something to wedge underneath it. Fraser might be being all helpful now, but could she really trust him?

*

Despite the lodge being in the grounds of the Lochy House hotel, and Effie having a coat, she was still drenched by the time they got inside. Dolly wasn't as wet because she always had her large black waterproof poncho with her; it was one of the many essentials she kept on the scooter along with a slab of Scottish tablet and a toilet roll. Once inside Effie helped her grandmother take off her poncho and Dolly's old Scottie dog, Jock'O, came to meet them.

'Hello, boy,' said Dolly as the two greeted each other.

Jock'O proudly presented his mistress with a sock and jumped onto Dolly's lap – he loved to cadge a lift on the mobility scooter.

'Hey, Jock'O, that's one of mine,' complained Effie trying to take the sock but he'd only growl if she tried to reclaim it. She'd have to wait for him to abandon it somewhere and snatch it then. Dolly headed off to the kitchen and Effie tried not to drip water everywhere. Effie took off her wet layers and went through to the kitchen where Dolly was making their night-time drinks.

'What do you make of the English girl?' asked Dolly.

'I like her very much.' Effie was pleased to have another female around, who was of a similar age to her. 'I hope she stays.'

Dolly gave her a look that Effie was very used to seeing from a lot of people – a mix of pity and tolerance. 'I'm afraid that once she remembers who she is she'll be off.'

'I wonder where she's from. Do you think she's foreign? She could have travelled thousands of miles only to get knocked over by Ginger.'

'I doubt it,' said Dolly giving Jock'O a stroke. 'From her accent I'd guess Manchester or Liverpool. I always get those two mixed up.'

'Still, that's a long way away.' It was further than Effie had ever been. She had dreams of going on epic journeys to far-flung places. The celebrity television travel documentaries were her favourite. Effie had plans. One day she'd do it. She'd be like her mother and leave Glendormie and see for real the things she'd only seen through a TV screen. But for now, Dolly needed her, so this was where she had to stay. She didn't begrudge being her grandmother's carer. There weren't many jobs locally that she'd want to do. Most of them came and went with the tourist seasons. And as she didn't drive, working from home was very convenient.

Effie helped Dolly make the drinks and they went through to the small living room. Jock'O made the short jump from Dolly's lap to the sofa and while he settled down with his night-time biscuit, Effie stealthily repossessed her soggy sock.

'Jings!' said Effie as a thought struck her.

Dolly put her hand to her chest. 'Goodness, Effie. You gave my pacemaker a start! What is it?'

'We could have asked the girl to stay with us.' Effie was thoroughly disappointed that she'd not thought of this earlier. 'Should I call Fraser to bring her down here?'

'And where would she sleep?' asked Dolly blowing on her cocoa.

Effie mentally went through the house. There was Dolly's room, which was the largest but it didn't have a big bed. There was Effie's tiny bedroom with a single bed. 'There's the sofa.' The dog finished his biscuit and eyed her suspiciously.

'And where would Jock'O sleep?' asked Dolly, looking put out on his behalf.

'He has a bed in the kitchen.'

'And when has he ever slept in it?' asked Dolly. 'I'm sure the English girl will be just fine with Fraser.' There was a brief pause. 'I'm just not that sure how our Fraser will be with her.'

They both winced at the thought.

8

Liv took off her wet things, dried herself and got changed under the covers because the room was so chilly but once she was in bed she was actually quite cosy. The sheets were a high thread count and despite the pillows being a bit lumpy, and her various body parts aching, she managed to get comfy. She'd found a box in the corner of the room, torn off a flap of cardboard and after folding it multiple times it made a good wedge for the door. She'd placed the biggest of the books, she'd found inside the box, on the bedside cabinet so if she needed to defend herself in the night it would make a good impromptu weapon.

Despite everything she wasn't worried about being murdered in her sleep by Fraser. Her brain was unhelpfully thinking about Janet the witch. She wasn't usually spooked by ghost stories but now she'd seen the painting it seemed to come to life in her mind, which wasn't helpful. She squeezed her eyes tight shut. She was tired and she needed to get to sleep.

She must have nodded off because she turned over and something pulled her awake. She plumped her pillow and snuggled down again. That was when she heard it. A sort of rhythmic moaning noise. Was she dreaming it? She gave her arm a pinch. Nope, she was now wide awake and there was the noise again. Was it Fraser messing with her? That must be it.

There was only one light switch and it was by the door. She swung her legs out of bed and crept across the room. She'd show him she wasn't that easily spooked. She stood by the door waiting for the noise but when the moaning started again it was behind her. Liv spun around, her heart thumping.

She squinted across the dark room. There was nothing there but the moaning continued. She crept towards the end of the bed where another piece of furniture was still covered in a dust sheet. A shiver ran through her. What had her mother said to her about following strange noises? But she had to investigate. She tried to keep her nerve. What had Fraser rigged up under there to scare her? She grabbed the sheet and with a tug it came free. With that something burst from under the sheet right at her face. Liv screamed louder than she thought possible. She waved her arms about in panic. What was it? Was it Janet come to claim her soul?

There was a thudding sound and someone tried to push the door free of the cardboard wedge. At last the door swung open, the bedroom light came on and a panicked Liv turned around. 'What the hell is wrong with you?' asked Fraser, looking tired with his hair all dishevelled.

'There was a thing. It was moaning and then it came at me out of the darkness and it freaked me out.'

The moaning started again. 'Shhh,' whispered Liv. 'Did you hear that?'

Fraser's expression changed from annoyed to intrigued. He crept past her and around the bed. He crouched down and when he stood up he was grinning. That annoying smug grin she'd seen earlier. 'I think I've found the culprit,' he said, holding a pigeon in his hands. He pulled back the curtain to reveal the window had sprung open again. As an icy gust came in he put the pigeon out and shut the window. This time double-checking the catch. He didn't say anything as he left the room. Liv muttered a reluctant thank you and went back to bed.

She didn't have the best night's sleep. As well as the pigeon incident, different parts of her ached at different times and her brain kept going over everything: how come Fraser didn't seem to recognise her? Why had he let her stay? Was he being kind or was it all part of an elaborate master plan that her tired brain couldn't work out? The rain continued to lash it down, which sounded like someone had a hosepipe trained on her bedroom window. At one point it had sounded like gravel being thrown at the windows. It was cold and there was a draught coming from somewhere because the tassels on the four-poster bed kept moving. On top of that she was starting to think the place was haunted. Every time she was dropping off to sleep there would be another creak, bump or noise, which would freak her out.

The sound of the dawn chorus woke her and she took stock. She'd made it through the night without being murdered or having her soul sucked from her. There was a bump on her head that was tender to the touch, but the throbbing had stopped. Her ankle was stiff but not as painful as the previous night, and whilst her body felt a bit achy, she was otherwise fine. She lifted the covers. She'd spent the night wearing Fraser's T-shirt and underwear, which was not how she'd expected her day to end when she'd set off from Lancashire. She was very confused about Fraser. He had seemed grumpy and aloof but then, in his defence, she had almost taken him out with the long pole thing. But carrying her upstairs, finding her a room she was happy with and lending her something of his to sleep in were really kind things to do.

The cold light of day was an actual thing in Scotland, she discovered as she opened her curtains and the source of the chill became abundantly clear. Outside, the windowsill was covered in snow. She looked beyond to see that it wasn't just the windowsill. The view from her window was stunning and only enhanced by the frosty coating. The trees were all coated in nature's icing sugar and the sun glinted off the icy water like a mirror. Then she snapped out of the fairy tale. 'Shitting hell. Snow!'

She'd survived the night, now all she had to do was find her mobile that she'd dropped when she fell, sort out the ripped tyre, give Fraser a piece of her mind and get the hell out of the haunted hotel and forget all about Fraser. It seemed like a daunting list of things. Liv picked up her clothes that she'd hopefully placed on an ancient-looking radiator the night before. They were no longer dripping wet but they weren't dry either. She was hunting for a hairdryer when she could hear someone knocking but it wasn't on her door so she carried on. The knocking got closer until it was at her door and it abruptly opened, making her jump.

'Here you are!' said Effie marching over and wrapping

her in a hug. 'I'm so glad you're still here. Do you know who you are yet?'

'Err.'

'Don't worry. Doc McLeod will check you over and you'll be fine. I brought you some of my clothes. You're sort of the size I was last year. I've put on a couple of pounds since I discovered chocolate Brazil nuts. Have you tried them? They're moreish. Here, try this on.' She thrust a black dress and thick black jumper at Liv, followed by a carrier bag. 'There's underwear, a new toothbrush that I was saving for when I go travelling, and hiking socks because I know Southerners feel the cold more than we do.'

'Thanks, this is really kind of you.' At least she wouldn't have to put on her damp pants and jumpsuit. 'I feel fine now, so I think we can cancel the doctor.'

'But you still don't know who you are. Do you?'

Liv had no option but to carry on with the lie. 'No, but I'm sure I'll be okay.'

'I don't think you will. You see, head injuries are dangerous.' Effie was looking serious. 'I saw a programme. They can cause all sorts of things like percussion.'

'Concussion,' corrected Liv.

'That too? You see it's important you see the Doc. Anyway has Fraser offered you breakfast?'

'I've not seen anyone,' said Liv.

'Typical Fraser. I'll get you something to eat. Back in a jiffy.' And with that she was gone. Effie was a bit of a whirlwind, if a whirlwind talked as fast as it twirled.

Liv put on some borrowed flowery pants from the bag Effie had given her and the black dress, which was quite long with a white collar and cuffs. She pulled the black jumper on over the top but the white collar was still showing. A glance in the mirror made her think she looked like a vicar. She found the bathroom and felt better for a wash and for brushing her teeth. She made the bed and tidied the few things she had. She moved her car keys out of her hoodie and into the dress pocket. With any luck she'd be able to escape later on.

The hotel was eerily quiet as she walked carefully downstairs so as not to agitate her ankle. How come it was now completely silent and yet last night there were so many noises? She realised that whilst her sister's place lacked character there were lots of benefits to a new build, not least the lack of ghosts.

Once downstairs Liv headed in the direction of the voices that were coming from the back of the building. As soon as she got the chance she was going to find her phone, because she'd need to call her mum and sister soon or they'd start to worry about her. There was a door with a porthole window, which she had a little look through. She was about to go inside when Fraser's face appeared on the other side. She smiled. He scowled back at her. Fine, if that's how he wanted to play it. She tried to push on the door but it wouldn't budge.

'Stop pushing,' said Fraser from the other side. Liv did as she was told and the door instantly swung in her direction whacking her. Thankfully her forearm took the brunt of it. 'Shit. I'm sorry,' said Fraser, coming through the door looking concerned. He took in her outfit. 'Good morning, Wednesday Addams.'

'I'm fine, thanks for asking,' she said giving her arm a rub.

His tone seemed to change. 'You shouldn't be in the kitchens. It's for staff only. See...' He tapped the sign on the door.

'There was nobody about.'

He took a breath as if resetting himself. 'Fine. Good morning, I trust you slept well?'

'Yeah, I did actually apart from the whole freaky pigeon interlude. Thanks for your help with that.'

'My pleasure,' said Fraser with a smile at the edge of his lips.

Effie came through the door with a tray. 'Stop bickering, you two. Daphne needs her breakfast.'

Liv stepped out of the way and Effie walked past. 'Come on, Daphne, this way to the dining room.'

Liv wanted to know what the next level up from confusion was because she was definitely in a very strange place. 'Is Daphne another ghost?' she asked Fraser.

'That's what Effie has decided to call you,' he said with a grin.

'What now?'

'Because you cannay remember your name, she's decided that *to her* you look like a Daphne.' He seemed to find this hilarious.

'I don't know what to do with that,' said Liv. 'I don't mean to be rude but is Effie okay?'

He pursed his lips and leaned closer. 'Effie is a kind soul but she just takes a bit longer than most to work stuff out. Because of that she had a tough time at school. She has a good heart but that means she can be easily hurt. So please be kind to her.'

'I will. Thanks for putting me in the picture.' They stayed

looking at each other. Those were the words of a kind and caring soul. Fraser was beyond baffling.

'Daphne!' called Effie from the other room.

'You'd better go, Daphne,' said Fraser failing to hide a smirk.

Liv followed the sound of the tray being unburdened and found herself in a lovely room, high ceilings, recently decorated, two complete and sparkly chandeliers with a number of tables and chairs but only one with a tablecloth.

'Here you go, Daphne. Porridge with salt or sugar followed by a morning roll.'

'A morning roll, I should be so lucky,' said Liv with a chuckle but Effie was frowning at her.

'You *are* lucky because there's your morning roll.' Effie pointed at the plate.

Liv looked at the white roll and what looked to be something square inside it. 'What's in it?' she asked.

'Lorne sausage,' said Effie. 'You'll like it, Daphne. Trust me.'

'Actually, hang on,' said Liv. 'I'm pretty sure my name's not Daphne.' Effie looked disappointed and for a moment she thought about what Fraser had said about being kind to Effie but even if she was only going to be there for a couple more hours she wasn't sure she could stand being called Daphne. Perhaps she could lure Effie down another route. 'I think my name might be something beginning with L.'

'Ooh I love guessing games. Lucy, Lottie, Lewis, Lesley?' said Effie excitedly taking up the challenge.

'Nope. Maybe not something that obvious.'

'Lettuce, Lego, Ladle, Leaf?' Effie was frowning hard with the effort. 'Lurpak?'

Okay, this wasn't going quite how she'd hoped. 'I don't think so. Something like Liz maybe?' suggested Liv, hoping Effie would land on the right answer.

Effie scowled at her. 'People called Liz are usually horrid and unkind.'

'Okay, not Liz. Maybe um... Liv?' She looked hopefully at Effie.

'No, I don't think so; that's not even a name,' she said with a giggle. 'Tea or coffee, Daphne?'

Effie returned with a pot of tea, took the seat opposite Liv and watched her eat her breakfast. Liv found she was ravenous but when she thought about it she'd not had a proper meal the previous day, assuming she didn't count all the packets of crisps she'd consumed. She chose to have sugar on the porridge because salt was just plain weird and the roll was surprisingly delicious even if the sausage was square. All washed down with a cup of builder's tea. Liv felt ready to face the day.

'Good?' asked Effie.

'Yeah. Great. Thanks. What was the crumbly stuff on the top of the square sausage?'

'That's haggis.'

Liv froze. 'And what is that exactly?'

'It's a mixture and it includes Fraser's secret mix of spices and herbs. Along with onions, oats, suet and sheep's pluck.'

'Sheep's pluck? What? Something that's been plucked from a sheep? Like wool?' She asked the question, unsure whether she wanted to hear the reply.

'No silly. It's things from inside the sheep. Usually, lungs, liver, heart, tongue. And it's encased in the sheep's stomach,' said Effie happily.

Liv gagged as she went through the ingredients. 'Oh my life, I'm Hannibal Lecter.'

'Anything else to eat?' asked Effie.

Liv held up her hand like a stop sign. 'No. Thank you.'

'My pleasure. It's what I make every morning for my granny, Dolly.'

'Then she's very lucky,' said Liv. Effie began loading the tray up. 'Effie, do you think you could help me with something?' asked Liv.

'I'd love to. What do you need? Map, supplies, headtorch?'

Liv blinked; it was hard to keep on her own thought path when Effie seemed keen to take her down a weird and wonderful one of her own. 'I was thinking that it's likely I would be the sort of person who would have a mobile phone. But there wasn't one in my pocket. I'm wondering if I may have dropped it when I had the run-in with the cow. Would you help me look around for it, please?'

'Ooh a treasure hunt – I love those. Where shall we start?'

'I thought maybe in the yard where you found me?'

'Good idea,' said Effie pointing a finger at Liv. 'Follow me.' She picked up the tray and set off.

Effie gave Liv Fraser's coat to wear and they went outside. Liv had seriously misjudged what she thought was a coating of snow as she stepped out and her boots disappeared. 'Chuffing heck, that's quite a bit of snow.'

'Noooo, that's barely a flurry,' said Effie striding out in her wellingtons. 'Now where shall we start?'

Liv pointed to where the crates had toppled over and then moved her finger about so it was more of a general area.

After twenty minutes Liv couldn't feel her fingers. It had started to snow again and there was no sign of her phone. Liv was getting fed up and a little fraught. There was a distant rumbling sound, which made Effie stand up straight.

'That'll be Doc McLeod.'

Liv wanted to find her phone but she really had no choice but to give up for now, so she had one last look around before heading inside.

It wasn't a lot warmer inside until Effie took her through to the library. She could hear Fraser greeting someone at the door and was keen to listen to what he said, but unfortunately they were a bit too muffled. Liv sat down on the window seat.

'This is my favourite view,' said Effie.

Liv followed her gaze. Down a sweeping lawn, some stone steps drew the eye to a gap in some trees and a vast expanse of water, with impressive mountains beyond. 'Is that Loch Lochy?' she asked.

'Ahh now that is a good sign,' said an older gentleman joining them. 'Don't get up. I'm Doctor McLeod, but you can call me Doc. Everyone does. Now tell me what happened.'

'You see I heard a scream like this,' began Effie. 'Arrrrrrgh!'

'Thank you, Effie. But it would be best if I heard it from this young lady. Perhaps you can tell me your version later.'

'Let's leave them to it, Effie,' said Fraser. He nodded at Liv and shut the door once Effie had reluctantly left.

Liv kept things sketchy and told the Doc what happened from after she came round. She was fairly certain that she had managed to knock herself out but for how long she wasn't sure. Given Effie's account it was likely she'd come outside not too long after she'd heard the scream, so Liv couldn't have been unconscious for more than a couple of minutes. The Doc examined her head and ankle, took her temperature and blood pressure, and checked her pupils and reflexes.

'Any dizziness or nausea?' he asked.

'No. I felt a bit sick last night when it happened but I feel fine now.'

'I don't think there's any cause for alarm. You have concussion and I suspect in the next day or so your memory will come flooding back. If you do feel dizzy, have any head pain or pass out, you must go directly to hospital. Understood?' he asked getting to his feet.

'Yes, Doc. So I'm good to go then?'

'Well you can't drive, if that's what you mean. You need to stay put until you are fully recovered.'

'But there might be people worried about me.'

'I'm sure there are. But I understand the police are already aware.'

'The police?' Liv barely managed to squeak the word out. This was getting out of hand.

'Yes, the police. Robbie Williams. Cheerio.'

Why did he keep naming musicians? Liv was beyond baffled.

9

Liv waited, thoughts swirling in her mind like a snowstorm. Fraser saw the doctor out and after a few minutes, where she assumed he was getting an update on her condition, he came back into the library.

He pouted. 'Got concussion then,' he said.

'So it would appear.' Liv wasn't sure if she'd successfully hoodwinked the doctor or if she did actually have concussion. She didn't feel great about either option. But she had been honest about banging her head, blacking out and feeling queasy.

'I'm sorry if it ever came across that I doubted you.' He looked sheepish. 'Doc says you need to stay put for a couple of days.'

She couldn't stay for a couple of days. For one the whole deception thing was getting out of hand. For another she needed to get in touch with her family and let them know she was okay. They were expecting her home later that day. 'I'll stay in a Travelodge or something,' she said getting to her feet.

'Nearest one of those is at Fort William.'

'Great,' said Liv, heading for the door.

'Which is just over twenty miles in that direction,' he said pointing over his shoulder.

'Right.' Liv was trying to work out how she was going to get to the car and then find someone to sort out the flat tyre and then she wasn't even sure if she was meant to drive or not.

'You'd better stay here,' he said.

Was he telling her or was he just being nice? Her head started to hurt again but possibly for different reasons. 'I couldn't impose any longer,' she said.

'I don't think you have a lot of choice. But it's up to you,' he said.

She didn't like that he was right and she wasn't keen on staying in such close proximity to him, but even if she just stayed long enough to find her phone and work out an exit strategy. What choice did she have? 'Okay. Thanks.'

He nodded before reaching for the door. 'Seeing as you're staying for free you may want to pitch in and help. Just a thought.' He opened the door and Effie almost fell inside.

She did a very bad mime of someone dusting the doorframe without a duster. 'What's happening? I guessed you're not going to hospital. Are you staying? Please say she's staying.' She looked from Fraser to Liv and back to Fraser.

'Daphne's staying,' he said with a roll of his eyes and he left the room.

'Yay!' squealed Effie clapping her hands together. 'We are going to have the best time.' She wrapped Liv in an unexpected hug. For a moment Liv was resistant but then she relaxed and it was really quite nice to be held. After the roller coaster of the last twenty-four hours she'd been so caught up in everything she'd not realised that what she really needed was someone to hold her. Effie pulled away. 'Dear Daphne, what's wrong?'

Liv wiped away a tear from her eyes. 'I don't know. Must be the knock on the head.'

'You're going to be fine. Me and Fraser are going to look after you. You're safe now.'

'Thanks,' said Liv. Effie's kindness made her smile despite everything. 'Fraser said I could help out. I thought the hotel was closed. What did he mean?'

Effie became animated. It didn't seem to take much to get her excited. 'It's the build-up to the big launch of Fraser's new restaurant. We're holding a showcase dinner on the twenty-third of December, assuming everything is ready.'

Liv didn't want to be the voice of doom but from the bedrooms she'd seen last night they were a very long way from being able to have paying guests. 'I think the bedrooms need quite a bit of attention. One of them has water pouring through the ceiling.'

'It's only the restaurant that's opening, not the hotel. But if that makes money Fraser might be able to open the hotel again but then it's really only the cooking he's interested in, so maybe not. He's focused on the kitchen, the dining room and the menu. And I'm going to be a waitress and maybe help a bit in the kitchen when I'm not caring for my grandmother. And now you're going to work here too. This is so exciting!' She began clapping her hands again.

'It's only for a couple of days remember.' Effie looked instantly deflated and Liv felt bad. 'But we'll make the most of it, okay?'

'I can show you where everything is in the kitchen. I can show you now.' She turned to leave.

'Actually there was something else I wanted to ask,' said Liv. 'Doc said something about Robbie Williams. Does he live around here?' She knew he'd lived in LA but she remembered reading something about him moving back to the UK.

'Yes he does. He lives at Invergarry, which isn't far. He's kinda cute.'

'My mum likes him,' said Liv, thinking that an autographed something would make an excellent extra Christmas present as she'd only got her smellies so far.

Effie frowned at her. 'Your mam knows Robbie?'

'She's never met him. She's just a fan of his music. You know,' said Liv breaking into a hummed version of 'Let Me Entertain You'.

Effie started to giggle. 'You are silly. Not *that* Robbie Williams. He doesn't live around here. The one you met last night – *that* Robbie Williams.'

It was Liv's turn to frown. 'The bloke who was laughing with Dolly?'

'Yes. He's Robbie Williams. And so is his dad, and his grandad and his great-grandad too but he lost the family bakery in a game of cards so we don't talk about him. But none of them are the pop star.'

'Right. And The Police?' Liv thought it best to get everything cleared up while she was at it.

'Robbie works for them. He's taking his sergeant's exam in the new year. He would have sooner but he managed to get stuck in a pair of his own handcuffs, so he said it was best to let that blow over first.'

'Ah.' At least a few things were starting to make more sense. 'Then there's nobody famous around these parts?'

'No.' Effie pulled a sad face. 'Susan Boyle lives near Edinburgh but that's like a hundred and fifty miles away. I wish we had some celebrities. Are you one? You might be.' Effie leaned very close and studied Liv's face.

'No, I think I'd remember that.'

'Let's wait and see,' said Effie hopefully. 'Do you think the new restaurant will bring some in? The lawn is easily big enough for a helicopter to land on. I'd love to meet Jedward.'

'You never know, Effie. We can only hope.'

Effie had to go and check on Dolly, so Liv was left alone. Liv slunk out of the library checking all around her. She felt like a cartoon villain. The reception and hallway were quiet. She went behind the reception desk and to her relief found a telephone. She quickly dialled her mum's home number. She kept scanning the reception area because she didn't want to get caught. Someone with amnesia wouldn't remember any phone numbers to call.

'Hello, I don't need any insurance and there's nothing wrong with my computer,' said her mum.

'Mum it's me,' whispered Liv, scanning the area like a rubbish spy.

'Oh Liv. Thank heavens! I thought you'd been kidnapped. No actually Charlotte thought you'd been kidnapped; I thought it might be worse and that you'd let this loser sweet-talk you around. I do hope it's neither of those things.'

'It's not. Listen I—'

'Good. Where are you? Because it said number withheld, which was why I let whoever was calling know I was onto them from the get-go.' Goodness her mother talked more than Effie.

'Mum, this is a really quick call. I'm fine but it's taking longer to sort things out than I thought—'

'How long does it take to tell someone off?'

'Mum, I have to stay here for two days. I love you. Don't worry about me.'

'Now I'm worried!' said her mum.

'Trust me, I'm fine. I have to go,' said Liv putting the receiver down. She needed to call a tow truck but with no phone and no internet how was she meant to get a phone number for one? She needed to find her mobile – that was the easiest solution. She could hear voices approaching as she came out from behind the reception desk. The front door opened and a cold blast quickly made its way through to her. Dolly and Effie came in, mid conversation, covered in snow like a bad case of dandruff.

'I think my new year's resolutions are to help the bees, to be less political and to understand more about pineapples.'

'Hi,' said Liv as Effie helped Dolly take off her coat.

'I've just been telling Granny all about you,' said Effie. Liv wasn't sure there was anything to share. At least that was one benefit to her imagined amnesia.

'Hello, how are you feeling this morning?' asked Dolly.

'Okay. A bit awkward about staying here but the Doc didn't give me much choice.'

'Don't worry about that,' said Dolly. 'It's good to have people about the old place again. Are you sure you are up to helping out a little?'

'Apart from being a bit sore in places I'm fine. And I'd feel like I wasn't a complete freeloader.'

'Excellent. Don't let Fraser intimidate you; he can be a bit of a grump but he's a pussy cat really.'

'Uh-huh,' said Liv. She wasn't sure about that.

'Before you actually start work I think you need an orientation. That's when someone shows you where everything is and how everything works,' said Effie.

'Yep, got that,' said Liv.

They went through to the kitchen and Effie began pointing out obvious things like the cookers and the hobs.

This seemed to be the end of Effie's kitchen tour so Liv jumped up to sit on the worktop.

'We're not meant to sit on the worktop. Fraser doesn't like it,' said Effie, checking over her shoulder as if expecting him to jump out at them.

'It's not doing any harm though.'

'I guess.' Effie ran her bottom lip through her teeth before hopping up to sit next to Liv.

'What do I need to know about Fraser before I start working for him?' asked Liv. 'Any wife or girlfriend who might be unhappy about me stopping here alone with him?'

'No he's single.'

That's what his profile said too, thought Liv. 'Anything else?'

'He wanted to be a cricketer when we were kids. He used to practise on me and I used to get loads of bruises.'

'Practise on you how?'

'He'd bowl and I'd try to hit it but I wasn't very good and those real cricket balls are hard as rocks. They really hurt if they whack you.'

'Okay. Does he have any bad habits, pet hates and any topics I should avoid?'

Effie pouted hard. 'He's not a fan of Jennifer Lopez.'

'Right. I was thinking more about his management style.'

'He can be quite bossy. He likes his kitchen staff to say "*yes, chef*" when they answer him. They're really nice – you'll meet them later. I'm going to feed Ginger. Want to come?'

'Okay.' Liv wasn't sure about meeting the beast who had attacked her but she figured if she kept a safe distance away she'd be fine and it was an opportunity to find out more about Fraser.

Outside the weather was getting worse and it battered Liv despite the very large borrowed coat she was wearing that felt almost as heavy as she was. They trudged across the yard at the back of the hotel towards some stables. She looked about for any sign of life. At least she would have looked about had the hood of the coat not been completely rigid, so that when she turned her head she ended up looking inside the hood.

The falling snow with the sweeping mountain backdrop was like looking at a Christmas card. Liv wondered if her mum was worrying about her. She felt bad but she'd got herself in a mess that she wasn't sure how to get out of. At least the hurried phone call should buy her the couple of days she needed before she could drive again. Although the car wasn't driveable, which was another conundrum she needed to solve.

The stables had an overhang, making them a little more

sheltered, and it was good to get out of the wind that was battering them with snow. They walked into one of the stalls. Effie pulled off her hood and stamped her feet to get off some of the snow. Liv looked around; the stable was empty.

'Looks like Ginger has gone walkabout again,' said Effie, grabbing a bucket from the wall and striding off. Liv waited in the stall as her face was stinging from the icy weather. Effie came back. 'Come on, I've got some carrots. They're her favourite.'

'Should she not be inside in this weather?'

'Nah, she's hardy. Some breeds would likely die but not Highlands; they're used to it. But it's better that she's not wandering about. It's only a scowtherin now but there's more forecast.' With that she pulled her hood back on and left, making Liv feel that she should follow although she really didn't want to. Her face was stinging and her ears were numb with the cold.

They seemed to trudge around for a while with Effie calling out the cow's name. Liv hadn't realised they would be doing this much walking. She'd assumed the cow would be nearby or at least come when it was called. She was about to declare defeat on the grounds of this not being the sort of rest she thought the Doc had meant, when an odd sort of wheezy honk could be heard.

'There she is. That's her bellowing,' said Effie, spinning around and stomping off across the snow. Liv looked but could see nothing but snow, it was really coming down now. As far as she looked in every direction it was white. She hoped Effie knew where they were, because Liv had absolutely no idea.

10

Effie had no idea where they were. She didn't want to let on to Daphne that they were lost, so she kept on walking in the direction of the bellow. She already knew that most people thought she was an idiot and she didn't want to give her new friend any reason to believe them. She'd never ventured this far away from the hotel, at least not for many years and certainly not in bad weather. All she could see in every direction was whirling snow. She'd not known Ginger to stray this far from the hotel either.

Ginger was attached to Lochy House because it was where she'd been hand-fed by her, Dolly and Fraser on a twenty-four-hour rota. Ginger's mother had had a bad birth and immediately rejected the new-born calf. She had quickly got used to life inside with warm fires, blankets and Jock'O to learn from. Being put out to grass had been a nasty shock for Ginger that Effie was pretty sure she still didn't understand.

Effie looked around. She called Ginger but there was no

reply. She was starting to panic. She was worried for Ginger but she was also worried for her and Daphne. Where was Daphne? Effie scanned in all directions. It was hard to see through the snow but she could make out a figure far behind her. She knew Daphne didn't know which way to go either but she somehow felt safer when they were together. She checked her pockets. She'd forgotten to bring her mobile with her. She thought back to when she'd had it last. She'd been checking her messages while she was getting Dolly's breakfast. She must have left it in the kitchen at the lodge.

Effie tried to walk a little faster but the snow was getting deeper and she needed to take bigger steps. These were all the things she'd always been told to avoid. She was beginning to panic. What if this was how she died? Would her ghost be forever roaming the hills lost? She thought of her secret boyfriend, John. It was who she'd been texting. Nobody knew about him, so he'd never know what happened to her. Her dad's voice came into her head and she savoured it, despite what he was saying not being that helpful: '*Only a fool ventures into a blizzard, Effie. And that's why they frequently don't make it back alive.*' She gulped, turned around and upped her pace to shorten the gap between her and Daphne.

*

After walking for what felt like ages Liv's ankle started to complain. Unlike most of the rest of her it wasn't numb with the cold. It felt like snow was now coming from every direction, not just above. She had to keep blinking because it was pelting into her face. All around them was white. Effie was heading back towards her, which was a relief.

'Effie, I'm sorry but I can't walk any further,' called Liv over the wind.

'You're meant to be resting,' said Effie her tone quite accusatory.

'I didn't realise we'd be going this far. I think I might head back.'

'Okay. See you later,' said Effie.

Liv turned around. She had no idea where she was. All she could see was snow and trees, but her footprints were still visible in the snow so she began following those. She trudged on with her head down to avoid getting a face full of snow. She hoped it wasn't as far back to the hotel as it felt, because her ankle was throbbing. Liv was concentrating hard on following the footprints in the snow, which was getting more difficult the further she went as they were being blurred by the snowfall. Staring at all the white was also making her eyes go funny. Then all of a sudden she stopped because there was something very different in front of her.

She followed hairy ginger legs up until she was nose to very large wet nose. 'Eurgh, snotty cow,' said Liv.

The cow let out the same noise they'd heard earlier – sort of a wheezy honk but it was very much louder now she was this close to the beast. Ginger stepped forward and Liv tried to reverse away but stumbled and landed on her bum in the snow.

'Argh!' she yelled. She didn't care what they said about her being small; this was a big fat cow and she feared she was about to be trampled. 'Effie, help!'

She heard the squeak of wellies on snow before she saw Effie. A bucket came over the top of Liv's head and the cow immediately stuck her face in it and started to munch away.

'You found her,' said Effie. 'Well done. She's hard to find when she's out roaming.'

'She kind of found me really,' said Liv.

'Why are you sitting down?' asked Effie.

'Just checking gravity still works,' said Liv, rolling over and very inelegantly getting to her feet. The bottom of her borrowed dress was now covered in snow and sticking to her legs. 'I'm going back.'

'We're coming too, because it'll be dark soon,' said Effie. 'Come on, Ginger.' She walked off with the bucket, much to the cow's disgust.

By the time they got back to the stables Liv was freezing cold, her ankle was pounding and she was getting a bit grumpy. Effie walked into the stall with Ginger close behind. Liv went to follow but Effie pushed the top of the stable door shut, smacking Liv in the face and sending her flying onto her backside for the second time that day. Thankfully the layer of snow was a softer landing than the concrete underneath.

'Ow! Bloody hell, Effie. I'll have another lump on me now.' Liv sat in the snow holding her cheek. The cold of her palm felt quite nice.

Effie closed the bottom half of the door, opened the top and peered out. 'What are you doing?' she asked.

'Looking for my bagpipes,' said Liv.

'Ooh do you play?' asked Effie now leaning on the lower section of the door.

'No!' said Liv trying not to get cross. 'You smacked me in the face with the door.'

'That's good. Sometimes another knock on the head can bring memory back. We should have done it earlier. Can you remember anything, Daphne?'

'I remember that I'm definitely not called sodding Daphne.'

'That's progress!' said Effie. 'Well done me,' she added turning her attention back to Ginger.

Liv went inside and found Fraser in the kitchen humming 'Fantasy' by Mariah Carey but he stopped and did a double take when she walked in. 'What happened to you?' he asked failing to hide the smirk on his face.

Liv could imagine she looked like the abominable snowman. 'I got knocked over by Ginger, *again*. And then Effie smacked me in the face with the stable door.'

Fraser spluttered a laugh. 'Sorry, it's not funny,' he said although he was grinning.

'It might be a little funnier from where you're standing.' Liv touched her puffy cheek and winced.

'I promise not to laugh.'

She gave him a look.

'Well, I promise not to laugh anymore. I think I have something of yours.' He opened a cupboard and took out a jar. He unscrewed the top and let Liv look inside. Surrounded by rice was her mobile phone.

'My phone!' She went to grab it but he pulled the jar out of reach. Why had he done that?

'It's drying out,' he said. 'It was frozen in a lump of ice that I guess was a puddle when it landed in it. I moved a crate in the yard and there it was.'

'Does it work?' she asked feeling worried about whichever answer he gave. If it didn't work she had no phone and if it did had he been spying on her stuff?

'It wouldn't switch on but then if it's been out there all night; the battery is probably dead.'

'Let's charge it then.'

'Nobody has a new iPhone like that here. So there's no charger to match it I'm afraid. I think it needs to dry out first anyway.' He put the lid back on and returned it to the cupboard. Liv watched forlornly as he closed the cupboard door.

'Have you come to lend a hand?' he asked.

'I've come to defrost with a hot drink. I'm frozen. And to make one for Effie too.' She wasn't completely selfish.

'Is that my coat?' he asked peering at it.

'Effie said I could borrow it. Thank you,' she said.

Fraser took it from her and muttered to himself as he went to hang it up.

Liv decided that whatever happened she needed to get her charger from the car. She was already cold and wet; a few more steps couldn't do much harm. She grabbed the soggy coat off the hook, hastily dashed through the hotel and with her cheek stinging she set off down the drive. The wind was biting and the snow harsh. The trees were swaying wildly and the noise of the wind was more than a bit creepy. A picture of Janet the witch popped unhelpfully into her mind.

The light was starting to fade as she trudged on trying to think about anything other than Janet. On the plus side she was feeling okay and Fraser had found her phone, even if it wasn't currently useable. On the not so plus side she had failed to do what she had come to do but did it really matter? She hadn't challenged Fraser yet but she could hardly do that if she was going to be stuck there for a couple of days – how awkward would that be? No, she needed to bide her time and once she was able to leave that was when she could read him the riot act – and not before.

At least spending more time there than she'd planned meant she could find a bit more out about Fraser and try to work him out and what game he was playing. So far she'd discovered that he was a bit different to how he'd portrayed himself on the app. He was definitely grumpier although also more thoughtful than she'd imagined. Kind of funny in his own way. But definitely as good-looking as his photograph. And she enjoyed the banter between them.

Liv rounded the bend away from the hotel and that was when she saw it. A hunched figure in black was gliding through the trees and she could hear a low moan in the air.

'Shitting hell!' said Liv turning around and walking back as fast as her gammy ankle would let her. She got back to the hotel steps a lot quicker and was about to dart straight inside – she was sure the moaning was following her.

'Wait up!' called someone behind her as she was closing the door. Liv looked up the darkening driveway. There was Dolly on her scooter almost all covered by a large black mac. The moaning got closer. It was the scooter – not Janet at all. Liv breathed a sigh of relief and held the door as Dolly trundled up the ramp and inside. It looked like Liv would have to wait for another opportunity to sneak back to the car for her phone charger.

Effie came to help Dolly get her mac off. Liv was surprised to see what was underneath it. Not only was it Dolly but there was also a little black dog lying on her lap. She had to look twice to check it wasn't stuffed.

'Utter disaster at the lodge,' said Dolly. 'The boiler's packed up.'

'It does that,' said Effie joining them. 'It'll need a whack with a mallet and it'll be fine.'

'It won't. It's properly died this time. So there's no heating and no hot water.'

'Sorry to hear that,' said Liv. There was an awkward silence. 'Who's this then?' asked Liv pointing at the dog.

'Jock'O,' replied Dolly.

'What's the O for?' asked Liv reaching out a hand to see if he was friend or foe.

Dolly closed her eyes as if in deep thought. That or she'd nodded off. At last she opened her eyes. 'I've absolutely no idea,' said Dolly looking puzzled. 'Got him from a chap in Invergarry who called the whole litter that and I thought it was a good name.'

Liv gave him a stroke and he lifted his chin to show off a greying beard. 'He's a cutie.'

Fraser appeared with a pot of tea. 'I thought you were making tea?' He shook his head at Liv but seeing Dolly he turned his attention to her. 'What's up?' he asked.

'The boiler at the lodge has finally given up the ghost,' said Dolly. Effie opened her mouth. 'Nothing to do with Janet,' she added and Effie looked a little disappointed.

'You can stay here until it's fixed,' said Fraser. 'I'll go over with Effie and bring back whatever things you need.'

'Ooh can I have Janet's room?' asked Effie clapping her hands together.

'See, some people aren't scared of paintings,' he said placing down the tray and unloading the teapot.

Liv pointed at the teapot. 'Here I am. What are your two other wishes?'

'Sorry?' Fraser looked perplexed.

'You're like Aladdin,' said Liv. Fraser frowned at her. 'With the lamp.' She pointed again at the silver teapot, but he was still frowning at her. 'Never mind.'

'Daphne's remembered things,' said Effie happily and all heads spun in her direction. 'I gave her another bump on the head and it worked.'

'Not exactly what happened,' said Liv.

'Who are you then?' asked Dolly.

'Please be someone famous, please be someone famous,' whispered Effie standing next to her with her fingers crossed.

Liv decided that the best option was to tell the truth. 'I've remembered that I'm called Liv.'

'Liv's not a proper name,' said Effie, shaking her head. 'Sorry, Daphne, try again.'

'No, that really is my name. I'm Liv.'

'Is Liv short for Livid?' asked Fraser. 'Because that's what you are most of the time.'

'No it's short for—'

The front door slammed open, interrupting Liv, and in came Robbie wearing his police uniform bringing in an arctic flurry of snow. 'There's an emergency!'

'Goodness me, shut the door!' called Dolly as the icy gust hit them and they all shivered.

'Sorry,' said Robbie, looking a little deflated as he shut the door and joined them. 'A weather warning has been issued. The road's blocked in both directions and there's a car in the ditch. I need all of you to help,' he said. Everyone rushed out into the blizzard.

11

Once outside they'd had a moment of clarity that they needed some equipment so had all marched back inside to grab useful items, shovels mainly but Effie was carrying a bucket and Robbie had a hammer, which were interesting choices. Despite the awful weather it was quite exciting striding along with Effie, Fraser and Robbie. Dolly had had a last-minute realisation that her scooter wasn't great in the deep snow and that it was probably best that she cover the phone, although Liv had never heard the thing ring once.

The drive climbed up to the road and that was when it became even more apparent how bad the weather was. The wind was hard to walk against and the snow was like someone was jet-propelling it into her face. Fraser looked like he was out for an afternoon stroll, the weather and hill not seeming to interrupt his stride.

'Does this happen often?' she asked, her voice almost swallowed by the wind.

'Only when there are tourists involved.' He gave a look.

'I'm not a…' As she'd now revealed that her memory had returned, if she wasn't a tourist then what was she? 'Not alone in wanting to see this beautiful country,' she corrected with a sweep of her arm. They both glanced about the landscape, obscured by the blizzard. Fraser was giving her an odd look so she put her head down and ploughed on.

'It's this way!' yelled Robbie, who was striding past a snow-covered mound. Liv wasn't entirely sure what triggered the thought; it was probably a combination of things. Fraser and Effie started to jog and that was when it hit Liv. The snow-covered car they were running past was her sister's.

'I remember that that's my car. I hit a pothole and got a puncture.'

'English drivers,' he mumbled.

'What?' Liv didn't quite catch what he said but she had a good idea and it irked her.

'Nothing. Carry on.'

'When I realised the tyre had blown I pulled over and left it there to get help.' They both surveyed the snowy mass. 'Can you help me dig it out?'

Fraser called to Robbie. 'Shout if you need me. Else I'll clear the snow around this one first.'

'Sure thing, be careful,' replied Robbie as he and Effie went off down the lane.

Fraser started to shovel away the snow and Liv joined in. The passenger side was a little more protected from the elements thanks to it being parked near the bushes, so when enough snow had been moved Liv got out the car keys, unlocked the car and squeezed around to try to open the door. She tugged hard but it wasn't opening.

'It'll be frozen,' said Fraser. 'Let me.' As he leaned close to the iced-up window his eyes widened. That was the moment when Liv remembered Stan. 'There's someone inside,' said Fraser. 'Have they been stuck here this whole time?' He looked suitably shocked at the prospect.

Liv swallowed hard. 'Not exactly. It's not a live person…' she began. Fraser's alarmed expression made her speed up. 'It's also not someone I've killed, or that *anyone* has killed. There are no dead bodies in the car.'

Fraser didn't look in any way calmed by her explanation.

She'd hoped there would be a way for her to avoid Fraser and Stan meeting, but that was no longer the case. When Fraser pulled on the door, there was a crack as it released. Fraser stuck his head inside and Liv wanted to spontaneously combust with embarrassment. 'What the hell?' he said through a burst of laughter. 'Is this your boyfriend?'

'He was a present for my birthday,' she said trying to reach inside and pull Stan out. She couldn't leave him there for fear of a passer-by assuming there was someone trapped in the car and setting off a full-scale rescue mission.

'You like the silent type do you?' asked Fraser moving out of the way.

'Very funny.' Liv had to lean inside to undo Stan's seatbelt, which must have made for an odd picture with her face in Stan's lap. Fraser snorted a laugh behind her and she tried hard to ignore him. The seatbelt finally released and she reversed out with Stan in her arms. In her haste to hide him she dragged him along the bushes and he started to make an elongated fart sound as the air escaped. 'Shit,' she said.

Fraser turned away and failed badly to stifle how funny he was finding her predicament.

She tried to get to the boot but there was too much snow. 'Do you think you could help me? My stuff is in the boot.'

He came to join her and a floppy Stan at the rear of the car and they started to dig again. With the two of them, and Liv driven by embarrassment, they cleared the snow quite quickly and, thankfully, with a shove from both of them the boot opened. Liv got out her bag. She was just about to put Stan inside when someone called.

'Hello!'

'Bloody hell,' said Liv wrestling Stan into the boot and slamming it shut. She glanced at Fraser who had a grin like a boomerang.

They turned to see two women and a man approaching them through the flurry of snow. One of the women was wearing a floaty dress and matching jacket and carrying a fancy holdall. She was strikingly beautiful despite being blue with the cold. The other two were bundled up against the weather in matching puffer jackets.

'Hiya,' said the man. 'I'm Aaron and this is my wife, Kacey.' They both giggled. 'It's going to take a lot of getting used to.'

'We got married at Gretna Green this morning,' said Kacey, pulling off a glove to stick her ring hand under Fraser's nose, making him recoil.

'Aww congratulations,' said Liv.

'Thank you,' said Kacey, batting her eyelashes at her husband. They were clearly smitten.

'Our car ended up in a ditch and the copper told us there's a hotel we can stay in.'

'That's not exactly what happened is it?' The other woman had joined them and did not look happy. 'You swerved because of a sparrow and stuck the bleedin' car in a ditch.'

'He couldn't help it,' said Kacey clutching Aaron's arm. 'He's an animal lover. We both are and the snow was everywhere, so you couldn't tell what was road and what wasn't.'

'But nobody's hurt?' asked Fraser.

'We're all good. Not sure about the car,' said Aaron.

'I may have whiplash,' said the woman in the floaty dress and thin-looking jacket. 'I'm Shanie Cortina.' She scanned their faces as if expecting a response. 'The reality TV sensation?' Fraser and Liv both slowly shook their heads. '*Beach Babes?*' The frustration was evident in her voice. 'For heaven's sake do you not have television up here?'

'Oh the reality TV show,' said Liv as realisation dawned. 'My sister watches that sometimes. It's on one of the obscure channels late at night,' explained Liv while Shanie's glare intensified. 'What year and where did you come?'

'Two years ago and I don't think it's when you leave that matters; it's the impact you make while you're there. Anyway, where's this hotel? I'm frigging freezing,' she said with a shiver. Liv stepped away from the car, making Shanie do a double take. 'What the hell?'

Shanie's eyes widened and Liv followed her gaze to where an arm was sticking out of the car boot. Liv quickly opened it, ignored the fart noise that came from within, shoved Stan's arm inside and shut it again as fast as she could. 'The hotel is this way,' said Liv guiding them all away from the car and up the track.

'Hang on,' said Fraser. 'The hotel's not open. It's not guest-ready. It's… nobody is listening are they?'

'Have you come far?' asked Liv, keen to distract the woman who was now looking over her shoulder at the boot of the BMW.

'Essex,' said Shanie, still distracted by what she'd seen.

'Goodness did you drive all the way up here from Essex?'

'We're not together,' said Aaron. 'Me and Kacey picked the hire car up in Dumfries and Shanie was trying to hire something because her driver was a no-show but there were no cars left. So we offered to give her a lift.'

'That's kind,' said Liv.

Shanie didn't look like she agreed as she huffily swapped her bag to the other hand. 'I had a chauffeur booked and paid for. My manager will be complaining. You can't just abandon someone in a frozen wasteland.'

Fraser chuckled behind them and Shanie spun around to glare at him. 'Who are you exactly?'

'It's his hotel,' said Liv, thinking that however pissed off Shanie was she really didn't want to fall out with Fraser or she'd be sharing a stable with Ginger.

'Here you go,' said Shanie handing him her bag. Fraser seemed surprised to now be holding two shovels and a designer bag. 'Careful that's got my eye massager in.'

'Ooh I've heard about those. They're meant to give you a great night's sleep,' said Liv.

'I don't share personal items. Sorry,' said Shanie with a look of fake commiseration.

'I wasn't asking you to.' Liv was starting to think that maybe Shanie was a bigger cow than Ginger. They walked on in silence apart from the rhythmic crunch of shoes on fresh snow. The snow was still coming down thick and fast.

'This is so exciting,' said Kacey finishing her sentence with a small squeak.

Shanie huffed. 'How much further?' she whined as they reached the sign for the hotel. But in her defence it was partially covered in snow, as was she and her thin jacket.

'Not far now,' said Liv. 'This is the driveway.'

'It had better be worth it,' muttered Shanie.

Liv very much doubted that it would be.

12

It was a relief to get inside. Liv took off the borrowed coat and marvelled at how much snow was on it, which was now sliding onto the entrance hall floor. Aaron helped Kacey off with her puffer jacket.

'Aww this is dead nice,' said Kacey taking it all in.

Shanie pouted as she scanned her surroundings with a critical eye. 'It's old,' she said.

Fraser shook his head, dropped Shanie's bag in the puddle Liv had created and began pulling off his wellies.

'It dates from the seventeenth century with some Victorian additions,' said Liv, quite proud that she'd remembered what Fraser had told her.

'Like I said, *old*,' said Shanie.

The door opened and an icy draught blew in Effie and Robbie.

'Where's the body?' asked Effie in not very hushed tones, making Aaron and Kacey both stop what they were doing to listen.

Liv saw Fraser's shoulders start to shake. 'What now?' And there was she thinking she'd only have to face humiliation once.

Robbie shut the door. 'Effie thought she could see someone wearing a baseball cap in the passenger seat of that other car.'

Liv bit her lip. Despite the cold her neck prickled with the scrutiny of a dozen eyes. This was awkward. 'Nope, we checked and there was definitely no one there. It was just a top and a baseball cap.'

Robbie appeared puzzled. 'Are you sure? You did take a bang to the head.'

'There was nobody in there, Robbie. I saw for myself,' said Fraser. 'The car has a puncture, so the driver has abandoned it.' He glanced awkwardly at Liv.

Liv held up a hand. 'I'm the driver.'

Robbie still didn't look like he was buying it but was distracted by Effie's sudden gasp. 'What?' he asked, visibly checking her over.

'Do you think Janet has taken them?' asked Effie with wide eyes. 'She could have, you know.' Effie made hand gestures nobody understood.

'Who's Janet?' asked Kacey.

Effie opened her mouth, but Liv was already escorting people into the hallway.

'Hello and welcome to the Lochy House Hotel,' said Dolly from behind the reception desk. 'If you'd all like to sign in.'

Fraser came striding after them. 'They can't stay here.'

'Sorry, mate,' said Robbie. 'There's nowhere else. It's a matter of public safety.'

Fraser shook his head and Liv decided distraction was probably the best approach to avoid any conflict. 'Bring your bags and everything through, and we'll get a fire lit in the library.' Everyone filed into the library, heads twisting in all directions as they checked the room out.

'Is that a video player?' asked Aaron.

'This place is out of the Dark Ages,' muttered Shanie.

'At least there's a telly,' said Kacey switching it on. The TV blared out a hissing noise accompanied by a black and white screen that looked like it was also snowing a blizzard in the TV.

'Aerial blew down in a storm last Christmas,' said Fraser.

'Would anyone like tea or coffee?' asked Liv trying to distract them.

'I'll have a soya cappuccino no foam,' said Shanie.

'Um, I think it's instant,' said Liv.

Shanie's lip curled.

Fraser butted in. 'Actually we have an espresso machine so we can stretch to a cappuccino but there's no soya milk. However, there is some straight from the cow if you'd prefer.'

'Eww how unhygienic,' said Shanie.

'Take it or leave it,' he said.

'Fine. I'll have mineral water. Sparkling. Chilled. Ice made from mineral water not tap.' Shanie flicked her hair over her shoulder and narrowly missed swiping Fraser in the face. He did not look impressed. While everyone else muttered about the choices, Dolly moved her scooter between them to get to her grandson.

'Fraser, this is an opportunity,' whispered Dolly. Despite his eye-roll she continued. 'Think about it. You could be the hero here. That's good publicity.' Dolly tilted her head. Fraser's jaw was tense. 'Your decision.'

Fraser clapped his hands together. 'Right, can I have your attention?' When everyone finally stopped grumbling and turned to face him he lifted his chin. 'This hotel is not open.'

'What?' Shanie turned to Robbie. 'Why on earth did you send us here then?' There were noises of agreement from the others.

'There's been a weather warning,' said Robbie. 'They don't issue these for fun. It means there's a very real risk to life.'

'Surely we can get a cab?'

'You'll not get one locally because Wylie Harris ran the nearest taxi firm and he retired this summer gone, and as the road is blocked they'll not be able to get here from Fort William,' said Dolly calmly. 'Your choices are stay here or risk your life in a raging blizzard. It's up to you.'

'I'd rather take my chances out there than stay in this dump,' said Shanie.

'Qui-et!' said Fraser. 'I get that this is nobody's first choice. You are also not my—' Dolly cleared her throat behind him, making him take a pause. 'You are also not alone in being in a difficult situation. The hotel has been closed to the public for some three years now. However, as a gesture of community and Scottish hospitality, we're happy for you to stay here, but you need to understand that you are staying as our house guests and that everyone will have to muck in. Okay?'

'Sounds like fun,' said Kacey. 'Blitz spirit and all that.'

'The blitz spirit sounds so lovely,' said Effie. 'Strangers all coming together, united in their efforts and making friends for life.' She looked hopefully at Shanie, who actively avoided eye contact.

'I'm calling my agent,' said Shanie. 'It's like being held hostage but without hope of someone paying the ransom.'

'I don't want to be awkward or anything,' said Aaron looking incredibly awkward. 'But we just eloped because we couldn't afford a big wedding.' He wobbled his head. 'Or any size wedding actually. So I'm just wondering if you're going to charge us for staying here?'

'He had better not be,' said Shanie. 'It's a prize dump.'

Fraser sighed. 'Drinks you can have on the house but we'll need to work something out for everything else.'

This set off the disgruntled chatter again, making Fraser throw up his arms and storm off towards the kitchen.

This was a moment where Liv could take the easy option and slink out but the new Liv didn't dodge things, and whilst this wasn't her argument she did feel for the situation Fraser and his family had been forced into.

'Seriously, how ungrateful are you lot?' asked Liv.

Dolly looked impressed whereas the stranded folk didn't seem that pleased to have their behaviour called out.

'If it's a hotel, and we're expected to pay then I don't think it's unreasonable to expect half-decent facilities and a little customer service,' said Shanie, folding her arms.

'If the hotel is not flaming well open and hasn't been for years, then it's not a hotel. It's just that Fraser has more bedrooms than most people, it's blowing a freaking blizzard out there so he's been asked by the police to take you in so that you don't end up frozen in ice like this century's Ötzi the ice mummy.' She pointed at Robbie who stood up a little straighter. 'All Fraser is saying is that you staying here is going to cost him money, so it's not unreasonable to expect you to pay him something so he's not out of pocket.'

'My grandson is a trained chef,' put in Dolly. 'He's well-regarded locally. I guarantee the food will be amazing.'

'I have allergies,' said Kacey looking apologetic.

'If I was cooking for this many people it'd be beans on toast all round,' said Liv. She was met with stony faces. 'Are we all agreed that staying here for free is not an option?'

'Fine,' said Shanie. She was the last person Liv had expected to agree first.

'Great, thanks, Shanie.' Liv eyed the other sheepish-looking faces.

'But I'm not paying until we leave so I can assess how much I should pay. I'm not an idiot,' she added.

'Fine,' said Liv. She'd done her best.

'What's the Wi-Fi code?' asked Shanie.

'You've got to be joking. All one word,' said Liv before leaving the room. She wondered how long it would take them to work that out.

Effie and Liv got everyone settled in the library with drinks. Even Shanie seemed mollified by her soda water despite the ice cubes being made from tap water. They were all playing the 'find the phone signal game' which would keep them amused for a short time at least. Liv and Effie joined Dolly who was sitting by reception with a selection of room keys in front of her.

'What's the plan?' asked Liv.

'Assuming we don't want to share—' began Dolly.

'Ooh I'll share with Daphne!' said Effie.

'But you wanted the Janet the Ghost room. I definitely won't sleep a wink in there,' said Liv. 'And my name's Liv.'

'Sorry, but now I know you as Daphne it's hard to change. I guess I can share your room, Da-liv.' She grinned at her.

'Let's see if we can work something out so that nobody has to share,' said Liv looking hopefully at Dolly. 'I'm settled in my room now I've managed to jam the window shut.'

'Where do you want to sleep, Granny?' asked Effie.

'There's no downstairs bedrooms and no lift,' said Liv, thinking out loud.

'There's a reclining chair in the snug. I'll be fine in there. I've slept on worse,' said Dolly. Dolly pushed the keys for the already occupied rooms to one side. 'Here you go,' she said handing over the remaining six keys. 'You'd best go and make three of these habitable.'

'What a stroke of luck, our boiler breaking,' said Effie.

'Is it?'

'Ye-ah. Because now we get to work together *and* stay here together.' Effie seemed so pleased at the prospect.

'I guess,' said Liv, sounding a little more sceptical. She would have far rather have been on her way home. 'Is Robbie staying too?' She looked about but there was no sign of him.

'He's probably gone to rescue some other poor souls,' said Effie wistfully. 'Putting himself in danger as he battles against the storm to seek out the lost.'

Dolly tutted. 'His mam rang to say she'd made a casserole and not to get snowed in here so he headed home on foot.'

'See, brave explorer,' said Effie.

'It's only a couple of miles to Invergarry,' said Dolly with a tut.

'Still, in this weather,' said Liv, hoping Robbie was all right.

'It's barely a flindrikin now,' said Dolly turning her scooter around.

'A what?' asked Liv as Dolly headed off.

'We Scots have four hundred and twenty-one words for snow. Someone counted,' said Effie.

'And I will probably experience them all before I get out of here.'

'I could teach you what they all mean,' said Effie clapping her hands together.

'Come on, let's sort the rooms out first,' said Liv and Effie followed her upstairs.

The first room they came to was the one with the leaky ceiling and a selection of buckets on the floor and an increasingly wet patch where they had overflowed. 'Let's call this one a backup,' said Liv matching the room key to the room. The next two were full of stuff and one had a broken bed but Liv figured they could move all the boxes into the room with the broken bed, which would make for one decent room. Then there was the first of two rooms with deer heads. Not her cup of tea but otherwise fine. They checked out dead Bambi room one and that seemed all in order and just needed a clean and bedding. They walked into the second one and there was a large mounted stag's head right above the bed.

'This is a pretty room,' said Effie.

'If you don't mind being watched by him.' She pointed at the largest head. 'And his *deerest* friends while you sleep, then this is quite nice,' said Liv.

'It's not real,' said Effie, pointing at the head.

Liv moved a little closer. 'It looks real to me.'

Effie stared at the deer. 'It's definitely dead.'

'I figured that was the case.' Liv went to explore. 'Maybe we could give this room to Aaron and Kacey, sell it as the horny room.' Effie was giving her a puzzled look. 'Because of the horns,' she explained miming them coming out of her own head.

'But they're not horns; they're antlers.'

'I know but there's nothing funny about antlers.' Liv mulled over the options she had with the antler and horn puns. 'The feeling horny room or they've got the horn?' She opened a built-in wardrobe and got the shock of her life. Like something from a *Scooby-Doo* cartoon, bats took flight straight towards her.

'Argh!'

'Don't scare them!' snapped Effie.

'Scare *them*? What about me?' asked Liv who was now crouching on the floor checking none were caught in her hair as the bats flapped above her.

The bedroom door flew open and in marched Fraser. 'Heavens!' He came in and shut the door behind him just in time as one of the bats was swooping in that direction.

'She did it,' said Effie, pointing an accusatory finger in Liv's direction. 'She woke them up.'

'Not on purpose. Who keeps bats in a wardrobe?'

'I didn't know they were in the wardrobe,' said Fraser. 'This room is out of bounds.'

'Yeah because everyone would be queuing up to sleep in here,' said Liv starting to crawl towards the door.

'It's out of bounds because they're a protected species,'

said Fraser. 'Looks like they're in the loft,' he added pointing to a small hole in the ceiling.

'I like them,' said Effie, putting out her arms like a scarecrow.

'Then you can have this room,' said Liv, overjoyed to make it to the door. They waited for the bats to settle before dashing out, dragging a reluctant Effie with them.

13

It took Liv, Fraser and Effie a while to cart all the boxes and random stuff from one bedroom to the one with the broken bed. It was especially tricky as Effie was excited to look in every box and ooh and ahh over the old artefacts they uncovered. Liv had spotted a small bedside lamp that she might bagsy later on, so she didn't have to fumble about for the light switch in the dark.

'I remember this teapot!' exclaimed Effie. 'Fraser, remember?'

'No,' said Fraser, taking it from her and putting it in the top of a box before carrying it out.

'You do. We used to use it for tea parties in the garden with our teddies,' said Effie.

'Teddies?' queried Liv with a grin.

Fraser's lips made a flat line as he paused with the box in his arms. 'They were Effie's teddies,' he said.

'And yours!' said Effie. 'Remember you had Floppy Teddy and Pink Ted who you always said needed extra biscuits.

I think Fraser used to eat them,' she added with a wink for Liv's benefit.

'Pink Ted,' said Liv. 'Now I'm guessing here, but was that a pink teddy by any chance?'

'It was very pink,' said Effie. 'It had a bow on its head too.'

Liv spluttered a laugh.

'I won it at the village fair raffle,' said Fraser sounding defensive.

Liv started to properly laugh and had to adjust her grip on her box.

'You should take that into the other bedroom before you drop it,' instructed Fraser looking vexed.

As Liv turned she caught sight of the little black dog darting past her and he had something in his mouth. Was that her sock?

Once all the stuff was out of the room it looked okay. There were no scary dead animals, no leaks or holes in the ceiling, the bed was sound and even had a little canopy above it, making it seem fancy. Liv bounced up and down on the bed a bit. 'The bed works. Once we've hoovered and sorted out the cobwebs I think we should give this room to Aaron and Kacey,' she said.

'Because spiders are lucky?' asked Effie pointing at a large one hanging from the canopy.

Liv shot out from underneath it. 'Not exactly.' Effie seemed puzzled. Liv didn't want to have to spell it out. Instead she said, 'That leaves leaky room or The Night of the Living Heads for Shanie.'

'Difficult choice,' said Fraser, deadpan.

Effie looked shocked. 'You can't make her sleep in the leaky room.'

'He won't,' said Liv.

'I might,' muttered Fraser.

It took some time to clean the room properly but it did look good and smelled a lot fresher. Liv was coming out as Fraser was leaving the bathroom wearing yellow rubber gloves.

'Marigolds? I'd never have guessed,' she said.

'I'm not cleaning toilets with my bare hands.'

'Of course not but *yellow* marigolds. I'd have thought you'd have gone for pink to match your teddy,' she said.

'Do you think you could maybe forget that?' he asked.

'Nope. Sorry, that's indelibly etched on my brain.'

'Mind you don't get another bump on the head then,' he said with a grin as he went past.

Was Fraser Douglas actually starting to get playful?

Fraser went off for a shower before starting on dinner and Liv and Effie decided to show the reluctant guests to their rooms. None of them seemed that happy to have been left in the library while they got everything ready.

'Hi, everyone, we have good news,' said Liv.

'The Wi-Fi is back on?' asked Aaron hopefully.

'Better than that. Your rooms have been cleaned, fresh bedding has been put on and they're ready now,' said Liv with a forced smile.

'Here,' said Shanie, offering her bag to Liv who just looked at it. Shanie waved it at Effie but when Effie went to take it Liv stopped her.

'I think you can manage to carry that up a few stairs. Follow me,' said Liv leading the way.

'The service here is the worst,' muttered Shanie.

'The service here is blinking well excellent seeing as I don't actually work here and it's free,' said Liv.

'Do we not have to pay now?' asked Shanie sounding cheered.

'You need to pay for the room and the food. My service is free,' said Liv.

Upstairs Effie opened the door to the best room with a bit of a ta-dah motion. 'This is Aaron and Kacey's room because it's the nicest and has spi—'

'Spice,' shot in Liv, desperately trying to avoid Effie saying the word *spiders*.

'Spice?' Kacey was pulling a face.

'It's for good luck for a long and happy marriage. Very old ritual and ancient Scottish tradition,' said Liv.

Effie looked more confused than usual.

Kacey walked inside and sniffed the air. 'I can't smell anything – only furniture polish.'

'It's a delicate scent,' said Liv nodding sagely.

Aaron walked around the bed. 'I can smell it. It's nice.'

Liv breathed a sigh of relief.

Shanie cleared her throat and when Liv turned she beckoned her to one side. 'I know they're just married and all that,' she said in hushed tones. 'But why have they got the best room?' Liv opened her mouth to answer but she continued. 'I think I was clear when I said I have a lot of Insta followers and I'm an influencer.'

'Sorry, I'm not that bothered because newlywed trumps whatever you are,' said Liv and went on to the next room, leaving her looking stunned.

'Shanie, this is your room.' Effie did the honours by opening the door.

Shanie tentatively put a designer-clad foot inside. 'Bloody hell. It's basically indoor camping.' She fixed Liv with an unblinking stare.

'Do you like camping?' ventured Liv.

'I hate it with a passion.'

'I had a feeling you were going to say that. Consider it an experience. Like being on reality TV. *Big Brother's Haunted Scottish Hotel*,' said Liv.

'There must be better rooms than this,' said Shanie.

'Trust me there's not.' Liv pouted and then decided to tell her the truth. 'Your choices are this one or there's a leaky room, which is not actually leaking at the moment but only because the snow and ice must have stopped anything coming through.' Liv didn't want to think what was likely to happen once things started to melt. 'Or there is a room with taxidermy deer heads and a colony of bats, or one with a broken bed and lots of boxes or one without a mattress.'

With a sniff Shanie said, 'I suppose it'll have to do.'

'Here's the key, but the lock's a bit dodgy so mind you don't get trapped in here forever,' said Liv humming the tune to 'Hotel California' as she left the room and was pleased to see the slight look of alarm on Shanie's face.

*

Effie was ushered back downstairs by Liv. Effie was having the best time. Getting her head around Daphne's new name was going to be tricky, but she could tell her new friend preferred to be called Liv so she was really going to try. She'd been so busy she'd barely checked her phone and there had been too many people in the library to be able to get in the right spot for the signal. She pulled it from her pocket. No messages. Her heart felt a little sad but then she knew John was busy and in a different country, which meant the time difference didn't help. She decided to go and have another root through the boxes they'd discovered earlier because along with a ton of memories there were also some useful bits she thought she could use to brighten the place up a little.

The hotel had been empty for such a long time and Effie had been so excited when Fraser had said he was going to open up the restaurant, but this was even better. The hotel had been her dad's pride and joy. It had also been a huge pull on his time and something, at times, Effie had felt she had to compete with. But now she was feeling differently about it. Like it was a long-lost relative and they'd been reunited. She was going to make it her job to look after everyone. She liked caring for Dolly. How hard could a few more be?

Effie's idea of going through the boxes had sent her back down memory lane. Each box was like a portal to another world. It was as if her childhood had been packed away with the lifetime of collected clutter. Effie pawed over long-forgotten treasures of moneyboxes, beaded purses and her much prized keyring collection. She'd bought one every time they went away and there had been quite a few family holidays as the collection bore witness to. She had been a traveller and maybe she could be again.

An old clock that had once stood on the mantelpiece in the dining room brought back a memory of her dad checking its accuracy to the speaking clock. A large hunting picture used to have pride of place in the entrance hall where the umbrella and coat stand also used to be kept.

Reams of tartan bunting that came out for Burns Night along with forgotten Christmas decorations filled two more large boxes. It reminded her of how the hotel used to be and of happier times. Was she really thinking about leaving all this behind?

14

Liv wasn't sure why she was creeping about but it was probably because she wanted to get her hands on the old bedside lamp she'd seen when they'd been moving the boxes and feared that if she asked for it one of the others would decide they were more deserving than her. She also wondered if there was anything that might uncover a bit more about the mysterious Fraser. She crept into the room now full of boxes. It was getting dark and she knew she'd trip over something if she started moving around so she put the light on. That was better.

But there were so many boxes, she had no idea which one the lamp was in. This was getting more and more like the story of Aladdin and that made her chuckle to herself. The chuckle seemed to echo in the room. Or was there someone or something else in there? Liv's skin prickled. This place gave her the creeps, but it was something she had to get over. She steeled herself and inched forwards. Her heart started to thump and it annoyed her. What was she scared of? A picture of Janet the witch loomed unhelpfully into her mind.

'There's nobody here. You're imagining it,' she whispered in an attempt to refocus. 'Janet doesn't exist.'

There was a brief pause before a reedy voice whispered, 'Yes she does.'

'Shitting hell!' shouted Liv, turning around and promptly tripping over a large box and landing with a thud.

'What's going on?' said Effie popping up from the other side of the bed looking startled.

'Effie! You'll be the death of me.'

'What are you doing?' asked Effie, craning her neck.

'I'm just looking for a um…' Something in the box she'd tripped over caught Liv's eye. 'This lamp,' she said holding it aloft like a prize trophy.

'You made me jump,' complained Effie, hauling a box into her arms and making her way around all the detritus.

'Me? What were you doing sitting in here in the dark?' *Who voluntarily did that?* thought Liv.

'I like the dark; it's comforting. I was looking for some decorations and I've found them.' Effie stepped over Liv like she were another box.

'Great. The fact you almost gave me heart failure is okay then.' Liv got to her feet and followed Effie out of the room, but not before she gave it a cursory check and put the light out.

Liv took the lamp back to her room and popped it on the bedside cabinet. She'd sort it out later.

Downstairs Fraser was in a huddle with Dolly and they both stopped talking when she approached – not off-putting at all. She poked a stray piece of hair behind her ear. 'What do you need me to do now?' she asked.

'I like her,' said Dolly as if Liv wasn't there. 'She has a good work ethic.'

Fraser seemed doubtful. 'There's not much else to do when you're snowed in.'

'I could be outside making snowmen. We don't see snow like this my way.'

Effie popped her head above the large box she was sorting through. 'I'd be up for making snowmen,' she said.

Liv glanced at her to see she had lots of strands of fairy lights around her neck.

'You okay?' she asked.

'I'm sorting out the decorations,' she said holding up a large knot of lights.

'Fraser's kitchen staff aren't due in today so he needs help in the kitchen,' said Dolly.

'Sure. What can I do?' asked Liv, but Fraser was already shaking his head. She was starting to lose her patience with him. 'What now?'

'I don't have time to train you,' he said.

Liv hated being underestimated. She put her hands on her hips. 'I might be a Michelin-starred chef for all you know. You've not bothered to ask.'

'Are you?' asked Dolly, her eyebrows and expectations raised.

'No, but the point is he didn't ask.'

Fraser threw up his hands. 'Okay so what do you do for a living?'

'I'm an SEO expert.'

'That sounds made up to me,' said Fraser. 'Or is it like when they call a window cleaner a transparency enhancement engineer?'

'I am a very good search engine optimisation expert, but I guess it could also be called online marketing.' Fraser clicked his fingers in a 'there you go' fashion, which annoyed Liv. 'But I do have other skills and to put those into fancy terms I am also an underwater ceramics technician with additional domestic water-erasing abilities.' She left a pause where they looked at her blankly. 'I can wash and dry dishes.'

'That's useful,' said Dolly. 'Isn't it, Fraser?'

He did not look impressed. 'Barely,' he said. 'We have two commercial dishwashers.'

'I can also peel and chop things.' *Including you into little pieces if you don't stop being an arse*, she added in her head.

Fraser did not look convinced. 'It doesn't look like I have a lot of choice.'

'I have rarely felt so valued and welcome,' said Liv. 'Shall we?' She stood back and elaborately waved for Fraser to lead the way to the kitchen. He stomped off in that direction.

Liv found him in the kitchen banging about. She put on an apron and joined Fraser where he was scanning a handwritten menu. 'What are we cooking, boss?'

'Cullen skink to start, venison with Hasselback potatoes or foraged wild mushroom and truffle ravioli, and for dessert cranachan with a pistachio crumb.'

'Nothing fancy then?' Liv grinned at him.

She received a stony face in response. 'And it's *yes, chef.*'

Liv snorted a laugh. 'Blimey, you're serious. Nah, that's not happening, Fraser. Remember I don't actually work for you. I'm the one doing *you* a favour here.'

'You're doing *me* a favour? That's rich. You turned up here with amnesia. We looked after you, I carried you to your room, arranged for medical attention and now you are stranded by the snow, and I have given you a room and board for as long as you need. I also suspect you will be looking to me to find someone to sort out your blown tyre once the weather lifts?'

'Fair enough. I'd say that makes us quits. Shall I start on the skink or the cranancanahan thing?' He shook his head and hauled a sack of potatoes onto the counter. 'Fine. I'm not too proud to peel spuds.'

'Do not peel them,' said Fraser. 'Do you even know what Hasselback potatoes are?'

She briefly considered giving a smart-arse response along the lines of them being a distant and slightly less glamorous relative of David Hasselhoff, but given the ferocity of Fraser's frown she thought better of it and shook her head. What followed was a cooking lesson worthy of any TV chef. He was less cranky when he was talking about cooking and surprisingly patient as he explained things. Liv forgot it was Fraser showing her what to do and got caught up in her job as commis chef.

*

Effie was quite pleased with the things she'd rediscovered and spent a happy couple of hours getting the dining room ready for dinner. As Fraser was planning to open a restaurant this was the one room that had been recently decorated, but she wasn't a fan of the stark white finish. Fraser called it classic, clean and sophisticated. Effie thought it was bland, boring and sterile.

With a bit of effort Effie had pulled some tables together to make a table for three and another for four as that seemed a lot cosier than the restaurant set-up Fraser had explained to her. It wasn't open yet so this seemed more friendly to Effie and it meant she could sit next to Liv. They'd not had a chance to get the new linen pressed so they were straight out of the packets with creases included. She laid the places and then went to choose a selection of plants from the lean-to greenhouse. She'd been nurturing them for some time. Some she'd planted from seed and others she'd picked up from neighbours and brought on. She picked the best of the pots and gave them a wash in the utility.

The smells coming through from the kitchen were tempting, but she made sure to keep out of Fraser's way. He took his cooking seriously.

With a few choice items the room seemed more inviting. Dolly wheeled in with Jock'O on her lap.

'Does it look okay?' asked Effie.

Dolly gripped her hand. 'Magnificent. You've done a fine job.'

'Thanks.' Effie was pleased and relieved. She didn't always get it right but she could trust her grandmother to tell her the truth, even if sometimes it wasn't what she wanted to hear. A little voice in her head made her wonder if that was why she'd not told Dolly about John.

'How long until dinner?' asked Dolly. 'The natives are getting restless.' She pointed a thumb over her shoulder where grumbled conversation was coming through from the library.

'I'll go and see,' said Effie.

'I'll give them wine, which should keep them quiet for a bit.'

Effie got an update from Fraser and went to tell the guests. The dishes he had cooked were some of the specialities he was going to have on his menu, and he'd been fine-tuning them with his kitchen team ahead of the restaurant opening.

She went through to the library where she was met by hopeful faces.

'Dinner will be ready in a few minutes,' said Effie.

'We'd planned to have fish and chips on our wedding day,' said Kacey looking glum. 'Is it fish and chips?'

'No. It's Cullen skink for starters, venison with Hasselback potatoes or foraged wild mushroom and truffle ravioli for mains and cranachan with a pistachio crumb for pud.' She was very proud of her cousin.

'I only understood potatoes and ravioli,' said Kacey.

'The rest didn't sound like food at all. I think we're being experimented on,' said Shanie.

Dolly wheeled into the room and Jock'O announced their arrival with a sharp bark. He fixed his eyes on Shanie and growled. 'It's all cooked fresh from locally sourced ingredients and would cost you an arm and a leg in that there London, so think yourselves lucky. If you take your seats in the dining room I'll take your choice of main course, either meat or vegetarian, unless you want to take your chances and walk fourteen miles that way to the twenty-four-hour garage that may or may not be open where you might be able to buy one of their out-of-date sausage rolls.'

Nobody replied. They all filed through to the dining room in silence with a flea in their ear, and Effie left Dolly to take orders.

Liv did a quick change and she and Effie ferried in starters to the dining room. The guests peered at the bowls in front of them.

'What's this?' asked Aaron, fishing about with his spoon.

'Cullen skink,' said Dolly, sounding even more Scottish than usual.

'It's fish and potato soup,' said Liv.

'Ahhh,' said Aaron. He had a small taste and the others watched him closely as if expecting him to convulse and die in front of them. 'That's all right that is,' he declared and the others picked up their spoons.

15

The main courses seemed to be going down well. Liv thought it was some of the best food she'd ever had, but then she wasn't very adventurous in that department and rarely could afford to eat out unless it was a cheeky weekend Maccy D's.

'Everything okay?' asked Dolly, which Liv thought was asking for trouble with this lot.

'The beef is really tasty,' said Kacey.

'It's venison,' said Dolly. 'Free roaming from the nearby estate.'

Kacey looked confused. 'Are cows free in Scotland?'

'It's venison,' repeated Dolly. 'Deer meat, which we pay a fair price for,' she added.

'Deer?!' Kacey dropped her cutlery. 'I'm eating a fawn?'

'It's why I went for the ravioli,' said Shanie.

'I think I might be sick,' said Kacey rushing from the table.

'Staggering,' said Dolly shaking her head.

Liv clicked her fingers. 'Aww good pun. I wish I'd thought of that one.' Shanie was the only one who laughed.

After the main courses Liv went to give Fraser a hand in the kitchen. 'Go and eat,' she said.

'No, I'll just—'

'Go,' she said trying to shoo him with a tea towel but he didn't budge so she felt a bit foolish flicking the cloth against his thigh. 'I mean I can't make you but I'm offering to clean up in here and that offer might not last long if I have much more wine so...' She pulled a face.

With a reluctant twist of his lips he muttered, 'Thanks.' And left the kitchen.

Effie came to help her and before long the dishwashers were full and they were making cups of tea and coffee.

'You should have your pudding,' said Effie. 'It's really nice. If you don't eat it I will and I need to watch my weight.'

'Why's that?' asked Liv.

'Boyfriend,' whispered Effie. 'Goodness it feels so good to finally tell someone. But you mustn't say anything. Not a word to anyone. Especially not Fraser or even worse my grandmother. Promise?'

'Sure,' said Liv, unsure why it would need to be all hush-hush. 'Why is it a secret?' Liv was already conjuring up a *West Side Story* rival family tale in her mind and a clan battle involving the ancient pike.

Effie bit her lip and Liv prepared herself for top-level gossip. 'He doesn't live near here.'

Liv was thoroughly disappointed. 'Right. Long-distance thing then.'

'You could say that. He's in Burkina Faso.'

Liv spun around. 'Blimey, that is long-distance. How did you meet him?'

'Online.' Effie whispered it like it was a bad swear word.

'Lots of people do these days. You just need to be careful. Make sure he's legit.'

'Burkina Faso is a real place. It's in Africa. I looked it up.'

'I know,' said Liv. 'But be on your guard because they make other stuff up, promise you things, let you hope that this time you've found someone who gets you and Mariah Carey but then they steal your heart and ghost you.'

'You can't get ghosts on the internet. They can't press the keys,' said Effie.

Liv chuckled and then paused because she wasn't entirely sure if Effie was joking. 'No, *ghosted*. Like when they suddenly unfriend you and completely disappear, making you feel worthless and questioning what the hell is wrong with you.'

'Right. I'd not heard of that.' Effie scrunched up her features. 'Actually I had heard of ghosting but I thought it was the same as being haunted.' She pulled out her phone. 'I might need to delete something I posted on a forum.'

'What's he like?' asked Liv, still a sucker for a romance story even if her own love life was like a disaster movie.

'Kind, selfless, cute. He changed his email address to John loves Effie at gmail. Isn't that romantic? He sent me a photo. Let me find it…' Effie was scrolling with Liv at her shoulder. There were lots of pictures of trees, Jock'O and Ginger.

The door swung open, interrupting them, and Dolly came in. Effie quickly shoved her phone in her pocket.

'You two look mightily suspicious,' said Dolly eyeing them knowingly.

'Nope,' said Liv. 'Effie was trying to explain haggis to me again. How are the prisoners?' she asked in a bid to distract her.

'Restless. Kacey is still upset about eating Bambi, Shanie can't function without the internet and Aaron was hoping for mints after his meal and possibly a turn-down service.'

'I'll happily turn him down,' said Liv with a smile.

*

Effie was rummaging in the cupboard when Fraser came into the kitchen. 'What are you looking for?' he asked.

'Shortbread. I thought you made some.'

'Top cupboard in a Tupperware. Are you still hungry after dinner?'

'No, it was lovely. But Aaron seems unhappy and I thought one might cheer him up.' Fraser's cheeks twitched. 'Stop being such a grump.'

'It's called being pragmatic,' he said with a harrumph.

'Whatever you call it you've been cranky with Liv.'

He waved his hands and his head trembled. 'That's all her doing. She's driving me nuts.'

Effie pointed wildly. 'This is just like Fiona Smith!'

'What?'

'You remember. Fiona with the wonky fringe and patent shoes? You used to throw paper at the back of her head on the school bus.'

'So?'

'You did it because you liked her but didn't know how to talk to her. And this thing with Liv is the same. Just without the bits of paper.'

Fraser gave a croaky laugh like it was getting stuck in

his throat. 'Oh no. This is definitely not what this is. Fiona was shy and had jellybeans. Liv is completely unpredictable and…' He stopped speaking.

'Has no jellybeans?' offered Effie as Fraser seemed distracted by the worktop.

Fraser's head snapped up. 'Exactly. She's just the same as the others.'

'But these people are potential customers.'

'You've got that from Granny and no they're not. As soon as the snow melts they will clear off and we'll never hear from them again, Liv included. Don't tell me we'll get repeat business because we won't. Especially not as they're all English. It's like another invasion.'

'You never know. If they have a good time here they might tell people about this amazing place in Scotland that you just have to visit.'

Briefly there was a smile on his lips. 'You are an eternal optimist.' He reached up, opened a cupboard and pulled down the box. 'If you're doing it then do it right. Put a couple of shortbread fingers on one of the fancy side plates and then dust them with icing sugar.'

'Thanks, Fraser. You're the best.'

'I think that's very much you, Effie,' he said as she got on with what he'd suggested.

Effie was carefully transporting the biscuits upstairs when she saw Liv coming out of the bathroom. 'Wait there, I need your help,' said Effie.

Effie knocked on Shanie's door. It opened to her stern face. 'Yes?'

'I thought you might like some of Fraser's special homemade short—' but before Effie had finished the sentence she'd taken it from her and shut the door.

'Rude bugger,' said Liv. She sucked her lip as she turned away and then back again. 'I don't like to see injustice and I'm not someone who dodges difficult situations.'

Effie wasn't sure if Liv was talking to herself or not so she nodded anyway in case she was talking to her.

Liv lifted her chin, marched over and banged on Shanie's door.

Shanie opened it again, looking bored. 'What now?'

'There's no excuse for rudeness. The word you are looking for is, thanks,' she said and she pointed at Effie.

Shanie glared at Liv. Licked her icing-sugar-coated lips and eventually managed to force out a mumble that might have been, 'Thank you.'

'Our pleasure,' said Liv as the door closed in her face. She turned to face Effie. 'What can I help you with?'

Effie felt a rush of something, possibly admiration. She wasn't sure what it was but she'd never met anyone like Liv before. Nothing and nobody seemed to faze Liv and here she was sticking up for her when they'd barely known each other for twenty-four hours.

'Thank you,' said Effie.

'No worries. Miserable cow wants to learn some manners.'

16

Effie was pleased with the results of the dining room and had an urge to make the rest of Lochy House Hotel feel more welcoming now they had some guests. Effie went looking for Liv and found her trying to get an old lamp to work. 'Hiya, what ya doing?'

'Well, I got changed.' She indicated that she wasn't wearing Effie's dress anymore. 'And now I'm trying to fix this but I'm probably wasting my time.' Liv flicked the switch on and off but nothing happened.

'Want to help me with something?'

'Sure. What is it?'

'Now the guests have gone to their rooms I want to decorate the library.' Liv looked interested. Effie went on. 'I'm thinking bringing nature inside, embracing the natural beauty of the woodland and calmness of spirit.'

Liv looked less keen. 'You want to go out in a weather-warning-level snow blizzard to get bits of twigs?'

'It's a bit calmer out there now.'

'Is it melting?' asked Liv.

'No, the temperature is dropping so it's turning to ice.'

'We won't be getting out of here anytime soon then.' Liv seemed to say it more to herself than Effie. She let out a sigh. 'Go on then. What's the worst that could happen?'

'My...' Effie counted them off on her fingers. 'Great-great-great-great-great-great-great-Aunt Tilda was lost in a snowstorm and they didn't find her body for three weeks. They thought she'd run off with a highwayman so nobody went looking for her.'

'Ri-ight,' said Liv slowly. 'Not really selling it to me there, Effie.'

'You won't die. On my dad's side there was a relative who lived for three months in a shepherd's hut with only foraged food and water. So we'll be fine.'

'You have lots of weird stories, Effie.'

'I know – aren't they great? I love things like that. You must tell me all your family tales,' she said as they left the room.

'Apart from the time my nan got locked in Woolworths and ate her own weight in Pick-A-Mix I'm not sure I have anything remotely similar,' said Liv.

They went downstairs to put on coats and wellies. Effie went in search of the tools she'd need to forage the decorations. Liv was pulling on her borrowed wellies when Effie tapped her on the shoulder, having found what she needed.

'Bloody hell,' said Liv lurching out of the way.

'What?' Effie looked at the bag she was holding.

'No, other hand,' said Liv slowly pointing with wide eyes. Effie waved the axe she was holding. 'You're quite safe.

I've used one of these loads of times. You can carry the bag. Come on.' It took Liv a moment to do up her coat. The whole time she seemed very interested in the axe because she didn't take her eyes off it. Effie was aware that she led a more rural lifestyle than most and it was likely Liv hadn't ever seen a real axe before.

They ventured outside. It had stopped snowing but it was dark and the temperature had dropped. There was a bit of a drift in the courtyard so they had to lift up their knees to get through it.

'This had better be worth it,' mumbled Liv. She stopped. 'Tell me you can hear music,' she said twisting around.

'Yes, it's Ginger,' said Effie.

'If you tell me that cow plays the accordion I'll know that bump on the head was a lot more serious than I thought.'

'Noooo, that's a cello.'

'You're winding me up,' said Liv, and under her breath added, 'Or I am going to need sectioning because I have properly wandered into La La land.'

'No. Ginger likes listening to classical music. She finds it calming. And I think she gets lonely.'

'It's a radio then,' said Liv.

'Of course it is. You didn't think she could play the cello, did you?' Effie got a fit of the giggles. Liv was funny.

'Probably a daft question,' said Liv as they continued out of the courtyard and towards the woods with Effie leading the way with a torch. 'But why don't you put Ginger in a field with other cows? Then she wouldn't be lonely.'

'We have tried that a few times with different herds but the problem is she doesn't know she's a cow. I think she thinks she's a dog because she spent the first few months at the lodge with Jock'O but then she got too big for the garden there and she was eating the herbs, the ivy and mother-in-law's tongue.'

'Eww that's an image I'll struggle to get rid of,' said Liv. 'Hang on, I'm guessing that mother-in-law's tongue is a plant?'

'Yes, a bit of a toxic one too. It gave Ginger diarrhoea.'

'That's also not a nice thought. A cow with the runs. That would take more than a couple of Imodium to sort out.' Liv seemed to find that funny. They trudged on a bit further. 'Are we there yet?' asked Liv.

'Almost,' said Effie pointing the way with the axe.

'I wish you wouldn't wave that thing around. I'm worried I'm going to go home looking like Van Gogh.'

They made it to the woodland where there was a little less snow, thanks to the tree cover, and Effie began searching.

'Effie, my teeth are actually chattering here.' Liv did a demonstration.

'It's okay. I found something.'

Liv went to join her. 'What is it?'

Effie stood back to proudly reveal her find. 'Mistletoe. Isn't it beautiful? I think it's quite romantic how it needs the poplar tree to survive. It draws on the tree's nutrients and water.'

'Sounds like a parasite to me,' said Liv who was visibly shivering. Fraser was right about one thing: southerners were definitely not as hardy as the Scots.

'The ancients believed it warded off evil and kept witches at bay.'

'Great. That'll keep Janet out of our hair. Chop a load down and let's get back.'

'Have you ever seen it in the wild before?' asked Effie selecting where best to cut without killing off the plant or the tree.

'Nope, ours comes from B&M Home Bargains. It's cheap, everlasting and it has added glitter. I highly recommend it.'

'You can chop down some of that holly,' said Effie pulling out the old curved machete they kept for jobs like this.

'Bloody hell,' said Liv staggering backwards away from the blade and reversing hard into a tree. 'I swear I'm going to die in this place.'

'Are you okay?' asked Effie offering her the knife again.

'Yep. All good. Nothing wrong with me. *I'm* perfectly sane,' said Liv. 'Thank you,' she added as, at last, she cautiously took the machete and backed away, this time avoiding the tree.

Effie concentrated on the mistletoe until she heard grumbling from Liv.

'Ouch, this stuff is vicious. I think it knows I want to cut bits off it.' Liv was getting her gloves and coat caught up in the holly bush. She looked like she'd been velcroed to it in a number of places.

'Here,' said Effie, coming over and taking the machete. 'Look for the newer branches. They're not as thick and woody. Take hold of a section where the leaves won't spike you and then...' Effie brought down the blade and cleanly cut the branch from the bush. 'See?'

'You make it look easy. I mean menacing but also impressive. Who showed you how to do that?' asked Liv taking back the knife.

'My dad,' said Effie, the familiar sense of loss gripping her. It wasn't true that time eased the pain, she simply had more distractions so she thought of him less, and that in itself made her feel guilty.

'He must be cool. Is he outdoorsy like you?' asked Liv.

'He died,' said Effie, and she went back to chopping the mistletoe.

17

Liv was glad to be back in the relative warmth of the hotel. Whilst Effie seemed nice, Liv had watched possibly too many horror films to be comfortable being out in the woods with someone with an axe and a machete, because in the films it usually didn't end well for the one without any weapons. Now safely inside and the sharp implements put away, she was feeling calmer and more rational. She went through to the kitchen and automatically got a mug out to make a drink. Fraser was leaning over a piece of paper on the counter.

'You English are obsessed with tea.' He said it like it was a bad thing.

'It could be worse. It could be deep-fried Mars bars.'

He raised an eyebrow. 'Urban myth,' he said.

'Aww I was hoping they'd be for dessert tomorrow.'

'You staying are you?' He lifted his chin to look at her. Those eyes were even bluer than his profile picture. They seemed to see into her soul and she did not like the sensation one little bit. How could he look at her like that and yet have no flicker of recollection? Or was he just very good at hiding it? Whichever it was, it pissed her off.

She folded her arms. 'Not a lot of choice given the weather forecast says more snow is coming, which won't help on top of the ice. Trust me I'll be out of here as soon as physically possible.'

'Robbie rang to check we were all okay and to say that the snowplough should be able to get through in the morning. There'd be nothing to stop you leaving then.' His expression was unreadable.

'Now don't you go getting my hopes up. Did you want a cuppa?'

'No thanks.' He tapped his water bottle and went back to his notes and his chewed pencil.

Curiosity got the better of Liv so she made her tea and came to stand next to him. 'Is this tomorrow's menu?'

'I thought I should plan ahead in case our guests are staying. I need to defrost ingredients.'

Liv considered biting her tongue instead of blurting out what she was thinking, but this was the new Liv, so what the heck. 'I don't know why you're going to so much trouble. They are an ungrateful bunch. I mean Aaron and Kacey are all right, but I doubt they'd be bothered what you served them, and Shanie doesn't deserve anything so I'd be giving her shop-bought lasagne and baked beans.'

He seemed mildly amused. 'I'm a chef,' he said as if addressing someone a bit dim.

'I know. Doesn't mean you have to cook all the time. I doubt Bear Grylls drinks his own wee when he's at home on his sofa watching the footie.'

Fraser put down the pencil and walked off. 'Follow me,' he said belatedly.

Liv walked over to where he opened the freezer. It was a large walk-in affair, which she'd seen him briefly open earlier when he'd labelled and stored some of the leftover cooked venison.

'What do you see?' he asked.

'The inside of a giant freezer,' she said. 'Brrr, it's almost as cold as outside.'

'But what's in it? And don't say food,' he said pre-empting her answer.

Liv tentatively stepped inside. She had a fear of being shut in one of these things. Now she thought about it she was definitely watching far too much scary stuff. She made a mental note to check out some romcom films for a change. She scanned the shelves and gave a brief commentary. 'Different sorts of fish. Joints of meat. Herbs. Vegetables.' She wasn't sure what he was getting at.

'Do you see a ready-made lasagne?'

'Ahhh I get it now,' she said exiting the freezer. 'You're being all hoity-toity because you make all your own food. Well, I think that's just poor forward planning. I always keep a pizza in the freezer for emergencies.'

Fraser huffed and slammed the freezer shut, making Liv shudder – she was glad she was on the outside. He tutted and went back to preparing his menu.

'Everyone likes pizza. Just saying,' she added and she made a hasty exit, taking her mug of tea with her.

She found Effie lugging a couple of boxes into the library.

'What is his problem?' she asked.

Effie looked up. 'Who? Fraser?'

Liv nodded. Effie paused as if considering whether to explain or not.

'I'm not imagining it, am I? He is more grumpy with me than anyone else, isn't he?'

Effie carried on dragging the box into the library. 'Come in,' she said. Liv gave a half-hearted attempt at helping with the box, but she didn't want to spill her tea. Once inside Effie shut the door and looked around as if double-checking there was nobody there. 'You're English,' said Effie in a way that implied that that one thing explained it all.

'I know that. Does he hate everyone who's not Scottish? Is he that prejudiced?'

'It's just that...' Effie chewed her lip.

Did she know something? Liv was beginning to wonder if Fraser had shared anything with his cousin. Perhaps he did remember who she was and that was why he was keen for her to leave. It was starting to make her cranky. 'Has he said something? Please tell me, Effie.'

Effie went over to the window seat and flopped down. 'It's a long story.'

Liv sat down next to her. 'Then just give me a trailer-length version.' Effie's face contorted at the request. This was obviously a big ask. 'Okay but try to keep it short.'

Effie took a deep breath. 'Fraser went travelling a few years ago and met Lizzie. I don't think she liked me.'

'Is that why you said people called Liz aren't very nice?' asked Liv, remembering the odd conversation she'd had with Effie about names.

'She used to laugh at things I said and say things to make me look stupid.'

'That's not nice,' said Liv, already not liking the sound of Lizzie.

'They met in Barcelona but Lizzie isn't Spanish. They fell in love and when he came home Lizzie came with him. He changed when he was with her and that made him act differently around everyone else – and not a good different, but he was still Fraser and she seemed to make him happy.'

'Where's Lizzie now?'

'I'm getting to that part,' said Effie with a finger wiggle of irritation. 'They had plans to move back to Spain and open a restaurant there but... Fraser felt he should stay here. Lizzie got really cross and I thought they were going to split up.' Effie visibly brightened. 'But they didn't. The compromise was that they decided to open up a restaurant at the hotel, but Lizzie was never really on board with it.'

Liv failed to hide a yawn. It had been a long day and it felt like Effie still had a lot to tell her.

Effie continued. 'Anyway, they got the right permissions and everything and then Lizzie dumped Fraser and went off with his best mate Callum, and Fraser didn't want to continue with the restaurant on his own so he got a job in a pub in Fort William. Then two months ago we found out that Lizzie and Callum were opening up a restaurant a couple of miles away, and it's basically what she and Fraser were going to do here. That upset him a lot. I mean like proper crazy upset.' She twirled her hands at either side of her head.

'I can imagine,' said Liv.

'I've not finished.'

'Sorry.'

'Fraser left the pub and started making plans to open

the restaurant here on his own. He sold his flat and moved in here. There's meant to be a big pre-launch event on the 23rd – I like to call it Christmas Eve Eve. It's to gain support, but that doesn't look like it will be able to go ahead if the snow sticks around.'

'That it? Anything else?' Liv was no wiser as to Fraser's attitude towards her.

'Um. No that's everything. The end,' said Effie, sitting up straight.

'Thanks for telling me, but I'm still not entirely sure why he's so pissy with me. Do I look like Lizzie?'

Effie laughed. 'Noooo, Lizzie is really glamorous. Very pretty. Actually she's more striking than pretty. The sort of face that makes men turn their heads to watch her walk by. She looks a bit like Blake Lively, and Lizzie's super stylish too,' she added with a glance over Liv's jumpsuit.

'Thanks for that,' said Liv, feeling like a swamp monster.

'And,' said Effie, as if something important had struck her, 'Lizzie is English.'

'There we are,' said Liv feeling a little vindicated. At least that explained why Fraser was frequently having a dig about the English and generally off with her. And now Liv was starting to make other connections. Was this why he'd ghosted her? Was it some sort of revenge plot on English girls? Maybe she wasn't the only one. That would explain why he didn't remember her. Or perhaps he didn't remember her because she wasn't that memorable and didn't look like Blake Lively, but she couldn't help that.

'Don't take it personally,' said Effie. 'Fraser doesn't mean to be bad-mannered. He's really kind.' Effie lowered her voice to a whisper. 'I think you remind him of Fiona Smith.'

'And what was she like?' asked Liv.

'Terrible fringe and very shiny shoes.'

'Ri-ight.' Liv decided to change the subject. 'What's with the box?'

'Christmas decorations! I thought it would cheer the old place up and get us all feeling festive, and then everyone will be less crabbit, that means grumpy.'

'Good idea,' said Liv although she wasn't as sure as Effie that a few bits of tinsel would be enough.

They spent an hour arranging bits of the foliage they had gathered, entwining them with the strands of fairy lights that they could get to work. They hung a piece of mistletoe from the chandelier and some other sprigs all around the hotel as there was quite a lot of it. When Liv came back into the library, Effie had a string of tartan bunting draped around her neck and she was adjusting the mistletoe. 'I guess only Aaron and Kacey will make good use of that,' said Liv with a little sigh.

'We'll all benefit from the mistletoe,' said Effie sounding extra earnest and making Liv wonder what sort of party games they played in these parts.

'I'm not kissing anyone this Christmas,' said Liv. The statement pulled her up short. Sure Christmas was a time for kids and families, but it was also special if you were in a relationship. There was something about being with someone at this time of year that made it feel extra special. Perhaps it was because each Christmas was a milestone; a marker in life that she pinned things to. And this would be the year she was on her own, double ghosted and most likely having Christmas dinner with her mum and sister. She loved her family with all her heart and would always want to be with them at Christmas, but how nice to have someone else to share that with too. Cuddling up with them to watch a soppy film and eat too many chocolates with and open thoughtful gifts you'd got each other.

She realised Effie was watching her closely. Maudlin wasn't going to do her any good. 'How will we all benefit from the mistletoe?' she asked. If the answer was some sort of orgy then she was going to dig her way out with her bare hands if she had to.

'The ancient Celts gathered mistletoe to ward off evil spirits and bring good luck,' said Effie.

Liv was much relieved. 'That's good then. Might keep Janet away. Perhaps the holly will ward off pricks,' she said with a smile.

'Holly brings peace and fertility,' said Effie.

'Yeah that too. Why do people kiss under mistletoe and not holly then?' she asked.

'Because a couple of centuries ago someone decided a man could kiss any woman he liked if it was under the mistletoe and it was bad luck for her to refuse.'

'I might have known it would have something to do with some chancer.' Liv shook her head.

'It's kind of nice if someone wants to kiss you though,' said Effie looking out of the window dreamily.

Liv took hold of the end of the tartan bunting they'd been pinning into the picture rail, got onto the chair and reached up.

'Is this a Scottish tradition?' asked Liv shoving a drawing pin into the end of the bunting with a sore thumb.

'My great-grandmother, Ailsa, made it from soldiers' kilts. When they came home from World War Two they handed in all their kit in exchange for a new suit. A lot of the clothes were good for nothing but rags, but the kilt is a hardwearing material so a lot of those could be used again. Those that couldn't went to the needy. Ailsa made some of them into clothes for children because there was still rationing, and the bits that were left over she made into bunting.'

Liv looked at it afresh. It was all one type of tartan: navy and dark green with a yellow thread running through it. The thought that every piece had seen military service made it quite a piece of history. 'The tartan is pretty. Is it all from one regiment?'

'The Gordon Highlanders,' said Dolly proudly as she entered the room and put down a mug.

'It's lovely. I like the colours. I noticed the curtains in my room are the same.'

Effie gasped and stood up very straight. 'They are not,' she said jutting her chin out.

'It's blue and green,' said Liv.

'The curtains are clan Campbell,' explained Dolly. 'The red and green tartan in the entrance lobby is Robertson, and the black and white with a thin red thread is Macpherson.'

Liv got the feeling she'd uttered something akin to blasphemy. 'Sorry,' she ventured.

'We take our history and traditions seriously,' said Dolly.

'I'm learning that. No offence meant.'

'Och, none taken,' said Dolly.

'I was expecting more men in kilts though,' said Liv thinking out loud.

'It's more ceremonial these days,' said Dolly.

'Does Fraser have one – a kilt?' Liv's mind was painting interesting pictures.

'Of course,' said Effie. 'He's got a sporran and a *sgian-dubh*.'

'What like a jet ski but for snow? They look cool,' said Liv now picturing Fraser on a snowmobile with his kilt blowing in the wind.

Effie got a fit of the giggles. 'No, silly. Not a skidoo, a *sgian-dubh*. That's a knife. All the men have them.'

'Ri-ight,' said Liv. Things were quite different this far north.

Dolly did a lap of the room. 'You've done a lovely job here, girls. But you know what this room needs?'

Dolly was looking towards the large window at the end of the room. 'A Christmas tree,' said Liv and Effie together.

'Goodnight, girls,' said Dolly, kissing first Effie and then to her surprise she wheeled over to Liv and held out her arms. Jock'O eyed her suspiciously as she tentatively leaned over him to accept the hug. As she pulled back she saw Jock'O had a sock under his paws.

'Hey, is that my sock?' said Liv but Jock'O quickly lay down.

18

Liv slept better than the previous night and was woken by the sound of Kacey either being strangled or hitting a particularly intense orgasm. Liv unkindly hoped it was the former. She was single and facing Christmas alone, but that wasn't the biggest of her issues. She walked over to the window, pulled back her Campbell tartan curtains and looked out. It was exactly the same as the previous day – wall-to-wall snow. She puffed out a sigh. She hoped Robbie was right about the snowplough getting through, otherwise it looked like she was going to be stranded with Fraser Douglas for a bit longer. Although she had to admit she'd warmed to Effie and Dolly, so it wasn't all bad, and the area was incredibly pretty even when it was covered in a few feet of snow and ice.

In the kitchen Effie and Fraser were preparing breakfast, so Liv mucked in where she was needed.

'You okay?' asked Fraser.

'Yep, not been pillaged by Janet for my soul.'

'Yet,' said Fraser with a wink. 'Almost like you're settling in.'

'I could certainly get used to the view from my room. It's out of this world. I thought the scenery on the way up here was impressive – all hilly and green – but out there is spectacular.'

'Trossachs,' said Fraser.

How rude, thought Liv. She was about to argue with him when the door opened and Dolly came in on the scooter. 'Slight problem,' said Dolly. 'There's no sign of our guests.'

'I hope they've all left,' said Fraser stroking his beard like a Bond villain.

'You're not the greatest host given you want to be a big thing in the hospitality industry,' said Liv.

Fraser blinked at her. 'Who said anything about a big thing?'

Liv smirked at the innuendo and was pleased to see a little colour come to Fraser's cheeks. 'I understand you're building up to a big launch. And you want to beat your… um… rival restaurant.' She pointed like she knew where Lizzie and Callum's place was although she hadn't a clue about the geography of where she was. In her head there was no north, south, east or west; only abandoned car, mad cow, loch or mountains.

'It is quite a big thing,' said Effie and Liv failed to hide her grin.

'Could you have this discussion later?' asked Dolly drawing everyone's attention. 'I think the guests have all slept in and as we didn't give them a time for breakfast we had better tell them that it's almost ready.'

They all looked at each other, hoping one of the others

was going to be the first to volunteer. Eventually all eyes were on Liv. 'Fine. I'll get everyone up.'

The others were visibly relieved. Liv pulled back her shoulders and headed out of the kitchen. 'Wish me luck.' There was no reply. As she walked up the hallway she was met by a sound she could only imagine was the result of a cat playing a recorder out of its bum. There was a brief interlude when the front door slammed open and the awful noise restarted, but now much louder and shriller. Liv stuck her fingers in her ears and approached with caution to find a red-faced Robbie puffing into bagpipes in the entrance lobby. She waved at him to stop.

'Was it "Wake Me Up Before You Go Go"? Am I right?' asked Liv.

Robbie's brow furrowed. 'It was "Scotland the Brave".'

Liv snapped her fingers. 'Shucks, that was going to be my second guess. Come properly inside and let's hear it again,' she said, immediately ramming her fingers in her ears. Robbie seemed confused by the gesture but he puffed up his cheeks and with a waggle of his arm he started playing again. Liv reversed into the hallway. From a glance over her shoulder she could see Effie and the others coming from the kitchen.

Doors began opening above her.

A dishevelled and confused-looking Kacey tiptoed out of her room with her hands over her ears, looking concerned. 'Is that the fire alarm?'

Shanie came marching out of her bedroom. 'What the actual f—'

'Okay, you can stop now, Robbie. Thank you.' Liv looked up to the top of the stairs. 'Breakfast is being served shortly in the dining room.' She turned around to face Fraser, Effie and Dolly. She waved an arm towards the angry-looking guests. 'Job done.'

Effie started an enthusiastic round of applause. Nobody joined in but Robbie did look chuffed at the gesture as he pulled his shoulders back a little and almost dropped the bagpipes, making them let out a sad, elongated final note. Liv walked proudly back to the kitchen.

Breakfast service was quite straightforward and bar the grumbles about being woken by bagpipes, the guests seemed okay. Even Shanie seemed mollified when Effie explained that the royal family were woken daily by a piper when they stayed at Balmoral. Robbie came in as they were clearing away. Liv had an armful of plates.

'I'm afraid I've just received a call. The snowplough has broken down so we're looking at a further day's delay.' There were huffs and protests from everyone, including Liv who almost dropped the plates. This was not the news she wanted to hear. 'But the good news is that I have logged you all on the waiting list for your vehicles to be recovered.'

'Waiting list?' queried Liv.

'Yes, there's not many companies with the right equipment out this way and they're all incredibly busy. Lots of abandoned cars on the A roads.'

Once the tables were cleared Liv was having a consolation cup of tea in the kitchen with Robbie, who was munching on a morning roll that Effie had made him. 'Thanks for getting us on the list. When do you think we'll get out of here?'

Robbie wobbled his head. 'Late tomorrow, best case. If not the following morning.'

It was hard not to feel a bit down about it. She was missing home. Maybe if she'd been stranded somewhere in the middle of summer it might have been different, but it was the run-up to Christmas and she was virtually confined to an old crumbling hotel with complaining guests and the man who'd ghosted her. It was very different to what she'd hoped she'd be doing. She'd been looking forward to a break from work. She'd planned a trip to a Christmas market in Chester and some evening shopping with her sister. Plus she had lots of plans for wrapping presents in front of cheesy festive films with a large glass of knock-off Baileys from one of the cheap supermarkets, because who could really tell once it was poured over ice cubes?

The kitchen door swung open and Effie bounded in. 'Are you coming with me and Fraser to get this tree then?'

'I don't think it'll take three of us to choose a Christmas tree,' said Liv.

'No but it will to chop it down and drag it back,' said Effie cheerfully. 'You're welcome to join us too, Robbie.'

'I'm on call,' he said importantly. 'But thanks for the offer.'

'No worries,' said Effie before disappearing.

The thought of venturing out in the cold yet again sent a seismic shiver through Liv. She wasn't sure she'd fully defrosted from yesterday's expedition. Liv dragged herself to her feet.

'Have fun,' said Robbie in a far too jolly tone.

'Have the emergency services on standby,' said Liv and she left a worried-looking Robbie sipping his tea.

*   *   *

Liv went to use the telephone on reception. Now she officially had her memory back she could at least openly call home.

'Hello?'

Liv had not been expecting her sister's voice. 'Hey, Charlotte, how are you?'

'What the hell are you playing at? I need my car back. And Mum is worried sick.'

'I miss you too. There's been like a gazillion feet of snow in the last couple of days, the roads are impassable and the snowplough is broken so I'm stuck here.'

'Is it awful?' came her mum's voice. 'Make yourself useful. Don't be the first one to be eaten.'

Liv rolled her eyes even though she was on the phone. 'I'm not in a film, Mum. Nobody needs to eat anyone. Actually the food is excellent. I just can't leave for a bit longer.'

Fraser gave her a look as he strode past. He was difficult to read. 'Sorry, I need to go and cut down a Christmas tree, but I'm fine.'

'Just get my car back safe,' said Charlotte.

'Love you too. Bye.'

Liv went through to the boot room and put on the now familiar borrowed coat and wellies before sullenly following the others outside. Effie was almost skipping and Fraser was carrying a large rucksack on his back like he was going camping. The wind had whipped up and it was snowing again. 'Come on, seriously?'

'It's a wee bit oorlich,' said Fraser.

'It's a wee bit nothing. It's a whole huge great snowy…

Nobody else is bothered, are they?' She looked at the other two who simply pulled on their hoods, shrugged and marched out into the weather. 'They're all blinking nuts,' she said pulling the door closed behind her as she followed them out into the cold. They passed Ginger who today was listening to Alexander Armstrong – she clearly had varied taste. It didn't seem quite as far to the woodland, but once there time seemed to drag as the first section was full of ridiculously large trees, so they had to keep walking.

'We could have a Griswold Christmas and get this one,' said Liv stopping and pointing at one of the monster trees. Effie and Fraser viewed her with blank faces. 'From the film,' she added. They both shook their heads. '*National Lampoon's Christmas Vacation?*' More shaking. 'Blimey, I might as well be at the North Pole.'

'Hey, don't disrespect my homeland just because I've not watched some stupid cult English film,' snapped Fraser.

'I'm not disrespecting anything. I'm sure it's lovely here when it's not minus twelve and trying to bury me alive in snow. But who hasn't heard of that film?' Effie unhelpfully put her hand up. 'Apart from you two, hardly anyone, because it's massively famous and for your information it's an American film.' Fraser's snowy eyebrow twitched. 'Now you know it's American you might even enjoy it.' She went to walk away.

'What do you mean by that?'

Liv turned to look but the ruddy hood stayed still and she ended up looking inside it, which was infuriating. She had to turn around an almost full circle to face Fraser again. 'You hate the English.'

He looked taken aback but that might have been because

she was twirling around like a Scottish dancer. 'I've never said that. It's not personal. It's in our history.' He clenched his jaw.

'That has nothing to do with me. No ancestor of mine has ever picked up a long spiky pole, let alone marched all the way up the sodding country with it to prod one of your family tree in the arse. You can't take it out on every English person. You had no right to—' A little voice in her head willed her not to show her hand now. She still needed somewhere to stay. This was not the right time to bring up the ghosting, although the fire in her gut said otherwise. Liv took a breath. 'You didn't need to be mean to me. It is not my problem that your ex-girlfriend turned out to be a cheat. I'm not related to her either!'

Liv was so cross she turned around and stomped off, almost walking straight into a large tree trunk. She skirted around it and carried on tramping ahead, hoping very much that the others were following her because she really didn't want to get lost and freeze to death like poor old Aunt Tilda with too many greats to mention.

A few paces deeper into the woods, she was aware that Fraser was walking alongside her. 'It was hundreds of years of persecution—' Liv shot him daggers. 'But I get your point. I'm glad this one's not on the end of a pike.' She carried on walking. 'That was a joke. Point of a pike. Probably not a good joke if it needs signposting.' They walked along in time and Liv had to slow her pace because the anger that was fuelling her was abating and the snow made it hard going, even if there was less under the trees. 'Sorry,' added Fraser.

Liv stopped and looked back. Effie was a few metres

behind them still checking trees for their suitability. 'Sorry for what?' For a moment she wondered if he was going to confess all.

'I'm sorry that I made you feel that I was pissed off at you because you were English.'

'If *I* feel?' She stared him down. That was not an apology if he was putting it back on her.

'Okay. I was pissed off,' said Fraser. 'But I was pissed off with everyone. You sort of took the brunt of it. I don't know why. Maybe because you turned up out of the blue and stirred up all these feelings. Everything. You stirred everything up.' He glanced down at his wellies before looking her in the eye. 'I'm sorry. Can I stop saying sorry now?' Those Nordic blue eyes held her gaze as snowflakes caught in his eyelashes.

'You can.' Now *she* felt bad. 'I'm sorry if I've overreacted. It's been a tense time with... everything.' They stared at each other for a moment longer than was comfortable. The tension was broken by a large snowball whizzing between the two of them. They turned to see another one coming and Liv just managed to dodge out of the way. Fraser balled up some snow and hurled it back at Effie, who squealed and ran off. The tension broken they put the quarrel behind them and began looking properly for a suitable tree.

'I think this one,' called Effie and they went to see.

'Nice tree but it's a bit too big,' said Fraser.

Liv was craning her neck to try to see the top of it as snow was blown into her face, making her cheeks sting. Liv had her head so far back she started to topple. She staggered a bit before strong arms grabbed her and kept her upright.

'You okay?' asked Fraser looking concerned.

'She does that,' said Effie. 'She's just checking that gravity still works.' She nodded wisely.

Fraser was still waiting for a reply. 'I'm fine thanks,' said Liv. She was glad she'd not fallen over and there was something lovely about being held by strong arms. Self-consciously Liv pulled herself free.

'This one?' shouted Effie pointing at another fir tree.

'I bloody well hope so,' said Liv and a smile tweaked at Fraser's lips.

'That's perfect, Effie. Let's chop it down,' he said.

Liv was relieved but she had to admit the tiny tree was somewhat of a disappointment, so dwarfed by all its fellow firs, but she was far too cold to argue.

Chopping the tree down was not like Liv had seen it in the films. Out of the rucksack Fraser pulled another horror film staple, the chainsaw, and proceeded to effortlessly cut wedges out of the tree from alternating sides. She and Effie stood well back until Fraser put his boot against it and pushed it over. He chiselled little grooves in the trunk before putting the chainsaw away and tying ropes around the bottom, which held firm in the cut ridges. They each took a rope and set off for the hotel.

Trudging through the snow with thoughts of a nice hot drink in her head, Liv had that sense that someone was watching her. If it was Janet she was so cold she was almost at the point of being happy to surrender her soul. But she glanced across the bushy branches to see Fraser looking at her, and for the first time there was no air of contempt in his gaze. He smiled, which caught Liv by surprise, and she instantly tripped over and face-planted in the snow.

19

Back at the hotel Liv made a cup of tea and went through to the library where the men had already got the tree up and were adjusting it in the base.

'Chuffing heck. Is that the same tree?' asked Liv scanning the giant fir up and down. 'Did that grow like six feet between the woods and here?' The tree, which had seemed dwarfed by its peers in the woodland, now looked huge as it reached almost to the high ceiling and filled the bay window. 'It is a Griswold tree,' she said and then remembered the earlier conversation. 'I just mean—'

'I loved that film,' said Robbie, sticking his head from underneath the branches. 'Absolute Christmas classic. I must dig it out this year.'

'Thank you, Robbie,' said Liv, feeling vindicated. 'Please can you strap Fraser and Effie to a chair and make them watch it too, because they've not seen it.'

'Restraining people without consent is against the law—'

'It's okay,' said Fraser. 'She didn't mean literally. And

I *would* like to watch it.' There was a quick glance in Liv's direction. Was the tide changing with Fraser Douglas? Liv was still very much on her guard.

Effie hugged herself as she grinned at the tree. 'It's so pretty. All it needs is a sprinkle of reindeer dust.'

'What would that be exactly? Deer dandruff?' asked Liv. Effie shook her head at her.

Robbie had set a roaring fire in the library and Liv was starting to defrost while she gave Jock'O a tummy rub. The mission to make the guests enjoy themselves was taking shape. Effie invited them all downstairs with the lure of Drambuie laced coffees and presented them with the box of ornaments she'd discovered.

Dolly beckoned Fraser and the others out into the hallway, leaving the guests in the library. For once she didn't have Jock'O on her lap; he'd been replaced by a radio and the sound of someone speaking was a little distracting. 'Listen to this,' she said, turning up the volume. A radio presenter with a thick Scottish accent was enthusing about how the snow was bringing people together. He was finishing a story about a rural community who were delivering food packages by tractor. 'And now the story I was teasing you about. I have Hamish MacNeish…' Dolly grumbled something at the surname. Fraser gave an imperceptible shake of his head which Liv took as 'Don't ask.' So she didn't. The radio host continued. 'And he is live now from The Grog and Scran pub. Hello, Hamish, I understand you've taken in some stranded travellers?'

The noise level changed when Hamish came on and it sounded like a full-scale party was underway. 'Aye. It's like Hogmanay has come early. We rescued eight poor folk from the terrible weather. Some were trapped in their cars and we brought them here. It's a snow-in but we have food and beer, so everyone is happy.'

'That's Scottish hospitality right there. Can we speak to one of the guests please, Hamish?'

'Sure thing.'

'Hiya,' came a female voice.

'You're live on the radio. Can you tell me a little about your experience?'

'OMG. We are all getting on so well. When our car conked out and ended up in a snowdrift little did we know we would all be having the time of our lives. I have met people here at the Grog and Scran that I know will be friends for life.'

Dolly turned the sound back down. 'The presenter wants people who are in a similar position to phone in. What do you think?'

'Could be good PR,' said Liv. 'The Grog and Scran just got a good few mentions in just a couple of minutes.'

Fraser was looking sceptical. 'It's not exactly a party here though.'

He pushed the library door gently open and they all surreptitiously peered inside. Shanie was sitting on the rug with Jock'O, mug in one hand and pointlessly waving her phone in the other, while Aaron and Kacey were diligently placing baubles on the tree. Aaron looked a bit precarious on a chair as he reached for the higher spots and Kacey looked on in awe, her pride in the smallest of her new husband's abilities very apparent. It was a picture-perfect scene.

'I'm going to ring in,' said Dolly decisively.

After a few minutes Dolly was on hold to the radio station and the excitement in the hallway was palpable. She put her hand over the receiver. 'They're putting me through to the host,' she whispered.

Effie was bouncing on her heels. She gripped Liv's hand. 'We're going to be famous,' she whispered in her ear. Liv smiled at Effie's endless enthusiasm.

Fraser was chewing at a hangnail and Robbie had wandered off. Dolly's eyes suddenly widened. 'Hello, Gordon, this is Dolly Douglas,' she said, her voice a little stilted. 'Aye, we're here at Bonnie Scott's restaurant, part of the Lochy House Hotel, and we have four stranded people with us. We've given them shelter and top-class food from locally renowned chef Fraser Douglas.

'Right now they are drinking Drambuie coffees and decorating a local fir that has been felled in their honour,' said Dolly.

She's laying it on thick, thought Liv.

'Of course you can speak to them. I'll just—'

But Dolly was interrupted by all hell breaking loose in the library. Fraser opened the door and they all watched as Aaron lost his balance, fell forwards and the Christmas tree came crashing down on Shanie, and Jock'O fled.

'Shit,' said Fraser running to help with Effie close behind.

Dolly was frozen with her mouth open. Liv took the phone from her and, grabbing a sheet of paper from the reception desk, she made a crackling sound into the receiver. 'I'm afraid...' crackle crackle '...breaking up. Sorry...' crackle crackle. 'Best time... Bonnie Scott's restaurant.' Crackle. 'Bye.' And Liv hastily ended the call.

'Thank you,' said Dolly looking a little stunned.

'No worries,' said Liv and she went to see if she could help.

Thankfully only Shanie's coffee was spilled but she was complaining about the bits of fir tree in her hair and Liv removed a large spider on the sly. Aaron had landed on his side and was hugging his ribcage, which was likely bruised along with his pride, but Kacey was giving him a lot of fuss so he too seemed okay. Robbie took charge of the situation and ascertained that the size and weight of the tree meant it should have been tethered.

'Thank goodness everyone is all right,' said Dolly, her hand on her chest.

Liv did a scan of the room. 'Where's Jock'O?' she asked. Everyone did the same scan followed by a shrug.

'He was on the rug with me,' said Shanie.

'Och my poor wee boy,' said Dolly, visibly upset.

Effie was quick to comfort her. 'I'm sure he's okay.'

'He's just had a bleeding great tree land on him, so I doubt it,' said Shanie Cortina, still pulling bits from her hair.

'We'll find him,' said Liv.

Fraser and Liv went through the door from the library to the dining room and began checking under tables and behind curtains. 'He can't have gone far because of his arthritis,' said Fraser as he looked in the corner by a large sideboard.

'I think having a tree land on your bonce would make anyone find their running legs,' said Liv.

'I guess.'

They thoroughly checked the kitchen including in boxes, cupboards and drawers but there was no sign of him.

'He could be anywhere,' said Liv, starting to realise that the hotel was actually quite big if you were trying to find a little dog. 'But at least he has to be inside, which is good.' She wasn't sure she could face the icy weather again.

They both went upstairs but with all the bedroom doors firmly closed there were few hiding places, even for a small black dog. Liv pushed on her own door and thanks to the dodgy lock it opened. Fraser followed her inside and she was glad she had done a half-decent job of making the bed. Liv got on her knees and lifted up the bedcovers and peered under the bed. Fraser's face appeared on the other side at the same time. And there was that smile again along with the chamber pot – not exactly a classic romantic moment. Liv hastily put the bedcovers back. 'Where the hell is he?'

'Unless he's recently joined the magic circle he can't have just disappeared. We'd best look downstairs again,' said Fraser opening the door. 'I'm going to check outside.'

'Is there any point? How could he have got out?'

'I don't know but he's not here,' he said walking off.

'Fine,' said Liv feeling she'd have to go with him. A shiver came over her at the mere thought of the temperature outside. They went to get their coats and the one she usually borrowed was on the floor. She went to pick it up but it was considerably heavier than usual. 'I think I've found him. He's in my coat,' said Liv crouching down. There was a large lump in the sleeve making it look like a snake had eaten a watermelon.

'Thank goodness for that,' said Fraser crouching down next to her. 'Hmm,' he said.

'Exactly.' It looked like Jock'O had tried to hide in the coat and in his keenness to feel safe had burrowed down the sleeve. 'Come on, out you come,' she said but received only a whimper in reply.

After a few minutes of trying to coax the dog out, it became clear that he was stuck. 'We'll have to cut him out,' said Liv.

'You could hurt him,' said Fraser.

'No choice. We can't hand him back to Dolly like that. What do we tell her? He's taken up modelling?'

'Fine. But be careful.'

Liv came back with the largest pair of scissors she could find and began carefully cutting through the thick material. It was tough but the fancy kitchen scissors were up to the job. Halfway up the sleeve they found a nose and soon had cut through enough for the little dog to wriggle himself free. He seemed very pleased to be rescued and wanted to shower them in doggy kisses.

Fraser picked him up. 'Thanks, Liv. It was good of you to sacrifice your coat like that,' he said.

'My pleasure. Not my coat,' said Liv wielding the scissors.

'What?' Fraser did a double take. 'That's *my* coat!'

'Whoops,' said Liv with a shrug. 'Still, it died for a good cause.'

Dolly was overjoyed to be reunited with Jock'O, who seemed happy to be back in the safety of Dolly's lap. 'Right, now he's safe we have another issue.'

'What now?' asked Fraser.

'The guests are a bit... well one of them used the word "traumatised" by the toppling Christmas tree episode and Shanie was encouraging Aaron to look into solicitors. She said where there's blame there's a claim.'

'You see. I said no good would come from this.' Fraser

began pacing. 'You try and help people and this is the thanks you get. We should have left them in the snow,' he muttered.

Dolly gave him a hard stare. 'I think we need to do something,' she said. 'But what can we do?'

'We need to find ways to turn this miserable moment into a memorable one for the right reasons,' said Liv.

'Ooh like when I gave them shortbread,' said Effie.

'Exactly. Any ideas?' She was met by blank faces. She decided to reword it. 'What can we do to make things even better for each of the guests?'

'Ooh,' said Effie thrusting her hand in the air.

'You don't need to put your hand up.'

'Sorry,' said Effie. 'Robbie could play the bagpipes for them.' Robbie sat up straight and grinned.

'Nooooooo,' said Liv turning it into a cough when she saw the disappointment on Robbie's face. 'I think that's a um... special occasion thing. And we should save that for when they leave as a proper Scottish send-off,' she said, pleased with her improvisation.

'Maybe see if we can get a television signal,' said Dolly.

'I'll take a look,' said Robbie and he and Dolly left.

'Shanie is desperate to get on the internet because she's bored. What could she do instead?' asked Effie.

'Read a book,' said Liv with a shrug.

'Genius!' said Effie. 'I'll show her the library.'

'She's seen the library, Effie. And I'm not being mean but the books you have in there are not exactly TikTok's finest. I've a steamy romcom in my room; I'll see if she fancies reading it.'

'Great idea. What about Aaron and Kacey? What can we get them?' asked Effie.

'They're *in* a steamy romcom so maybe an annual subscription to Lovehoney?' said Liv with a grin.

'I don't know if they even like honey but if you think—'

'It was a joke. Lovehoney is a... well, it's a website for um... This is like explaining the birds and the bees to Winnie the Pooh.'

'Pooh knew all about honey. You'd not need to explain it to him,' said Effie.

'You're absolutely right. Let's give Aaron and Kacey the gift of private time.'

'Good idea because they're probably having lots of sex,' said Effie.

Liv laughed. 'Got it in one.' Effie was clearly more worldly-wise than Liv had given her credit for. 'Anything else we could do?'

'Point out that they're not freezing to death in their car,' suggested Fraser.

'Nope. Try again,' said Liv.

'A hot bath with candles always cheers me up,' said Effie.

'Great idea,' said Liv. 'Let's run a bath and offer it to Shanie. And if we've got something fancy to put in the bath and some candles around the edge that would be great.'

'On it,' said Effie.

'I've a suggestion of something special we could do for Aaron and Kacey but, Fraser, I'm going to need your help,' said Liv.

'I'm all yours,' he said and they both smiled and then looked quickly away.

20

Robbie returned from fixing the aerial and he and Effie righted and tethered the Christmas tree. They tried the television but the reduced number of channels did not impress the guests. Shortly afterwards Dolly was telling Aaron elaborate stories of long-fought battles while Kacey put baubles on the tree, but only as high as she could reach, and Effie swept up the last of the mess that was created when the tree had fallen over.

Effie hoped Liv's plan was going to work. Effie had sorted out the bath for Shanie. There was little else to do when you were stranded for the day and had no internet connection, although she did seem to be enjoying Liv's book. Effie wasn't a reader. She didn't feel she needed to be. She had enough stories going on in her head. There were all the very many tales that her granny had shared with her plus all of those she'd been told by others in the village. On top of that she also liked to make up stories. She might see someone waiting at the bus stop and that would make her wonder who they were and where they were going and why. Her brain would then fill in the blanks and a little story would play out in her mind. So she was never bored.

Effie went to sit in her favourite spot to admire the Christmas tree. Despite being a little crushed and losing most of its baubles it was still impressive. The smell was amazing and she loved trees so what could be better? Apart from the decorations there was something else missing. She studied the tree. Presents! She had an idea. A few minutes later Effie was settled by the fire with a pile of wrapping paper, bows, ribbon and sticky tape.

Robbie stood and watched Effie for a moment, his brow furrowed. 'What's the matter?' she asked.

'Why do you have all these boxes of cereal, cushions and packs of toilet rolls?'

'I'm wrapping them up,' she said trying to reach the tape while she held the Christmas paper in place around one of the sofa cushions.

'For who?'

'Christmas,' she said pulling off far more tape than she needed and watching it curl around her fingers and stick itself together.

Robbie took the tape from her and without asking cut her a good length and held the paper in place while she secured it. 'When you say Christmas... Do you mean Father Christmas or someone else?' he asked.

'Not Father Christmas silly. We leave a mince pie and a whisky out for him. No, these are pretend presents for under the tree. To make it look more Christmassy.'

'I see.' Robbie looked relieved. He scanned the tree. 'Back

in a mo,' he said and he disappeared, leaving Effie to her next parcel.

'Right,' said Robbie coming back into the room a couple of minutes later carrying a small stepladder. 'Shall we finish decorating the tree?' he asked.

'Ooh yeah,' said Effie.

'These people who aren't health and safety aware are a danger to themselves,' he whispered and she nodded her agreement. She liked that Robbie was trusting her to do it properly.

Effie passed him the baubles and directed him to where to put them, and very soon it was transformed from average woodland fir to stunning Christmas tree. Robbie came down the ladder and flicked the switch on the lights.

'Aww that makes me feel so Christmassy,' she said.

'I liked it better when we did it,' said Kacey looking at her husband. There was no pleasing some folk.

★

Liv was trying to persuade Fraser to do something when they came face to face with Shanie who stopped and appraised them both. 'This is why you're not interested.' She wiggled a finger in front of Liv but she was staring at Fraser. What was Liv missing?

'Er, no,' said Fraser. 'We're... um just discussing something.' He sounded cagey.

'Yeah, right. Likely story,' said Shanie. 'I was told there was a surprise for me in the bathroom. I was hoping it was going to be you.' Fraser looked quite embarrassed. 'Oh well, can't blame a girl for dreaming.' And off she went upstairs.

'What's that all about?' asked Liv.

'Nothing. Why do you want to look in the tower?' asked Fraser.

'Can I just look and then I'll tell you?' Liv didn't want to declare her ideas too soon because if the tower wasn't what she hoped then her idea wouldn't work and it would be another opportunity for Fraser to deride her.

'Maybe later because I—'

'Sorry can we do it now? Please. It's to do with turning our guests' miserable moments into memorable ones.' She looked hopefully at him.

'Those people cause their own miserable moments. They like being like that. You won't get them to suddenly be happy.'

'But I can try. Only I need to see in the tower so...'

Fraser gave her an indulgent smile. 'And then you'll leave me in peace?'

'I'll try. Promise.' Liv offered her hand for him to shake.

'Fine. Come on.' He grabbed a rusting set of keys from a hook behind reception and went up the stairs two at a time so Liv had to run to keep up with him. At the end of a long corridor he unlocked a door that was exactly like the panelling around it, so almost hidden. He pushed the door open and it creaked in protest as it revealed a dusty spiral staircase. 'There you go,' he said standing back.

'You not coming up?' asked Liv leaning forward and peering into the darkness.

'No.'

Liv shrugged and went through the door, but she had a thought so she reversed back. 'Is there a reason you're not coming up?' He pushed out his bottom lip and shook his head. 'Spiders? Ghosts? Oh it's not flaming Janet again is it?' she asked.

'No, I just don't like it up there, that's all. Are you going up or what? Because I've things to be getting on with.'

'Fine.' Liv pulled back her shoulders more times than was necessary as she readied herself for whatever was up there. Tentatively she took to the stairs. A few steps up she realised Fraser was watching her closely. 'You sure it's not haunted?'

'No idea.'

'Great, that's helpful.'

'There's a light switch on the right when you get to the top.'

'Thank you,' she said as she followed the stairs round until she came to an archway. She felt around for the switch and flicked it on. The light blinked a couple of times before coming fully on and revealing a small circular room sprinkled with cobwebs and dust. There were a couple of boxes and an old easel but otherwise it was empty. Liv went to the window and rubbed at the grimy pane to reveal a stunning view over the loch. 'You should come up; it's really—' She spun around to find Fraser was standing right behind her. 'Argh! Shit! Don't creep up on people like that.' Her heart was hammering in her chest.

'I didn't creep anywhere. I can't with size-twelve feet.' They both looked at his boots.

'You gave me a fright.'

'Have you seen enough?' He turned to go.

'I have. Here, take this.' She passed him one of the boxes. 'I've a job for you while I get this place spick and span.'

Fraser took the box and mumbled as he went back downstairs. 'Because what I need is more stuff to do,' he muttered to himself. But Liv didn't care; her idea was coming together.

An hour later Liv was fit to burst with excitement. With some help from Effie they had cleaned the little tower room until it sparkled and smelled of cleaning products. The windows were once again transparent and the wooden floor dust-free. There was now a small table with two chairs in the tiny space and a candle flickered. 'It needs something else,' said Liv. 'I know, music!' She dashed downstairs and without thinking ran out into the yard. The bite of the wind took her breath away but she wasn't going back. She crossed her arms to hug her body and she dashed across the yard to Ginger's stable where the cow was having a snooze. 'Don't mind me,' she said fumbling with the lock. Ginger gave her a wide-eyed look as she came into the stable. 'I'm just borrowing this,' said Liv grabbing the radio and exiting. 'Thanks!' she called as she locked the stable door. She got back inside the hotel as quickly as she could.

'How's that?' asked Fraser as she went through the kitchen. Liv turned to see a three-tier cake stand filled with delicate finger sandwiches, scones and cakes.

'Blimey, that's amazing,' she said. She'd asked him if he could rustle something up for an afternoon tea but she'd not been expecting the full works. 'It's absolutely perfect. Thank you.'

Fraser went a bit coy. 'It's nothing. And it was your good idea. Any fool can make a sandwich.'

'True,' she said and his head shot up. She pointed at him.

'Gotcha. You're very good at what you do. A real talent.' *Credit where it was due and all that*, she thought.

'Thanks. It's what I love to do so that makes it easy.'

'I love chocolate but there aren't many jobs in that. I know because I've looked,' said Liv.

'I did a course in chocolate making once. It's quite tricky but if you're interested I could maybe—'

'Quick!' yelled Effie. 'They're coming!'

Liv darted off to the tower room and put the radio out of the way as it wasn't the prettiest object, but the lilting classical music was just right to finish the scene. She stood back when Aaron and Kacey arrived at the top of the winding staircase, looking a little bewildered.

'Aww this is adorable,' said Kacey taking in the space.

'Wow, look at that view,' said Aaron.

'Take a seat,' said Liv. 'Tea will be served shortly.'

Fraser and Effie arrived with the cake stand and teapot and the three of them had to do an uncoordinated manoeuvre to let Liv out and get themselves in without overcrowding the couple. 'Enjoy,' said Effie and they all left.

'It's a nice thing to do but I'm not sure I see the point,' muttered Fraser. But he was interrupted by giggles from above them.

'Aww,' said Effie. 'Now they're having a lovely honeymoon.'

Liv smiled at him. 'See, happy customers.'

'I guess I'll have to concede that one.' He continued downstairs and Liv felt like she'd received the best praise ever. Was Fraser Douglas starting to mellow?

Robbie met them at the bottom of the stairs. 'What's happening?'

'We've created a magic moment for the honeymoon couple,' said Effie. 'They're having afternoon tea like a princess in the tower.'

'Aren't princesses usually imprisoned in towers?' asked Robbie.

'Not this one,' said Liv.

'Ooh,' said Robbie. 'Shall I serenade them with my bagpipes?'

'No,' the others all chorused.

Effie and Robbie went off and Liv cornered Fraser at the bottom of the spiral staircase. 'Could we make some fudge to put on pillows instead of a chocolate,' she asked. It seemed a good opportunity if she was finally in favour.

'Fudge? No way,' he snapped. 'In Scotland we make Scottish tablet.' The words making his accent seem even stronger.

'Tablet – that sounds so much nicer.' She tilted her head at him.

'Well it *is* nicer. I guess the name could be better but that's not my doing.'

'So can we make Scotch tablet then?' asked Liv.

'Scottish,' corrected Fraser. 'I suppose so. I'll need to check—' He stopped talking because they were both distracted by the sounds coming from above. Aaron and Kacey were kissing. Fraser pulled a face. Liv shrugged her shoulders and grinned. She was pleased that Aaron and Kacey were doing what they should be on honeymoon. She and Fraser smiled at each other as they listened. Then the noises changed. Fraser frowned. Liv listened. The sound of groans of pleasure had Fraser and Liv almost barging each other out of the way in their haste to get away. They shot through the doorway and Liv quietly shut the door to both their relief. Fraser started to laugh. 'I think they're enjoying that too much.'

'No such thing,' said Liv as they went off to the kitchen.

Fraser jumped up to sit on the worktop. 'I thought we weren't allowed to do that,' said Liv putting her hands on her hips.

'You're not allowed. It's my kitchen so I can do what I like.'

'Not fair.'

'Did you want to learn how to make Scottish tablet or not?'

'Learn? I was hoping you'd be making it. You're the chef.'

'But I know how to make it. And I'll need to get on with dinner. Your call.'

'Fine. What do I need?' Liv grabbed an apron and tried not to look petulant as she put it on.

'Granulated sugar, whole milk, a tin of condensed milk and butter.'

'Right.' Liv turned in a couple of circles while she worked out where to go first.

'And scales, a bowl, spoon, saucepan and a deep baking tray.'

'Shall I put the oven on?'

Fraser laughed. 'No, you don't bake it.'

'If you're going to laugh at me.' Liv fixed him with a hard stare. It was impossible not to take in his striking features: those eyes, strong jawline and sturdy physique.

He held up his palms as if surrendering. 'Sorry. No offence meant. Ready?'

'Obviously not,' said Liv and she began amassing all the things he'd listed. She soon had everything laid out and she felt a bit like one of those TV chefs who has all the ingredients set out for them, although her pile looked a lot less orderly.

He explained what to do at each step and she melted the butter, sugar and milk together before adding the condensed milk and watched it vigilantly while it boiled. She feared it was going to come over the top of the pan at one stage but Fraser's calming tones meant she held her nerve.

Before she knew it, it was in a tray cooling and she was helping Fraser with that evening's far less demanding meal of asparagus and mint risotto, although Fraser was making a big thing about how adding the stock slowly was key to the end result. She was in charge of making a blackberry version of Eton mess, which was thankfully straightforward. And Effie was making a warm winter vegetable salad for the starter under Fraser's guidance.

They served the starters but Dolly called them back. 'Look at this,' she whispered and she pushed the door into the dining room open a fraction. The guests were all chatting and they sounded jolly. The group of listeners all sighed in unison.

While the guests were eating their desserts, Fraser cut the tablet into cubes and Liv wrapped a few in greaseproof paper and tied them with some raffia they'd found in one of the boxes in the tower. The little parcels were rustic but cute. Liv and Effie delivered the packages to pillows while the guests chatted amiably over coffees and whisky in the library, and Liv felt like it was a job well done. The television was working again but there was nothing on worth watching. Instead Dolly and Effie told some tales by the fireside as everyone listened intently and Liv tried hard not to nod off. Kacey did some terribly fake yawns and stretches before announcing she was worn out and virtually dragged Aaron from the room, but it was the cue everyone needed to turn in for the night.

Liv was tired as she flicked on the bedroom light. There on her pillow was another little package of tablet and it made her smile to see it. She assumed Effie had left it there but when she picked it up she could see there was writing on the paper which read – *It's definitely nicer than fudge!* It didn't take a genius to work out who had done that. Liv pulled her curtains closed for the last time. Tomorrow, all being well, she could leave. But not until she'd told Fraser Douglas what she thought of him. The question was after three days in his company what did she think? That was something she would have to sleep on.

She opened the small, wrapped package of Scottish tablet, popped a piece in her mouth and savoured the crumbly sweetness. 'Not bad, Fraser. Not bad.'

21

Liv was dreaming of being fed Scottish tablet by Fraser who was wearing a kilt and nothing else. She was abruptly pulled from her dream by something. She opened a blurry eye to see a shadowy figure all in black standing at her bedside.

'Shitting hell!' she said trying to reverse away, which was harder than you'd think. She was thoroughly wrapped in the quilt like a giant maggot and therefore not the most agile of things. By the time she'd squirmed as far as the other side of the bed she was worn out, but she was also far enough away to see that it wasn't Janet the witch come for her soul; it was in fact Effie. 'What are you doing?' asked Liv, wriggling her top half out of the duvet and trying to calm herself down because her heart was still in fight-or-flight mode – the latter not having worked well at all.

'Waiting for you to wake up,' said Effie, her tone very matter-of-fact.

'Mission accomplished.' Liv patted the bed for Effie to sit down. 'What's up?'

'I've had a message from John. He's in danger.'

'What's happened?'

'The refugee camp where he's working was raided by gorillas.'

'The hairy sort or the soldiers?' asked Liv with a smile, trying desperately to lighten the mood.

'I'm not sure,' said Effie, frowning hard. 'But he escaped in a truck.'

'That's a relief. Is he okay?'

'I think so. But it's frightened me,' said Effie, her lip wobbling.

'Of course it has. Come here.' Liv opened her arms and Effie inelegantly crawled towards her. 'It's okay. I'll get up and give you a hug, otherwise it's weird.' Liv untangled herself from the duvet and dashed across the cold floor and around the bed to embrace Effie. 'He'll be fine. He must know what he's doing. Hopefully he'll be home soon. If not you're flying out there to meet him, aren't you?'

Effie pulled away and wiped away a tear. 'I'm scared.'

'Of course you are. It's horrible to think of people you care about in danger.'

Effie shook her head. 'I'm scared of going out there.'

'Then don't go. It is a long way. I'm sure he'll understand,' said Liv.

Effie bit her lip. 'I'm scared of going anywhere. Not just Burkina Faso.'

'Why's that?'

'My dad was killed in a car crash three years ago, and

I've only been as far as the dentist's since then. I just can't…'
She looked agitated just at the thought of it.

Liv held her hand. 'I'm so sorry, Effie; that must have
been so hard for you.'

'I'm lucky really. I've got Granny here and Fraser came
back from Barcelona.' A few things started to make more
sense to Liv. 'But I'm worried I won't ever be able to
leave here.'

'Maybe starting off with short trips is the answer. You've
been to the dentist so that's a start. Perhaps you need to
plan small outings and each time go a little further. I'm
sure there are lots of people who would come with you and
support you.'

'I guess.' Effie didn't look sure. 'Would you come with
me?'

'Um, well,' began Liv as Effie fixed her with big puppy-
dog eyes. 'Has the snow thawed?' asked Liv.

'Ooh let's see,' said Effie, thankfully easily distracted.
She dashed to the window and Liv followed her. Oddly
her tummy felt tight. She was apprehensive, unsure what
she wanted Effie to find. Effie pulled back the curtains
and they both looked out. The hills were breathtaking, the
morning sun highlighting the dips and curves of the land
and scattering a sparkle on the loch. There was still a lot
of snow, but there were patches of colour where it was
melting. 'Aww, the snow's thawing,' said Effie sadly. 'Maybe
there'll be more later. Shall we get breakfast?'

'Err, yeah okay.' Liv wasn't sure how she felt as she got
dressed and made her way downstairs. Was this her last
meal at Lochy House Hotel? she wondered as she was

overtaken by Jock'O with a sock in his mouth. Belatedly she realised it was one of hers. 'Hey!' she called. The dog ignored her but Robbie turned in her direction.

Robbie was pacing the hall as he spoke to someone on a walkie-talkie. 'My civilians need to be a priority,' he said giving Liv a firm nod. She responded with a weak smile.

She was going home. That was a good thing, she told herself. She'd missed her mum and sister and their usual madcap pre-Christmas festivities such as wrapping, shopping for the stuff you only bought at Christmas like shelled nuts, brandy butter and the extra strong indigestion tablets.

It also meant that the moment she could rant at Fraser, and lay the ghosting debacle to rest, was fast approaching. It had seemed like a good idea when she was driven by anger and hurt and had a fire in her belly. Now she was full of Fraser's good food and her own couldn't be arsedness it was a lot less appealing. There was also the niggle in the back of her mind that none of it really added up. But she couldn't really go home without saying something, otherwise what was the point of the whole trip? And what would she say to her mum and sister? She could hardly confess that she'd been won over by a lump of hard fudge so had let him off.

There was an amazing smell wafting from the kitchen. On the stove was a big pan that smelled delicious. 'Is this mulled wine?' she asked.

'Yep,' came the clipped response from Fraser.

'Mulled wine for breakfast. I'm starting to like Scotland,' she said. It struck her that she really did like it, despite everything, and soon she would be leaving.

'It's not for breakfast.' He gave her a frustrated look. 'Dolly wants us to help these freeloaders enjoy their stay so I thought...' He went back to what he was doing.

'Good idea,' said Liv.

She helped with breakfast and joined the others in the dining room where excited chatter filled the air. Aaron and Kacey were eating their breakfasts with one hand so that they could hold hands under the table; Shanie was discussing books with Dolly and getting recommendations of her favourites. Robbie strode in. 'If I could have everyone's attention please.' The chatter stopped abruptly and everybody turned to look at Robbie who seemed to swell with the authority he now held. 'I am pleased to inform you that the snowplough has been through from Fort Augustus to Fort William.' It meant nothing to Liv but the others seemed pleased. 'There's a tractor on its way to recover your vehicle.' He pointed at Aaron. 'And you are on the list of emergencies with the local garage,' he said pointing at Liv.

'Oh I'm not an emergency,' she said and surprised herself that she felt that way. It was a surprise to her that she wasn't already skipping up the driveway but she wasn't.

'That's good,' he said with a wince, 'because there are quite a few ahead of you on the list.'

'No problem,' said Liv. 'Thanks.' It looked as if her departure wasn't imminent and she was relieved. At least it would give her time to get her final speech straight in her head.

'You're welcome,' said Robbie. 'I'll let you know when the tractor arrives,' he said to Aaron.

'Is there a charge for that?' asked Aaron.

'It's local goodwill,' said Robbie. 'But perhaps a charitable donation to a local cause might be a nice gesture.'

'I did you a morning roll,' said Effie, presenting Robbie with a brown paper bag. 'I know you've been up a few hours so I thought…' She shrugged as she handed it over.

Robbie looked like he'd been presented with a prestigious trophy. 'Goodness. I don't know what to say. He clipped his walkie-talkie onto his uniform, took the bag and peeped inside. 'It smells divine.'

'It's nothing really,' said Effie going coy.

'It's very much appreciated, Effie. Thank you,' said Robbie with that air of earnestness that he managed to convey without sounding patronising.

'It's important to support the emergency services,' she said matching his tone.

'Actually, Effie, I was wondering if you'd like to—'

'We've had a great idea,' said Kacey, waving her hands about. 'Aaron, my husband,' she said and Shanie rolled her eyes, 'thought we could pay like that TV programme where you pay what you think the stay has been worth. What do we all think?' She bit her lip as she scanned the other faces excitedly.

'Great idea,' said Liv.

'Fine,' said Shanie. 'As long as I can pay by card. I don't carry cash.'

'That's if it's okay with you,' said Kacey to Fraser.

'Seems fair,' said Fraser.

'I'd best fire up the card payment machine,' said Dolly wheeling herself and Jock'O out of the room.

*   *   *

The guests all lined up at the reception desk. Aaron and Kacey were instantly distracted by the mistletoe hanging above them. Liv stepped back. 'I guess I should wait until the car's fixed before I pay and check out, shouldn't I?' she asked Fraser.

'From what Robbie says, you could be here for another night at least.' This didn't fill her with dread as it would have done a couple of days ago; in fact she felt quite the opposite.

'It's not a problem,' she said trying to sound nonchalant. 'As long as it's okay with you, of course.' She watched him for a response.

'Makes no odds to me. Just one more for dinner.' Was he playing it cool or did he really not care?

Aaron and Kacey were so focused on snogging under the mistletoe that Dolly had to keep tutting to get their attention long enough to complete the transaction.

Shanie tapped in her PIN. 'I've had an unexpectedly good stay. Thank you all.'

'It's been a pleasure,' said Dolly, and Jock'O barked his agreement.

'I'll put our luggage in the car,' said Aaron.

'Miss you already,' said Kacey.

'Miss you too,' replied Aaron.

Dolly tutted and shook her head.

'Someone's here!' called out Kacey from the entrance and everyone went to see except for Liv, because Fraser took hold of her arm and held her back. The touch of his hand on her skin gave her goosebumps.

'I think I know why I was a wee bit off with you before,' he said looking sheepish.

'A wee bit? A great clonking… yeah well, I think I know why but let's hear your version.'

'I've been hurt. And I mean real heart crushing, stomp all over ma feelings level of hurt.'

'Not by me,' pointed out Liv.

'I know. But there's something about you. I don't know what it is but…' Fraser looked deep into her eyes as she waited for him to finish the sentence. A shudder went through her and it was nothing to do with the weather. 'Do you not feel it?' he asked.

She took a moment. Did she feel anything? Confusion mainly. She had come to roast the guy who ghosted her but she couldn't deny that the Fraser she'd met here did have a certain attraction. He was gorgeous and kind so despite everything she knew about him she was still attracted to him, which was very inconvenient. However she felt, Liv was not going to show her hand. 'I do feel something,' she said and his features lifted. 'But I figured it was because of the bang on the head.'

'Can you not be serious for a second. I'm trying to be honest here.'

He seemed unsure as he slowly looked up. Liv followed his gaze to the mistletoe hanging above them. 'Ah the famous evil spirit and witch repellent. Are you checking to see if I shrivel into a ball?' she asked.

'It's also known for its romantic properties. I thought I might see if it worked.'

'Ah the male clause of I can kiss whoever I like as long as it's under a poisonous plant in December. So romantic,' she said.

'I think so.' Fraser had a glint in his eye. 'But only if they want to be kissed.' It went against everything she knew about the man who had ghosted her, but at that moment she really did want to kiss him. He leaned forward until their lips were so close she could feel the warmth of his breath on hers.

22

Their fleetingly brief kiss was rudely interrupted by Robbie shouting up the hallway. 'Fraser, you need to see this. Now!'

Fraser pulled back from Liv and she instantly missed him. Her lips tingled from the contact. Something was zinging around her bloodstream and this time it wasn't too much sugar from the Scottish tablet.

'Sorry, it sounds urgent. Don't go anywhere,' said Fraser, letting her go and striding off towards the entrance.

What the hell just happened? She felt like she had an angel and a devil on each shoulder who were both perplexed by her actions. This was the guy she hated, right? Then why had that kiss felt so right? This was a big pile of twisted wreckage that was going to short-circuit her brain if she tried to work it out. After a moment she pulled herself together and belatedly followed him.

Liv pulled her clothes tight to her as she went to join the others outside. Liv grabbed a blanket and slung it around her shoulders before following them. She found them all watching someone holding a for sale sign as Fraser stood nearby looking cross. 'What's going on?' she asked.

'That's what we all want to know,' said Dolly scooting her wheelchair next to Fraser and almost spilling a precariously held mug of tea. 'You need to do something,' she told him.

'Like what?' Fraser threw up his arms.

'Is this a mistake?' asked Liv. 'Are you not putting the hotel on the market?'

'It's not mine to sell,' replied Fraser, his jaw tight.

Liv looked about her at the others. 'I thought he owned it,' she said.

'His dad is the owner,' said Robbie. His walkie-talkie crackled into life with something inaudible. 'Tractor ETA five minutes. I suggest we head off,' he said already shooing Aaron away.

Kacey welled up with tears. 'Aww, I'm going to miss you guys so much. We were like a little wartime family all thrown together.'

'Minus the bombs and rationing,' said Liv, giving her a hug and getting her breath squeezed from her lungs in response.

'We must keep in touch,' said Kacey wiping away a tear.

'Uh-huh.' Liv nodded but felt it was very unlikely.

Kacey followed Robbie and the others out of the driveway waving all the way. When Liv's arm started to ache she turned to go back inside. The blanket was next to useless at keeping her warm.

'You going in?' asked Effie.

'Yeah, I'm frozen and I don't think that poor estate agent needs everyone to watch him while he bangs in a sign.'

'Thanks,' said the estate agent seeming a little awkward. 'But I'm here to value the property. I can't officially put the sign up until the paperwork is completed. Unless you're happy for me to–'

'No, we are not!' said Dolly. 'And you'll not be valuing anything without an appointment.'

'It'll only take a few minutes.'

'Did you not hear what she said? You'll not be valuing anything today,' said Fraser.

'Right. I'll be in touch but I'll leave the sign if that's okay.' The estate agent leant it against the portico. 'It was quite a struggle getting it in the car.' He grinned but nobody replied. He gave a brief nod and almost ran back to his car that was parked nearby.

Fraser stepped forward, grabbed the sign and attempted to snap it in two. Liv paused, expecting to see something impressive but unfortunately the sign was sturdy. Fraser made a sort of growling noise as he wrestled with the post, his muscles bulging under his top. Everyone watched in silence. Eventually he let go, looking red in the face. After a bit more of a tussle he finally slammed it down on the ground. He turned around to look at the reaction of the estate agent but he was long gone. It was a bit of an anti-climax.

Fraser cracked his neck, pulled back his shoulders and strode inside. Nobody said a thing as they all filed after him. They walked back into the hotel in silence. Liv wondered what was going on, but it wasn't really her place to say anything. She supposed this meant they wouldn't be resuming their kiss anytime soon and she was a little disappointed about that. Liv held the door for Dolly who was behind the others as she had to come the long way around via the ramp.

'What was that all about?' asked Liv.

'Families,' said Dolly with a tut. 'Nothing for you to worry about.' She patted her arm as she passed.

Liv didn't need to worry; it was nothing to do with her. *Fraser* was nothing to do with her, but she was intrigued all the same. She went down the hallway towards the kitchen and was intercepted by Effie. As she came out of the kitchen there was the sound of someone banging pots and pans behind her. She shook her head firmly. 'I'd stay out of his way for a bit. He's crosser than a cat in a thunderstorm,' said Effie as there was an almighty clang from the kitchen making them both jump. They crept away. Perhaps now wasn't the best time to ask Fraser what was going on.

Robbie came back and announced that Aaron's hire car had been successfully pulled out of the ditch and the occupants had departed. He had no update on when Liv's car would be looked at, but Liv wasn't in a rush to go anywhere. She wanted to know what that kiss meant almost as much as she wanted to know why Fraser had ghosted her. Liv busied herself with tidying up the turret. She realised poor Ginger had been without her radio all night so she felt that she should return it to her. With no coat on she made the trip as quickly as possible. 'Hi, Ginger. Bye, Ginger,' she said putting the radio back where she'd found it and exiting the stable, pulling the door to behind her and hotfooting it back across the yard into the warmth of the hotel.

*   *   *

'Fraser!' came a panicked shout from Dolly, which got Liv's attention, so she left tidying the tower and headed to the top of the stairs to see what was up.

'Coming!' called back Fraser as they all headed in Dolly's direction.

Dolly was in the hallway below and her shouts had also alerted Robbie. 'What's wrong?' he asked as Fraser, Effie and Liv all came barrelling into the hallway.

'Ginger has escaped,' said Dolly.

'Not again,' said Effie.

'How?' said Fraser. 'I checked that stable door was bolted after I fed her first thing. Someone must have let her out.'

'Do you suspect foul play?' asked Robbie looking eager and a little fired up as he pulled his notebook from his pocket.

'Lizzie wouldn't do something like that, would she?' asked Dolly.

'I wouldn't put it past her,' said Effie. 'She's not nice.'

Liv had a little flashback to her being keen to get back in the warm as she'd gone out without a coat on and of shutting the stable door. Or did she just pull it closed? She couldn't be sure. Liv cleared her throat and all eyes swivelled in her direction. 'I think it might have been me, sorry,' she said in a small voice. Robbie put away his notebook. 'You see the little tower room needed some music and I thought of Ginger's radio, so I borrowed it, and this morning I returned it...' The faces were not looking sympathetic. 'I'll find her. Don't worry. I'll get her back,' said Liv sounding surer than she felt.

'You can't go out alone. You don't know the terrain or the area,' said Robbie.

'He's right,' said Effie.

'Fine, I'll go with her,' said Fraser stomping off up the hallway and Liv sheepishly followed.

They walked into the utility together. 'I am really sorry. I know I pulled the stable door shut. But I guess that wasn't enough.'

'You think?' He was cross again. Gone was the gentle man who had kissed her under the mistletoe.

'I'm not going to beg for your forgiveness,' she said looking for the coat she'd used the previous day and realising it had been shredded thanks to Jock'O. 'But I need a coat if I'm going to help you look for her.'

'Bloody hell. Here, wear Effie's,' he said taking it off the hook.

'Thanks. I don't know what's going on with the estate agent and everything, but it's not my fault.'

They didn't speak as they donned their wellies and once again headed out into the wintry weather. Fraser sniffed the air. 'It's starting to thaw.'

'Only a little bit.' Liv looked around at the white landscape.

'Yep, with any luck you'll be out of here by this afternoon.'

'Good,' she said with feeling, and Fraser twitched as he did a double take. She stomped off across the yard.

'What are you doing?' he called after her.

'Checking she's not in the stable.' Liv was ever hopeful that the daft cow had come back of her own accord.

'She weighs about four hundred kilos – she'll not be hiding in the hay.'

'I know that!' Liv was getting ratty and as she approached where the stable door was swinging wide open it was obvious the heifer wasn't in there. But still, to make a point, she went into the stable, gave a theatrical performance of looking around before coming back outside to where Fraser was watching her with a smirk on his lips. 'Right, best we find her then,' said Liv. She marched past Fraser and mumbled under her breath. 'Perhaps we can hunt down your sense of humour while we're at it.'

'And your sense of responsibility. I mean who leaves a stable door open?'

Whoops, he'd clearly heard her but now she was properly riled. 'Responsibility? I could teach you about responsibility!'

Fraser laughed. 'You have no idea.'

'Try me.' She beckoned him on with her hands.

'I've been looking after Granny and Effie for the past three years since...' His jaw was tense like he'd clamped his teeth together. He swallowed. 'No matter.' He walked around the side of the hotel and Liv went after him.

'I know about your uncle being killed. And I'm sorry. But that doesn't give you an excuse to be an arsehole.' That probably wasn't the best way to show her sympathy for his loss.

'You are completely and utterly unbelievable.' He shook his head and stormed off.

'Me? You're the one who...' But she couldn't see him

anymore, which was particularly frustrating when she was finding her stride. He'd disappeared through the steam billowing out from the boiler vent on the wall. There was no snow here either thanks to the warm air. 'Fraser?' She stood and waited for a moment, seething gently.

He strode towards her through the steam like a hero in a film, and she had to check herself so that she didn't swoon. This was the bastard who had ghosted her. But he was also the person who twenty minutes ago tenderly kissed her but now he was back to being a grumpy arse. Perhaps it was a bit like Stockholm syndrome when people who were kidnapped fell in love with their kidnappers. She was being forced to share space with him so that was kind of the same. It was hard to deny that she definitely felt a flutter of something at the sight of him, although it was confusing because she also wanted to deck him. There were a lot of emotions fighting for attention and the dry ice effect of the steam wasn't helping.

'What?' said Fraser throwing up his arms.

'You're an arse,' she said.

He seemed taken aback. 'I've done nothing but help you.'

'I know. You keep reminding me of that.'

'You're infuriating!' he said getting quite close.

'Hi!' called Shanie, interrupting them as she tottered across the yard in very high heels. 'There's a car on its way for me, ETA thirty minutes, so I just wanted to ask—'

Shanie didn't get to finish her sentence because they were all alerted to the sound of fast approaching hooves on stone as Ginger came thundering across the yard towards them. Instinctively Liv went to grab Shanie and pull her out of danger. The only trouble was Fraser had had the same thought and he made a lunge for Liv. The force of them both pulling and the muddy ground underfoot sent them all flying backwards. Fraser hit the sludge with a squelch. Liv landed half on him and half in the mud with Shanie on top of her.

'Argh!' screamed Shanie as Ginger hurtled towards them and they tried to scramble out of the way.

Ginger came to an abrupt halt. Snorted at the sight of the three of them writhing about in the mud and trotted off to her stable.

23

They looked like an upturned caterpillar with all the many legs that were waving about. 'Do you think you could get off me?' asked Fraser testily.

'Do you not think I'm trying?' snapped back Liv, writhing about and a little conscious that she was probably grinding her shoulder blade into his groin.

'I'm all muddy,' moaned Shanie with a wobble in her voice. 'And my car is on its way. I can't look like this. What did you do to me?'

'Silly cow,' said Liv with feeling.

'Excuse me?' Shanie was disgruntled and dug an elbow in Liv's middle as she tried to get up.

'Ow! I was saying Ginger is the silly cow that caused this. Nobody else.'

'But still. It's your fault that I'm all messy. You pulled me over. I've got an important interview and I've no time to change. This is a disaster.' Shanie's voice was rising rapidly.

'Don't panic. Can you at least get up?' Liv asked Shanie.

Shanie nodded and with a bit of effort and more mud on her hands she scrambled to her feet. She stood there looking sad with her hands bobbing in front of her. 'I'm so muddy.'

'That can all be sorted out. If I can just…' Very inelegantly Liv stuffed her hand into the mud and pushed herself up and off Fraser, although on her first attempt she flopped back down and landed in his lap with a thud.

'Oomph,' was all that came from Fraser.

'Whoops, sorry,' said Liv having another go. Each time getting more and more muddy.

'I'm so cold,' complained Shanie.

'We all are,' grumbled Fraser clambering to his feet.

'What am I going to do?' asked Shanie, pointing at her ruined clothes.

'We'll have you Insta-ready in no time,' said Liv as Fraser squelched past them to go and bolt in Ginger who was watching them with curious eyes.

'Ooh Instagram,' said Shanie brightening up immensely. 'Once I finally get some coverage this could be an amazing before and after. Even a viral tap to tidy,' she added excitedly.

'I don't know what that means but I bet we can get you showered and changed in a flash.'

'Hang on,' said Shanie. A very muddy Fraser went to walk by and she grabbed him by the arm. 'Just a couple of selfies of my rescuer.' Shanie linked a muddy arm through his and he scowled at the phone camera now pointed in his direction. 'I am *so* digging the moody look. That is sexy,' she said as she let go of Fraser and began tapping on her phone.

'Come on,' said Liv, guiding Shanie back inside. It seemed it didn't take much for people to revert to type.

Liv had washed her hands, put Effie on notice to stall Shanie's driver before sorting out a shower for Shanie and within record time she was clean, dressed and Liv had blow dried her hair to the best of her ability. Shanie was now hastily reapplying her perfect make-up.

'Car's here!' bellowed Effie from downstairs.

'I'll be two minutes,' called back Shanie.

'Right, well I need to dive in the shower too,' said Liv indicating her now crusty state as the mud was starting to dry.

'Uh-huh,' said Shanie distracted as she reapplied her lipstick.

Liv turned to go and then she changed her mind. 'Look I know you're going back to your world but do you think you could take a minute to rate the restaurant online and remember what a good time you had? I mean before you fell in the mud.'

Shanie turned and looked Liv up and down. 'Okay and thanks for helping me. Sorry if I was a bit of a diva.'

'A bit?' said Liv with an arched brow. 'You're the full Celine Dion!'

'I love that for me,' said Shanie. 'You are a sweetheart.' She went as if to hug Liv and then thought better of it. 'Don't worry about Fraser and the restaurant; I'll make sure he gets the best sort of exposure.'

There was the sound of an impatient car horn outside and Shanie grabbed her bag and dashed past Liv.

Liv didn't know exactly what Shanie meant but she hoped it would get Fraser a few more customers when he opened. Whatever he had done she had to admit that he had looked after her since she'd turned up and that kiss... She shook her head as if trying to disperse the memory. It felt like she'd dreamt it. The window of Fraser being anything other than annoying and grumpy had been brief.

Liv trudged back to her room, took off her muddy clothes and then realised she'd get mud on a towel if she used it to wrap around herself. She poked her head out of her door. The coast was clear. There was nobody around and the bathroom was next door. Could she risk it and make a naked dash? The corridor wasn't visible from downstairs and all the guests had gone. She reasoned that if she heard anyone coming it would take two steps and she'd be back in the safety of her room. She took a breath and darted into the corridor. She grabbed the bathroom door handle and dashed into the safety of the bathroom. *Made it*, she thought with relief.

'What the hell are you doing?' came Fraser's cross voice.

Liv instinctively spun around to see Fraser stark naked standing in the bath. She was mortified. At the same time they both realised their mistakes and covered their modesty with their hands. It was hard to look away so she closed her eyes. 'I needed a shower,' she said groping for a towel off the nearby stand. 'Sorry, I'll come back.' She hastily wrapped the towel around her and left.

Liv waited by her door so that as soon as Fraser had finished she could get clean. At last she heard the bathroom door click open so Liv opened hers a fraction to see a wet and naked Fraser prance across the landing. She noted his lean figure and peachy bum. At least she wasn't the only one making an arse of themselves. Liv crept out, went into the bathroom and shut and locked the door. She let out a huge sigh. Mission accomplished.

Liv wasn't looking forward to facing Fraser but she figured she'd brazen it out. The thought of his bare backside creeping across the landing made her smirk. At least she could use that as a counter-offensive if she came under attack for having walked in on him in the bathroom. An image of his naked body swam into her mind. It was very distracting. He had a beefy physique that she definitely favoured. She'd always been more attracted to the muscular build like The Rock, rather than the pretty-boy Ryan Reynolds type. She was about to dismiss the image but she let it linger in her mind just a moment longer – no one could tell her off for that, although it probably wasn't healthy.

It was usually about this time that she would have been helping Fraser in the kitchen with the dinner. She'd enjoyed doing that over the last few days. She guessed it wouldn't be the same with the guests gone. There'd definitely be less to do. She may not have been needed but she decided to check, just in case. She was no chef but she'd surprised herself by how much she'd enjoyed learning about the different dishes and helping where she could. Liv was also looking forward to surprising her sister with making Hasselback potatoes when she got home. She opened the kitchen door to be met by silence – there was nobody there. As she walked back along the hallway she almost bumped into a distracted-looking Robbie who was coming out of the library.

'I know, I know,' he said holding up his palms. 'You wanted to be out of here but there have been so many cars covered in snow for hours that they couldn't get started. You'll be number-one priority tomorrow – I'll make sure of it.' He pointed a finger at her, which she assumed was meant to be reassuring.

She'd have one more night at Lochy House. 'Thanks,' she said. 'Do you know where everyone is?' she asked.

'Having a bit of a discussion in the dining room.'

'Right.'

'I've got to dash. I'm needed on important police business.' He gave her his serious look.

'Sure,' said Liv.

Robbie's walkie-talkie burst into life and he marched off. Liv wandered into the dining room where there was an intense discussion going on, which halted abruptly as she walked in. Effie, Fraser, Dolly and Jock'O all turned to glare at her.

'Everything okay?' she asked scanning the flustered-looking faces. She and Fraser looked directly at each other and Liv couldn't help smiling at the thought of their bathroom run-in.

'Yep, fine,' said Fraser getting up and shoving his chair under the table before walking out.

'Was it something I said?' asked Liv, taking his vacated seat.

'It's not you,' said Effie. 'The thing is…' She tailed off and Liv could see it was because Dolly was signalling to her to stop talking.

'The thing is?' encouraged Liv.

'Um…' Effie seemed torn. 'The Thing is a hand in the Addams Family. Sorry I need to get on.' And she hastily left the table and rushed from the room, followed by Dolly at a much slower pace. Liv sat at the table alone and pursed her lips. There was definitely something going on and she was now itching to find out what it was.

Liv tracked down Effie to the reception desk where she appeared to be hunting for something and almost knocking over the mugs of half-drunk tea Dolly had abandoned there. 'Hey, Effie, what's going down?'

'Nothing. Absolutely nothing at all.'

'Nice try,' said Liv. 'But I know there's something up. That or my deodorant stopped working because I don't usually have the effect of everyone leaving a room when I enter it.'

'It's not you,' said Effie.

'That's good. What is it then?' Liv leaned forward with interest.

'I can't say. It's family business.'

'Okay,' said Liv. She didn't want to make her feel uncomfortable. 'But if you change your mind and want to offload to someone who has absolutely no vested interest and won't repeat a word of it, then you know where I am.' Liv turned to leave.

'Actually...' began Effie slowly. 'You promise you won't say anything to anyone?'

'Scout's honour.'

'You're not a Scout are you?'

'No, but it's the thought that counts.'

Effie looked momentarily confused. 'Okay but if you repeat any of this then I'll be forced to wish bad things for you.'

Liv chuckled but Effie looked stern. 'Right,' said Liv trying to look serious. 'Sure, I don't want Janet after my soul.'

'Exactly,' said Effie making Liv swallow hard. She didn't believe in all that stuff, but still she'd not want to take any risks and be proved wrong. 'Fraser is upset about the hotel being put up for sale.'

'Yep, I'd gathered that much.'

'He doesn't own it,' said Effie.

'And I'd worked that out too.'

'You're very clever,' said Effie.

'I'm not but thanks. Robbie mentioned that Fraser's dad owns it. If that's the case how come you're all using it?'

Effie pulled up the reception chair and sat down, and Liv leaned on the counter. 'My dad and Fraser's dad owned it. Together. Jointly.' Effie was pointing at invisible people. 'You see his dad is my uncle and my dad was his uncle.'

'They're brothers. I get it,' said Liv, amused by the effort of Effie's explanation.

'You are smart. Anyway, they were in partnership together. My dad ran the hotel side and Uncle Rory ran the restaurant and any events. Back then it was thriving. Always full of people. We had lots of tourists, regulars who came back year after year, plus this was the place the locals came for special meals. You know the sort of thing: birthdays, anniversaries, first dates. Then Dad had his accident and Uncle Rory disappeared.'

Liv leaned forward. 'Disappeared?'

Effie nodded. 'One night he was here drinking whisky and singing "Shang-A-Lang" by the Bay City Rollers and the next morning he was gone.'

'I can see why the Bay City Rollers might drive you to that, but still a bit extreme. Then what happened?'

'We don't know. The estate agent is the first contact we've had in three years.'

Now she really had Liv's attention as there was most definitely a mystery to solve.

24

Liv found Fraser in the kitchen scowling at his phone. 'Something interesting?' she asked.

'If you think my ex getting in touch is interesting then yes.'

'Actually I do. What does she want?' she asked, coming closer and snatching a look at his screen before he rapidly put his phone away.

'It doesn't really make sense, perhaps the message wasn't for me.'

She sat on the worktop and Fraser shook his head at her. 'What did it say?' she asked.

Fraser busied himself with getting out pans and then changing his mind and putting them away again and choosing different ones. 'Something about me looking cheap on the internet.' He dropped a pan with a loud clatter, making Liv put her hands over her ears. Fraser spun in her direction. 'You didn't take a photograph of me earlier when I was...' He waved a hand up and down his body.

It took Liv a moment to cotton on. 'Oh, when you were naked you mean?'

'Shhh, voice down,' he said. 'If Granny hears you she'll start asking awkward questions. Anyway stop dodging the issue. Did you take a photo?'

Liv gave him a look. 'Do you recall what I was wearing at the time?'

Fraser looked to the ground for a second then looked up. 'Not a lot.'

'Exactly. I didn't happen to have my Nikon with the paparazzi super magnifying lens on me.'

Fraser's expression changed to one of thunderstruck. 'There's no need to be rude.'

'I wasn't,' said Liv. Then she went over what she'd said. 'I didn't mean I'd need a powerful lens to see your... um...' She pointed at him, making them both look down at his trousers. Liv whipped back her finger and folded her arms to stop herself doing anything similarly embarrassing. 'I didn't mean it like that. There were no size issues that I witnessed.' Fraser blinked. 'Not that I was looking obviously,' added Liv hastily. 'Anyway let's tiptoe out of this minefield. To answer your question. No, I did not take any photographs of you naked or otherwise.'

'Then I don't know what she's going on about.'

'Did the intensive care work on my phone?' she asked.

'Dunno, have a look.' He got out the jar of rice and passed it to her. She hoicked out her phone. It seemed okay.

'I'll get my charger,' she said getting off the worktop but Fraser didn't reply.

A few minutes later she returned to the kitchen and plugged in her phone. They both watched it and waited.

At last a red battery sign appeared. 'Yay! It works. You're a star,' she said automatically throwing her arms around his neck. There was a tricky moment where they both froze as if suddenly remembering they were mortal enemies. Liv let him go and they both became intensely interested in staring at her phone.

The staring was interrupted by the beep of Fraser's phone. He snatched it from his pocket and his eyes pinged wide as he looked at the screen. 'Bloody hell.'

'What?' said Liv trying to get a look over his shoulder.

'How on earth…' He appeared stunned as if he'd been whacked in the face with one of his heavy-based pans but at the same time he couldn't seem to take his eyes off his screen.

Liv was more than curious. 'For heaven's sake what?' Fraser turned his phone around so that she could see. There was a photograph of a muddy Fraser with Shanie Cortina stood right in front of him pouting. It was surprisingly flattering given the situation. Fraser looked ruggedly handsome and Shanie only had the tiniest mud splatter on her cheek, making it look almost strategically placed and you couldn't see the mess the rest of her was in. 'What's wrong with that?' she asked as he whipped his phone back.

'It's got over twenty-one thousand likes and the caption reads: *Got saved by a real-life hero today. He's handsome, fit and the best chef ever. Check out Bonnie Scott's restaurant at the Lochy House Hotel. Things are looking up for me.*' Fraser looked up from the screen. 'And then she's put a heart emoji.' He shoved his phone in his pocket and went back to banging pans.

It was Liv's turn to look like she'd been smacked in the

face with a pan, which was also exactly how she felt. How those two had slipped under her radar she wasn't sure. 'What did I miss then?' she asked feeling and sounding narked. There had been that odd moment when Shanie had said something when she'd seen Liv and Fraser together. Had Liv inadvertently got herself in a love triangle?

'Nothing. She's deluded.' He ran his hands through his hair and left a bit sticking up.

'Is she?' asked Liv, feeling strangely defensive on Shanie's part. 'Or did you also kiss her under the mistletoe?'

'What? No. Is that what this is about? You're jealous. Jeez.' He threw his head back and blew out a breath. 'I don't believe this.'

'Nor do I,' said Liv. 'Why do you lead women on and then deny everything? What is your problem?'

'I didn't do anything. Shanie has got it all wrong. She said a few things and maybe there was some flirting.'

'Is that all?'

Fraser looked sheepish. 'She came knocking on my door the other night and her intentions were pretty clear.'

'What did you do?' Although Liv wasn't sure she wanted to know.

Fraser looked embarrassed. 'I pretended to be asleep. There really is nothing going on, so I don't know why she put a heart or why she thinks... Heavens, I don't know what she thinks.'

Liv made a heart shape with her hands.

'She doesn't love me; she doesn't know me,' said Fraser.

'Did you exchange phone numbers?'

'Yeah.'

Liv gave him her 'there you go then' look.

'Come on.' Fraser was looking exasperated. 'That is not the universal sign for "I love you".' That was the moment Effie chose to walk in.

'Yay! My two favourite people are in love! Well, apart from Jedward, David Tennant, Taylor Swift and Dolly – and Jock'O, who technically isn't a person so doesn't really count. Oh and Sharleen Spiteri.' Fraser and Liv were both staring at her aghast. 'But yay two of my top-ten people are in love.'

'Na-huh,' said Liv shaking her head so fast it made her ears ring.

'Definitely not in love with *her*,' said Fraser stabbing a finger in Liv's direction.

'Hey!' said Liv. 'You don't need to be mean.'

'I wasn't being mean; I was simply agreeing with you.'

'But you said you loved her.' Effie looked beyond sad.

'No, he meant Shanie Cortina,' explained Liv.

Effie's sad expression instantly evaporated. 'Yay! Shanie would be in my top ten too. And she's famous. This is the best news. Wait 'til Granny hears.' Effie turned to leave.

'Stop!' Fraser held up his palm. 'Please can we stop all the madness – it's making ma heid mince. Let's keep this simple and get something very clear.' He glanced at Liv and then focused on Effie. 'I am not in love with anybody.'

'Except maybe yourself,' muttered Liv, seeing if her phone had a smidgeon enough charge for her to use.

'Hang on,' said Fraser. 'Can you please stop sniping at me for one—'

'Bloody hell,' said Liv. 'You've gone viral. Look at these numbers. Instagram. TikTok. Thousands and thousands of likes and going up all the time.' She showed them both her phone where she'd been searching on social media.

Fraser ran his hands through his hair. 'How do we make it stop?'

The phone in reception started to ring and all three heads turned in that direction.

'I'm not sure we can,' said Liv. She was left wondering if this was Shanie's response to her asking if she'd give Fraser a good review or had there been something going on between them all along?

The next hour was quite wild where the hotel phone was constantly ringing with people asking to book a table or speak to Fraser about his relationship with Shanie Cortina. Dolly was fielding most of the calls and was taking their details if it was for a booking and saying 'no comment' for everything else. When it got too much they put on the answerphone.

Fraser had been hiding in the kitchen for the most part. Robbie had turned away one local reporter at the front gates and had pulled them shut in anticipation of the masses of paparazzi, which had made Fraser go a little pale and Effie squeak with excitement although it turned out it was purely a precaution and thankfully there were no photographers. Another definite benefit of living in the wilds of the Scottish Highlands.

They all convened at reception with Fraser the last to join the group.

'At least we'll be fully booked for the showcase dinner,' said Dolly. 'In fact we could probably do two – we've had that much interest in bookings.'

'Slight problem,' said Fraser.

'What now?' Dolly sounded exasperated.

'I've just had phone calls and two text messages...' He was frowning as if struggling to know how to finish the sentence.

'From who?' asked Liv.

Fraser looked at her for a moment before he spoke. 'All my kitchen team and waiting staff. They've all said they're not coming back. Every single one of them.'

'Are they all sick?' asked Effie. 'Do you remember when Donald's diarrhoea did the rounds?'

'They've quit, Effie. Left. Resigned.'

'That's more than fishy,' said Dolly.

'Donald's diarrhoea wasn't fish; it was out-of-date Scotch eggs that...' Effie noticed everyone was staring at her and she stopped speaking.

'Did they give any reasons?' Liv asked Fraser.

'I didn't think the first one was anything odd. He said he'd got a new job so I wished him well. But by call number five I knew there was something up.'

'Number five?' queried Liv.

Fraser scowled at her. 'Kitchen and waiting staff.'

'Got it. Sorry, you were saying?'

'I asked her where she was going and she said Lairds and put the phone down.'

Effie gasped. 'That's Lizzie's restaurant.'

'And you think they've all got jobs there?' Fraser wobbled his head. 'Blimey, she knows how to get revenge,' said Liv. Perhaps she could give her a few pointers.

'Revenge for what?' said Fraser throwing up his hands. 'I didn't do anything wrong. It was her and Callum who were off shagging behind my back.'

'She's trying to scupper the showcase dinner. That's what she's doing,' said Dolly.

'I think it's fair to say that she has,' said Fraser. 'There's no way I can get enough staff in and trained by tomorrow. In fact I doubt I can get anyone at all. That's it. I'm screwed.'

'We'll help, won't we,' said Effie, grinning at Dolly and then at Liv.

Liv felt a wave of something unpleasant come over her as she realised what Effie was suggesting and wondered for a moment if she'd got Donald's disorder. 'Oh no, I can't stay any longer. I have to get back for… um…' What did she have waiting for her at home? She thought of her sad little single bed at her sister's. 'My sister! And my mum. I need to—'

'It's okay,' said Fraser. 'There'd still not be enough of us.'

'We could stagger the service,' said Dolly, pushing out her lip. 'Surely we have to try.'

'We'd definitely need Liv and even then it's probably impossible,' said Fraser in a small voice. He turned to face Liv. 'I know we've not always seen eye to eye. Because quite honestly I don't know what you're going to come out with from one moment to the next. But that aside, you're a good worker, you know the dishes and I'll need your help if we're even going to consider going ahead.'

'Err…' Liv looked at the hopeful faces of Effie, Dolly and Fraser all waiting for her reply. At that moment her mobile sprang into life and she'd never been so relieved for the interruption. Even if it was a scam call she'd be forever grateful. She looked at the screen. 'It's my sister. I need to take this.'

25

Liv rushed out into the hallway, letting the kitchen door swing closed as she put the phone to her ear. 'Charlotte, you will never know how pleased I am to hear from you—'

'What the hell are you doing? Mum is beside herself with worry. Is he holding you hostage? Actually don't say anything because if he is then he's probably listening in—'

'Honestly, I've not been kidnapped. I'm here of my own free will. Well, that and the shitload of snow that came down. Seriously, I thought we had a lot of snow that year the shed roof caved in and we had to dig the guinea pigs out. But up here it's on a biblical scale.'

'Is my car all right?' asked Charlotte.

Liv winced. 'Don't worry but—'

'You know I'm now instantly worried. You've totalled it and that's why you've not come home. Good grief, that's it, isn't it? You're not in hospital are you? If you're lying in a hospital bed and—'

'Stop! I am fit and healthy and your car has a puncture but it's being fixed tomorrow… hopefully.'

Liv heard Charlotte sigh into the phone. 'Bloody hell, Liv. As long as you're okay, that's the important thing. So you'll be coming home tomorrow?'

'Um…' Liv looked over her shoulder. She could just see Fraser through the glass in the kitchen door. 'Thing is there's a bit of a crisis here and they need me to stay and help out with this big event on the twenty-third.'

'An online marketing crisis?'

'No, a cooking one and—' Liv didn't get to finish her sentence because Charlotte was laughing so hard on the other end of the line.

'You? Cooking?' was all Charlotte managed to say before she dissolved into more hysterics.

It wasn't *that* funny. When Charlotte had got her laughter under control Liv tried to explain. 'Fraser is about to launch his new restaurant with a showcase dinner tomorrow night, but his ex has just hired all his staff in an attempt to sabotage everything.'

'Good,' said Charlotte. 'That's called Karma. It saves you taking him down but I can see why you'd be keen to watch him go down in flames.'

'That's not why I want to stay.' She'd not heard herself say that out loud before and it solidified something in her. 'I want to stay and help him.'

'Why on earth would you do that? Why?' Charlotte sounded exasperated.

Liv thought about the Fraser she'd got to know, him losing his uncle and his dad disappearing the way he had had definitely softened her view of him. Plus he had let her stay for free. 'Nothing's ever straightforward. And I've kind of got to know him.'

'But this is the guy who ghosted you, right?'

'Yep.'

'Then he's a shit. That's as straightforward as it gets. Come home.'

Liv sighed. She understood Charlotte was only looking out for her, as she always had done, but sometimes you had to go with your gut and staying to help felt like the right thing to do. 'I know you don't get it, Charlotte, but I need to do this. I'll be home soon and we'll have a great Christmas. Give Mum my love.' And before Charlotte could protest any more, Liv ended the call.

Fraser strode out of the kitchen pulling on his coat. 'Everything okay?' he asked.

'Yes, I'm staying,' replied Liv and Fraser smiled. 'Just until after the showcase dinner, then I really need to get home and get ready for Christmas. Or we'll be like the Cratchits.'

'Thanks, I appreciate it,' he said, moving to one side as Dolly joined them. 'But I'm not sure it'll be enough,' he added.

'But there's us too,' said Dolly pulling back her shoulders, which pushed her tummy out and gave Jock'O an unwelcome nudge up the bum.

Fraser looked at Dolly in her wheelchair and Effie, who was staring at the chandelier above them as she twirled her hair around a finger. Liv knew exactly what he meant. 'The four of us can't manage alone, can we?' Liv looked from Fraser to Dolly.

'No.' Fraser looked defeated.

'Goodness me, Fraser,' snapped Dolly. 'You're a Douglas,

with a large dose of McNab running through those veins. We do not give up.'

Liv looked to Effie for an explanation. 'Granny comes from a long line of McNabs,' she whispered with an expression that said Liv should be wildly impressed by that fact. She would have been more impressed if she'd come from a long line of McVities.

'Sometimes you need to know when to graciously step down. I think there's a difference,' said Fraser. 'I have to face it. Lizzie knew what she was doing. She set out to derail the restaurant and she's done it.'

'But if it's just staff that you need,' said Dolly sounding a little desperate.

'I need a kitchen team and waiting staff. There's simply not enough time to get anyone else hired.'

'Then we'll have to rope in as many locals to help as we can to make up the numbers,' said Dolly. 'I'd best get on it right away.' She headed for the reception desk.

'Granny, that's sweet of you but—'

Dolly spun her chair around making both Liv and Fraser step back. 'Sweet?! I've been called some things, Fraser Douglas, but never sweet.'

'Kind, thoughtful then,' said Fraser. Dolly was still glowering at him. 'Also determined and tenacious.' Dolly seemed mollified by this. 'But I need trained staff, otherwise it will be a complete and utter disaster. 'We have to face it.' He looked up at the ceiling. 'Bonnie Scott's is on hold. Possibly indefinitely.' Fraser turned up his collar and strode off.

'Where are you going?' called Liv.

'Delivery van has made it here but the gates are shut thanks to Robbie and his paparazzi paranoia. And it couldn't get up the drive anyway.' He rolled his eyes. 'To add insult to injury I'll have to pay for all this food when I won't be able to serve it,' he added and carried on walking.

The front door banged closed, which seemed to snap Effie from her daydream and she looked around like she'd been teleported somewhere unfamiliar. 'What?' she asked, her eyes darting from Dolly to Liv and back again like a startled rabbit.

'Effie dear, we're in the middle of a family crisis. Please try and stay with us,' said Dolly.

Liv's mind was buzzing. There had to be an easy solution. 'I'm thinking out loud here so hear me out,' said Liv and Dolly nodded. 'There have to be people around with the right skills. We just have to find them. Put out an advert maybe. A plea for help. Like a Just Giving page but we need people instead of cash. Or a lost dog.' Dolly and Effie were looking at her like she'd grown a beard. 'Okay maybe something else.' Liv's brain was whirring with the effort. 'Someone stole Fraser's staff. I'm thinking maybe he could borrow someone else's. He needs trained staff so something in the same or similar business. How about a local pub?'

'The Saracen's Head will be full every night – they'll need everyone they've got,' said Dolly.

'Ooh are they burning rowan again this year?'

'Blimey who's Rowan? Another witch?'

Effie giggled. 'No silly. It's a tree. They burn a branch of it to—'

'Ward off evil spirits?' offered Liv, sensing a theme in this neck of the woods.

'Actually,' said Dolly. 'It's to eradicate bad feelings between friends and family. Still pagan in origin though so it was a good guess. And the locals love it so the Saracen's will be busy tomorrow night.'

'Okay.' Liv wasn't giving up. 'Anywhere else that's already shut up for Christmas? Coffee shop? Fast food outlet? Garden centre? Pet shop? Anything really.' At the end of the day they were desperate.

Effie shook her head. Dolly held up a finger. 'The Little Loch Tearooms. My friend Winnie said they were going to be closed over Christmas and Hogmanay. I suspect they've shut up already thanks to the weather.'

'Perfect,' said Liv feeling like she might actually have a grip on something useful. 'How do we get hold of the boss or the staff?'

'I'll call Winnie,' said Dolly continuing towards the reception desk.

A few minutes later the front door banged open and Fraser put down a crate of food. 'Please can someone give me a hand?'

'Coming,' said Liv almost skipping up the hallway until she was stopped in her tracks by an arctic blast. 'It's not warmed up yet then.'

Fraser blinked at her. 'It won't until April when the temperature might make it into double figures.'

'Fair enough,' said Liv going to pick up the crate and realising it was heavier than she was expecting.

'You can leave it. I'll sort it once I've brought everything down from the gates.'

'No, it's fine,' said Liv, her voice squeaking under the strain of lifting the heavy box. She wasn't going to be shown up as a wimp even if it meant a hernia. She waddled up the hallway with the heavy load, but as soon as she heard the front door close she put it down with a jolt. 'Bloody hell that's heavy.'

'Did you want a hand?' called Effie.

'Please.'

Together they carried the crate through to the kitchen and began unpacking it. Effie didn't say anything, which Liv realised was quite unusual. Now she watched her she seemed preoccupied. 'Everything all right?' asked Liv as Effie passed her far more garlic than anyone could ever need.

'Me?' Effie looked around and then pointed to her chest.

'Yeah, you. Are you okay?'

'Yep,' she said as she put the empty crate in the freezer.

Liv retrieved it. 'You're not okay. Sit down. What's the matter?'

'Nothing.' Effie perched one bum cheek on one of the high stools.

'Is it John?'

Effie breathed out in a gush. 'It is and I don't know what to do. I can't tell Dolly or Fraser because they don't know about him and they wouldn't understand.'

'What's happened?'

'He sent me this.' Effie pulled out her phone and bit her lip as she passed it to Liv.

Liv read the message: *This might be goodbye, my love. Almost out of money. You've brought me so much happiness and joy. I only wanted to help the needy but I can't do any more. Please pray for me. All love John x*

Alarm bells were starting to ring in Liv's head. She looked up at Effie's expectant face. 'What do you think?'

'I need to help him. But how? He's so far away.'

'Yeah. I think that's how he wants you to feel. At least he hasn't asked for money.'

'But he does need money. Maybe I should offer to send him some,' she said.

'No, no, no. Don't do that.' Liv was struggling – she wanted to alert Effie to a possible issue but at the same time she didn't want to burst her bubble. 'I'm sure he'll find a way to sort things out. Have you got any photos?'

'Ooh yes.' Effie's mood lifted as she showed Liv on her phone. Up popped a picture of a smiling young man with short cropped hair and what looked like an American army uniform.

'Is he in the army by any chance?' asked Liv.

'He is. He's taking a sabbatical to help people after he was on a dangerous mission and suffered trauma.'

'Right,' said Liv no longer able to hide her cynicism. 'And you believe him?'

Effie pulled her chin in. 'Of course I do.'

'You see I'm not so sure. You get a lot of men claiming to be American generals but they're con men and I'm worried that—'

'Stop it!' Effie's voice was almost a shout. 'John's not like that. He's lovely.'

'But what if he isn't?'

Effie shook her head. 'I thought you were my friend. I told you because I thought you'd understand but you're just like everyone else. You think I'm stupid and that I don't know my own heart. But I do.'

'Effie, look—' But Liv didn't get to say any more. With tears welling in her eyes Effie stormed out of the kitchen and Liv was grateful that it was a swing door because otherwise she knew it would have slammed. Liv sighed. Perhaps she could have handled that better. Poor Effie. The door opened again and a large crate came in with Fraser carrying it. He plonked it on the counter. 'What's wrong with Effie?'

Liv opened her mouth but engaged her brain in the nick of time. She couldn't tell Fraser the truth without revealing Effie's secret boyfriend, but which was worse? 'She's a bit sensitive.'

'Heavens, Liv! What have you said to upset her?' said Fraser.

'Thanks for assuming it's my fault!'

Fraser shook his head. 'I've one last crate to get,' he said and he left.

'It's not my fault by the way,' she called, but he was already gone.

26

Effie couldn't think straight and didn't know where to go. She dashed through the hotel with hot tears stinging her eyes. She wasn't sure what she was most upset about: Liv's hurtful and unjustified words or the thoughts they were triggering. But she knew in her heart that John was the real thing. He'd been able to connect with her like nobody else had. He seemed to know what she was thinking before she did and he always made her feel better about herself. She took a breath, she had no reason to question John, he'd only ever been lovely to her and he was selflessly giving his time to help others for goodness' sake. She shook any doubts from her mind.

John was real. But then did that mean that her relationship with Liv was fake? The woman she thought she'd found a friend in had very quickly turned on her. Maybe she was jealous. Liv didn't have anyone special in her life – she'd told Effie that. But it didn't give her the right to say unkind and untrue things about John. Effie felt betrayed – she'd trusted

Liv with her darkest secret. Well, apart from the time she ate the golden syrup and replaced it with cod liver oil – she'd never told anyone that. But she was pretty sure Dolly had worked it out quite quickly.

When Effie slowed down she found she was in the lobby where a draught from the front door made her shiver. She was about to go and curl up on her seat in the library when the door opened, giving her a start.

'Hello,' said Robbie, jolly as usual. His smile shifted. 'Is everything okay?' He looked past her furtively. 'Can I help in any way?'

Her lip wobbled and she had to fight the tears from escaping. Why was it that you were fine until someone said something kind to you? She needed to think quick – not something she was known for. Robbie was looking increasingly restless. 'I've a friend in trouble,' she said, realising as soon as she'd uttered the words that this was the worst thing to say to an alert police officer such as Robbie.

His eyebrows twitched. 'Trouble? What kind of trouble? Have they committed a crime?' He was already reaching for his notebook.

'No!' said Effie a little more forcefully than the situation warranted. 'They've just got themselves in a pickle really and they're a long way away so I can't help. That's all. There's nothing you can do.'

Robbie's hand moved away from the notepad and his face returned to neutral. 'That's tough but I'm sure there will be someone local who can help them. Would you like me to look up any agencies? There are all sorts of support systems available for a variety of predicaments. Women's refuge? Shelters? Citizens Advice?'

He made her smile even though he wasn't trying to. 'It's okay, Robbie. I'll work something out.' Although she had absolutely no idea how she was going to do that.

★

Liv unpacked the next crate and put away all the food. There was such a lot of ingredients. How many was he expecting for this showcase dinner?

'Right,' said Dolly wheeling herself into the kitchen. 'I've spoken to my friend Winnie who has called Meredith and she's put our plight on their staff WhatsApp thingy. I said for anyone who's interested to come here for six o'clock so Fraser can brief them for what's needed tomorrow.'

'You star. He'll be over the moon,' said Liv.

Dolly held up a hand. 'I think we wait and see how many turn up first. If we raise his hopes it could be an additional blow.'

'Fair enough. But yay! Showcase dinner could be back on.' Liv crossed her fingers and Dolly did the same.

As the kitchen door opened it bumped into the back of Dolly's chair, making Jock'O bark his annoyance. 'Whoops, sorry,' said Fraser, squeezing past the wheelchair. 'What's going on?' he asked.

'Nothing,' said Liv putting some onions back in the crate and then taking them out again.

'There's something up.' He pointed at Dolly. 'Are you plotting?'

She held up her palms. 'Now there's a thing to accuse your grandmother of,' she said giving him a look worthy of Lady Violet Crawley. Jock'O barked again. Dolly lifted her chin and manoeuvred her chair out of the kitchen, giving Liv a sly wink as she left.

Liv got mugs out and without asking made Fraser a brew. She pushed the mug in front of him. 'Penny for them,' she said.

'Thank you. Sorry, what?'

'You were miles away.'

'Aye, I wish I was, that's for sure. I've been a fool.' He looked downcast and she so wanted to tell him about the rescue mission and the staff from the tearooms but perhaps Dolly was right – what if none of them showed up? She checked the clock. Only twenty minutes until, hopefully, they arrived.

'Don't go putting yourself down. Look what you've achieved.' Fraser snorted in response. 'You saw an opportunity and you took it. This hotel was sitting here doing nothing and you breathed new life into it.' He gave her a sideways look. 'Well, you made a good effort at CPR anyway and who knows? It may still be resurrected. There's still a faint pulse. I'm going to stop with the medical references now,' she said.

He scratched his head. 'I wish I knew what Dad was planning. Why is he selling this place now?'

'Ask him,' said Liv. 'Oh yeah, you don't know where he is. Sorry.' There was a moment's silence. 'But the estate agent must have contact details. Ask him to pass on a message or for a tenner he might give you some information.' Fraser looked aghast. 'Worth a try I reckon. If you don't ask, you don't get.'

Fraser sighed. 'But after all this time what would I even say to him?'

'Why are you selling the hotel?'

Fraser laughed. 'You see things very clearly don't you?'

'I guess. I'm one of those people where what you see is what you get.'

'It's a good trait to have,' said Fraser picking up his mug. 'I'd better draft a cancellation email and tell everyone the showcase dinner is postponed indefinitely,' he added.

'Ooh no, don't be hasty.' Liv chanced another glance at the clock. How had only three minutes passed since she'd last looked?

'I don't think I can give the guests less than twenty-four hours' notice that it's not going ahead. And it's only putting off the inevitable.'

'How long is it going to take you to draft it, do you think? You know, roughly? In minutes.' Liv fixed him with interested eyes.

'Err I don't know. Say ten minutes, fifteen maybe. Why?' He was giving her the same look he frequently gave Effie.

'Just don't press send until I'm back. Okay?'

'Why?'

Why did people always want a blinking reason? 'Umm because I'm sure there's a marketing spin we can put on this. I just need a few quiet moments to come up with something. Say until six o'clock? Promise you won't send anything before then?'

'O-kay,' he was more than hesitant.

'Fab! Thanks.' And she dashed off.

Liv was fit to bursting by the time six o'clock came. She stood by the large grandfather clock by reception and watched the big hand click into place and the clock let out a small peal of dings. Liv checked the time on her phone to be on the safe side – 18.01. It was gone six o'clock. Her heart sank. Was nobody coming? She looked over at Dolly who was behind reception busying herself with something.

'It's six o'clock. Where are they?' asked Liv in a low voice. Dolly looked up. 'They will come.'

'This is not a remake of *Field of Dreams* and I'm not Kevin Costner,' said Liv.

Dolly stared at Liv for a moment and sucked her bottom lip as if thinking. 'I have no idea what you just said.'

'Do you think it's the icy driveway?' asked Liv but she answered her own question. 'The bloody gates are closed. Of course it's the driveway!'

Liv dashed through the kitchen. 'Don't send that email. Don't do anything until I get back,' she said as she grabbed Effie's coat from the hook and ran from the kitchen, trying and failing to put it on as she went. She got it in such a tangle that she had to stop by the front door to sort it out and put it on properly, wasting valuable seconds. What if they all drove off again?

Liv went outside and started to jog up the driveway until her foot skidded on ice and she resorted to a strange waddle of a walk as fast as she dared. By the time she went around the bend her heart was pounding – partly with the effort but mainly with angst. But she needn't have worried. There on the other side of the gates was a minibus.

Liv waved and a lady about her mum's age waved back from the driver's seat. Liv badly mimed opening the gates as she skidded on the icy patches. The woman's expression changed to one of confusion. 'I'm open-ing the gates,' repeated Liv with more exaggerated actions. The woman didn't react. 'I'll just get on with it,' said Liv, undoing the bolt and swinging back the first gate. As soon as it was fully open the rickety minibus trundled inside. The woman wound down her window. 'Thanks. I'm Meredith. We're here to see Dolly.'

'I'm Liv. Careful driving up to the hotel; it's really slippy in places.'

'Righty oh,' said Meredith and the bus crawled past. Liv tried hard to see how many people were on board, but the bus was all steamed up. But as it rattled by Liv decided that the more steamed up the better because that meant there were lots of people in there. She had a cursory look out of the gates. There were no paparazzi about waiting to snap Fraser. She suspected his five minutes of fame, thanks to Shanie, was over.

Liv made her way back up the driveway as quickly, but as carefully, as she could. In her mind she was picturing school outings and trying to work out how many people could fit in a minibus. In her head she counted out the seats. She was sure there had been at least fifteen. She very much hoped that all the seats were full. At the hotel the minibus was parked right in front of the doors but Liv could hear excited chatter, which was promising.

Liv walked around the vehicle expecting to see lots of keen helpers but instead it was like the local nursing home was having a day out. Meredith was talking to Dolly as a stream of elderly people made their way painfully slowly from the minibus and up the ramp to the front door. 'Hi,' said Liv. 'What's um... going on here?' she pointed at the pensioners.

'These are the volunteers who run the tearooms,' said Dolly happily.

'We've come to your rescue,' said Meredith looking mightily chuffed with herself.

An old man made it to the top and clutched the front door for support while he caught his breath. 'Och, hello, Donald. Lovely to see you. Thanks for joining us,' said Dolly, as the man gave her a wave and shuffled inside.

'Donald?' Liv had a vague recollection of a story. 'Of Donald's diarrhoea fame?' she whispered.

'The very same,' said Dolly cheerfully.

Oh heavens, what have I done? thought Liv.

27

Being subtle wasn't one of Liv's talents but she needed to have a quiet word with Dolly. 'Dolly could I have a quick chat...?' She pointed inside.

'Go ahead. Meredith is a friend and I've explained to her exactly what's happened.'

'That Lizzie is the worst,' said Meredith. 'Imagine being so bitter that you wanted to take revenge on someone.'

'Well,' began Liv. Memories of being ghosted stabbed at her. Dolly and Meredith both watched her closely. 'Yeah, imagine that. How many staff have we got here?' she asked keen to change the subject.

'Seven but...' Meredith leaned forwards and lowered her voice. 'That does include Winnie.' She tipped her head towards the bus.

Liv turned to see a tiny lady who looked like she'd been sun-dried longer than your average raisin. She gripped a walking frame tightly as she slowly made her way up the ramp. If it had been warmer, snails would have overtaken her.

'And she's one of the helpers?' How on earth did someone like Winnie work in a tearoom? she wondered.

'She's very good at buttering bread for sandwiches,' said Meredith nodding enthusiastically.

'She's my oldest friend,' said Dolly proudly.

'I wish you wouldn't say that,' said Winnie who had a high-pitched voice that suited her. 'She makes it sound like I'm the oldest person she knows.'

'She is,' whispered Dolly.

Liv tried to get her head around the situation. She had to somehow reverse this and fast. There was no way the showcase dinner could go ahead staffed by diarrhoea Donald and the Golden Girls. First thing was to get Fraser to send the cancellation email so that notifying attendees wasn't delayed any further, and then she needed to keep him occupied and away from this fiasco.

'Hello, what's going on here?' asked Fraser strolling outside to join them.

Bugger it, thought Liv. She needed to think on her feet. 'You've got a lot of food so we thought—'

'That I could feed some of the locals?' Fraser was already nodding.

'Yes,' said Liv.

'No,' said Dolly and Meredith together both scowling at Liv.

Fraser turned towards his grandmother. 'They're your staff,' said Dolly proudly. 'We used our initiative and we rounded up local people with the right skills.'

Fraser was looking mightily confused, as well he might.

'We're from the Little Loch Tearooms,' said Meredith. 'We've come to save the day.' Meredith seemed mightily pleased with herself.

Fraser looked at Liv. She shrugged as if she hadn't a clue what they were talking about. 'How exactly?' he asked.

'These are your kitchen and waiting staff for the showcase dinner,' said Dolly. 'They're here for you to brief them ready for tomorrow. It was Liv's idea.'

Great, thrown straight under the geriatric minibus. 'More a random thought,' said Liv. 'But what's important to focus on is…' She wagged her finger like a back-bench politician. 'Is um… nope I've got nothing.'

'Let's get Winnie inside before she catches hyperthermia,' said Meredith, putting an arm around the lady who had almost made it to the top of the ramp and looked like she'd run a marathon. Liv feared for poor Winnie. It appeared walking was her kryptonite.

'Hello, Fraser,' said Winnie, instantly brightening. 'Ooh and who is this gorgeous creature?' she asked fixing Liv with interested eyes.

'It's Liv,' said Dolly. 'I told you about her over the phone.'

'The mysterious young woman. I've been looking forward to meeting you,' she said. 'Now, Dolly, who does she remind me of?'

Liv felt like everyone was now scrutinising her.

'I canna say she resembles anyone I've seen before,' said Dolly.

Liv wasn't sure whether to be offended or not.

'I know who she looks like,' said Winnie letting go of her

frame for a moment to click her old fingers. 'Amy Pond! She's her double. I thought I knew her from somewhere.'

Liv was none the wiser. Fraser leaned in close and whispered in her ear. 'In case you're wondering She's a character from *Doctor Who*.'

'Oh great,' said Liv as Winnie walked in with Dolly, leaving the others to follow. 'I look like some alien creature do I?'

'No,' said Fraser. 'Amy is Doctor Who's sidekick and played by the Scottish actress Karen Gillan. She's human.'

'I'll take that as a win,' said Liv.

Once they were finally all inside, Dolly and Jock'O began corralling everyone in the library. It was like watching a slow-motion version of *One Man and his Dog* but with people instead of sheep and the dog was working from a wheelchair.

Liv went to join the others in the library but Fraser took her arm and held her back. 'What is going on? I genuinely have no idea what's happening.'

'Err well...' She decided coming clean was the best option and her shoulders seemed to release tension as soon as she'd made the decision. 'I thought if we could find a local workforce who had already been stood down for Christmas they could fill in for the staff you've lost and the showcase dinner could go ahead as planned.' Fraser was looking at her blankly. 'Dolly said she'd try the tearooms and their staff were all available. Yay,' she said somewhat half-heartedly.

'I can't... But... Those are all...' He seemed to be struggling to find the words.

'I know. It wasn't exactly what I had in mind either. And

with hindsight I didn't ask as many questions as I could have done when Dolly said the tearoom staff were available.'

'You think?' said Fraser sarcastically.

'I'm sure we can sort something out. I think offer them a free dinner and then they'll go home quietly. Maybe after a nap but it'll be fine,' said Liv.

Fraser opened his mouth but Dolly interrupted them.

'Fraser! Come on. Your team are waiting to hear from their leader.'

Fraser was turning an unhealthy sort of reddish purple colour. 'You'd better go,' said Liv, using her fingers to mime walking into the library. He looked like there was a lot he wanted to say but thankfully he shook his head and went inside. Liv decided to hover near the door.

'Welcome, everyone,' began Dolly. 'Thank you so much for responding to our call for help.'

'Actually, Granny,' said Fraser. 'Can I just step in?' Dolly waved for him to come forward and looked on proudly as he addressed the room. 'I'm really sorry but there's been some sort of mix-up. I needed experienced kitchen and waiting staff and—'

'That's what you've got,' said Meredith.

'You're not about to be horribly ageist, are you, Fraser?' said Dolly fixing him with a steely eye.

Liv winced on his behalf. He briefly turned to scowl at her and she held her hands up in surrender. 'Your call,' she mouthed from the safety of the doorway.

Fraser ran a hand over his face. 'Okay let's look at it another way. For a start I need an experienced sous chef who can prep, take orders from me, and deliver top-quality cuisine.' He looked at the expectant faces.

Donald cleared his throat. 'I used to work as a chef de partie at Balmoral.'

Liv had no idea what that was but she was impressed. As did everyone else appear to be, even Fraser. It did cross her mind as to how Donald may have come to leave that job, but perhaps that was a question for another day.

'Right,' said Fraser. 'Okay, that is really useful, Donald, thank you – but we can't pull this off just the two of us.'

'You'd have Effie and Liv in the kitchen too,' said Dolly.

'And me,' said Winnie, with a wave. She was quite adorable.

'That leaves Meredith, Hester, Audrey and Sheena to wait the tables, which I'll supervise,' said Dolly. 'I think we have our team.' Meredith started a round of applause and everyone happily joined in. Apart from Fraser who looked like he'd just landed in his own personal hell.

To his credit he was professional as he went through the planned menu, explained dishes and the roles that needed fulfilling. Everyone was keen, even the lady who fell asleep part way through the briefing and had to be nudged awake. At the end Dolly suggested that everyone came to have a look at the kitchen and dining room set-up so that they would be familiar with it ahead of tomorrow and, despite her best efforts to overtake, Liv found herself caught behind a slow-moving Winnie with Fraser next to her.

'Could we not carry her or something?' Liv whispered.

'What, in a backpack like Yoda?' Fraser gave her a pointed look.

Liv shrugged. 'It's not the worst idea and she's small

enough. She'd look kinda cute.' Liv mimed her peeping out of a backpack. Fraser snorted his derision. Maybe it was too soon for jokes. 'Look I'm sorry about...' She twirled a finger behind the line of old people heading for the hotel kitchen. 'I was only trying to help.'

Fraser took a very deep breath and Liv waited for the verbal backlash. 'It's not your fault.'

'It kinda is.'

'Okay, yes it is but it's Lizzie who's caused all of this. The problem now is do I cancel and call a halt to everything or do I go ahead and...' He sucked his lip. 'Who am I kidding? I can't go ahead. My dad is selling the place. Come spring the hotel will likely be sold, so it's all pointless.'

'Really? You're going to cave in just like that?' Liv gave him the side-eye.

'What?'

'I just thought you were a bit more maverick, the do-or-die type. Are you more Jim Carrey than Mariah Carey?'

'Mariah's formidable so I'd happily be compared to her...' He wobbled his head as if questioning his own words. At least the bit about him being a fan appeared to have been true.

'Me too,' said Liv. 'I love her. Some people just don't get her but...' He was starting to frown. 'Sorry, I'm getting carried away. Back to the issue in hand.'

'Thanks,' said Fraser.

Liv put her hands on her hips. 'Okay, Mariah. What'll it be?'

'You really expect me to go ahead with the cast of a Victoria Wood sketch? How do I explain that away?'

'You could be honest and tell the truth. You didn't get

yourself in this situation, but showing that you're doing all you can to get out of it shows what you're made of.'

'And what if it goes spectacularly wrong? That's what I'll be remembered for.'

'True but I think the Fraser I thought I'd got to know would at least channel his inner Mariah and give it his best shot. Because what if it actually works? What if the showcase dinner goes well and the great and the good are interested and want to back you? That could open up the doors you need to get another premises if your dad does sell this place. I mean, I don't know what he's asking for it but it needs a heck of a lot of work doing. I'd be amazed if it was snapped up. More likely it'll be on the market for ages and in that time you could build your business. And deep down don't you want to show Lizzie that she's no longer working your strings?' Liv gave a little smile at the end of her speech.

'You are so...' Fraser clenched his fists '...bloody annoying.'

'Thank you,' said Liv sensing a victory of sorts.

28

The next morning Liv tapped on Effie's bedroom door. She figured she would give her overnight to calm down and think things through. Liv wasn't holding out much hope that Effie would have come around to her way of thinking, but she wanted to smooth the waters all the same. Liv didn't like that she'd upset Effie but, she still felt she'd done the right thing by flagging the potential issues with John. In the cold light of day Liv felt slightly less certain about her convictions. John hadn't directly asked for money so perhaps he was genuine and just unfortunate that his profile screamed fraudster.

There was a long wait before the door opened a crack and Effie's unsmiling face came into view.

'Good morning, I brought a peace offering.' Liv held up a breakfast tray. 'It's to say I'm sorry for upsetting you yesterday.' And she *was* sorry for that. She liked Effie and didn't like to see her upset. 'Shall I put it down here or can I bring it in?'

Effie stood back and let Liv inside. Liv went in and placed the tray on the bed. 'Shall I pour you a cuppa?'

Effie wrapped Liv in a hug and she hugged her back. 'Let's not argue again,' said Effie releasing her.

'I mean it wasn't an argument as such,' said Liv. 'But okay. And just look out for yourself. I hate to think of anyone taking advantage of your kind nature.'

'I will. I'm okay with John.'

'Hmm.' Liv had heard the expression biting your tongue and she feared she may have to do exactly that in order to stop herself from commenting. She took a breath instead. 'I find my mum is always good to talk to when I'm having man trouble. Can you speak to your mum about John?'

'I would love to,' said Effie. 'But she moved to France and I don't hear from her very much. She's busy. I imagine her like an older Lara Croft; venturing into ancient, booby-trapped tombs and crumbling ruins searching for priceless artefacts.'

'Is she a rebel archaeologist?' asked Liv already impressed.

'No, she's a hairdresser.'

Liv didn't know how to respond to that. 'Anyway, tea?'

'Please,' said Effie sitting down on the bed. 'I miss my mam doing my hair too.'

'Your hair is lovely. Great colour.' Liv took in the rich chestnut shade as Effie swished it about.

'It's out of a box. Well, everyone's ginger aren't they.' Liv was considering how to reply when Effie went off at a tangent. 'I am so excited about today. Aren't you?'

Excited probably wasn't the first word that sprung to mind. 'I'm more apprehensive, worried even and a little nauseous if I'm being honest.' She'd persuaded Fraser to go ahead with the showcase night and now a lot was riding on them and the local geriatric community pulling it off.

'Don't be silly. It'll be fine. Robbie says we have experience on our side.'

'I'm not sure what else we have though.' Liv feared they may not all stay awake for the duration and, if they did, were they capable of helping Fraser to produce an exemplary four-course meal with top-class service? Only time would tell.

Robbie stopped by to tell Liv that her wrecked tyre had been replaced and to hand her a hefty bill. She made a phone call to the garage and settled up. She was not looking forward to her January credit card bill. But at least now with the car fixed she could make a quick getaway the next morning or whenever it suited her.

Most of the day went by in a whirl of cleaning, laying tables and food preparation, until a couple of hours before guests were due to arrive Dolly appeared in the kitchen looking flustered. 'There's a problem,' she said.

Fraser put down the knife he was holding and shut his eyes tight. 'What is it?' he asked.

'The helpers have just arrived and the good news is we've still got Donald.' Liv wasn't holding out a lot of hope if Diarrhoea Donald was the good news. 'Unfortunately Meredith has a migraine so she couldn't come and nobody else is insured to drive the minibus. So Donald has had to drive.'

'Who've we got?' asked Liv.

'Hester, Sheena and Winnie,' said Dolly.

'Yay, we still have Winnie,' said Effie. 'I love Winnie – she's the cutest.'

Fraser rubbed a hand over his face. 'I canna believe it. It's like there's a force trying to block me at every turn.'

'Och for goodness' sake, that's enough of the dramatics,' said Dolly. 'Effie and Liv will have to double up. They'll need to help in here as well as serving.'

Liv scratched her head. 'Look, I'm all for working hard but I just don't think that'll work.'

Fraser stood up straight. 'Then Effie you're in the kitchen,' he said. 'And Liv you prep and then shift to waiting tables.'

'That could work.' Liv tried to look enthusiastic. Dolly crossed her fingers but even she didn't look convinced. Dolly left. Fraser had his hands on the counter and looked like he was about to have a panic attack. 'It'll be okay,' she said.

His head snapped in her direction. 'How?'

'Because everyone here wants it to be a success. We are all rooting for you. Even Gordon Ramsay doesn't have that most of the time – all his staff think he's a prize dick.'

Fraser snorted a laugh. 'And I'm not?'

Liv thought for a second. 'No, you're not. I mean you're a bit of an arse but you'd not win prizes for it.'

Fraser belly-laughed in response.

'So we're good?' asked Liv picking up his scarily big knife and presenting it to him.

There was a small pause before he took it from her. 'Yeah, we're good.'

They all worked like demons and got as much prepared and on the cusp of ready as they could to minimise effort when it was time to cook and serve. Liv was getting plates lined up so that serving was swift when Dolly came in wearing black and white and looking very smart, and she was also minus Jock'O.

'Right, you need to get showered and changed,' said Dolly shooing Liv out of the kitchen to get ready.

'It'll be fine,' said Liv as a passing comment to Fraser. 'Okay?'

He gave her a nod. 'Thanks.' It wasn't a big word but the expression it came with meant a lot. They made a good team.

Liv liked a shower. She usually liked to spend longer under the water than she could today, but she found it was a great place for thinking. And today her thoughts were on Fraser. How could this be the same person who had ghosted her? It didn't make sense. Unless it was some weird retaliation for the way Lizzie had treated him but that was feeling less and less likely the longer she knew him. Perhaps there was someone else behind the Fraser profile. Maybe someone had just used his photograph but then surely all the other information wouldn't match to the real Fraser. Not that she was trying to find reasons to let him off the hook, but it was at least something she felt she should explore. But if there was someone else behind it, who could that be?

When Liv came out of the bathroom, Effie was waiting for her. 'I've got you a black skirt and white shirt to wear, and I thought I could do your hair.' Effie held up a hairbrush.

'Thanks, Effie, that's kind but I'll be okay sorting out my hair. Can I ask you something?'

'Of course. We're friends, you can ask me anything.'

'Do you know anything about an online dating profile

for Fraser?' Liv watched Effie's reaction closely in case she gave anything away.

Effie's eyes pinged wide and she put her hands to her mouth. 'Show me – I have to see this. There was me thinking he'd laugh at me and he's been doing it himself. Do you think he has a John too? Well, not a John, but a Judy? What about poor Shanie? Uh I hope he's not two-timing Shanie and Judy.'

Liv wasn't sure how things seemed to escalate so fast with Effie but at least she had her answer – Effie clearly hadn't set up the profile on Fraser's behalf, either with or without his knowledge. 'It was a hypothetical question, Effie. Sort of a what if he did have one.'

'Right. Do you mean he *doesn't* have an online dating account?' She seemed confused.

Maybe now was a good time to explain the whole situation to Effie. 'No not now but you see—'

There was the sound of a text arriving. 'Hang on,' said Effie pulling her phone from her pocket. The happy-go-lucky expression slid away as she scrolled.

'What's wrong?' asked Liv, giving her hair a rub with the towel.

'It's John.'

'Right. And let me guess: things have got worse and now he needs money?'

Effie's mouth fell open. 'How did you know?'

Liv scrunched up her eyes. 'Because that's usually the next move...' Effie's fingers were skidding over her phone screen. 'What are you doing?' asked Liv.

'He needs money and I can't log in to my online bank account and—'

Liv had been waving her hands for some time before Effie eventually paused for breath. 'What exactly does he need money for?' she asked as a room full of alarm bells rang in her head.

Effie opened her mouth, but for once nothing came out. There was a long pause before she spoke again. 'I'm not sure. To get away? What should I do?'

'For a start, don't send any money,' said Liv.

Effie frowned. 'But he's in danger.' She looked genuinely panicked.

How did Liv tell her that this perfect boyfriend she'd put on a pedestal was a con man? It would be like kicking a puppy. 'You only have his word for that.'

'Why would he lie?'

Liv tried hard to think of a nice way to break it to Effie gently, but there didn't seem to be one. 'I'm sorry, Effie. He's lying because he's trying to con you out of money.'

Effie laughed. 'No, he's not.'

'Effie, it's not your fault. I got conned too, in a way. These men – they don't care about us. They pretend they do but they don't. And John is just the same. He's spun you a story and now it's payday.'

'That's awful.'

'I know. Some men are.'

'Not John. You! You're awful. How could you say such horrible things?' Effie rushed downstairs leaving Liv on the landing dripping wet and feeling that, yet again, she'd handled that badly.

By the time Liv had got ready and made it downstairs guests had started to arrive and Dolly was showing them into the dining room on her scooter. The slow speed seemed to make it feel more of an occasion. Fraser had spared no expense on the quality of the table linen and the silverware had come up well after a good polish. The décor was slick and minimal, and the few sprigs of holly, mistletoe and ivy that Effie had insisted upon worked very well and hopefully would also bring peace and good luck to the evening – Liv could only hope because at this stage that was all she had left.

She walked into the kitchen and all eyes swivelled in her direction. 'Right, where do you want me?' she asked clapping her hands together.

'Out,' said Fraser.

'What, in the dining room already?'

She sensed something was wrong. Fraser stared her down. 'No, I want you to pack your stuff and leave.'

Stunned didn't quite cover how Liv felt in that moment. It was like Ginger had sat on her as all the air seemed to have been punched from her lungs. 'Why? What have I done?'

Fraser shook his head. 'You know what you've done and I canna deal with this right now, so I'm politely asking you to leave.'

The kitchen door opened and an ominous-looking Robbie stood in the doorway and beckoned Liv out. 'Is this about Effie because—'

'See you do know,' said Fraser. 'Don't make this worse. Please just go.' The way he looked at her hurt her more than she cared to admit. But above all, the unfairness of it all overwhelmed her. After everything that had gone on she was gutted that he could dismiss her so easily. The last few days had been intense and certainly they'd had their ups and downs, but to be so blunt and final without giving her any opportunity to defend herself was too much.

There were so many things she wanted to say but emotions were bubbling too close to the surface and she feared as soon as she tried to explain she'd turn into a snotty, gibbering mess – why did that always happen? She would not give these people the satisfaction of seeing her cry. Instead she lifted her chin, turned around and stormed past Robbie. She fled upstairs and threw her things into her bag. Where the hell were all her socks? She knew she'd upset Effie but what Fraser obviously wasn't aware of was that she was trying to help Effie, yet she couldn't explain without breaking Effie's confidence. The injustice of it burned her gut. As she came out of the bedroom still fuelled by anger she almost sent Robbie flying.

'Can I help?' asked Robbie, stretching out a hand to take her bag. He froze as his radio crackled into life. All she could make out was something about graffiti, but Robbie seemed to understand every word. Perhaps it was like mums and toddlers where they were so used to hearing the incoherent babble that only they could decipher it. She lifted her bag higher onto her shoulder and marched past him. This was not how she wanted things to end. Poor Effie, she was about to get her heart broken and most likely her bank account wiped clean, and Liv was powerless to stop it. Halfway down the staircase Robbie overtook her. 'Emergency,' he said as he raced by.

At the bottom of the stairs she turned to follow him. The front door slammed behind Robbie and the loud noise made Liv jolt. She was Olivia Bingham. She'd done nothing wrong so why was she skulking about? This wasn't how the new Liv would behave.

She pulled back her shoulders ready to face the

opposition but there was nobody about; everyone was busy. Her shoulders slumped down. The front door opened and as she assumed it was Robbie coming back to make sure she was leaving she dashed behind the reception desk and bobbed down. She would leave when she was ready and not when Robbie and the Bonnie Scott's clan decided. She wasn't entirely sure why she was hiding. Did that make her look more guilty? She heard footsteps. It definitely wasn't Robbie, unless he'd popped out to put on a pair of heels. The heels click-clacked over the parts of the hallway that were uncarpeted and then nothing. Was the mystery woman walking on the carpet or had they stopped?

Liv was about to peep over the top of the reception desk when someone repeatedly and incredibly annoyingly tapped the reception bell in quick succession. Liv jumped up and was pleased that her sudden appearance made the woman gasp and flinch.

'Hello, welcome to Lochy House Hotel. How can I help?' asked Liv.

The woman in front of her was very well made up with long golden blow-dried hair and sharp eyes. 'Who are you?'

That was an odd question to ask someone on a reception desk. 'I'm Liv and I'm here to help.' *Probably only for about another minute before someone forcibly evicts me*, she added in her head.

'I need to see Fraser. It's important.' Her voice had a hard edge to it and her eyes conveyed her instant disdain for Liv.

Liv heard the kitchen door open and as she glanced in that direction she saw Effie looking wide-eyed at the new visitor. 'I'm afraid he's rather busy this evening. If you tell me who you are I'm sure I can help you?' said Liv.

The woman scanned Liv up and down. 'I doubt that very much. You have ten seconds to get Fraser or I will find him myself.' She had even more of a resting cow face than Ginger. She turned away from Liv and the kitchen door swung too and fro rapidly, as Effie made a hasty retreat.

'I'm happy to ask Fraser but I'm going to need some information from you, otherwise he's not coming out because like I said he's very busy this evening with—'

The kitchen door swung open with force and Fraser came storming out. His face was stern but he looked impressive as he strode towards them. His eyes were fixed on the woman but there was a moment where his gazed flicked to Liv and he looked surprised to see her manning the reception desk, which she had to concede was probably understandable. Liv began to hum 'Emotions' by Mariah Carey, which made Fraser do a double take before turning his attention back to the other woman.

'What are you doing here, Lizzie? Have you not done enough?' asked Fraser.

Lizzie! This was the famous ex-girlfriend. Liv was enthralled. She would not have put those two together in a million years.

'Fraser darling, I am here to put things right between us,' said Lizzie, her voice now lacking the hard edge of earlier. 'Perhaps I could have a quiet word?'

'And what would Callum have to say about that?'

Lizzie contorted her pretty features and put on mock-sad eyes. 'I'm afraid we've split up.'

Fraser snorted and shook his head. 'You just screw people up and throw them away, don't you? It's like a hobby for you.'

'Sometimes things just don't work out. But it's important to recognise your mistakes, which is why I'm here. Come on, Fraser, this is me waving the white flag.'

'I don't have time for whatever your latest game is. I'm busy with the showcase dinner.'

'It's going ahead?' She seemed surprised.

'Really none of your business, but if you thought stealing my staff would stop me you sorely misjudged my Mariah attitude and resilience.' There was a brief moment where his eyes flicked in Liv's direction. She would take that as a tacit acknowledgement that her pep talk had worked.

'Of course not. Remember, I know you well,' said Lizzie her voice a little husky. 'I don't want to fight with you. I think we are both wasting time being enemies.' Liv mimed sticking her fingers down her throat. And Fraser smirked at the gesture. Lizzie shot a look at Liv and she quickly pretended to do something on the ancient computer. Surprisingly the screen sprang into life. It wasn't even password-protected.

'Lizzie, I literally don't have time for this,' said Fraser.

'And that is exactly why I am here. I'm sure you understand that employing the best staff is merely a smart business decision; however, I concede that my timing could have been better. I'd like to propose a compromise.' She lifted her chin and, looking rather pleased with herself, she clearly felt she had the upper hand in whatever she was about to negotiate.

'No,' said Fraser and he stared her down.

Lizzie pouted. 'But you've not heard what I'm—'

'Not interested,' said Fraser and he turned to walk away. Lizzie grabbed his arm and he froze. He stared pointedly at where her hand was gripping him tightly. 'Would you please let go of me. I need to get on.'

'Fraser, don't be so hasty. This is cutting off your nose to spite your face.'

'My granny used to say that,' said Liv but when all eyes darted in her direction she returned to randomly tapping away on the keyboard. The autocorrect was having a field day.

'Read my lips,' said Fraser. 'I'm not interested in anything you are offering.' His eyes swept over her outfit.

Ouch, burn, thought Liv and she gave Fraser a thumbs up, although this time she only received a scowl in response.

'Fraser, I hate to see what you've worked for fail. Remember this was my dream too. I am offering you a partnership. I would buy ninety per cent of the business, you retain ten per cent and would have a job here for as long as you want it and, if you agree, you can have your staff back. Tonight.' At that she let go of his arm.

This was tense. Liv was fascinated. Fraser scratched his head. He leaned in and spoke softly. 'I don't need your money or your flaky staff. Now please leave before I call the police and have you removed.'

Lizzie laughed and an image of Cruella De Vil popped into Liv's head. 'You mean Robbie. That dim-witted yokel couldn't undo his own handcuffs.'

The kitchen door swung wide open and Effie came barrelling out looking thunderous. 'Don't you dare bad-mouth Robbie. He's worth ten of you.'

'I'd be surprised if either of you could count that high,' said Lizzie. She turned back to Fraser. 'It's a one-time offer. Don't be a fool,' she said.

'I was a fool once,' he said. 'Thank you for teaching

me a valuable lesson, because I'll not be fooled by you again. Now please leave.' The level of menace in the last three words was quite impressive. It sent a shudder down Liv's spine. There was something wildly attractive about a forceful Fraser, as long as she wasn't on the receiving end.

'Fine,' said Lizzie. 'You'll regret snubbing me. This place will never be more than a cheap canteen.'

Fraser looked as if he was going to retaliate but instead he turned and went back to the kitchen. Lizzie turned to Effie who stuck her fingers in her ears and began humming as she followed after Fraser. Lizzie then turned to Liv, who picked up the telephone and pretended to tap in numbers. 'I don't know why I wasted my time with these halfwits,' said Lizzie and, with a click clack of her heels, she left.

It was all quiet after the drama. Liv needed to think through what she was going to do. Leave with her tail between her legs or stand up for herself? She definitely needed a better plan than walking into the kitchen and shooting her mouth off. She picked up her bag and headed into the library which, thankfully, was empty.

Liv put down her bag and climbed onto the window seat holding her phone over her head. The elusive single bar popped up. 'Ah-hah,' she said, like a pantomime pirate. A quick bit of investigation on Google and she had what she needed.

With renewed energy she strode to the dining room door and was about to enter, but Fraser was in full flow speaking to the roomful of guests, making her feel compelled to listen.

'You can see I've not been the luckiest, but I wouldny be beaten by circumstance or people who would enjoy seeing me fail, so this is me giving it a go. The local community has rallied around and tonight we are going to do our best to present to you a sample of what Bonnie Scott's restaurant will be capable of. I hope you enjoy it.' There were murmurs of interest from the group.

As he left the room he almost knocked Liv out with the door. The look he gave her was one of contempt. 'Seriously, you're still here?'

Liv straightened her spine and stared him down. 'Yes, because there are a few things I'd like to say.' Robbie was out of the picture, so at least she wouldn't be arrested. 'Firstly—'

'I dunny care,' he said.

It stopped her speech dead. 'What?'

'Whatever it is you think you need to say. I dunny care. I've got meals to prepare.' He turned and walked into the kitchen with Liv close behind him, her temper rising to the challenge.

They entered the kitchen and people glanced up and then away, including Effie who blushed crimson at the sight of Liv. Liv looked at all the expectant faces including an angry-looking Fraser who picked up a particularly large knife. Liv took a deep breath. It was now or never.

29

It felt like a long time that Liv stood there with everyone
staring at her. She could feel herself sweating and the
kitchen wasn't even that hot. This was why she shied away
from confrontation. It was horrible.

'Can't you see we're busy?' said Fraser.

'Er yes but I have some things I want to say before
I leave.' She held her chin high and ignored the wobble in
her voice.

'Please don't,' said Effie, looking pleadingly at her.

Liv glanced around. Donald looked embarrassed; Winnie
was agog. There was no benefit in doing this in front of
everyone. The important thing was that she told Fraser
what she thought of him; she wasn't like Lizzie and out for
revenge. 'Can we talk in the hallway?' she asked, reversing
out of the kitchen.

Fraser slammed down the knife, which she was grateful
for. No point in toying with an angry man wielding a
weapon. He followed her out of the kitchen, as did Effie.

She looked at the two of them. She'd only known them five days but it felt like so much longer. Then she corrected herself. It was longer with Fraser but she'd really got to know the real him since she'd been in Scotland, both the good and the bad. And this was the end.

'Firstly,' said Liv, 'Effie, there's no shame in being the victim of a con man. These people are professionals.' Effie was shaking her head. Liv handed her her mobile. 'These are pictures of John. But here he is also known as Rick.' She flicked to the next exact same photograph as the one Effie had shown her. 'And Paul, Kyle, Christopher, Rocco and TJ.' All the pictures were identical.

'How have they got John's photograph?' Effie sounded bewildered.

'I'm sorry, Effie. His real name is Zach Rodriguez and his identity has been duplicated multiple times by con men, most notably those undertaking romance scams. John is just a name used by some chancer trying to wheedle money out of women. He's the worst.'

Tears welled in Effie's eyes. 'No, you're lying.'

'What are you doing?' asked Fraser.

'I'm stopping your cousin from sending money to a confidence trickster who claims to be a US army veteran taking a sabbatical to help people in Burkina Faso.'

At least it raised a derisory snort from Fraser. 'She'd not fall for a…' He ran out of words when he saw the look Effie was giving him. 'Effie, you haven't—'

'You're siding with her without even hearing what I've got to say? Or what John might have to say?' Effie swallowed hard at the end of the sentence. Liv hated to see her hurting.

'Go on then,' said Fraser.

'I met John online. We've been messaging. He's real and he's genuine and—'

'But, Effie, John clearly doesn't exist,' said Fraser. 'Liv's just shown you his real identity.'

Tears slid down Effie's face and Liv reached to comfort her but she shoved her away. 'I hate you both,' she said, pushing past Liv and running up the hall.

They both watched her go. It was horrible to see her so upset. Fraser turned. 'Right. I suppose I should thank you for sorting that out.'

'And apologise for blaming me for upsetting Effie.' Liv folded her arms and stared him down.

Fraser lifted his head as realisation dawned. 'That's what you said to her that upset her? I assumed you'd insulted her.'

'No!' Liv was wounded. 'Come on, what do you take me for?' His eyebrow twitched. 'Don't answer that. I might have implied that con men preyed on lonely people but it was me outing John as a no-good crook that upset her.'

'Then I'm sorry.' He held her gaze a fraction longer than she was comfortable with.

'Apology accepted.' Awkward glances darted between them. 'What do we do now?' asked Liv.

Fraser twitched a shoulder. 'I dunno. I guess there's no need for you to leave anymore. Service in twenty minutes?'

Fury erupted inside her. The cheek of him! 'Seriously. You think I'm going to stay and help you after this?' His expression gave him away. 'You're bloody unbelievable.' Liv was actually grateful for his attitude because it made what she was about to say, so much easier.

'I thought you were treating Effie how Lizzie had, and

I couldn't let that happen again. But I really don't have time to grovel and keep apologising.' He pointed over his shoulder towards the kitchen.

'Tough,' said Liv staring him down.

'What?' He almost choked on the word.

'You heard me. Tough because I've got something else to say and you're going to listen.' Liv pulled back her shoulders. 'Have you ever had an online dating profile?' she asked.

His cheek twitched and he moved his neck as if trying to make it crack. 'Why?'

'Simple question. Yes or no?'

'Then yes. Who hasny had a bash at it? It's about as much fun as chilli in your underwear but I—'

'Deleted the account?' suggested Liv, feeling her temper hitch up a notch.

'Yeah.' Boom. There it was – the admission she'd been after – but it still hurt her to hear it. Now was her opportunity to say her piece. She'd waited five days to say it. 'I'm Olivia Bingham. You connected with me on a dating app. We communicated regularly, like all the time. We got... close. And then you ghosted me. And I am here to tell you that you are a prize shi—'

Fraser was waving his arms in front of her. 'Stop. I have no idea what you are talking about.'

'Don't deny it. It's ridiculous to deny it now. We...' She rapidly pointed between the two of them. 'We're a match. On the app, not in any other sense. You're rude and grumpy while I'm—'

'Also rude and...' He waggled his head. 'Possibly not quite as grumpy.'

'We are not the same,' she snapped. 'Although we do have some things in common. Like Mariah.' He was frowning at her. 'Anyway that's irrelevant. The relevant part is that we both swiped the right way, we connected and then we contacted each other through the app.'

'No, we didn't. You're deranged and I don't have time for this.' He turned around.

'No!' snapped Liv. She'd got this far and heaven knew it had taken her long enough to drag up the courage to confront him. She wasn't going without telling him what she thought of him. He looked over his shoulder. Those icy blue eyes fixed on her and after everything they still managed to make something stir inside her. *Ignore them*, she told herself. She took a deep breath. 'You're the worst. You're...' Why had her brain gone blank? 'You're a shit,' she said.

He shook his head and went through the swing door. Liv watched the door swing back and forth a couple of times. That didn't go remotely how she'd imagined it in her mind. For a start she'd been a lot more colourful with the name-calling. A better phrase popped into her mind. She pushed open the kitchen door.

Fraser glared at her. 'What now?'

'Cock womble!' And with that she made a hasty retreat.

By the time Liv had got to the car she'd come up with at least five better insults she could have thrown at Fraser. Why was that always the way? She'd also forgotten that she'd planned to shout them at him for maximum effect and empowerment. But at least she'd done it. She'd called out his bad behaviour and told him what she thought of him. Although it hadn't gone exactly how she'd hoped and she certainly didn't feel as she'd thought she might. She was hoping for empowerment on an epic female scale. Images of Beyoncé, Mary Earps and Michelle Obama swam into her mind – maybe she'd been aiming a tad too high.

And why had Fraser denied it? Could he not at least have let her have her moment? Say, 'Yeah you got me, I'm a nasty bastard. And now I've lost you and that makes me an idiot.' Although would he think the last bit? She doubted it. But she had confronted someone who had wronged her and that was definitely progress. She would cling on to that fact. Although her brain was still unsettled about it all. It still felt like there was something amiss.

Liv was shaking as she got out the car keys. She popped the boot open and had the fright of her life at the sight of deflated Stan lying there. She put her hand to her chest. 'Bloody hell, Stan. You almost gave me heart failure.' She hauled her bag in next to him. 'Anyway, we're heading home at last. You might as well stay there. You look comfortable.'

Someone cleared their throat and Liv almost jumped in the boot in shock. She spun around. 'I'm glad I caught you,' said Robbie.

'Caught me? What am I meant to have done now? Because it wasn't me. Whatever it is. I didn't do it.' She realised she was gabbling and it was only piquing Robbie's interest. 'I'm going to shut up now.'

Robbie's eyes narrowed and she felt that uncomfortable sweaty sensation on her neck despite the cold. He couldn't arrest her for calling someone names could he? 'Does cock womble mean something different in Scottish?' she asked, which intensified Robbie's squint. 'I'm pretty sure shit's the same in both languages.'

Robbie opened his mouth but there was a long pause before he actually spoke. 'How about shite?' he asked. 'Is that the same?'

'I think so,' said Liv. This was a very strange conversation.

'Like in – the food's shite. Avoid like the…'

'Plague,' added Liv to finish his sentence.

'Yes, I thought that,' said Robbie getting a bit more chatty. 'But that was all it said.'

'I like things like that. Missing words,' said Liv, unsure why she was having this superficial chat in the icy wastelands of the Highlands when she should be heading back down the country to lovely Blackburn where there was less snow and people who understood her.

'You admit it then?' said Robbie. 'And now you're about to take off back to England.'

'Yes, I called him a shit and a cock womble and now I'm off home.'

'You're not denying the defamation then?' He watched her, unblinking. It was both mesmerising and off-putting.

Liv shuffled a few things around in the boot so that Stan wasn't quite as obvious. 'Robbie, I literally have no idea what you're talking about. I mean really not got a clue.'

He raised an eyebrow, old James Bond style, and it quite suited him. He whipped out and pulled on a single blue latex glove with a snap, leaned past her and moved Plastic Stan to one side. He reached in the box underneath and held up a spray can. He pulled a plastic bag from his pocket and dropped in the can – the whole time not taking his eyes off Liv.

'Hang on, that's my sister's property. What do you want with a spray can anyway?'

'Evidence.'

'Of what? That my sister is a forward-planning freak who has touch-up paint in every colour of car she's ever owned?'

Robbie was sealing the evidence bag. 'I'm arresting you for criminal damage. Anything you—'

'What now?' But Robbie carried on with the full statement while Liv continued to ask him what she was meant to have done.

'You'll need to accompany me to the station,' said Robbie, removing his blue glove with a snap, which made an unpleasant shiver go down Liv's spine.

'Robbie, this is bonkers. I don't know what you're arresting me for.'

'The graffiti on the hotel sign.'

Liv's blank expression must have matched her brain. 'Nope. Not got a scooby-doo what you're going on about, but I am not going to the cop shop. I need to get home. It's nearly Christmas.'

She closed the boot and went to get in the car but Robbie put a hand firmly on her shoulder, making her turn around. He unclipped something from his belt. 'Have you been in handcuffs before?' he asked.

She stared at him. 'Sexually or criminally?'

Robbie blinked a few times. 'I'll take that as a no. Please put your hands out in front of you.'

'Seriously?'

'I can call for backup,' he said, his face stern.

Liv let out the deepest sigh as she did as he asked, and he slapped on a pair of handcuffs. This really was the day from hell.

30

Effie didn't have long to wallow, because they sent Winnie to find her and bring her back, and that in itself must have taken quite a while given Winnie's lack of speed. Effie was both upset about John and about Liv – she'd made a real mess of things. By the time she had dried her eyes and got back to the kitchen, the starters were ready to go out and from then on the kitchen was busier than a hive in summer and the evening flew by in a whirl of plates. Dolly did a great job of directing the mish-mash of waiting staff from her scooter and keeping everything on track, and whilst it wasn't as slick as Fraser would have wanted it to be, it hopefully seemed good enough from the diners' point of view. Fraser had set Winnie up in the kitchen doing a final quality check before the dishes left the service counter, and while she was slow on her feet she had an eagle eye and made sure everything looked exactly like the example dishes Fraser had shown her.

The atmosphere in the dining room was infectious

as everyone tucked into the food. The diners were making the right noises and gestures and some were taking photos on their phones. There was lots of happy chatter too, which Effie took as a good sign. The foliage was doing its job.

As they cleared away dessert dishes and brought out trays of coffee and Scottish tablet, Fraser came into the dining room to speak to the guests and potential investors and was met by a round of applause. Effie was puffed up with love and pride for her cousin. Dolly wiped a tear from her eye and Effie turned to say something to Liv but found Sheena next to her instead. The events of earlier came rushing back and threatened to overwhelm her. Liv had gone and, despite everything, she missed her.

'Are you okay, Hen?' asked Sheena.

'Head rush,' lied Effie.

'You can probably duck out and have a sit-down. There'll only be the clearing away to do now.'

'Okay, thanks. I'll come back for that,' said Effie and she slipped from the room.

In the library she checked her phone. Another desperate message from John. She bit her lip. She had a decision to make.

About ten minutes later Fraser put his head around the door. 'Here you are.'

Effie stood up. 'Do you need me to help tidy up?' she asked.

'Nah, I think the guests are going to linger a while longer. That's positive right?' He looked unsure.

'I think so. You did brilliantly tonight. If you don't find investors then they're nincompoops.'

Fraser chuckled. 'I agree. Everything okay?'

Effie flopped back down on the window seat. 'Not really.'

'Is it Liv?'

'It's John.'

'You know that's not his real name, right?'

Tears stung Effie's eyes and she had to take a moment to control them before she could speak. 'I do but I don't want to believe it. Is that crazy?'

'Noooo,' said Fraser, sitting down next to her. 'Maybe a little,' he added as he gave her a nudge. 'It's not your fault. This is this person's job. This is what they do. They defraud people in the worst way possible.'

'It's horrible. John asked me for money again.' She looked sheepishly at him.

'Please tell me you didn't send him any.'

'I was tempted but I didn't. He keeps messaging.'

'Have you not deleted and blocked him?'

Effie stared down at her phone but didn't answer. She wasn't a good liar and Fraser had known her her whole life so it was pointless even trying to hoodwink him. 'Effie?' he prompted.

She looked up. 'Do I have to?'

'You must or they'll just keep badgering you. I can do it if you'd rather.' He held out his hand.

'No, it's okay.' She unlocked her phone, and blocked John's number and email.

'Well done.' Fraser patted her arm. 'Feel better?'

'Not really. Now I feel awful for what I said to Liv. And there's no way to put that right because she's gone.' She looked at Fraser.

He rubbed a hand over his chin. 'Sometimes you just have to let people go.'

'Even the good ones like Liv?'

He scratched his head. 'I don't know with Liv. I know what your dad would have said.'

Effie chuckled. 'That bird's a rocket; she's tuned to the moon,' she said mimicking her father's strong Scottish accent. 'But I liked that about her.'

'I suppose.' He didn't sound convinced. 'She's about as stable as Bitcoin. One minute she was batshit crazy and doing my nut in and the next…'

'She is one of a kind,' said Effie. 'Look how she stepped up to help – and I know I didn't behave well but she was trying to protect me from John. She has a good heart. We need people like that in our lives. Don't we?'

'I suppose we do,' he said.

*

Liv found herself sitting in a tiny room at a small police station with only a plastic cup of water for company. She'd never been in trouble before and she didn't like it. Well, nothing serious anyway: scrumping apples, late return of library books and the one time she was evicted from McDonald's for accidentally chucking a chicken nugget at someone's baby.

Now she'd somehow found herself arrested and detained at a police station. She'd almost laughed when Robbie had arrested her, but it had quickly become apparent that it was no joke. She'd pleaded her innocence but Robbie was having none of it. He'd locked up her car and taken her to the police station. He'd had to rush off before she was checked in so he'd left her with an unsmiling bald policeman who had thankfully removed the handcuffs, taken all her details and got her a cup of water. Now she was sitting in a featureless room feeling like she was in a TV cop drama.

Robbie had said that if she'd done nothing wrong then she had nothing to worry about, but as a police officer he had to investigate thoroughly. Her brain started to escalate the situation. What if nobody believed her? What if she'd been framed? Did that mean a trial and a criminal record? The door opened and she jumped. Immediately she feared that made her look guilty.

'Miss Bingham, I'm Sergeant Robertson. I'd like to ask you a few questions.'

She swallowed hard. This was scary. What if she got them wrong? She really didn't want to spend Christmas in a cell. Did you even get a Christmas dinner? And if it was would it be haggis?

'Okay, but can I just say I didn't do it. The graffiti. It wasn't me.'

'Do you know who did do it?' he asked.

'No. Can I go now?' She stood up and the sergeant motioned for her to retake her seat.

'Just a few more questions.'

She picked up her water with a shaking hand. They both looked at the water jiggling inside and she put it down again. Why did she feel like she was a criminal?

'Why do you have a spray can in your car?' he asked.

'It's not my car. It belongs to my sister – Charlotte. She always buys one to match the car because she's an obsessive forward planner and she likes to be prepared for everything. So if she dings it she can fix it straight away.' The words tumbled out like toffees out from a Quality Street tin. She realised she'd be rubbish under interrogation.

'And what colour is the spray paint in the can that Police Officer Williams retrieved from the car?'

'It's black. But it won't be called black. It's a BMW so it's probably called dingy midnight charcoal or something stupid.' She smiled but Officer Robertson didn't smile back. 'It's black,' she added just to be clear.

Sergeant Robertson stared at her and her pulse picked up. Had she said something wrong? At last he spoke. 'You're free to go.'

The relief was huge. 'Oh thank heavens for that.' It was a rush of joy like she'd never experienced before, almost worth the stress of being interviewed but not quite. She got up and the sergeant showed her to the front desk where she had to sign a form to get her car keys and spray paint back.

'Thanks and merry Christmas,' she said suddenly feeling like Scrooge on Christmas morning now that life was as it should be.

The desk sergeant walked away. Liv turned around to be met by a very empty police station. 'Um, excuse me. Is someone taking me home. Not all the way home because that's in Blackburn but back to my car?'

'It's not a taxi rank; it's a police station,' said the desk sergeant. Not exactly helpful.

'Can you direct me to a taxi rank?'

'It's in town. About two and a half miles that way.' Again no help at all.

'How do I get back to my car?'

'Call someone to get you.' He shook his head like this was a very stupid question.

'Can't Robbie take me. It's his fault I'm here.'

'PC Williams was called to an RTA.'

'Fair enough. That's definitely more important.' She realised her phone was in her bag, which was in the boot of the car. 'I've not got my mobile.' Maybe she was going to be stranded there. 'Can I use your phone please?'

He huffed and puffed before passing her a handset. 'Thanks. Um sorry to bother you again but could you look up a phone number for me please? It's the Lochy House Hotel. Actually it's the restaurant bit if that has a different number.' There was lots of tutting as he took the handset back, looked in his computer, tapped a number into the phone and grumpily gave it back to Liv. 'Thanks – you're very kind. Definitely on Santa's nice list,' she said with her sweetest smile. There was an awkward pause as the phone rang out and the police officer stared at her. At last it was answered. She mouthed what was happening and he shook his head slowly.

'Good evening, Bonnie Scott's. How may I help you?'

Liv wished she had taken a moment to plan out what she was going to say but then why change a habit of a lifetime? 'Effie, thank heavens it's you.'

'Who is this?'

'It's Liv. Please don't put the phone down.' Liv crossed her fingers. 'I'm really sorry about the whole John thing. I shouldn't have interfered.'

There was an unnervingly long pause. 'It's okay. Fraser agrees with you. He thinks John is a fraud. I think Janet might have cursed me. A couple of months back I was in the woods and I heard—'

'Sorry to interrupt you, Effie, but this is kind of urgent. I got arrested and I'm—'

Effie gasped. 'What did you do?'

'I was done for cattle rustling.'

'Really?'

'No! Robbie arrested me on false pretences and now I'm stranded in a police station in…' It dawned on her that she had no idea where she was. She put her hand over the receiver and whispered to the bored-looking police officer. 'Where am I?'

'Planet earth,' he replied.

'You should do stand-up. You know if you ever stop loving this job as much as you clearly do now.' She gave him a cheesy grin. 'Location, please.'

He shook his head at her. 'Fort William.'

'Thank you so much.' She removed her hand from the receiver. 'I'm at Fort William police station and I need a lift back to my car.'

'That's good because Robbie works there. He'll bring you back.'

Why were things so much harder than they needed to be. 'He's been called to an accident.' The officer cleared his throat and tapped his watch. 'I really need someone to come and get me. I don't know anyone else around here. Sorry.'

'Okay. Um, I'll sort something out.'

'Great, when do you think they'll get here?' But as she

was asking the question she heard an ominous click. 'Effie, are you still there?' There was no answer.

Liv handed the phone back to the police officer. 'I love what you've done with your hair,' she told him as she smoothed a hand over her own head. 'So shiny.' He shook his head at her. 'I'll wait over here.' She pointed at two sad-looking chairs.

'No. I'm already late locking up.'

'Police stations don't close do they?'

'This one does. I'm sorry but you'll have to wait outside,' he said with a shrug.

Outside it was cold and dark. This wasn't funny.

'You okay?' asked the officer as he locked up. Apparently having a brief moment of concern.

'Absolutely fine. Thanks for asking.' She grinned at him whilst trying to hide her chattering teeth.

'Goodnight then,' he said pulling up his coat hood and striding off.

Time ticked by. She had no idea how long she was standing there but it felt like forever. In reality it was probably only about forty minutes. She had visions of Effie appearing through the darkness riding Ginger. But would Effie be able to venture that far given her issues? Liv wrapped her arms around herself and hugged her coat in an attempt to keep warm. Could she trust Effie to sort something out? Or was hypothermia going to set in and she'd be like a human ice pop?

31

When a white van came into sight Liv had a sinking feeling she knew who would be driving it, and when it pulled up next to her she was right. A weight hit the bottom of her stomach like a frozen haggis as Fraser buzzed down the window. 'Get in,' he said and she was too cold to do anything else. She crunched her way along the icy pavement and got in. Inside the van was quite small and Fraser was a bear of a man so she was very aware of how close together they now were.

She put on her belt and found herself leaning slightly away from him. Thoughts of their earlier conversation made her grimace. Conversation was probably pushing it. She'd called him out for ghosting her and he'd denied it. Pretty much nothing about her trip to Scotland had gone to plan. But then had she ever had a plan in the first place? Maybe that was at the root of her problem. They were both silent while he turned the van around. Liv wasn't a fan of silence. 'I've told the police and now I'm telling you that I had absolutely nothing to do with whatever this graffiti is on the hotel sign.'

'They let you go didn't they?'

'Yeah.'

'So it wasn't you.'

She guessed it was a fair logic. 'I'm glad you agree. And thanks for picking me up.'

'It's okay.'

They both stared straight ahead out of the windscreen. It was dark so there wasn't much to see apart from occasional car lights. The snow was thawing a little although there were still great mounds of it on the sides of the roads. There weren't many cars about but then the conditions were still quite iffy and Liv reasoned that normal people would already be in Christmas mode with a large glass of their tipple of choice and their face in a tub of chocolates. The roads were awash with water as they made their way back to Glendormie, and the rhythmic sound of the tyres in the puddles was almost sending her to sleep. She had that horrid sensation of her head dropping forwards a couple of times. She'd need to wake herself up before she drove all the way back to Blackburn. Maybe she'd stop at the first garage and stock up on energy drinks and crisps to keep her going.

Liv had never been so happy to see her sister's car as when Fraser pulled up alongside it. 'Did you want to get a hot drink or something before you set off? I can find some scran for you for the journey.' He shrugged. 'You know, if you like.'

'Scran?' It didn't exactly sound appetising whatever it was.

'Snacks. I was thinking there's some leftovers from the dinner. I can make you a sandwich.'

With everything that had happened she'd almost forgotten it had been Fraser's big night. 'How did it go?' she asked belatedly.

He nodded. 'Good. I think. A couple of people seem serious about meeting up in the new year. But I need a far bigger investment than I first thought now that I'll need premises as well.' They looked at each other and then quickly away.

'I hope that all works out for you. Anyway…' She pointed at the car. 'I'd better go. Thanks for the offer of a snack, but I'll probably stop on the way home.' He didn't say anything. 'Right. Bye then.' Liv reached for the door handle but something stopped her. She turned back and Fraser pulled away slightly. Was he expecting her to take a swipe at him. She knew she probably came across as unpredictable but really? 'Look it's only you and me. There's nobody here to overhear anything. Please tell me straight: was it just me or were there loads of women that you did it to?'

Fraser frowned. 'Did what to exactly?'

'Ghosted. When you ghosted me was I the only one or was it some sort of revenge on English people because of Lizzie?'

'Honestly, Liv, I'm hearing the words but I canny make any sense of them.'

'You're still going to deny that you were ever on that dating app and that we connected. You can't just say,

"Hands up, yeah you got me. I led you on and then I deleted my account."'

He shifted in his seat so he was looking straight at her. 'Do you really believe that I knew you before you came here?'

'Yes! Because you did.'

'Right and what? We went out and then I chucked you?'

'No, it was only on the dating app. We were a match. We messaged for a few weeks and then a few days ago you deleted the account…'

Fraser's eyes were getting wider and wider. 'I deleted my account over a year ago because I didny match with anyone. Callum said it was because I'd used Ginger as my profile picture. I thought it was funny but apparently it's not.'

Either he was an exceptionally good actor or she had to face the fact that Fraser Douglas really didn't seem to know anything about having the account she'd been interacting with. 'You really don't know what I'm going on about do you?'

He waved his hands about. 'Have I not been saying exactly that?'

'You have but quite honestly I didn't believe you. Until now. But it was all of your details and your photo that was on there.'

'Well it wasnay me. Can you show me on the app?'

'No because you del— *Someone* deleted the profile and when that happened I lost all the messages log. And before you ask, no I didn't take a screenshot.' Not that she hadn't thought about it, but it had seemed a bit sad to screenshot someone when it was barely a relationship. Although talking about it now brought back those same feelings. She looked at Fraser. He was a pain in the arse but there was something about him.

'I'm a bit pissed off that someone used my details. I hope that doesn't mean I've been hacked somewhere. I'd best check my bank accounts when I get back.'

'Good idea. We probably need to find out who it was.' Liv was going into Miss Marple mode.

'I doubt we can do anything. And if the account's been deleted that's probably the end of it.' He checked his watch. 'Sorry, I should be getting back as I left everyone else with the tidying up. Have a safe journey home.'

'That's it?'

Fraser threw up his palms. 'What were you expecting? Hell, woman, you accuse me of all sorts, expect me to come out and collect you from the police station and now what? I don't know what you want from me.'

She didn't really know either but it just didn't feel like this was how it was meant to end. 'We kissed,' she blurted out. She wasn't sure where it came from.

Fraser opened his mouth a number of times, making him look like a just-caught trout.

Liv waited but no words materialised. 'Nothing?' she prompted.

'I don't know what you want me to say.'

'Forget it,' said Liv and she got out of the van, slammed the door closed and got straight in the car.

The BMW was literally freezing: the inside of the screen had ice on it. She needed to put on an extra jumper until she got the heater going. But she needed Fraser to clear off because she didn't want to get out of the car to go to the boot in case that meant she'd have to have another excruciatingly awkward conversation with him. Liv just needed to get away from Glendormie and Fraser as quickly as possible. She put the key in the ignition and turned it. Nothing happened. Had she done that wrong? She pulled the key out and peered around the side of the steering wheel. There was only one place to stick it so she tried again. Nothing. 'Shit.' She glanced over at the van and saw that Fraser was leaning forward and watching her. She waved at him. He buzzed down the passenger window and indicated for her to do the same. 'Oh great,' she muttered to herself. The window was too iced up so she opened the door.

'Everything okay?' he asked.

'Yeah. All fine and dandy.' Dandy? Who the hell said dandy? Nobody in this century, that was for certain.

'You sure?' Fraser seemed suspicious.

'Yes. Perfect. Just working out what tunes I'm going to listen to and then I'll be off. You can go. I'm fine.'

He paused and then shrugged. 'If you say so.'

'I absolutely do.' She just wanted him to leave.

'Bye then,' he said.

'Bye,' replied Liv and she closed the door. The van pulled slowly away and she let out a sigh of relief. 'Right, car, listen to me. I don't know what you're playing at but it's not funny. You have a new tyre that cost me a week's wages and you've had a rest sat here for five days and now it's time to go home. Ready? One, two, three.' She turned the key but nothing happened. She frantically tried it over and over again but it was completely dead. 'What am I meant to do now?' She gave a shiver. She was getting cold again, not that she was sure that she'd fully defrosted from standing outside the police station. 'Right, last chance.' Maybe it would be like it was in the films when the escaped dinosaur was bearing down on them and the car wouldn't start, but in the last moment it burst into life.

She took a breath and turned the key. Still nothing. That was when she noticed a shadow out of the window and she froze, staring straight ahead. Was it a person or Janet come for her soul? That was all she needed to finish things off. A tap on the window made her jump and squeal at the same time.

Fraser's face appeared. 'It won't start, will it?' She shook her head. 'We can get someone out to look at it first thing tomorrow but for now you'd best come back to Lochy House,' he said opening the car door.

For a moment she considered her options. There was only one she could think of, which was for her to sleep in the car, but her chattering teeth reminded her that there was no heat in the thing. She was out of options. She'd have to swallow her pride and accept Fraser's offer. 'Thanks,' she mumbled. Liv got out as he held the door open for her, and she went to the boot to retrieve her bag to find a smiling Plastic Stan looking up at her. She didn't know if the mechanic would need to go in the boot but she really didn't need any further humiliation, so she hastily folded up Stan who expelled a bit of air but otherwise didn't complain as she rammed him in her bag. She shut the boot, locked the car and got in the van.

'It's all been a bit shit, hasn't it?' said Fraser.

'I think that's a fair summary,' she said putting on her seatbelt.

As they trundled along the track the sign came into view and for the first time Liv saw the graffiti scrawled across it. In large spray letters that almost obliterated the Bonnie Scott's logo it read: *The food's shite. Avoid like the.*

At least it explained Robbie's very cryptic questioning earlier. 'That's not good and obviously not true,' said Liv. 'Did they get interrupted? Or is it like a competition? Finish the sentence and send answers on a postcard to a PO box.' Fraser glared and she stopped talking.

'Look over your shoulder now,' he said as they passed the sign.

Liv checked behind her and on the back of the sign was scrawled the word 'plague'. 'I'm guessing they're not professional graffiti artists then. I wonder who did it.'

'I've got a couple of ideas,' he said, his jaw tensing up. Maybe there were still a couple of mysteries that needed solving at Lochy House Hotel.

32

Fraser pulled the van up outside the front door. They both sat there with the engine running. Was he going to say something profound? She waited. 'Are you getting out?' he asked.

'I was waiting for you to switch it off, in case you drove off with me with one leg out of the car.'

He tilted his head in question. 'I was going to put this around the back in the cart shed in case the temperature drops again. That way it won't be as iced up.'

'Right. Good idea. I'll get out then.' Liv escaped from the van and watched it trundle off. This was all very awkward and a bit confusing. How did she feel about him now she was pretty sure he hadn't ghosted her? There was definitely something but it was hard to know if it was tainted by the fake Fraser. Maybe the best thing would be for her to forget all the Frasers.

She plodded up the steps and went inside. A waft of warmth and some now familiar smells greeted her. 'Hello!'

she called. There was no reply. That was odd. Liv walked through the hallway, passed the abandoned reception desk and pushed open the kitchen door. There was nobody around. She checked the dining room and the library – not a soul. Had everyone gone to bed? She hoped Fraser came back quickly because even an awkward silence with him was better than being in the hotel alone.

That was when she heard it. A tapping noise. Liv went rigid. This was not good. She wanted to dash outside to Fraser but she wasn't even sure if she'd seen a cart shed, so she didn't know which way to head. And if she found him she'd look like a twerp for having run to him. No, she needed to think logically and face her fears. Because facing up to things was what this trip was about. Although she'd not considered that it might include actual ghosts.

'Hello?' Her voice was a little wobbly. That wouldn't do. There was nothing to be scared of. 'Is this a joke?' She spun around expecting someone to jump out. 'Effie? If you're trying to scare me, it's not working.' She held her chin high. Silence. She listened hard and there was the tap again. Liv swallowed. She needed to find out what was making that noise. It had probably been doing it all the time she'd been at the hotel; she'd just not noticed before. Liv inched her way down the hallway, following the sound. She reached the reception desk and peered over the top. Nobody there. She heard the noise again and it was definitely a little louder, so she was getting closer. It was probably a window that had been left on the catch or a breeze making something rattle. There was bound to be a simple and non-paranormal explanation.

She moved around the reception desk and stood still. Nothing. She looked about her. There was more wood panelling behind reception but there was something that caught her eye. One of the panels had a join in an odd place and there was a tiny gap. She followed the line of the gap with her eyes. Was that a door hidden in the panelling? She was quite excited by her discovery. As a child she had read countless mystery books and had dreamed of finding secret doors and passageways. Although now she was presented with one she was thinking that maybe they didn't always lead to treasure, and she was fearful of what was on the other side of the secret door.

As she reached for the panel, the tap went again making Liv jump. It was definitely coming from the other side of the door. But most ghostly-sounding noises were actually plumbing and in a place as old and decrepit as Lochy House Hotel it was most likely the latter. But then what if it was Janet? She shook her head. That was ridiculous. Janet was a figment of Effie's imagination. Granted it was a vibrant one and based on local legend but most definitely enhanced by Effie's imagination. It was plumbing, plain and simple. This was most likely the boiler cupboard.

Liv ran her fingers over the edge of the rogue panel. The door was expertly disguised. How did it open? Liv felt around until she noticed a slightly lighter patch on one side where the colour looked faded. She pressed it and the secret door opened. Liv held her breath as she peered inside. There was nothing but darkness.

Liv pulled out her phone to use as a torch as a wizened old face loomed out of the darkness towards her. 'Shit!' said Liv stumbling backwards in her haste to get away.

'Hello, lovey,' said Winnie. 'Thank goodness for that. I thought I was sealed up forever like an Egyptian mummy.'

'Why didn't you say something?' asked Liv.

'Sorry? Battery in my hearing aid has gone. Anyway, thanks for coming to my rescue. Have you seen Donald? He's meant to be taking me home.' Winnie slowly shuffled out.

'Winnie, can you hear me if I shout?' tried Liv.

'Ooh did you say something?' she replied as she stopped to fiddle with her hearing aid.

'Yes. Why were you in there?'

'I was being nosy. I noticed the panel had a seam in it and when I looked closer I could see it was a hidden door. But when I got inside it was pitch-black. I felt around for a light and thought I'd found a pull chord but that must have been connected to the door, because it clicked shut behind me. I've lived to tell the tale and wait when the folks at Little Loch Tearooms hear this one.'

'I'm glad you're okay,' said Liv loudly.

'Oh, I'm fine. Nothing a daily dose of David Tennant in a kilt can't solve.' She cackled a laugh as she made her way slowly up the hall. She paused. 'Thanks for coming to my rescue, Liv. What exactly is Liv short for?'

'It's Olivia,' said Liv.

'No, can't hear a thing,' said Winnie. 'Cheerio.'

Liv let out the longest sigh. Her pulse was racing. It's okay, she told herself. It wasn't a ghost; there was a perfectly rational explanation. Although an old lady trapped behind a secret door hadn't been the straightforward explanation she'd been expecting. Liv switched on her torch and opened the door fully, revealing a bigger space than she'd been expecting and definitely a lot more cobwebs than she was comfortable with. She stepped inside.

'Just an empty cupboard. That's all it is,' she whispered to herself. That was when a hand gripped her shoulder. 'Arghhhhhh!' screamed Liv, spinning around ready to defend herself.

Effie wrapped her in a tight hug. 'You came back!'

'Bloody hell, Effie. You scared the life out of me.' Her pulse was off the scale.

'Why?' said Effie letting her go.

'Because...' Liv pointed into the darkness. 'I was concentrating on what is in here.'

'It's just an old cupboard. I used to play in here when I was little until I got stuck in there for five hours and peed my pants,' she whispered the last part and grimaced. 'I wasn't allowed in here after that.'

That put paid to any romantic notion Liv had of finding treasure. Liv scanned the space with her torch. It was empty apart from dust, cobwebs and an old box of papers.

Liv picked up a dusty document off the top of the box. It was addressed to Effie.

'Ooh this looks interesting,' she said.

'Hey, what are you doing in there? That box is private,' said Fraser, irritation heavy on his words.

'Don't start on me. I was only looking,' said Liv, although she was aware it was a bit snoopy but the owner of the letter was standing next to her.

Fraser stomped over, snatched the letter from her and stepped inside the cupboard to return it to the box.

'I hate you fighting with each other. Will you two just sort things out already?!' said Effie, her voice strident.

'But he was the one having a go at me,' said Liv, but at the same time Fraser was speaking over her saying something about wild accusations. They kept talking, their voices rising and becoming more and more heated until Effie gave Liv a shove, making her lurch towards Fraser and drop her phone.

'Hey!' he complained.

'It wasn't me!' Liv bent down to get her phone and was about to ask Effie what she was playing at when she pushed her again but harder. Liv toppled forward and had no option but to push Fraser backwards or she was going to end up in his arms. They were falling inside the cupboard. One more big push and Liv was up against Fraser's chest as the door panel closed behind them, plunging them into darkness.

'What the hell!' Liv was hopping mad. But she was also disorientated thanks to the dark. 'Effie!' she yelled.

Fraser cleared his throat. 'Do you think you could stop yelling in my face?'

'Oh sorry.' She realised she also had her hands pressed against his chest. She tried to step away but the door was right behind her. 'Can you back up? Because I've got nowhere to go.'

'And I've got loads of room?'

'Yeah actually you have. It's quite a big cupboard. Heaven knows what it was used for?' An image of Janet swam into her mind and she shuddered.

'It's an early example of an escape room. Remember this place was built in the seventeenth century when things were still pretty volatile. When the clans were fighting, things were unpredictable and with the English a constant threat, the owners had a secret room added that they could escape to if the worst happened.'

'Thank you for the history lesson. Now can you step backwards?'

There was shuffling and Fraser moved away from her and she felt she could breathe a little more normally. She felt another shudder like icy fingers creeping up her spine. 'When you say *if* the worst happened…'

'I don't think it was ever used, which I suppose is a good thing.' His voice had almost a melody to it, now it was all she had to focus on.

'Definitely. I'd not want to be shut in here for long. Talking of which how do we get out exactly?'

'Ideally we need Effie to open it from the other side,' he said. There was a pause. 'Effie? I know you're there and listening.'

There was a huffing sound. 'I'm not letting you out until you make up,' said Effie from outside.

'We already have,' said Fraser.

'Err, did I miss that?' asked Liv.

Fraser breathed out hard, ruffling his hair. She could imagine his exasperated expression. 'I just got you from the police station didn't I?'

'You did and I've said thank you for that. But I still think you're not being honest about everything.'

'See you've not made up,' said Effie from the other side of the door. 'I just want us all to be friends.'

'Effie, please can we talk about this?' asked Fraser moving forward and bumping into Liv.

'Hey, mind out.'

'Can you switch on your torch phone?' he asked.

'Nope, it's on the floor on the other side of the door.'

'Is it? I thought you kicked it in here.'

They both crouched down at the same time and banged heads. 'Bloody hell!' said Liv. 'I'd be seeing stars if I could see anything right now.'

'Sorry,' said Fraser. 'Start feeling around.'

'I am!'

'Don't get crabbit with me. It's Effie who's shut us in here.'

'Good point. Effie!' called Liv. There was no response. 'She's gone hasn't she?'

'I think so,' said Fraser with a deep sigh.

33

Effie was in the kitchen having a camomile and coconut tea to calm herself. Thankfully the banging and shouting from the cupboard had stopped. It had seemed like a good idea to put Liv and Fraser inside when they had all been standing near the cupboard. She wanted Fraser and Liv to make up because if they didn't she'd never see Liv again and she really liked her. The back porch door opened and in came Robbie, looking all official and serious.

'Hey, everything okay?' asked Effie. 'I heard you'd been called to a nasty accident.'

'You can only have received that information from Liv. Has she been released on bail?'

'No, she's completely innocent,' said Effie happily.

Robbie frowned hard. 'But I found the spray paint in her car.'

Effie shrugged. 'I don't believe Liv would do something like that.'

'Hmm.' Robbie didn't sound so sure.

'Did you want a drink?' she asked.

'I am in need of a large hot chocolate,' he said, leaning on the counter opposite her.

'Was the accident horrible?' she asked, unsure whether she really wanted to know any details as her mind found it easy to paint vivid pictures.

'Absolute carnage,' he said shaking his head and Effie feared the worst. 'Low bridge, large lorry, driver not paying attention and hundreds of adult toys and lingerie all over the road.'

That wasn't exactly what she'd pictured when he'd said carnage. 'But nobody hurt?'

'Thankfully not but it took a lot of sorting out, let me tell you.' Robbie got a mug out of the cupboard.

'I'm sure it did.' Effie tried not to giggle at the image in her mind. *Poor Robbie*, she thought as she passed him the cocoa and a spoon.

'Did the evening go to plan?' he asked, as he made his hot chocolate.

Effie had a think about all that had happened. 'Not entirely.'

'Poor Fraser – at least he tried,' he said.

'That bit was fine. It's the other stuff.'

Robbie looked interested. 'Do you want to share? Off the record of course,' he said, sitting down and hugging his mug.

She paused for a second. She did trust Robbie but she knew how quick people were to judge. 'I thought I'd met a decent man. One of the good guys, but he turned out to be a scammer and now I feel like a numpty. But I'm hoping to put a curse on him. Nothing deadly – just warts, scabies or athletes foot, that sort of thing.'

'Have you got his details? Because we can prosecute if there's any wrongdoing.'

She waved at him to stop. 'You said off the record. And he's not committed a crime exactly. He just said lots of nice things and like a fool I believed him. But thanks to Liv I didn't hand over any cash.' She rubbed at the corner of her eye where a tear was threatening to fall.

'There are some terrible people out there. I know. In my line of work you see the worst of society. I'm sorry this happened, but you mustn't blame yourself. Okay?'

She had been beating herself up but Robbie was right – she needed to stop. 'I'll try.'

'You need to do something that makes you happy, to take your mind off it,' he suggested. 'Are you still ghost hunting?'

'It's not exactly ghost hunting.' He gave her a questioning look. 'It's more trying to connect with the spirit world.'

'Most people are terrified of that.'

'But they've not lost someone,' said Effie. 'It's different for me because I've lost a loved one.'

Robbie seemed hesitant. 'Are you expecting to see their ghost?'

Effie sighed heavily. 'Wouldn't that be the loveliest thing? To see my dad again. Even if it was only for a moment. To see his face, his smile and maybe even hear his voice.' She saw Robbie's expression. 'No, I don't expect to see his ghost but if I saw someone else's ghost that would be cool too. Sort of proof that they live on somewhere, somehow.'

Robbie nodded. 'I see what you mean. But I always thought ghosts were troubled souls, in which case it's a good thing that your dad's not here. It means he's at rest.'

'I'd not really thought about it like that. I was a bit too caught up in what I wanted. But I definitely want him to be at peace.'

'I'm sure he is,' said Robbie. They sat in silence for a while. Each time they caught the other's eye they smiled. It was a comfortable, easy silence and for once Effie's mind wasn't too noisy.

'Thank you,' she said and she meant it.

Although she could hear muffled shouts. Were they in her mind? Robbie began frowning. 'Can you hear—'

'Whoops!' said Effie, hopping off the stool. 'I need to let Fraser and Liv out of the cupboard.'

Robbie opened his mouth but didn't reply.

*

Liv was fed up of crawling around the floor. Goodness only knew what dirt and grime she was getting on her clothes. She also was quite disorientated as it was so dark. She sat down where she was and reached out with her hands. Her fingertips touched something.

'Ow!' yelped Fraser.

'I'm sorry,' said Liv, biting her lip. 'Did I hurt you?'

'No, only kidding,' said Fraser.

'You're hilarious,' she said shaking her head, although there was no point because he couldn't see her. 'I guess Effie is right that we should stop arguing.'

'I'm not arguing,' he said.

'Yes, you are!' There was silence and then a snort of

laughter. 'Shall we agree we won't keep having a go at each other?'

'I will but can you do that because you seem quite fixed on me having ghosted you, which I haven't.' He said the last bit fast.

'Okay but someone did. I am happy to accept that it wasn't you.' She was okay about that because if he really hadn't done it then the Fraser she'd got to know was actually all right – a bit grumpy but then she had to acknowledge that she'd triggered some of that grumpiness. And it was this Fraser who had been kind to her, kissed her under the mistletoe and gave her goosebumps at his touch. He was also fit which was an added bonus.

'You sure?' he asked.

'Yeah I am. Thing is, if it wasn't you then who was it?'

'I don't know. Could be anyone. It could be someone like John.'

'But he didn't ask me for money. I don't understand what they'd get out of building a relationship with me only to ghost me. Makes no sense.'

'I guess we'll never know.'

'But don't you *want* to know who it was?' It was already eating away at Liv like she'd rechannelled her hurt and anger on to the person behind the fake profile.

'I guess. But I don't know how to go about that. And I've got quite a lot of other stuff on my mind right now,' he said.

'Like where your dad is?' There was a long pause and Liv feared she'd overstepped a mark.

She heard him take a deep breath. 'I know roughly where he is.'

Liv heard shuffling. Was he sitting down or standing up?

She couldn't tell. Then he stepped on her foot. 'Argh!' She automatically pulled it free.

'Whoa!' he yelled.

That was all she heard before he fell against her and pinned her to the wall. 'Ow! What are you doing?'

'You tripped me up!' he complained as he tried to right himself.

'Do not put your hands there,' she said into the darkness. He was half leaning on her. Her heart was thumping hard in her chest – but that was just the shock of a great klutz of a man falling on her, right? She got a waft of cologne mixed with something herby – a not altogether unpleasant smell.

'Sorry. I honestly can't see a thing. Is that your shoulder?'

His hand was resting on her shoulder and slightly touching her neck. She shuddered at the contact. It was a very different sort of shudder to the one she'd felt earlier. 'Yep,' she confirmed in a small, husky voice.

He adjusted his position and she could feel his breath on her cheek. If she moved her head slightly their lips would touch. 'Are you okay?' he asked, his voice soft and soothing.

Her heart continued to thump. 'I think so. You?'

'I'm good,' he said against her cheek.

Liv turned her head slightly and his beard grazed her lip. This was really quite erotic. 'Fraser?'

'Yeah?'

'Do you think there's any chance, despite everything, that we could—'

'I am soooooo sorry,' said Effie, opening the door and making Liv fall backwards out of the cupboard with Fraser virtually on top of her.

'Ah,' yelped Liv.

'You made up,' said Effie clapping her hands together. 'I wasn't expecting you to be getting it on in there. But yay! Whatever works for you. Shall I shut the door again?' she asked whacking Liv in the head as she tried to hastily close it.

'No!' they both said together.

'And we weren't getting it on...' said Liv scrambling backwards as her eyes adjusted to the light.

'Looks that way to me,' said Effie putting her hands on her hips.

'I sort of fell on top of her,' said Fraser, looking embarrassed.

'But you're friends now?' asked Effie, looking apprehensively between them both.

'Fine. We're fine. Right?' Liv looked Fraser square in the eye.

He nodded. 'Yeah we're good.'

34

Liv was about to head upstairs to bed when Dolly and Jock'O wheeled in front of her. Liv readied herself for an attack.

'Can I speak with you?' asked Dolly.

'Dolly, you can but I think it's probably best for everyone and Scottish and English relations if maybe I just go to bed, and tomorrow I'll be out of your hair and we can all go back to our lives. What do you say?' Liv looked hopefully at the older woman.

'I think it's better to speak out,' said Dolly.

Liv had feared that might be the case but didn't interrupt.

'I don't know what you came here to achieve and I certainly don't understand the ghost hunting aspect of it.'

Liv decided it was best to let that go than try to explain what ghosting was.

Dolly continued. 'But I do know you are a canny lassie with an infectious energy and you have brought out the best and the worst in my grandchildren. I've not seen Effie this engaged for such a long time. She retreated into her shell after her father's untimely death and has been closer to the dead than the living, but with you I've seen glimpses of the old Effie. Maybe there's a chance that she can get over this and eventually live out her dreams of travelling. Perhaps a visit to Blackburn might be a start?' Dolly tilted her head forward.

'Err.' Liv was a little taken aback at Dolly's words. 'Thank you, I think. You know Effie is a truly lovely person. She'd be welcome at mine anytime. It's been a long and weird day, so if that's all, I'll say goodnight.' Liv went to go past Dolly and her scooter but Dolly didn't move and Jock'O barked as if to tell Liv to stay where she was.

'There was one other thing,' said Dolly.

Oh great, here we go, thought Liv. 'What was that?' she asked, emphasising a yawn in the hope that Dolly would keep it short. It had been an emotional few days and she really was ready for her bed.

'You've stirred something in Fraser,' said Dolly. Liv couldn't help her eyebrows rising. 'Not in a sexual way,' added Dolly quickly.

'Good, that's good,' said Liv although on one hand she had to admit she was a little disappointed but on the other she did not want to have any level of discussion about Fraser's arousal with his grandmother.

'Fraser is a deep thinker. But when he thinks, he shuts others out. He broods. But with you he gets cross.'

'Yeah, I noticed that,' said Liv.

'But it's a good thing. He tends to bottle things up but not with you. I mean you fight far too much to be healthy, but I am grateful for you pressing his buttons, so to speak.'

'Right.' Liv wasn't sure what to say. 'You're welcome?'

'And my last point,' began Dolly.

Thank heavens for that, thought Liv.

'Maybe rethink rushing off in the morning. It would be better for my grandchildren if the last interaction with you was a positive one.'

'Okay. Like what exactly?' asked Liv.

Dolly set off down the hallway. 'I didn't have anything specific in mind. It was just an idea. You'll have to figure the details out for yourself. Goodnight,' said Dolly, leaving Liv standing at the bottom of the stairs bewildered and wide awake.

The next morning Liv was up bright and early. Partly because she knew she had to be up and ready for the mechanic, but mainly because Dolly's words had got her thinking and trying to figure out what she could do for the people of Lochy House Hotel so that she was remembered positively. Seeing as everyone had taken her in, she felt doing a little something in return would be nice. Liv fired off an email to an old friend who was a complete whizz when it came to computers and who had got her out of sticky situations with lost documents a number of times. He was quick to respond and excited about taking on the challenge that Liv had set him. One down. The others would need a bit more thought. She was getting herself a cuppa and some toast when the doorbell sounded. She took a slug of slightly too hot tea and grabbed her toast and dashed to the front door.

'Morning. You Olivia with the BMW?' asked a jolly man in a Rangers bobble hat.

'That's me.'

'Let's take a look then and we'll have you on the road in no time,' he said happily.

It turned out his optimism was misplaced because ten minutes later he sucked his teeth and declared that the battery was deid. Some phoning around established that the nearest one that would fit this particular model was at a garage near Inverness.

'Is that far?' asked Liv.

'About an hour and a quarter.'

'That's just one way is it?' asked Liv.

'I'm afraid so.'

She wasn't going to be getting away anytime soon. But perhaps this was the opportunity she needed to do as Dolly had suggested. 'Are there any shops on the way?'

'Erm, what like ladies' shops?' He seemed flustered at the prospect.

'Not exactly. I need to buy some last-minute gifts.'

He grimaced. 'There's a DIY store and a boat specialist.'

Maybe she could work with those. 'Okay, any chance we could call in at those on the way?'

'We?' He jerked his head like a seagull waiting for a chip to be thrown.

'Yes, I was hoping you'd take me with you. Please?'

'As long as you don't mind me having my music on.'

'Of course not,' said Liv. But once she was in his van and Nicki Minaj was playing at high volume, she knew it was going to be the longest journey of her life.

Despite the terrible tunes, Liv had a productive morning. She'd dashed in and out of the couple of shops on the way, they'd picked up the car battery and the journey back had given her a chance to take in some more of the stunning scenery. While the mechanic swapped over the batteries, Liv's plan was to get to work on the hotel sign with some rubbing alcohol she'd bought at the DIY store. She walked down to the hotel entrance and was taken aback to find someone was already scrubbing at the sign with a foamy brush. That was a bit annoying. She'd not banked on Fraser paying someone to clean off the graffiti.

'Hello!' she called and the man spun around, looking startled.

'I can explain,' he said, holding up one palm and a foam dripping brush in the other.

Liv's spider sense was piqued. 'You'd better explain and quick before I report you,' said Liv, trying hard to look like someone of authority.

The man was a similar age to her with light hair and a kind face with dark circles around tired eyes. 'I'm really sorry. I don't know what came over me. I was angry and I had a few drinks and then…' He looked back at the words scrawled across the sign.

'Name?' asked Liv.

He paused and swallowed. 'Are you some sort of undercover cop?'

'Name?' she asked more forcefully.

'Callum Stewart. When I said I could explain, I'm not sure I can. It was just a daft drunken revenge, a lashing-out thing. But I'm trying to put it right now.' He waved the foam-laden brush and splattered himself with water.

Callum. That name rang a bell. 'Are you a friend of Fraser Douglas?'

'I used to be.' He didn't seem confident about that.

A few things clicked into place. 'You copped off with Lizzie!' She did a gasp that was worthy of Effie, making Callum recoil slightly. 'You did this. You're the shite graffiti artist!'

Callum was giving her a strange look. 'You're not an undercover cop. Who are you?'

She was about to tell him and then had a thought. If this was the graffiti artist was he also the ghosting fake Fraser? 'I'm Olivia Bingham.' She watched him very closely. There wasn't even a hint of recollection. 'I've been staying and helping out at the hotel.' She held up the bottle she was carrying. 'I got this to clean the graffiti off the sign. Want a hand?'

He was a little hesitant but then shrugged. 'Yeah, why not? Thanks.'

It was hard work but the spray paint did start to disappear. It was also a good opportunity to get a bit more information.

'I hear you and Lizzie split up. Sorry about that.'

'Thanks.'

Liv had been hoping for a bit more. 'Can you explain something to me? You and Lizzie were doing the dirty behind Fraser's back and then you nicked his idea and set up a rival restaurant. But you were angry enough with *him* to deface his sign. What's that all about?'

Callum sighed. 'I'm not proud of any of that. It's not an excuse, but when Lizzie wants something she's a force of nature.'

'Blimey, she should be a politician.'

'She'd be great at that,' agreed Callum.

'So why the graffiti?' asked Liv.

'Lizzie and I had a massive row about her poaching all Fraser's staff and she said she was going into business with him...' He suddenly seemed aware that he was talking to a stranger. He cleared his throat. 'Anyway, I was hurting and I went out on the lash and somehow I ended up here.'

'With a spray can?' queried Liv.

Callum looked sheepish. 'I called at the petrol station to get more booze and they had them on offer. But when I sobered up I realised Lizzie treated us all badly and I'm ashamed for the part I played in it and for this. I regret it all.' He pointed at the sign. At least that was one mystery solved.

'Sometimes it's a shame we can't turn the clock back,' said Liv, and Callum sagely nodded his agreement.

'Any chance you know anything about an online dating profile for Fraser?' she asked.

Callum pulled his chin into his chest. 'Fraser, online dating? He doesn't seem the type.'

Liv felt a little defensive. 'The profile I'm on about was one Fraser didn't set up. Someone else did and then they pretended to be him.'

'Why?'

'That's the bit I've not worked out yet. Along with who did it. It's a puzzle really. Definitely not your handiwork then?'

'Nothing to do with me.'

'Right, let's get this sign sorted.' After a few more minutes of scrubbing they stood back to admire their handiwork. Not only was it graffiti-free, but it was also clean and gleaming. Hopefully Fraser would be pleased with that.

They were doing a bit of self-congratulation when a white Mercedes drove up the driveway too fast and Callum's head spun after it.

'Hell!' He started running after the white car.

'What is it?' called Liv.

'That's Lizzie!' he called back.

It looked like things were about to kick off again. Liv was contemplating whether she should stick her nose in or not, when Robbie's police car swung into the driveway and headed for the hotel. Liv had no idea what was about to go down but she was keen to find out, so she jogged after them.

35

Effie was a bit worried that Liv had left without saying goodbye because she couldn't find her anywhere, but a quick check in her bedroom revealed that her bag was still there. Seeing it lying on the chair gave her an idea. A few minutes later she snuck back in and slid the envelope into the bag and made sure it was right at the bottom so that Liv wouldn't find it until she was safely back in Blackburn and unpacking. Effie couldn't stop the sigh that escaped. She was going to miss Liv so much.

She made her way downstairs feeling quite pleased with herself but a little sad that Liv wasn't about and would be leaving soon. Dolly trundled up the hallway with Jock'O on her lap already standing up and wagging his tail at the sight of Effie. 'Morning,' she said to Dolly as she gave Jock'O a fuss.

'I've invited Winnie for Christmas so I need to let Fraser know there'll be an extra one for dinner.'

'Hmm good idea.' Effie couldn't focus on Christmas Day just yet.

'What's up?' asked Dolly.

'I can't find Liv but her things are still here so she's not left. At least I don't think she has.'

'The mechanic was coming early to fix the car. She's likely overseeing the repairs.'

'Ooh you could be right. I'll go and see.'

'Hang on.' Dolly jerked the scooter forward, which almost made Jock'O topple off and he lay down quickly. 'You're going to really miss Liv, aren't you?' said Dolly.

'You know sometimes you just click with a person. Like Ant and Dec, Tess and Claudia, Craig and Charlie from The Proclaimers – and that's how I feel about Liv.'

Dolly smiled. 'You know you could always go and visit her.'

Effie came over all sweaty. Her skin prickled and her chest felt heavy. 'I don't know about that.'

'There's always the train. I've a friend in Blackpool so we could travel together.' Dolly reached for Effie's hand. 'Don't go back into your shell when Liv leaves. Build on this.' She nodded and oddly Effie found she was nodding along. 'It was always your dream to travel. And this might be a start. Baby steps.'

She did feel braver when Liv was around. 'Baby steps,' she repeated. 'I guess Blackburn isn't Burkina Faso.'

Dolly gave her an odd look. 'It's a lot closer than that. Will you think about it?'

'I will,' said Effie, trying hard to ignore the slightly faint feeling that was coming over her. Dolly squeezed her hand and with that the front door opened and was flung so hard it banged into the wall.

'Where is he?' yelled an irate Lizzie.

Dolly and Effie went to see what she was shouting about. Callum came in behind her. 'Lizzie, what are you doing here?'

She glanced over her shoulder. 'Callum, you're like a bad smell. Please go away. This does not concern you.'

'There's no need to be rude,' said Callum.

'Talking of bad smells, you've not changed your perfume,' said Dolly scooting into the entrance hall. 'Why are you here, Lizzie?'

'Your grandson is playing games. My money is as good as anyone's!'

An out-of-breath Liv came running into the hotel and waved that she needed a moment to get her breath. 'What did I miss?' she asked.

'Nothing,' said Dolly. 'Lizzie is just leaving.'

'No, I'm not,' said Lizzie before filling her lungs and yelling, 'Fraser!' Everyone recoiled.

'Is there a problem?' asked Robbie, putting on his hat as he came inside and shut the door.

'Good grief, it's PC Plod,' said Lizzie.

'Can you arrest her for calling you that?' asked Effie.

Robbie shook his head.

'Shame,' said Effie.

The thud of footsteps announced Fraser's arrival. He took in the crowded entrance.

'You,' said Lizzie stabbing a finger in his chest. 'You can't refuse an offer. That's against the law in Scotland.'

'I can and I did refuse your offer of a job. I was very clear about that,' said Fraser.

Lizzie looked exasperated. 'Not that. The offer to buy this place.'

'That was you?' asked Effie.

Lizzie preened herself. 'It's what the big corporates do. They buy up the competition.'

'Just lately, women speak but I don't understand them,' said Fraser, looking around for some reassurance.

'I'll keep it simple for... all of you,' said Lizzie. 'I put in a pre-emptive offer on the hotel. But now Fraser's trying to worm out of it, saying it's not going up for sale but I will get my lawyer onto it.'

Fraser held his palms up in surrender. 'I don't know shit about an offer on this place.'

'Liar,' snapped Lizzie.

'He's not a liar,' said Effie. 'We didn't know.'

'Yes, well you not knowing something isn't unusual.' Lizzie rolled her eyes at Effie.

'Hey, let's keep things civil,' said Robbie, stepping forward in Effie's defence.

'Are you all going to play dumb?' Lizzie scanned the room of blank faces.

'Still no idea what you're on about,' said Fraser.

'Fine.' Lizzie threw up her arms. 'You'll be hearing from my solicitor. See if a day in court makes you remember.' She made for the door.

'Actually I did remember something,' said Effie and all eyes turned on her, Lizzie's being the last set, and they looked at her with derision.

'Was it to do with fairies or witches this time, Effie?' asked Lizzie.

'One witch in particular although I didn't know that at the time.'

'Ooh is it Janet?' asked Liv.

'No, I was trying to be sarcastic,' whispered Effie. 'It's Lizzie.'

'Ohhh,' said Liv. 'Carry on.' And she indicated that people were waiting. Dolly gave her a nod of encouragement.

'You see, we found a box in a cupboard and I started to go through it. There were some old paid invoices but there was other stuff including letters from the solicitor after Dad's death.' She took a moment to keep her composure. 'I remember signing a few things but I wasn't in a good place and couldn't look at them, so I shoved it all in the cupboard – until now that is. I read things I should have read a long time ago.'

'Like the Janet and John books?' asked Lizzie, chortling at her own joke.

'I don't know about those but I do know who owns the hotel,' said Effie.

'Fraser is the owner,' said Lizzie although there was doubt on her face.

'No,' said Fraser. 'I never said I owned it. I said I could use it.'

'Who owns it then?' Lizzie was getting more irate by the second.

'My father does,' said Fraser.

'Actually,' said Effie holding up her hand to get their attention. 'He does, but I do too.'

Everyone looked surprised. 'Effie, are you sure?' asked Dolly looking concerned.

'Yep. Dad left it jointly to Uncle Rory and me. Uncle Rory can run it and repurpose it with my approval but if it's to be sold then both of us have to agree. And I don't.'

Lizzie was going a strange colour. 'I'm speaking to my solicitor about this.'

'You should,' said Effie. 'I spoke to mine and he was lovely. I wish I'd done it years ago.'

Lizzie let out a frustrated squeal and marched out of the hotel, bumping Callum as she went.

'Woo-hoo!' yelled Liv starting to clap, and the others joined in. Effie felt her cheeks pink up. Liv wrapped her in a hug. 'You complete blooming star! You stood up to Lizzie.'

Callum stepped forward, looking apprehensive. 'Fraser, can I have a word?'

'I've nothing to say to you.' Fraser glared at Callum.

Liv leaned into Fraser's shoulder. She would have whispered in his ear but he was too tall for that. His shoulder was as close as she could get. 'Maybe hear him out?'

'I'll handle this, thank you,' said Fraser to Liv and she backed off. He turned to Callum. 'You'd better get after your girlfriend.'

'She's not my g—' but Callum didn't get to finish the sentence before Fraser was pointing forcefully at the door.

'Get oot!' Fraser's voice was getting louder.

Callum held up his hands. 'Fraser, I'm sorry about everything. I dunny want to make things worse. You know where I am if you…' Fraser's frown was deepening. Callum shrugged. 'You know where I am.' With that he turned and walked out.

Fraser looked visibly relieved as he turned to Effie. 'Is there anything else I should know?' he asked her.

'Sorry, I was going to tell you but it was all a bit crazy this morning with the solicitor and the estate agent and then Lizzie turned up.'

'That's okay. What are your plans for this old place?' Fraser looked apprehensive.

'I don't know, but I want you to go ahead with the restaurant and maybe if that goes well we could do some refurbishment and reopen the hotel.'

'Can you afford to do that?' asked Fraser.

'Yeah. Dad left a lot of investments. No wonder the solicitor kept writing to me. Whoops.'

'But you didn't put it on the market?' asked Liv looking confused.

'No that was Uncle Rory,' said Effie. 'Apparently he told the estate agent that I would sign whatever he told me to. I guess he thought he could treat me like an idiot too.' She didn't like how that made her feel.

'You're not an idiot,' said Liv giving her arm a squeeze.

'Very astute businesswoman I'd say,' added Robbie. 'Well done.' Everyone's words made her feel better, but Robbie's meant the most.

'Thanks,' said Effie.

'Actually I came over because I wanted to show you something,' said Robbie, guiding her into the library and leaving the others chatting in the entrance. Robbie put a video into the old player. 'Have a seat.' He pointed to the window seat.

Effie wasn't sure what was going on and wondered if maybe she should be doing something else rather than sitting down to watch a film. 'Is it going to take long because—' Effie was interrupted by her father's voice. She turned to watch the TV screen. There was her dad. She felt like time had stopped. 'Dad?' A much younger version of her father was looking at her from the television. His hair was longer than she remembered and he was holding a microphone.

'It was my mam and dad's wedding anniversary,' said Robbie leaning towards her and whispering.

'Uh-huh.' Effie couldn't take her eyes off the screen.

Her dad smiled into the wobbly video camera. 'And this one is for my little girl: Effie,' he said. A sob caught in her throat. She watched as a tiny version of herself, probably only about three or four years old, ran to her daddy who scooped her up into his arms and kissed her cheek. The music started and her dad started to sing 'Wherever I Lay My Hat That's My Home'. Effie couldn't look away. It was like a portal to the past. To hear his voice and see his face meant so much to her.

The song ended and he passed the microphone to Robbie's mother who started talking, but Effie was fixed on the figure of her dad carrying her off to one side. She noticed how her chubby fingers were gripping him tightly and she could almost feel how good that sensation was. That feeling of love and safety. And then he was gone and it was just Robbie's mam talking about cake. Robbie stopped the video.

'Robbie,' said Effie. 'That's amazing.' She tried to wipe away the tears but there were a lot of them. Robbie passed her a tissue, which she gratefully took. 'How did you find this?'

'My mam mentioned about him singing at their anniversary do years ago so I had a dig around and found this. There's a place in Glasgow where they can copy videos onto files, so we'll do that and then you can listen to your dad anywhere and anytime you want to.'

'Robbie, I don't know what to say.'

'You don't need to say anything. It's just nice to be able to help people. Well, you especially. You know I think you're great, don't you?'

Effie blew her nose. She didn't feel great. She felt all puffy-eyed and mixed up. She was happy to see her dad but sad too for what she'd lost. She was lucky to have a friend like Robbie. 'You're great too,' she said.

Robbie looked at the floor, seeming a lot less like his confident policeman self. 'Do you think maybe sometime in the future we could be great *together*?'

It took Effie by surprise but the notion made her a little giddy. 'I think maybe we could.'

36

Liv had paid the mechanic and hastily wrapped the gifts she'd managed to grab at the few shops they'd visited in the only remaining wrapping paper she could find. Vivid pink Christmas trees would not have been her first choice, but it was all they had. She'd brought them inside while everyone else was in the kitchen discussing the Lizzie outburst and Liv had wrapped them in her room. With an armful of presents she pushed the library door open with her bum.

'Can I help you with those?' asked Robbie, already intercepting the two gifts about to tumble from the top of the pile.

'Thanks,' said Liv, heading for the Christmas tree. The fake presents were already under the tree so Liv tried to hide hers behind them, which was hard thanks to the bright pink Christmas trees. She didn't want the embarrassment of the others seeing them and then feeling bad because they hadn't got her something. That wasn't why she was doing it.

Robbie hovered nearby. 'I think I owe you an apology.'

Liv stuck her head out from under the Christmas tree. 'For handcuffing and arresting me?'

'Yep, really sorry. The evidence seemed indisputable. My mistake and an important learn for the future.'

'It's cool. Think about the story I'll have to tell my mum when I get home.' She grinned at him.

'I suppose that's one way of looking at it. Thank you for being so gracious,' he said.

'No worries. At least that's one mystery solved,' she said as she tried to reposition one rather heavy fake present. What had Effie been wrapping up?

'Mystery solved?' Robbie crouched down to join her at tree-base level. 'What do you mean?'

'The hotel sign.'

'I saw that it had been cleaned but I didn't know by whom. Was it the perpetrator come back to undo the crime? Did you see who it was?' Robbie's questions were coming thick and fast.

'Hold on,' said Liv, waving a hand at him. 'I cleaned the sign because I thought it would be a nice thing to do.'

'But you didn't graffiti it – we've established that.' He was peering at her strangely. Far less *Poirot* and more *Dr Who* weeping angel. 'Do you know who did deface the sign?' he asked.

'I think it's more important to focus on the fact that that mystery is solved and to focus on the one that isn't. Could you hold this like that for a second?' she asked as she leaned what felt like a chopping board at a strategic angle.

'What mystery isn't solved?' asked Robbie.

'The ghosting. Actually I have a few ideas about who it might be but what with all the shenanigans earlier I was distracted and forgot to ask Lizzie outright, but my money is totally on it being her. Some sort of strange revenge thing.'

'Ghosting? Lizzie? I'm afraid I need all the details,' said Robbie getting out his notepad.

'No you don't and you can put that away. It's not a matter for the police. I was an idiot and I've learned my lesson. What do they say? If it seems too good to be true, then it probably is.' Liv reversed from under the tree and viewed it from standing up to see if she could see any pink paper.

'Maybe *I* should ascertain if it's a police matter or not.'

'I'm afraid however much it hurts ghosting isn't a crime.' Robbie put his notepad away. 'Ahh, that's tough. Who did it happen to?'

'Me,' said Liv, but she was pleased that she no longer had that instant feeling of shame and embarrassment. It really wasn't to do with her; it was someone else with far bigger issues than she had if they got some sort of pleasure out of what they did. And at least now she knew it wasn't Fraser.

'I'm sorry, I didn't realise. People can be unkind. I'm afraid I get to see the worst of society sometimes.'

'I bet you do,' said Liv, tilting to one side just to check the packages.

'Here,' said Robbie, handing Liv his business card. 'I know you're not local but I do have connections and if there's ever anything I can do to help, don't hesitate to call me.'

'Aww thanks, Robbie,' she said giving him a hug and feeling him tense under her embrace. Clearly hugging wasn't his forte.

Liv checked her pockets for one of her own business cards but she had none on her. 'If you ever have any search engine emergencies you make sure you call me. Effie has my details. I need to dash.'

Robbie looked serious. 'Will do.'

'Bye, Robbie. Nice to have met you,' she said pausing at the door. He was a funny one but she was still going to miss him.

She went into the hallway. After almost a week she was going home and leaving this odd place behind but that meant leaving the people too. Liv tried not to think too much about it as she took the stairs two at a time.

It didn't take a minute to gather her things together. Liv took one last look out of the window at the stunning view. She let out a little sigh as she left the bedroom. Despite it seeming a bit dingy at first, it had soon become cosy and she loved the history seeping from its walls. As long as that history didn't include ghosts, she would be forever grateful that she'd not met Janet in person.

Downstairs was quiet so she left her bag by reception and went to say her goodbyes to one local she knew wasn't inside. It was chilly outside but not quite as bitterly cold as it had been – that or she was hardening up. Across the yard it was as if Ginger had been expecting her. She had her head peeping over the bottom half of the stable door. Her big eyes watching Liv as Mariah Carey sung at them from the radio.

'All I want for Christmas is youuuuuuuu!' chorused Liv. Ginger eyed her suspiciously. 'Here you go,' said Liv offering her the carrot on her flat palm. Ginger's giant tongue swept it all away with one lick.

'Blimey you're a greedy cow!' she said with a chuckle.

'Have you gone all Dr Dolittle?' asked Fraser making her jump.

'Jeez, I thought I was alone.' She pointed at Ginger. 'Apart from my learned friend here.' She went to give Ginger a head rub but the cow was keen to check there were no pieces of carrot lurking anywhere, so Liv's hand got another slobbery lick.

'I was just checking for any English invaders,' he said pretending to look serious.

'Very wise,' said Liv. 'I hear there has been the odd one about.'

'Yeah, odd being the key word there,' he said with a laugh.

'Hey! I resemble that remark,' she joked and gave him a playful whack on the arm. Then it all felt a bit awkward so she turned her attention back to Ginger.

Fraser leaned in close and she could hear him breathing. 'Are you scared of spiders?' he asked.

'I know I'm an English jessie but no, I'm not scared of spiders.'

'That's good because…' He pointed above her head and they both looked up to see a spider's web sparkling in the daylight. The intricacies of the web made it quite beautiful.

'Is this where you launch into that famous Scottish poem. Wee tim'rous *beastie*?' she asked.

Fraser laughed. 'That was a poem about a mouse by Robert Burns. You're thinking of the Robert the Bruce story.'

'Too many Roberts,' said Liv returning to watch the spider making its web.

'It's stunning. Isn't it?'

'It really is,' she said aware that his face was close to hers and her heart was starting to thump a little harder. 'Amazing to think they make them with their bum.'

Fraser burst out laughing. 'Liv, you are the funniest, most...' He seemed to be searching for the right words when his phone rang and interrupted them. Fraser frowned as he cancelled the call. 'Lizzie?' asked Liv.

'Callum. I wish he'd just let it go.'

'Do you? I'm guessing you've been friends a while.'

'Since P1.' He must have seen her confused look because he quickly clarified. 'That's reception in England.'

'See, that's a blinking long time. You don't want to throw that away.'

'He threw it away when he slept with Lizzie.'

'Yeah. That takes two you know? I'm not defending him, and I know he wouldn't either. He knows he's been a shit but you have lots in common. Not least the fact that Lizzie has shafted you both.' Fraser's eyebrows jumped. 'As in treated you both badly as well as the obvious but don't think about that bit. Focus on the fact she was a nasty cow to both of you.'

Ginger made a low bellowing noise. 'Not you,' said Liv. 'You're a nice cow.' Fraser was giving her a strange look so she turned her attention back to him.

'My dad did the same to my brother.' He studied the floor.

Liv's brain was trying to work it out. 'He slept with his girlfriend?'

Fraser nodded. 'His wife, Effie's mum. The day Uncle Duncan found out about the affair was the day he died in a car crash.'

'Shit. Does Effie know?'

He shook his head. 'No and I don't want her to either. She lost her father and then her mam said she needed to get away. Shortly afterwards my dad walked out, leaving us to sort everything out here. But what did any of us know about running a hotel? We had no choice but to close the place down.'

'How did you find out about the affair?'

'Something didn't add up for me. I managed to track Dad down to France and guess who was there with him.'

'Effie's mum.'

'Spot on.' He sighed. 'I got angry but that only made things worse. Dad and I haven't spoken since.'

'Blimey. No wonder the Callum and Lizzie thing hurt. But Callum's not your dad and he is sorry for what he's done.'

'You won't tell Effie any of this, will you?'

'No, but maybe one day you should. She'll find out sometime and it would be better coming from someone who cares about her.' He nodded. 'Anyway, why were you lurking out here?' she asked.

'I wasn't lurking, I was waiting for a delivery. I'm doing a seafood platter for dinner. I hope you're not allergic?' He was smiling at her, which was quite a rare thing and definitely something she would have liked to have got used to. But she got the distinct impression that the kiss meant nothing; friends was all that was on the table.

'I won't be here for dinner. The car's fixed. So I'll be home for Christmas. Hurray.' It was probably the most unenthusiastic hurray that had ever been uttered. 'I was just saying goodbye to Ginger and then I was going to get off.' She did an impression of her driving for no apparent reason. Why did she turn into a bit of an idiot whenever she was feeling awkward?

His smile faded and his expression changed but to one that was difficult to read. Was that relief or disappointment? Most likely the former. 'Right, then,' he said. 'This is it. You're off.' He pointed past the hotel and they both looked.

'Yeah.' There was a self-conscious silence that seemed to stretch on. 'Right, well, thank you for everything. It's been um... interesting. If you find out who impersonated you on that dating site you let me know okay?'

'Why? Did you want to date them instead?'

Liv pouted as if giving it consideration. 'He was a nice chap. He was Scottish.'

'And you like that do you?' he asked sounding more Scottish than ever.

Liv felt heat rush to her cheeks. 'Nah, when you've heard David Tennant on every advert on TV it gets a bit much really.'

Fraser laughed hard. 'You crack me up, Liv. You'll be missed.'

What did that mean? 'I'll miss you too.' Fraser seemed surprised, which probably indicated he'd only meant it in a general way. Ugh how humiliating. She turned to Ginger. 'I'll miss you too,' she repeated in an attempt to hide her embarrassment. Ginger wasn't falling for it and eyed her suspiciously. 'I had better get going,' said Liv. She stood in front of Fraser for a fraction longer than was necessary. What was she waiting for? Him to gather her up in his arms and declare his undying love for her? Not likely and did she even want that? This was excruciating, and she needed to end it and run. But as Liv went to give him a quick hug he went for the handshake and ended up stabbing her in the stomach – oof!

'Hell, I'm so sorry,' he said. 'Are you okay?'

'Fine,' she squeaked. 'Bye then.' She rubbed her middle as she made a dash for inside.

When she came into the hallway there was a bit of a gathering: Dolly and Jock'O, Effie and Robbie were all waiting for her. It made her smile at the sight of them but her smile was soon raced away when Robbie pulled out his bagpipes and an awful din echoed off the walls. Jock'O yelped, jumped off Dolly's lap and ran upstairs. Dolly was grimacing but Effie was swaying from side to side as if she were listening to lift music. Liv feared her ears were going to bleed. Thanks to the bagpipes she didn't hear Fraser join them but she felt his arm brush hers and every hair stood on end. They looked at each other and smiled but then Robbie hit a particularly high note and they both winced at the same time. Fraser started a round of applause, Liv joined in and thankfully Robbie took the hint and stopped playing.

'We wanted to give you a bit of a send-off,' said Dolly.

'You certainly did that. Wow. Thank you.'

Robbie seemed coy. 'It needs some work but I'm sure you could tell what it was.'

Liv had no idea but she nodded earnestly. 'Definitely a classic.' She so hoped he didn't question her any further.

Dolly put down a mug of tea, wheeled over and handed her a package. 'That should keep you going. You drive safely now,' she said giving her hand a squeeze.

'Thanks, I will. My sister would kill me if I didn't.'

She turned to Effie but before she could say anything a puffy-eyed Effie pulled her into a bear hug, which she reciprocated. Effie had the purest heart of anyone she'd met and they'd grown close. 'You take care and please keep in touch,' said Liv.

'I wondered if in the new year I might catch a train to Blackburn.' Effie sounded very unsure and sunk her teeth hard into her bottom lip at the end of the sentence.

'That would be brilliant. I'd love to see you and you're welcome any time.'

'Bye,' said Fraser. 'Can I just check? Are we doing a handshake or a hug?'

Something inside her said she was going to miss this bear of a man the most. 'Hug?'

He held out his arms and she tentatively stepped into them. He gave the best hugs and with the whiff of cologne and a few added pheromones it was all a bit much. She had to pull away. Fraser was the one who never was and she was a little sad about that, but she was taking home a renewed sense of self-respect and a feeling of victory in that despite it being misplaced she had stood up for herself. Also unexpectedly she'd fallen in love with the beauty of the Scottish Highlands. She let out a breath. She was in danger of getting emotional so she grabbed her bag and pulled back her shoulders.

'You've all been marvellous. Thanks for everything. Have the best Christmas. Bye!' Liv couldn't look at Effie or Fraser so she turned away, but as she did something caught her eye. She stepped between Robbie and Effie, took Effie's arm and moved her closer to Robbie. 'Now look up,' she said. Everyone did and as they were all contemplating the mistletoe above them Liv walked away as fast as she could without it looking like she was running.

37

The journey home was just as tedious as the one up to Scotland. It was such a long way. Liv sang and shouted at the radio depending on what the programme was, rationed her drink intake and made one scheduled stop at one of the bigger services. When she got back in the car she decided to see what was in the package Dolly had given her, although she was pretty sure she could guess. She was right: it was Scottish tablet. At least the sugar high would help her stay alert.

Liv replayed all that had happened in the last six days. It seemed like she'd been there a lot longer and had come away feeling like she'd known the people forever. She finally pulled onto her sister's driveway at a quarter to eight at night. She was tired but oh so pleased to be home. That feeling didn't last long when she saw her sister's angry face as she stormed outside. 'Where the hell have you been?' she asked her through the driver's window.

'Scotland,' said Liv.

'We thought you'd emigrated!' Charlotte did a good impression of an angry person but there was something about sisters – however cross they were you knew deep down that they loved you and you were family, so they were stuck with you. Liv got out of the car and opened the boot. 'Where's the damage to the car?' asked her sister as she stalked around it like a rooster in a henhouse, her eyes homing in when she thought she saw something of interest.

Their mum came running out of the front door doing up her jeans. 'You would arrive when I'm having a wee,' she complained as she threw her arms around her youngest daughter.

'Eww too much information, Mum. I hope you've washed your hands.'

'You cheeky wotsit! Let me look at you.' She held her at arm's length and Liv felt like she was at primary school again. 'Are you okay?'

'I'm fine. All in one piece.'

'Come inside. It's blooming cold out here,' said Charlotte.

'Cold, you southern softie – this is nothing. It was minus twelve in Scotland.'

Her mum and sister looked suitably shocked.

They went inside and Liv regaled them with tales from over the border where she frequently was the hero in the story. She realised a lot had happened in six days. And the more she talked the more tired she got.

'So no men in kilts,' concluded her mum.

'Nope,' said Liv. 'The kilt thing is for formal occasions and apparently when they go into battle.'

'Disappointing,' said Charlotte. They all nodded.

When there were more yawns than words per sentence she conceded it was time for bed.

'Come on,' said her mum. 'Santa will be on his way.' Which received groans as a response. 'I'll see you at mine for present opening and a cheeky glass of fizz before we get the potatoes on.'

'Okay,' said Liv giving her mum a hug.

'I'm so glad you're home and I'm so proud of you for standing up to that horrid man.'

'But I explained he wasn't really horrid at all because it wasn't him who ghosted me.'

'Hmm,' said Charlotte. 'I reckon he's gaslighting you.'

'I'm too tired for this,' said Liv and she kissed her mum and sister. 'See you at Christmas,' she joked and she went to bed.

Liv was woken on Christmas morning by her sister grumbling about being late. She'd not managed to get as much sleep as she'd hoped. For one thing she'd had to do some last-minute wrapping and then when she'd got into bed her tired mind had decided that was a good opportunity to go over things and try to sort them out. But sorting things out wasn't that simple. She felt like she'd lost something, but if that was the Fraser from the dating app then she never had him in the first place. And if it was the Fraser she'd got to know in Scotland then he was juggling a wash load of baggage. Maybe some things just weren't meant to be.

Liv popped in the shower and before getting dressed she decided to unpack the bag she'd been too exhausted to attempt the night before. She was making a pile for the washing machine when she discovered an envelope. She took it out and sat down on the bed to look at it. On the front was LIV in capitals along with neatly drawn holly and bells. At the bottom it said: '*Do Not Open Until 25 Dec*'. Her heart gave a little flutter. Obviously someone in Scotland had put it in her bag, but who? She so wanted it to be Fraser but she couldn't imagine him colouring in holly. She was about to rip open the envelope when her sister banged on the door.

'Are you dressed yet? There's a mince pie and a glass of fizz with my name on it at Mum's.'

Liv looked at the envelope and then at the towel still wrapped around her damp body. 'Give me five minutes,' she called and she put the envelope in her handbag. She'd have to wait to open that later.

A few minutes later a damp-haired Liv dashed out of her bedroom pulling on her Christmas jumper whilst wrestling with her handbag and a big bag of presents. They were going to walk to their mum's so that they could both have a drink.

'At last,' said Charlotte, waggling the door key at her. Charlotte was fully made up, with blow-dried waves, wearing a stylish knitted dress underneath a winter coat and had a bag of neatly wrapped presents at her feet. How could two sisters be so different?

'You're wearing that?' Charlotte pointed at Liv's jumper, which proudly displayed a large turkey in a party hat.

'I am. And listen to this.' Liv groped around near her left boob for the little push pad and once pressed it started to play 'Grandma Got Run Over by a Reindeer'.

'It's a turkey, not a reindeer,' said Charlotte.

'Don't be picky. I got it at the market,' said Liv as she tried to switch it off again. Charlotte was still shaking her head as they left the house and began the short walk to their mum's.

'You were up late,' said Charlotte.

'I had a few things still to wrap. Were you spying on me?'

'I saw your light was still on when I went for a wee.'

'Old age catching up with you already?' quipped Liv. At least constant digs about her sister being older were a staple in their relationship.

'Ha. As long as it was just presents. I do worry about you, you know,' said Charlotte giving her an awkward one-armed hug as they walked along.

'Yeah I know. And you're all right too.'

'High praise indeed. You'll be fine – you know that don't you?'

Liv gave her the side-eye.

'I know I have a go sometimes but you're my little sister and that's kind of my job.'

'No it's not,' said Liv.

Charlotte puffed out a breath and it plumed in front of her in the cold air. 'I feel like I have to look out for you and Mum. But I know you'll be okay. Despite what you think you will find the right person for you if and when you're ready. You don't need someone to complete you – that's just trash they use to fill magazines.'

'I know that,' said Liv. 'I am a strong, independent woman.' She pulled back her shoulders, lifted her chin and walked with a swagger.

'You're also an idiot and I love you,' said Charlotte,

giving her a nudge. 'You had better have got Mum a good present in there.'

'I have,' said Liv defensively. She glanced at the jumble of bright pink paper. Oh well it was too late now.

★

It was Christmas morning and Effie was even more excited than the time she'd thought she'd seen Santa's reindeer on the lawn and it had turned out to be a plain old ordinary deer. She cannoned down the stairs and into the library to find someone had beaten her to being the first one up. The lights were all on and twinkling, and a new fire was just taking in the grate. The small pile of presents under the tree had grown as others had secretly added theirs before going to bed.

'Hey, no opening until everyone is up!' scolded Fraser from the doorway. 'Breakfast first.'

'Okay,' said Effie and once he'd gone she checked the tag on the nearest present and saw it was for her. She picked it up, held it to her ear and gave it a little shake.

'Oi, breakfast,' said Fraser reappearing and she guiltily put the present down and ran giggling from the room.

It wasn't long before they were all sitting by the fire with drinks in hand and Jock'O in pole position. They had opened a few presents and Effie was very pleased with her book on Scottish Myths and Legends and her witch's brew candle. Dolly was trying out a new hand cream and Fraser was sorting out the fake presents.

'Did you wrap up bog rolls?' he asked moving one of the large parcels.

'It was all to get the right effect,' said Effie.

'Are these fake too?' he asked holding up a very round package wrapped in pink Christmas trees.

'No, is there a label?'

Fraser turned it over and found a piece of white paper taped to it and read it out. '*To Ginger, you lucky cow. Love from Liv.*' He blinked as he said her name.

'Ooh that's kind of her,' said Effie. 'Can I open it?'

'I think it's pretty obvious what it is,' said Fraser passing it to her. 'And it will last all of five seconds like every other ball she's got hold of.'

At the mention of the word ball Jock'O lifted a lazy head but when there wasn't one in sight he flopped back down again as the fire cracked and sizzled.

Effie tore off the Christmassy paper to reveal something a little unexpected. 'It's a boat fender or buoy,' said Fraser.

'But Ginger doesn't have a boat,' said Effie. This was a weird gift.

'No but it's almost the same as a ball and given it's made of tough stuff it might actually last when she hoofs it around the yard. It's actually a very good present,' he conceded.

'Any more things wrapped in that paper?' asked Dolly, putting her hand cream away.

'Yep,' said Fraser, passing them to her.

Dolly unwrapped a pair of thick socks for Jock'O, which he instantly took interest in and for her a travel cup and cup holder that had a note with it saying – *It's really for a boat but I think it will also fit on your wheelchair from Liv.* 'Ooh what a good idea,' said Dolly. 'I'm always leaving mugs of tea places.' She looked at Effie. 'What did you get?'

Effie had opened a set of ghost fairy lights from Liv that

she was over the moon with and was now looking at the letter that was in with them.

'What's it say?' asked Fraser.

Effie swallowed and read it out. '*Dear Effie, You have quickly become my friend and I wanted to get you a little something to say thank you for being my bestie in Scotland. I saw the little light-up ghosts and thought of you and Janet. They were in the sale section with other Halloween stuff but it's the thought that counts, right? Anyway, I also did something else. I have a friend who is a whizz with computers. The judge called him a hacker but that's another story. He sent an email to "John" making out it was from you with details of a money transfer but it was really a virus. I'm pleased to report that John's computer has been wiped of all information, which hopefully is a giant pain in the bum for him and will stop him from conning women for a while. Lots of love and don't forget to visit, Liv x.*' Effie lifted her head and looked at Dolly and Fraser's faces.

'Well done, Liv,' said Fraser. 'She gave Karma a helping hand.'

'Um, who is John and isn't giving his computer a virus very illegal?' asked Dolly.

Effie felt sick she'd not thought through the implications before she'd read the note out, but Fraser was already coming to her rescue. 'John was a nasty piece of work who badgered Effie over the internet. But she's a smart woman and she blocked him. Liv was just stopping him from doing it to others.'

'I see,' said Dolly. 'Good thing she did – some people can be gullible.'

'They can,' said Fraser and he and Effie exchanged smiles.

38

Effie was blown away by what Liv had done. She loved that Liv knew someone who could wreck John's computer. Liv was right – at least now he'd lost all the information he'd probably built up, it would take a while before he was in a position to start approaching women again. Effie even hoped that perhaps this would be the wake-up call he needed to realise the error of his ways and get himself a proper job. She'd play that little story out in her head and hope it came true. She didn't like the thought of anyone else being upset like she had been. Although, even today it didn't seem quite the disaster it had first felt like.

She'd thought she'd found someone special in John but even in the midst of all the excitement and subterfuge she'd known it wasn't love. She'd liked the reassurance of him telling her she wasn't an idiot, but now she realised she was surrounded by people who didn't think she was daft and that was what really mattered.

Effie absent-mindedly flicked the ghost lights on and off. She felt her grandmother's hand on her shoulder.

'Are you all right?' asked Dolly, with a kind and knowing smile.

'I'm all good,' said Effie and she meant it.

Dolly turned her attention to Fraser. 'What did Liv give you?' she asked, nodding at the gift in Fraser's hands.

Fraser took a moment before holding up a deflated plastic man. 'Her note to me says: *Hi Fraser, I've done some tinkering and your website search engine optimisation should be better than it was. Your security is pants so you need to change your password.*' He rolled his eyes at that before carrying on. '*I'm also gifting you my friend Plastic Stan. He's not much of a talker but he's a terrific listener and will make a good stand-in until you realise how valuable your friendship with Callum is and that it's not something you want to let Lizzie ruin. All the best. Liv. P.S. It was nice meeting you for real.*'

'Good grief,' said Dolly, putting one hand over her mouth and pointing with the other. 'Is that a *sex* toy?'

Effie burst out laughing and Fraser looked decidedly uncomfortable. 'I think so, but it's just a joke.'

'Hmm,' said Dolly. 'It's an unusual Christmas present but I have to admit, I think what she says is true.'

'About Stan being a good listener?' said Fraser, tipping his head to one side and smiling.

'About you and Callum. We can all act like bampots now and again. And I don't want to play down what Callum did, because it was deceitful and the worst kind of betrayal. But there's no prize for taking the higher ground here. You'll only lose your friend for good. And I think it would annoy

Lizzie no end if you and Callum made up, so that's probably the best reason to give him a call.'

'And it's Christmas,' chipped in Effie. 'You shouldn't fight at Christmas.'

'I don't know. Maybe I'm not the forgiving type,' said Fraser.

'You forgave Liv for accusing you of being a ghost. And you forgave me for whacking you in the gentleman parts with a flowerpot.'

'You were only seven at the time, Effie.'

'Still, it means you can find it within you to forgive and forget. You just need to speak to Callum.' Effie put her hands on her hips.

Fraser looked Stan over and smiled at the note in his hands. 'I'll think about it,' he said.

The doorbell went. 'I'll get it. Do you think it's Callum?' asked Effie getting to her feet. 'That would be spooky,' she added as she left the room with Jock'O at her heels carrying a sock to greet the visitor with.

'It's Christ-mas!' announced Winnie in a very high-pitched attempt to mimic Slade's Noddy Holder. Unfortunately it set off a coughing fit.

'Goodness, Winnie. Merry Christmas,' said Effie trying and failing to hurry the old lady inside. 'Granny is in the library.'

'Wonderful,' said Winnie and she shuffled in that direction with a small bag of presents dangling from her walking frame. 'My chauffeur is just parking the car,' she added with a giggle.

Effie was about to follow her when the doorbell went again and she opened the door to a very large present, which moved down to reveal the deliverer. 'Yuletide felicitations,' said Robbie, who was wearing a Santa hat.

Effie was super excited to see him. She'd done some thinking since yesterday. The fact that he'd gone to the trouble of finding the video of her dad for her meant so much. It was the kindest thing anyone had done and when she took a moment to think about it, Robbie had only ever been lovely to her. 'Happy Christmas. Come in,' she said, unable to hide her grin. They walked up the hallway and both faltered near the mistletoe. 'Sorry about yesterday,' she said. 'I don't know what Liv was thinking.' Effie felt a little embarrassed when she recalled the moment they'd both looked up to find themselves directly underneath it. Obviously they hadn't kissed and now, if she was honest, she was a little worried about evil spirits but undeniably excited about the prospect of witches. She took Robbie through to the library where Fraser quickly bundled up Stan.

'I need to check on the roast beef,' he said. 'Hiya, Robbie. Did you want to stay for dinner?'

'Festive greetings one and all,' said Robbie. 'Thanks for the offer but my mother will roast *me* if I'm not there for Christmas dinner.' He chuckled and Effie giggled along.

Dolly turned her scooter in the direction of the door. 'I'd best give the lad a hand,' she said. 'Come on, Winnie,' she added. Winnie had only made it to the doorway anyway. They both followed Fraser out with a sock-carrying Jock'O at Dolly's wheels, leaving Robbie and Effie alone.

There was a moment of silence where Robbie seemed hesitant, and Effie took a moment to look at him. He'd always been just little Robbie Williams who lived in the next village and shared his chocolate biscuit with her at school break time. She'd never taken the time to appreciate the kind, quirky and well-turned-out man he'd grown into. When the silence got too much Effie jumped into action. 'I got you something,' she said grabbing a small parcel from under the tree and thrusting it at him. 'Open it.'

'Right. Thank you. You shouldn't have.' He put down the large package and took the offered gift. He carefully peeled away the tape, preserving the paper, and cautiously unwrapped the present. 'It's a keyring and sugared mice.'

'And attached to the keyring is a handcuff key. It's extendable so if you found yourself in a similar situation to, you know…' She mimed being stuck in handcuffs. 'You should be able to easily unlock them.'

'Thanks, Effie, that's thoughtful of you.'

'And mice because everyone needs sugared mice at Christmas.' It was all a bit tense and Effie wasn't sure why. It wasn't uncomfortable exactly but it was like waiting for the woosh of the firework after the tape is lit.

'And here, this is for you. It's just a little something,' he said picking up the rather large parcel and almost taking Effie out as he thrust it in her direction at the same time she stepped forward to take it. 'Sorry!' he added.

'Thank you.' Effie shredded the paper and instantly revealed a yellow suitcase. She looked at it and felt a little anxious.

'It's for when you firm up your plans to explore the world. I know it's something you're building up to.'

'I thought I'd start with Blackburn to see Liv and then France to visit Mum.'

'And when you're ready you'll have the right kit,' said Robbie.

'Thank you,' she said throwing her arms around him. He was a little taken by surprise and there was a delay before his arms wrapped tightly around her. They stayed in each other's arms, neither one wanting to pull away. She tilted her head back a fraction. Their faces were very close. Effie looked up and then back into Robbie's eyes.

'Is there any mistletoe?' he asked.

'No,' said Effie, her voice barely a whisper as her heart hammered in her chest.

'Good,' said Robbie and he kissed her.

*

Liv found something comforting about being back in her usual routine. Christmas at her mum's always started with pancakes for breakfast although now they had Buck's Fizz with them instead of chocolate milkshake like they had done as kids. The *Now That's What I Call Christmas* album was playing because it was their mum's favourite and even though it had some proper festive howlers they all hummed along to it. Charlotte and Liv both helped to get the vegetables prepared while the delicious smell of the cooking turkey filled the little kitchen. Their mum always got up early on Christmas morning to put it in the oven on low. When the kitchen was looking fairly tidy and everything was prepared it was finally time to start opening the presents.

As usual Charlotte must have spent ages wrapping hers because they were perfect with matching curly ribbons and tags and even little tinkly bells hanging from them. Everyone was pleased with what they'd been given, even if her mum was a little confused about the soft-close toilet seat

Liv had bought her from the DIY shop. Well, she couldn't just give her smellies.

Liv had been putting off opening the envelope she'd found at the bottom of her bag but now she'd opened everything, even the selection box her mum always bought them both, so there was nothing else for it. She ripped open the envelope. Inside was a gift card and instructions plus a brief note. It read: *Hello Liv, I wanted you to have this. I bought them for all of us months ago when there was an offer on and there was one spare. Sorry, can't lie, this one was for Lizzie but obviously I'm not going to give her a Christmas present when she cruelly cheated on my cousin. You never know we might be related. Love ya, Effie* – followed by too many kisses to count.

'What is it?' asked her mum, which made Liv take a closer look at the card. 'It's a heritage DNA kit. You do a swab test and send it off to find out your genetic make-up and where your predecessors originated.'

'Who's it from?' asked Charlotte.

'Effie, from Scotland. She must have put it in my bag when I was doing something.'

'A DNA kit from someone you just met – that's proper weird,' said Charlotte.

'No. It's cool. I like it and what's more I'm going to do it and send it off,' said Liv.

'Not until after dinner,' said her mum. 'That turkey should be done to perfection around about now.' And she hurried off to the kitchen.

Charlotte stared at her. 'What?' asked Liv.

'You're different since Scotland. I'm not sure what it is exactly.'

'I feel different,' said Liv, putting the letter away. Charlotte was still studying her closely. 'What now?' she asked.

'Just wondering how much Neanderthal is in your DNA.'

'Hey!' Liv whacked her with a cushion. It was exactly how Christmas should be.

39

Effie found Fraser in the yard feeding raw sprouts to Ginger. The sky was a clear blue and the air crisp. She watched Ginger inhale another sprout from Fraser's hand. 'You know that's probably not going to end well, don't you?'

'Sounds like the story of my life,' he said.

Effie came to lean on the stable door next to him. 'Why so glum?'

He sighed heavily. 'I dunny know. I have a lot to be thankful for. Especially now the hotel's not being sold and with a big heap of luck I should be able to get the restaurant off the ground. But you know when something feels off? Like you've forgotten something important but canny think what it is? I feel like that.'

'Is it Callum? Do you need to give him a call?'

'I don't know. That still feels pretty raw. But I do know I'll not be nagged into it.' He gave her a look and she nodded. 'We'd better get back inside.' He gave Ginger one last sprout and roughly rubbed the top of her head, which she leaned into before he and Effie walked back across the yard. 'What's the deal with you and Robbie?'

An instant giddiness came over her at the thought of it. 'I don't know yet, but it'll be fun finding out.'

'He's a great guy. A bit off the wall but nice all the same,' he said shutting the door behind them.

'I like off the wall. I guess I'm a bit like that too.'

Fraser looked up from pulling off his wellies. 'You dunny say?'

She nudged him and he almost fell over. 'It means he gets me. I don't think many people do. They think I'm a bit dippy, daft, kind of wacky. A reindeer short of a sleigh ride. You know?'

'You're you and that's a good thing,' he said. 'I'm going to check the roast tatties,' he added pointing into the kitchen.

Back in the warmth of the library, Jock'O was twitching in his sleep, Winnie was enjoying a glass of Scotch and Dolly was studying her DNA kit. 'Will this tell me all the clans I'm related to?' She seemed interested at the prospect.

'I don't think it's that detailed,' said Effie. 'But it will tell you different countries and civilisations and stuff. We might even be related to royalty or better still someone famous. I also read where this man found out his grandad had been switched at birth!'

'That's the sort of thing I'd not want to be finding out,' said Dolly.

'But you'll do the test, Granny, won't you?' Effie put her palms together as if sending up a little prayer.

Dolly smiled. 'If you want me to.'

'I do. And I've paid for super-fast responses so if we all do them and post them off we'll get the information really quickly as they upload it to an app,' said Effie, bobbing up and down in her seat.

'That's good then,' said Dolly although she didn't sound that pleased about it.

Effie was seeing Robbie out and catching a quick kiss under the reception desk mistletoe just to undo any bad luck they might have triggered the day before.

'Eww get a room,' said Fraser, walking up the hall. 'Is that what we've got to look forward to? You two being all loved up? Eurgh.' He pretended to feel queasy at the prospect.

'Truly sorry,' said Robbie. 'I've waited a lifetime to kiss your cousin.'

Effie spun around. 'Have you?'

Robbie went all shy. 'I think you're amazing. Always have, always will. Did you not know?'

Effie shook her head. 'You never said anything. All this time we could have been together.'

'I guess I hoped one day it would just all work out and it did.' He kissed her.

Fraser made retching noises behind them. 'Sorry,' he said with a grin as they pulled apart.

'Ignore him,' said Effie. 'He's jealous.'

'Let's call it a touch of envy. I'm really pleased for both of you,' said Fraser, reaching forward to shake Robbie's hand. 'And nice touch with the case – great idea.' Fraser's expression changed. 'I didn't get Liv a Christmas present. But then I wouldn't have known what to get her anyway.'

'Gift purchasing can be a minefield,' said Robbie. 'I just thought about what Effie wanted most in the world and how I could facilitate that.'

'Aww, you're so lovely,' said Effie giving him a tight squeeze.

Fraser snorted a laugh. 'What Liv wants most is to track down who set up the fake dating profile in my name and give them a piece of her mind. So that's a bit out of my reach.'

Robbie's expression changed to his serious police officer one.

'What's this?' he asked.

Effie took a deep breath. 'Liv, set up a dating profile in her full name – Olivia Bingham – and she was matched with Fraser Douglas.' She pointed at Fraser. 'But it wasn't *our* Fraser who set it up and whoever *did* set it up led her on a wee merry dance before deleting the profile. And—'

There was a dramatic gasp from the library doorway and they all turned to see a shocked-looking Winnie standing there gripping her frame so tight her knuckles were white.

'Are you all right, Winnie?' asked Fraser going over to her.

'Oh dear, oh dear,' said Winnie. 'That poor wee thing.'

'Don't worry.' Fraser waved it away. 'It's a long story about Liv being ghosted on the internet. But I'm sure she's okay.'

'I'd better get going before my mam's turkey is as dry as sandpaper,' said Robbie turning around.

'No wait!' said Winnie forcefully. 'I've done something terrible.'

Robbie seemed torn by the statement and the thought of his mother. 'Terrible as in committed a crime?' he asked.

'Did you say Olivia Bingham?' she asked, scanning their faces.

'Yep, that's right. Liv is Olivia. One and the same,' said Fraser. He and Effie exchanged glances. 'You okay?' he asked Winnie.

'No, I'm not. Not at all.'

There was a long pause like when they're about to announce the winner of a reality show, and Effie got butterflies.

'Did you want to sit down?' asked Fraser.

Winnie straightened her shoulders, took a breath and looked Fraser in the eye.

'It was me.'

Fraser scratched his head, 'Sorry, Winnie. What was you?'

'I set up the phoney dating account in your name,' she said.

Effie gasped. 'You're fake Fraser?' She leaned into Robbie who put his arm protectively around her.

'Why? I mean, but you don't use dating apps. Do you?' asked Fraser.

'There's no upper age limit,' she said. 'It does take ages to scroll down to my year of birth. But no, I don't use them for me. But I do know my way around the world wide web. I've not always been a little old lady. I was one of the first women to get a degree in computer science in the early sixties, I'll have you know.'

'Oh, that's clever of you,' said Effie clapping her hands but Fraser was glaring at her. 'But you did a bad thing.' She wagged her finger, making Robbie give her a look. Perhaps telling off an old lady wasn't a good idea. 'At least you're not another John,' said Effie.

Robbie was momentarily distracted. 'Who's John?'

'Long story,' said Effie and Fraser together.

'Robbie, I think you can go because your mam's turkey is bothering me. Turkey dries out really quickly.' Fraser rubbed a hand over his beard.

'I'll just stay a few moments more,' said Robbie, pointing at Winnie. All eyes turned back in her direction.

'Why did you do it, Winnie?' asked Fraser, softly.

'Dolly and I got chatting at the Saracens charity quiz and she was concerned about you after Lizzie and Callum did what they did. She felt you had gone into your shell. Said you were sucking your thumb again.'

Fraser's face was one of horror. 'Thanks for that, Granny. I don't do that by the way. It's a hangnail that I sometimes chew… anyway carry on.'

'Dolly said you needed to meet a nice Scottish girl but as you were throwing yourself into the restaurant you had no time. You might remember I suggested to you that online dating might be an option?' Winnie looked at Fraser.

'Don't remember that.'

'Anyway,' said Winnie. 'I thought if I could do the groundwork for you – find you a perfect match – there would be little for you to do other than meet her, and you would instantly charm her and then you'd be happy again and Dolly wouldn't have to worry about you. And I do like to have a surf on the internet.'

'Aww that's really cute,' said Effie, wriggling from under Robbie's arm.

Fraser abruptly folded his arms. 'But Winnie. That's not how it turned out. How did you find Liv? What happened?'

'There were a few no-hopers and a lot who were clearly not after anything long-term. Some of the messages were borderline pornographic, which I'll not go into. But Olivia, because that's what she called herself, Olivia seemed lovely. She was a little feisty but driven and kind. She was self-employed like you. She liked food, action films and was mad about Mariah Carey. I clicked the like button and so did she, which led to us corresponding. There were daily messages. I answered everything as closely as I could to how you would so that any connection was based as much on you as possible. And I *have* known you since you were in nappies.'

'That's okay then,' said Fraser looking dumbfounded.

Winnie brightened. 'There were some quite lovely discussions about things. She really did seem to like you in a big way.'

'Heavens, Winnie!' Fraser's voice was shriller than normal.

'Don't shout. New battery,' said Winnie pointing at her hearing aid.

Fraser lowered his voice. 'At what point did you think you'd maybe gone too far?'

Winnie took a moment to think about the question. 'I suggested that we meet up. And that's when I realised how far away she was. You see she said she was from Blackburn. Which I assumed was Blackburn, West Lothian.'

'It's nice there,' said Effie.

'It is,' agreed Winnie. 'I had a cousin Maud who lived there. And it's a perfectly acceptable distance. But it was actually Blackburn, Lancashire, which also meant she was English – and after what happened with Lizzie.' She pulled a face like an exaggerated version of the grimacing emoji.

'And what did you do then?' Fraser was staring at her hard.

'I did the only thing I could. I stopped replying to her messages and I deleted your profile.' Winnie blinked and paused. 'That's what you young 'uns call ghosting, isn't it?'

'Uh-huh.' Fraser shook his head and began pacing. 'How did you not recognise her when she turned up here?' he asked.

'The photograph on the dating app was very small. That reminds me, I'd best get booked in for an eye test.'

Fraser rolled his eyes.

'Anyway,' said Winnie continuing. 'The photo was of a young woman with more golden blonde in her hair than auburn. She looked quite elegant with a sort of film star quality about her. Although I did think Liv was familiar.' Winnie put a finger to her lips as if remembering. 'I thought it was just because she looked like Amy Pond.' Winnie giggled but stopped when nobody else joined in.

'And her name. Liv is short for Olivia,' said Fraser.

'That one passed me by completely,' admitted Winnie. 'But in my defence, I wasn't looking for a connection and she'd only been here a few days. I didn't spend that much time with her.'

Fraser shook his head. 'I don't believe this. Poor Liv. Hell, all the things I've said to her. All the times I thought she was a fruitcake and it was because of your meddling.' He stared at Winnie. 'This is not good.'

'I am truly sorry,' said Winnie. 'I was only trying to do a nice thing and to help you find someone lovely. And she was lovely, wasn't she?'

Effie and Robbie both nodded.

'I panicked when I realised she was English,' said Winnie. 'I didn't think through how she might feel. She did say some lovely things about you though.'

'Like what?' Fraser softened.

'That you have the loveliest eyes! Like when you go on holiday and you can't quite believe the sea can be that blue.'

'Aww that's adorable,' said Effie clapping her hands together. 'What else?'

'She loved how passionate you were about cooking and setting up the restaurant. She admired you for that. And she liked how you didn't judge her when she bought a jumpsuit like the one she already had. She was especially impressed that you were comfortable to share that you were a huge Mariah Carey fan.'

'Goodness, Winnie, did you tell her I suck my thumb as well?'

Winnie cleared her throat. 'No. Like I say I am really very sorry for upsetting you and Liv. She liked you. She really did,' said Winnie. 'I'm sure this can be fixed. Did I do anything against the law?' She looked cautiously at Robbie.

'Nothing criminal thankfully, Winnie. I'd hate to have to arrest you. My mother would be furious,' he said. 'And on that note, I absolutely have to go now,' he added making for the door.

'You do,' said Fraser. 'I hope the turkey's okay. If not tell your mam to add some butter to the gravy and brush that mixture over the top of the sliced turkey, cover it in foil and whack it back in the oven while she serves everything else.'

'Thank you,' said Robbie. He kissed Effie briefly and left.

Fraser and Effie turned to look at Winnie still gripping her frame in the doorway. 'I am truly sorry, Fraser. Liv was a lovely young woman and you two were an excellent match. The app said so.' She gave a stilted smile and shuffled off down the hall.

Once he thought Winnie was out of earshot Fraser turned to his cousin. 'What the hell?' he said. 'Now what do I do?'

Effie rolled her lips together and thought. 'I think only you can make that decision,' she said and she went back into the library, leaving Fraser alone.

'Don't be a choob! You need to go after her,' called Winnie from the other end of the hallway.

40

Liv's Christmas had been exactly what she'd needed. It was just her, her mum and sister and that was great. They didn't need men in their lives. Men just complicated everything. They made women have unrealistic expectations of life and themselves, and they left dirty socks lying around – eurgh. No, they didn't need that, especially not when they had Prosecco, leftover turkey sandwiches and a tin of chocolates.

Liv put her hand in the tin and pulled out a Snickers. She dropped it like it was a turd. Though in fairness Snickers bars did kind of remind her of poo. She tried again – Snickers. What the hell? She peered into the tin. There was just Snickers left and there were only four of those. 'Who ate all the chocolates?' she asked sitting up a bit straighter to identify the culprit. There were little piles of wrappers on the arm of her mum's chair, on the sofa next to Charlotte and on the floor by her own leg. Liv's pile was by far the biggest. She was surprised, also impressed and a little nauseous at the discovery. She hastily scrunched up the wrappers and clambered to her feet.

'I think I'm going home,' said Liv, nudging her sleeping sister as she headed for the kitchen.

'Huh, no more for me,' said Charlotte looking slightly dazed as she came to and tried to focus on the flashing lights of the Christmas tree. 'Did you put those on the psycho setting again?' she asked. 'You know that gives me migraines.' Charlotte always exaggerated.

'I'll watch the rest of this tomorrow,' said their mum switching off the telly.

'I was watching that,' said Liv, pausing in the doorway.

'You said you were going back to Charlotte's.'

'Yeah but I was going to watch the end of that first.' Liv tried and failed to stifle a giant yawn. She was tired. And as per tradition they would be doing it all again tomorrow but with cold turkey and no presents, so she might as well give in. She put the evidence of her chocolate feast in the bin and returned to the living room. Charlotte was already on her feet and had packed her presents neatly into the bag she'd brought with her. Liv's were still in a heap with a mix of scraps of wrapping paper and yet more chocolate wrappers – how many had she eaten?

'I'll leave my stuff so I can have a proper look at them tomorrow,' she said. 'But I'll post the DNA thing.' She picked up the envelope. She'd done the swab as per the instructions and she was quite intrigued to get the results if only to prove to Charlotte that she wasn't three parts Neanderthal. She grabbed her coat from the hook in the hall and put the envelope in her pocket. She chucked Charlotte's coat at her and it landed on her head.

'No plans to grow up anytime soon then?' asked her sister.

'Maybe next year if I've room on my resolutions list.' Liv grinned at Charlotte.

'Stop fighting, girls. Now give me a kiss. I'm going to make a hot water bottle and go to bed.' She hugged them both. 'Thanks for a perfect day and for all my lovely presents.' Liv could have sworn her mum frowned at the toilet seat she'd bought her.

There were more hugs before they were finally outside and could hear the sound of their mum rapidly bolting the door and putting lights out. They walked down the path and both did their coats up that last centimetre as the full force of the chill enveloped them.

'It's a bit parky,' said Charlotte.

'It's nothing compared to—'

'Scotland,' cut in Charlotte. 'Yeah, you said.'

'Are you sick of me going on about it?'

'Nah... Actually, maybe a bit. But I'm glad you stood up for yourself and got things sorted out.'

'Thanks,' said Liv although she wasn't entirely sure she had.

They walked and talked and soon they were nearing Charlotte's. They went back via the post box so Liv could deposit the DNA swab. A bit further on it started to spit with rain, which made them speed up.

'You never see rain on Christmas cards,' said Charlotte. 'Far more rain than snow this time of year.'

'Not in Scotland,' said Liv, and Charlotte shot her a look.

'Okay I get it.' Liv mimed zipping up her lips and

throwing away the key. 'Ooh funny story, this policeman I met—'

'Shit,' said Charlotte.

'Come on just one more Scotland story and then I'll shut up about it.'

'It's not that,' said Charlotte. 'It's that.' She pointed to her doorway where there was the shadowy figure of someone sitting on the doorstep and slumped to one side. 'Christmas drunk. That's all we need.'

'We should have brought the little Snickers chocolates.'

'Nobody likes those, Liv. Not even the homeless.'

'He might not be homeless. He might just have had too much turkey and needed a sit-down.'

'I can relate to that,' said Charlotte giving her middle a rub. 'What shall I say to him?'

'I'll do it,' said Liv.

Charlotte did a double take. 'Bloody hell, you have changed.'

Liv shrugged a shoulder but she did feel different after Scotland. Something had shifted a little. She liked the more ballsy version of herself and wanted to hang on to her. As they approached the doorway she stepped in front of her sister. 'Hiya, wakey, wakey. It's time to go to bed.'

The person sat up, pulled off their hood and stared at Liv. 'I hope that's separate beds.'

Liv was stunned for a moment. Was she seeing things? 'Shit, Fraser! What are you doing here?' But she was already giving him a hug. She was so pleased to see him. And then she felt a bit self-conscious. Perhaps a tad too much fizz had made her overfriendly. She pulled back to let him stand up. 'It's Fraser, the guy who... but he hadn't and I stayed in his hotel... well his cousin's. Anyway, it's Fraser. This is my sister, Charlotte,' she said as her sister held up the door keys.

'Hi. Nice to meet you. Let's get inside out of the cold,' said Charlotte.

'It's all right. I'm used to it,' said Fraser. 'It's not as cold as Scot—'

'Bloody hell, not another one,' said Charlotte unlocking the door and ushering them inside.

There wasn't enough space in Charlotte's tiny hallway for all three of them, especially not with Fraser. But they all started removing their coats, hats and scarves at the same time, making them awkwardly apologise as they bumped and prodded each other whilst trying to take things off. Fraser kept his coat on but took off his hat and scarf. Charlotte escaped from her coat first and hung it up triumphantly. 'Tea? Who wants a cuppa?'

'Please,' said Liv, finding she'd managed to pull both sleeves inside out and her arms were still inside; it was like wearing a straitjacket.

'Not for me thanks,' said Fraser before turning his focus to Liv. 'Did you need a hand?'

'Noooo, I'm fine.' Liv tried to shake off the coat. 'Actually, just a bit of help please.'

Fraser untangled her and she hung up her coat. She looked at him afresh and something leapt inside her. She'd hoped she'd see him again but this was unexpected. A thought struck her. 'Heavens, is everything okay? Nobody's ill are they. Or has Robbie got another warrant out for my arrest?' Liv laughed but Fraser's frown deepened. 'Shit, what's happened?'

'Is there somewhere to sit down?' he asked looking uneasy. That same sensation was now creeping over her. She showed him through to the small living room. And they both sat on the sofa.

Liv clapped her hands together for no apparent reason before putting them on her thighs and that felt really odd, so she folded her arms, and now Fraser was watching her, so she'd have to leave them there. 'What brings you to Blackburn on Christmas Day?'

'There's no easy way to soften this and I'm sure of that because I've had a six-hour drive and two hours sitting on your doorstep.'

'Ooh six hours – you made good time,' said Liv automatically and hated herself for sounding like her mum.

'Yeah, nothing on the roads. And before I forget, everyone sends their best wishes including Robbie Williams.'

There was the sound from the kitchen of a mug smashing on the tiled floor. Charlotte was clearly eavesdropping. 'Not *that* Robbie Williams,' called Liv. 'I'll tell you later.' There was some muttering from the kitchen by way of reply.

'And it was Winnie who ghosted you,' said Fraser.

'What?' Liv started to laugh.

'It was Winnie on the internet. She thought she was helping but obviously she wasn't.'

'Shit. You mean it was little old Winnie who set up the fake profile?' said Liv, quite bewildered.

'Yeah. I know. She feels awful. Turns out she's got a degree in computer science so she's actually dead smart and computer-savvy. She was trying to find me someone but then she closed everything down without thinking through the impact of that. Sorry.'

'You don't say.' Liv tried to process the information. 'How did she not recognise me?'

'She said the picture was of a blonde, elegant woman with film-star looks.' Fraser had the good grace to look a little uncomfortable. 'We thought maybe it wasn't your photograph.'

'Bloody cheek! That *was* me. It was taken last summer.'

'If it's the one of you at that party, I did your make-up and it did have a filter on it,' called Charlotte unhelpfully from the kitchen.

'Still. I thought it looked like me. Maybe a best version of me. But anyway, we've gone down a rabbit hole. Why did she ghost me?' This was the crux of everything. What was it about Liv that had made Winnie do this?

Fraser's discomfort was increasing. 'There's a little place on the way to Edinburgh called Blackburn so she thought you were Scottish. But then when she realised you weren't…'

'She ghosted me because I'm *English*.'

'Winnie deleted it all in a bit of a panic, I think. She is truly sorry and sends her apologies. Oh, and these.' He pulled a package from his pocket and handed it to Liv.

Liv read the wobbly handwriting on the label: '*With love from the world's worst matchmaker. Truly sorry. Love Winnie xx*'

Liv unwrapped a pair of tartan slippers, which made her smile.

'They're regifted. A present from Winnie's neighbour but they're a couple of sizes too big for her,' said Fraser but Liv was struggling to concentrate on what he was saying.

It was a lot to take in. More than anything she was relieved because she'd never felt Fraser was entirely convinced about her story and she could understand his scepticism when she had no proof. But best of all it meant it really was absolutely nothing to do with her. She couldn't change being English. And now she didn't want to change anything about herself at all.

'I wasn't expecting that,' she said. 'Not being funny or anything but you could have telephoned to tell me. Not that it's not great to see you 'cause it is.'

'I didn't get you a present so...' Fraser pulled another small neatly wrapped package from his pocket and handed it to her.

'Thanks,' she said as she pulled the paper off. She stared at the gift for a moment. 'A signed Mariah Carey album. I don't know what to say.'

'I won it in a competition when I was a kid. Listened to nothing else that summer.'

'I can't accept it,' said Liv trying to hand it back.

'No, I want you to have it. I know you're a fan too.'

Liv ran her thumb over the thick marker-pen signature. It was something she would treasure that was for sure. 'Thank you. I'm blown away. I mean it's a seriously close second to the slippers.'

'I get that. Nothing beats second-hand tartan slippers. I'm glad you like the CD though and I wanted to see you open it. Not everyone gets Mariah.'

'Thanks. I really appreciate you coming all this way on Christmas Day to play postman.'

'And I also needed to tell you that I like you.' Liv stopped staring at the CD. He liked her – this was huge. 'I'm not expecting anything in return,' he said hastily. 'Because I think I could have behaved better, been nicer. Listened more. But in my defence you were a bit full-on crazy most of the time and none of what you said made much sense to me. Anyway, I'm sorry and I need to pass on a big sorry from Winnie too. Or did I already do that?' He looked a little flustered, which was quite cute. 'And Effie says hello and wanted me to give you a big hug but you might not want that now.' It was funny to hear him ramble. It was the first time she could see the family similarity with Effie and it was endearing.

'Apology accepted. I know I can be a bit intense when I'm focused on something,' said Liv.

'She's the same with jigsaws!' yelled Charlotte from the kitchen.

'Ignore her,' said Liv. 'And I'm sorry too,' she added.

'It's cool. Right, I'd better get going. I'll leave you to your cuppa.'

He got to his feet and Liv felt a sense of loss hit her. This was madness. 'Where are you staying?'

'I was going to sleep in the van and then set off at first light. I slung a camping mat and a sleeping bag in the back.' He'd thought it all through.

'You can't sleep in the van; it'll be oorlich.'

Fraser chuckled. 'Och I'm used to it.'

'Charlotte!' yelled Liv making Fraser flinch. 'Fraser can stay the night can't he?'

'If you want him to!' she called back.

Fraser was watching her closely. Liv took a moment too long to answer and he got to his feet.

'Nah, I'll not impose.' She followed him into the tiny

hallway and he paused at the door to put his hat and scarf back on.

'You can stay. It's fine – really it is.'

'I know. Take care, Liv,' he said.

'Thanks for coming and for my present. I love it.' He nodded and reached for the door. She felt like she was losing him all over again. 'Actually,' said Liv. 'I will have that hug. The one from Effie. I'll have it now please.'

He turned to face her, opened his arms and she stepped into the warmth of his hug. It felt so right and safe. And yes he annoyed the crap out of her, but there was something there and she wanted to know if that something could be significant if it was nurtured. And he liked her – that was a very good start, especially when he'd seen her at less than her best. At last she pulled back from him and he looked down at her. 'I would like you to stay because I like you too,' said Liv. 'Not fake Fraser.' She wobbled her head. 'I did like him a lot. But I like you too… a lot.'

Fraser looked up. 'You don't have any mistletoe,' he said.

'Don't need it. I already live with a witch,' she said.

'I heard that!' shouted Charlotte.

'I knew you would,' said Liv and she mouthed, 'See she's a witch,' to Fraser and he laughed. 'Why did we need mistletoe?' she asked, her heart picking up its pace.

'I was looking for an excuse to kiss you.'

'You don't need one of those,' she said. 'Because all I want for Christmas is you.' She leaned in and kissed him. He held her tight and her jumper burst into song.

Epilogue

L iv pulled up outside the Lochy House Hotel. She was full of excited butterflies. It felt so good to be back. A beaming Effie raced down the steps and across the gravel to meet them. Liv buzzed the window down but before she could say anything Effie had almost launched herself through the window.

'Hiya, Effie, this is my sister and my mum,' said Liv trying to point.

'Hello, I am so excited to see you all. I was worried I might actually spontaneously combust,' she said with a deadpan expression.

'If I can open the car door, we'll get our stuff,' said Liv.

'Come in. Everyone is excited to meet you. It's going to be wild tonight. There will be dancing, Robbie on the bagpipes at midnight and there's soooo many people coming.'

'Hello! Will there be men in kilts?' asked her mum.

'Yeah, loads,' said Effie.

'Great,' said Liv, glancing past her. Whilst she was pleased to see Effie there was one other person she was longing to set eyes on.

'He's in the kitchen but he'll be out in a mo,' she said reading her mind.

They took the bags inside and Effie gave Charlotte and her mum the guided tour as well as introducing them to Dolly and Jock'O. Liv ducked out of the tour after greeting Dolly with a hug and giving Jock'O a chew stick in the shape of a sock. She pushed open the kitchen door to find a hive of activity. Donald and a couple of people Liv didn't know were busy chopping and cooking, and Winnie was stationed at the end of the service counter.

As she walked in Fraser appeared, took her in his arms and lifted her up, which made a happy squeal escape. It was a bit embarrassing but Liv reasoned it could have been wind, which would have been far worse. He kissed her and Winnie started to clap.

'I did that,' said Winnie, pointing proudly at the kissing couple.

Fraser put Liv down and Winnie waved to get her attention.

'I'm so very sorry about ghosting you. I really wouldn't have done if I'd thought it through,' said Winnie biting her lip.

She gave her a peck on the cheek. 'All forgiven. If it wasn't for fake Fraser I never would have gotten to know the real one so thank you. And thanks for the slippers too.'

'It's good to see you,' said Fraser, his eyes searching Liv's face as if taking in every detail. 'How was the journey?'

'Excellent, only three wee stops. A lot less than I was anticipating with Mum on board. How's it going in here?'

'All under control. Two staff have voluntarily deserted Lizzie in favour of my kitchen and stalwarts Donald and Winnie have been doing a splendid job. It's a buffet tonight and the audience is friendly so we're good.'

Fraser and Liv had been desperate to see each other and with Charlotte and her mum badgering her for details they had hit upon the idea of having Hogmanay all together at the hotel. Fraser and Liv left the kitchen to find Robbie was waiting for them in the hallway.

'Lovely to see you again, Liv,' he said.

'Glad you're here Robbie because I understand there's going to be lots of men in kilts this evening flashing their *sgian-dubhs*.' The thought of seeing Fraser in a kilt was already getting her excited.

'You don't need to worry. It'll be quite safe with me around,' said Robbie straightening his jumper.

Fraser wrapped his arms around Liv from behind and she hoped she always got that little shiver of pleasure from the contact.

Effie came back downstairs from showing Charlotte and Liv's mum to their rooms. 'Did you get your DNA results back yet?' she asked, rocking on her heels.

'I did. The app pinged me a message as we left home but I've not opened it yet.' Liv pulled her phone from her bag.

'Open it, open it!' chanted Effie as Robbie put an arm around her.

'Och it's all bunkum and nonsense,' said Dolly.

Effie leaned in. 'Granny's not happy about hers.'

'What did yours say?' Liv asked Fraser as she pulled up the app. 'I'll show you mine if you show me yours,' she added with a grin.

Fraser leaned over the reception desk and produced his own mobile. 'Go on then.'

Liv went to the results screen and read it out. 'I'm thirty-four per cent Scottish!' said Liv delighted with the finding. 'Twenty-one per cent English, fourteen per cent Welsh and nine per cent Norwegian with a sprinkling of French and lots of low percentages of African countries.'

Fraser's mouth opened and closed a couple of times before he spoke. 'Seventeen per cent.' He swallowed hard. 'I'm only seventeen per cent Scottish.'

'What? I'm more Scottish than you are!' Liv fell about laughing but Fraser didn't seem to think it was that funny and Dolly had definitely stopped smiling.

'I'm twenty-six per cent Spanish and twenty-five per cent Polish,' said Fraser looking at Dolly. 'What's that all about?'

'It means we're all European and it's just like I said, it's a lot of old bunkum.' She thrust out her chin.

'Effie was forty-six per cent Scottish,' said Fraser. 'Why aren't I?'

'That'll be my mam,' said Effie. 'She reckoned she could trace back her family tree to the Battle of Inverlochy. But didn't you say the same, Granny?'

They all looked at Dolly. 'It doesny matter,' she said. 'It's what's in your heart that's important.'

'My Spanish and Polish heart?' asked Fraser, with a grin.

Dolly reversed backwards a fraction quicker than was wise and bumped into the pike pole, which bounced back off the wood panelling and fell straight towards Fraser. With lightning reflexes Liv shot out a hand and caught it just inches from Fraser's head.

'Whoa! Thanks, that almost took me out,' he said.

355

'Handling pikes is probably in my DNA. Back when my Scottish ancestors were fighting off the Spanish.'

Fraser took the pike from her. 'Are you going to fight off the Spanish now?'

'Nope, I think it's time to cement relations.'

He grinned at her. 'To that I say *Sí.*'

'And I say ma heid's mince!' she said in a passable Scottish accent.

With that he picked her up into his arms and kissed her.

Acknowledgements

THANKS TO my agent, Kate Nash, for always being in my corner. Thanks to my editor Aubrie Artiano and all the team at Aria. Special thanks to Meg Shepherd for the fabulous cover art.

Thanks to my technical expert Julie Smith for information on hotel kitchens.

Special thanks to Sheila McClure for information on cows and also for sharing her DNA story and letting me fictionalise it.

I have been lucky enough to enjoy a number of holidays in Scotland and my last visit was the inspiration for this story. In particular the Glengarry Castle Hotel with its enviable position on Loch Oich was how I pictured the setting of the fictional hotel in the story, although I must point out that the Glengarry Castle Hotel is indeed stunningly beautiful and certainly not in need of repair!

Thanks to my writing friends for their ongoing support.

And huge thanks to my family for always being there and for so many wonderful Christmases.

Big thank you to all the book bloggers, booksellers and library staff for their support of not just my books but the romance genre in general. A special shout out for The Friendly Book Community Facebook group – check them out! And last but by no means least my wonderful readers – thank you for reading my books and passing on the love whether that's by word of mouth, review or social media. It means the world – thank you!

About the Author

BELLA OSBORNE has been jotting down stories as far back as she can remember but decided that 2013 would be the year that she finished a full length novel. In 2016, her debut novel, *It Started At Sunset Cottage*, was shortlisted for the Contemporary Romantic Novel of the Year and RNA Joan Hessayon New Writers Award. Bella's stories are about friendship, love and coping with what life throws at you. She likes to find the humour in the darker moments of life and weaves these into her stories. Bella believes that writing your own story really is the best fun ever, closely followed by talking, eating chocolate, drinking fizz and planning holidays. She lives in the Midlands, UK with her lovely husband and wonderful daughter, who thankfully, both accept her as she is (with mad morning hair and a penchant for skipping).